Also Available from Signet Eclipse

Avenger's Angel
Always Angel
(A Penguin eSpecial)

MESSENGER'S ANGEL

A NOVEL OF THE LOST ANGELS

HEATHER KILLOUGH-WALDEN

A SIGNET ECLIPSE BOOK

SIGNET ECLIPSE
Published by New American Library, a division of
Penguin Group (USA) Inc., 375 Hudson Street,
New York, New York 10014, USA
Penguin Group (Canada), 90 Eglinton Avenue East, Suite 700, Toronto,
Ontario M4P 2Y3, Canada (a division of Pearson Penguin Canada Inc.)
Penguin Books Ltd., 80 Strand, London WC2R 0RL, England
Penguin Ireland, 25 St. Stephen's Green, Dublin 2,
Ireland (a division of Penguin Books Ltd.)
Penguin Group (Australia), 250 Camberwell Road, Camberwell, Victoria 3124,
Australia (a division of Pearson Australia Group Pty. Ltd.)
Penguin Books India Pvt. Ltd., 11 Community Centre, Panchsheel Park,
New Delhi - 110 017, India
Penguin Group (NZ), 67 Apollo Drive, Rosedale, Auckland 0632,
New Zealand (a division of Pearson New Zealand Ltd.)
Penguin Books (South Africa) (Pty.) Ltd., 24 Sturdee Avenue,
Rosebank, Johannesburg 2196, South Africa

Penguin Books Ltd., Registered Offices:
80 Strand, London WC2R 0RL, England

First published by Signet Eclipse, an imprint of New American Library,
a division of Penguin Group (USA) Inc.

First Printing, June 2012
10 9 8 7 6 5 4 3 2 1

PUBLISHER'S NOTE
This is a work of fiction. Names, characters, places, and incidents either are the
product of the author's imagination or are used fictitiously, and any resemblance
to actual persons, living or dead, business establishments, events, or locales is
entirely coincidental.
   The publisher does not have any control over and does not assume any respon-
sibility for author or third-party Web sites or their content.

This book is dedicated to everyone who is waiting—for a letter, for a phone call, for a *message*.

Here's to the words that bring us hope.

ACKNOWLEDGMENTS

This book is a tapestry. It is a work of art hewn of the colors of a land so steeped in the richest history, no amount of time can unravel the threads of its creation. This book is the voice of ghosts caught between the now and then of the Callanish Stones and Edinburgh Castle. It is the breath of a North Sea wind across a pale cheek, and the rolling approach of fog across the lonely Moors.

But this tapestry would never have been woven if not for the help of those precious, special few who live within the land and among the stories, both ancient and new, of our bonnie Caledonia—of Scotland. And so, I thank you.

I thank *you*, Susan Stewart, author in your own right, for your Scottish beauty, unrivaled kindness, and limitless patience as you took me to the corners of your Gaelic world and allowed me to touch upon the ancient history of the Outer Hebrides Islands. Thank you for letting me run between the Stones. Thank you for guiding me up the narrow stairwells of St. Clemens Rodel. Thank you for your continued friendship and the experience of a Scottish girl's lifetime.

I thank *you*, Bruce Officer, teller of humorous tales, for the history lessons you shared as I stood still at the threshold of Slains Castle and gazed out over the endless blue of a bottomless sea. Thank you for allowing me to walk the very same ground upon which my archangel and archess take their everlasting vows. Thank you for caring, for your gentle nature, and of course for your friendship.

I have been blessed with footholds in time and culture around the world: my *friends*. Without you, I simply would not be the author that I am.

INTRODUCTION

Long ago, the Old Man gathered together his four favored archangels, Michael, Gabriel, Uriel, and Azrael. He pointed to four stars in the sky that shone brighter than the others. He told the archangels that he wished to reward them for their loyalty and had created for them soul mates. Four perfect female beings—archesses.

However, before the archangels could claim their mates, the four archesses were lost to them and scattered to the wind, beyond their realm and reach. The archangels made the choice to leave their world, journey to Earth, and seek out their mates.

For thousands of years, the archangels have searched. But they have not searched alone. For they are not the only entities to leave their realm and come to Earth to hunt for the archesses. They were followed by another....

CHAPTER ONE

Juliette sidled back on the massive four-poster bed, a remotely hesitant part of her still wanting to get away. But the angel smiled a rakish smile and moved over her like a massive cat, graceful and deadly, and she didn't get far. He skillfully caught her wrists in firm grips and had her pinned before she could blink.

Juliette lay there, her breathing quick and sharp, and stared up at the taut muscles of his arms, chest, and torso. Her gaze boldly trailed across the tanned expanse of toned flesh . . . to where the rest of his body was hidden beyond the unbuttoned waistband of his blue jeans.

Her mouth felt both wet and dry; her heart hammered; her hands flexed beneath the viselike grips he had on her delicate wrists. The castle around them loomed in her periphery, empty yet protective. It felt both ancient and brand-new; its walls were crumbling, enshrouded by the echoes of the tapestries and torch sconces they once held.

The master's chamber was warmed by the crackling of the flames in the giant stone hearth. And it was chilled by the North Sea wind that ripped through the timeworn windows and raced through the empty, ruined room.

The castle was a skeleton and a ghost, broken down

to its barest bones and draped in the memory of what it once was.

The angel, though—he was warm. He was not a ghost. His body was hard and insistent and very, very real above her. He lowered his head to slide his gaze down the length of her slim body, and as he shifted, she once more caught sight of the massive black and silver wings at his back. Their feathers shimmered, iridescent in the shafts of moonlight that speared the empty windows and lit the stage of their clandestine play.

So beautiful, she thought absently.

He looked up and met her gaze, and she found herself at once lost in the strange glowing silver of his eyes.

They're glowing, she thought in awe.

He pinned her to the bed beneath him with that look; it claimed her, possessed her, and she was certain that no man in the world had ever looked at her—not really— until the angel had.

Juliette knew she was blushing. Her cheeks were hot, and her chest was flushed. Her breasts felt warm and heavy, even as her nipples hardened to painful nubs that scraped the inside of her shirt. Breathing was hard. She wanted to arch beneath him, close the gap he held above her. She wanted to touch him as she'd never wanted anything before.

He stared down at her forever, watching her, taking her in. He was eating her with his eyes, and her chest felt tight. She couldn't take it. His control over her body was absolute. It was as if he willed it and wetness gathered between her legs. As if he knew it was there, he chuckled. The sound rushed over her skin like a caress, deep and deliciously wicked. She shuddered and closed her eyes, fighting the urge to writhe beneath him. She almost broke then. She almost begged him to take her.

What's wrong with me? she thought. This wasn't like her. She never gave in easily. She was stubborn to the core. What was happening? How had she let this angel get her into bed? Hadn't she just met him?

I don't even know his name. . . .

Her eyes flew open when she felt the butterfly softness of his lips brushing against hers. Teasingly, he pulled back and once more locked her in his inhuman gaze. He said not a word, but smiled that faintly cruel smile of his, flashing teeth both straight and white. In the frame of his too-handsome face, it was nothing short of predatory. And then he put both of her slender wrists in one of his strong hands and used the other to grab the front of her button-up shirt.

The material pulled taut in his grip, scraping her tender nipples and ripping a gasp from her lips. Slowly, almost menacingly, he popped the buttons on the shirt, one after another. And then he let the material slide across her rib cage, opening her body to his stark, hungry gaze.

Now she did moan. The wind rushed across her exposed skin, licking at it hungrily, tightening her nipples beneath him to a painful degree.

He's going to devour me, she thought. And she didn't care.

His wings lowered gracefully over the edges of the bed, their silver and raven feathers blocking her from the wind. Then he lowered his head and she felt his hot breath, in stark contrast to the cold, across the hypersensitive flesh of her right breast. She tensed in his grasp, pulling hard against the hold he had on her arms. He held her easily, though, and his tongue flicked out to brush across the tip of her nipple. She jumped in his grasp, crying out at the sensation, but again he held her tight, and again his chuckle rumbled across her skin like silken thunder.

"Please," she gasped. She didn't even know what she was begging for. This was just too much. Too strange and

perfect. Too much. Angels weren't supposed to torture people, were they?

With that, the angel lowered himself closer. She felt the tips of her erect nipples brush the hardness of his chest and nearly jumped again. But he distracted her when he used his free hand to shove her tiered miniskirt up her slender thigh. She groaned once more in longing as his hand then roamed across the taut cheeks of her bottom. No underwear . . .

She felt his breath at her ear, cascading goose bumps over her skin. "My pleasure," he whispered. His hand sank lower.

". . . tray tables stowed and seat backs in an upright position . . ."

Juliette jolted awake in her seat as the pilot made the announcement that they were coming in for a landing.

The man seated beside her gave her a knowing sideways glance. Juliette blushed, swallowing a groan of embarrassment, and turned to steadfastly stare out the window. Her reflection stared back at her: long, rich brown waves, big hazel eyes that were mostly green at the moment, and flushed cheeks and lips—remnants of her dream.

It wasn't the first time she'd dreamed of crumbling castles and ghostlike figures. Some nights, she was walking through a Scottish kirkyard, ancient, worn, and collapsing, yet filled with fresh graves and newly chiseled headstones. Other nights she made her way through castles, as she had in this dream. They were ruins and yet they weren't—she saw the images of what they had once been draped over them like the cloying memories of glory days.

She'd always had dreams like this. Dreams of the past and the present, intermingling and poignant. It was one of the reasons she'd decided to become an anthropologist. The past and its stories intrigued her. It was more than that, even. . . . They *called* to her.

But this was the first time her dream had included a man. Or an angel.

Her reflection blinked, long lashes brushing against the tops of her cheeks.

"Good afternoon, ladies and gentlemen, this is your pilot speaking." The intercom sliced through the air, back to life once more, the static cutting through the dialogue and musical scores of every movie playing in the plane. Juliette glanced around and watched as people's heads jerked under the volume before they quickly yanked the headsets off their ears. "We're about six hours and thirty-eight minutes into our flying time now and twenty-three minutes outside of Edinburgh. It's a brisk March day, forty-one degrees Fahrenheit or four degrees Celsius; wind coming out of the northwest at fifteen miles per hour. . . ."

Juliette let the pilot's voice drift to the back of her consciousness and continued to gaze out the window at the green and black landscape below. She'd been traveling a lot lately. In the last year, she'd studied in Australia through an overseas program, visited New Zealand, and flown to both coasts of the US, and now she was about to land in Scotland and would be there for several weeks. She was a PhD student in anthropology and was working on her thesis; the travel was mostly for research, and it was her fellowship at Carnegie Mellon that paid for it all.

But Scotland was different for two reasons. For one thing, Juliette had wanted to visit Scotland since she was a little girl. Her parents were Scottish; her mother was a MacDonald and her father was an Anderson. It was in her blood.

The other reason Scotland was different was due to a fairly new development. Juliette had planned on going anyway in order to do ethnological research on the Outer Hebrides islands, where her father's side of the family originated. And then Juliette's adviser had contacted her with news: Samuel Lambent, the wealthy and prominent media mogul, had offered Juliette a deal. He would pay her a hefty royalty and foot the bill for the remainder of her research if he could use the information she gleaned for a television miniseries about the legend and lore of Scotland's more remote areas.

Juliette was so mind-blown by the offer, she hadn't even thought to ask why Lambent had chosen her, specifically, when there were other students in the world who either were currently studying Scotland or were already well versed in its history. She, of course, jumped on the opportunity.

Obviously there were stipulations. She had to make certain to thoroughly research the kinds of material that would "sell" to a television audience. She also had to meet with one of Lambent's representatives in person once a week to assure him that enough progress was being made.

Part of Juliette felt like this was a dream. It was too good to be true. She'd never had much money. Though both of her parents were professors, as she would be one day, their fields fell on the poorer side of the financial spectrum of academia. Plus Juliette had what an accountant would no doubt call a "nasty habit" of giving away most of her money. She was just too sensitive. She hated to see people suffer, and whenever she could possibly give something to someone that could alleviate even a little bit of that suffering, she did so.

As a result, she lived modestly.

However, now Juliette could afford just about anything she wanted. Of course, she couldn't buy a mansion in Beverly Hills, but she didn't *want* a mansion in Beverly Hills. And if the miniseries took off, even that mansion might find a place on her list of possibilities if she decided she ever wanted it.

It really was like a dream. The offer had come at a time when Jules was beginning to doubt herself and her sanity. She'd been nearly destitute for so long and grossly overworked between her thesis and her volunteer jobs. She thought she might be reaching a breaking point, because something strange happened during her stay in Australia.

She had been on the beach alone, enjoying a few rare minutes to herself. She'd been staring out over the waves when she saw a surfer go down and not come back up. Somehow, despite her diminutive size, she'd managed to drag his unconscious body out of the water and onto the beach. She could see the head injury and knew he was in bad shape, and then—and then she did something she could not explain. She put her hand to his chest and imagined that she'd healed him.

In retrospect, Juliette thought she understood what had happened. She must have been hallucinating. It was the logical explanation. The jet lag, the pressure of her studies, and the responsibilities she'd taken on as a volunteer at the local children's home—it all must have come to a head. Most likely, the man survived only because Juliette got up after her imagined "healing" and ran to the nearest lifeguard station to alert the authorities to the surfer's accident.

For days and nights, Juliette had thought on those strange, surrealistic minutes and wondered what the hell was happening to her. What kind of a breakdown was it that made a person imagine she was healing someone? She'd thought of dropping out of the program and quitting her volunteer positions. She'd considered telling her parents that she just couldn't handle it all anymore.

And then Samuel Lambent came along, a saving grace and guardian angel, and he'd offered her this deal. When the contract arrived via FedEx, she'd opened it, grabbed her pen, and signed it after barely reading it.

Almost immediately after scrawling her name on the black line, she'd felt her stress levels drop. It was as if a massive weight had been lifted from her shoulders and chest—a dark veil pulled from her mind.

She could kiss Lambent.

Juliette couldn't wait to get started. Her best friend, Sophie Bryce, was watering her garden for her and had agreed to stay at her rental home, as it was preferable to Sophie's tiny apartment anyway. Jules was well aware of how lucky she was to have a friend like Soph. The girl had a hard life of her own, yet she had never even blinked before agreeing to help Jules out while she flew around the world to do this research. If Soph was jealous, she didn't show it.

Juliette smiled and made a promise to herself to buy something special for Sophie in Edinburgh. Or maybe Glasgow. She wasn't exactly looking forward to renting a car and learning to drive on the wrong side of the road, but everything else about her life in that moment sounded just about perfect.

Och, not again. "Bloody hell," Gabriel muttered under his breath. He couldn't believe it was already happening again. He'd been in Rodel, Scotland, for only a few months!

"Get the nuts!" someone in the pub yelled. A few of his mates laughed. "Stoke the bloody fire!" another shouted.

Gabriel ran his hand over his face and tried to look properly embarrassed. It was hard, though. He was more frustrated and angry than embarrassed. He really hadn't meant for things to go so far this time. Whereas he'd always been admittedly a touch proud in the past when this happened, now it seemed a weary practice, both pointless and painful.

"Ye've gone tae far on this one, Black." Stuart leaned over and spoke softly across the table. "Dougal's got it in for yae. I dinnae like tae think what will happen if those fecking nuts don' meet this time." His accent was thick, as was normal for one who had lived on the islands all his life.

"They won' meet, Stuart. They never do," Gabriel replied just as quietly.

Stuart Burns was in his seventies and built hard as nails. He'd never done anything but fish in his life, and fishing on the Outer Hebrides of Scotland didn't make for an easy existence. It either killed you or made you stronger, and in Stuart's case, it had done a little of both. In fact, that was how he and Gabriel had met. Gabriel had pulled him out of the icy waters of the North Sea during a fishing accident in Stuart's youth.

The soft part of Stuart had died in that water. What was left was rigid and right and strong to an absolute fault. But he was a good man, deep down, and a dependable friend. Stuart was the only human alive who knew Gabriel's secret. He was the only one in Scotland who was aware that Gabriel Black was not in fact the son of Duncan Black, as everyone else believed, but was actually Duncan Black *himself*, because every member of that particular Black family was actually the same man. Stuart was the only soul privy to the knowledge that there was really no such thing as Duncan Black or even Gabriel Black—there was only *Gabriel*, the eminent Messenger Archangel and one of the four most celebrated archangels in existence.

Over the centuries, Gabriel had spent a lot of time in Scotland. Some of those times were less pleasant than others. Europe had gone through an Inquisition, a plague, and countless wars, and the tapestry of Scotland's history was woven from thorny thread. Nonetheless, when she was a fair land, she was a beautiful land, and Gabriel fell in love with his bonnie Caledonia.

However, he could never stay for too long, as he didn't

age, and people would begin to wonder why a fifty- or sixty-year-old man still looked to be in his thirties. Gabriel always left before this could happen. And then, twenty or thirty years later, he would return and pass himself off as the son of the man whose name he had claimed the last time he was in Scotland.

Gabriel's explanations were always generally the same. His "father" had eloped with a woman from another village or town or city—and Gabriel was the result. Again and again he did this, because not much could keep him away from Scotland. Not for long, anyway.

Gabriel had especially wanted to return this time around. Life had become surreal at the mansion he shared with his three brothers, and in the States, of late. Uriel, one of his brothers, had recently found his archess, and in her a taste of the true happiness so long desired by the archangels. For two thousand years, the former Angel of Vengeance had searched for the female archangel made solely for him by the Old Man. And a few months ago, he had finally come across her. Uriel was the first of his brothers to find his archess. The archesses were treasured, not only by their mates, the archangels—but by the Adarians, a separate and frighteningly powerful race of archangels. The Adarians wanted the archesses for their unique ability to heal. When Uriel located Eleanore, so did the Adarian leader. A series of battles ensued, both physical and mental, and the archangels won, more or less. Now Uriel and Eleanore were happily married in the US.

Gabriel was elated for his brother. Knowing that the feat was possible and that the treasured women they had all sought out for twenty centuries were in fact *real* filled Gabriel with a sense of promise after having nearly given up hope that he would ever find his own archess.

But at the same time, it was hard to see Uriel and Eleanore together and not wonder . . . would he have to wait a week for his own archess to come out of the woodwork? Or would it be another two thousand years? He wondered whether his brothers Michael, the Warrior Archangel, and Azrael, the Angel of Death, felt the same way.

The thought was too heavy to bear. So, he'd come back to Scotland, and he'd been welcomed by his homeland with open arms. Some arms more open than others.

Across the pub, the fire had been stoked and a metal grid tray had been placed across it as a makeshift grill. Gabriel stifled an inner groan when two large hazelnuts were extracted from the kitchen in the back and brought into the fray of Scotsmen out front.

"Christ," he muttered. It was a long-standing tradition in the Western Isles of Scotland, though it was supposed to happen only during Samhain, otherwise known as Halloween. However, the people of the Isle of Harris had changed their custom for this particular occasion, on account of one Duncan Black, a treacherously handsome silver-eyed, black-haired man whose existence had called for quite a few hazelnuts in his time.

Tradition stated that two hazelnuts were to be thrown onto the fire, one for each member of a couple. When the nuts heated up, they would pop and "jump." If they jumped together, the couple was deemed destined for a happy life together, and usually married shortly afterward. If, however, the nuts jumped apart, the couple had better break up. And soon.

Much to Gabriel's regret now, the late Duncan Black had been popular with the lasses, to say the least. Gabriel knew for a fact that none of Duncan's "nuts" had ever jumped together. Hell, if they'd even tried, he would have used telekinesis to keep them apart. He was a man with a man's needs, but none of the women he'd been with were meant to become his bride.

He knew this better than nearly any other man alive. And he'd never been more certain of the truth than he was now that Uriel had found his archess. There was hope where there frankly hadn't been for far too many years.

And so it was with very real chagrin that Gabriel realized he was right back in "Duncan" Black's shoes after a mere few months of residing once more in his hometown. It seemed the Black family line was doomed to drive women crazy and men insane with jealousy no matter what.

Gabe felt a little less at fault this time, however. He had had no idea that Edeen was Angus's sister and he'd heard well enough about Angus Dougal's reputation. Edeen had come on to Gabriel the first night he'd been back in Harris, when he was signing up for part-time work on Stuart's boat. She'd told him she had "family" here, but was unattached. Gabriel, of course, was interested. After all, Edeen was a beauty with that shoulder-length flaxen hair and those green eyes. He'd done what any red-blooded man would do! He was innocent enough in that, wasn't he?

Edeen Dougal was laughing. Gabriel could hear the light sound from across the room. She was seated with her friends at a round table near the window. When Gabe looked up and met her gaze, she offered him a teasing smile and a wink. It was a reassuring gesture to him, because it meant she thought this was funny. She wasn't taking it seriously.

Gabriel nodded.

At least there was that. Now the only one who would be truly disappointed would be her brother, Angus. Gabriel lifted his head and turned slightly until he had Angus in his sights.

Angus gazed back. It was a cold, hard, green-eyed gaze in a face that many women found nearly as handsome as Gabriel's. Gabe suspected that probably had something to do with the man's ire. Of course, the rest of the ire came from the fact that Gabriel had bedded Angus's sister. This was a very religious and superstitious community. People didn't generally go sleeping around—especially with the sister of one of the most dangerous men in town.

Angus was tall and solid and as hard in his musculature as Stuart Burns was in the bones. And he had a chip on his shoulder; that much was easy for Gabriel to decipher. If the hazelnuts didn't meet, he was going to try to prove something with Gabe.

And that wouldn't end well. Because there wasn't a human on earth who could best Gabriel in a fight—and at the same time, the last thing Gabe wanted to do was make real trouble by harming a clansman four months into his stay in Harris. Especially when that clansman also happened to be a cop.

"Get me out o' this," he whispered to Stuart, his own accent barely discernible when compared with the accent of the man beside him.

When Stuart laughed, it sounded like autumn leaves scratching across the ground in a gust of wind. "Yae got yerself into this, Black. Ye'll get yerself out."

Gabriel shot him a look and took a deep breath. He was about to stand up and make some sort of case for not using the hazelnuts as his father and grandfather—and great-grandfather—had done, when Edeen, herself, stood up and waved for everyone's silence.

"Listen up!" She got on her chair and then, with the help of a few men around her, stood on the table next to her. "Ye've all had yer fun!" she said, putting her hands on her hips and eyeing the men dead-on. "Now enough's enough! This is tae be a Samhain tradition, not a March tradition, and I fer one don't take kindly to yae suggestin' I marry a man based on what a fecking nut decides tae do!"

There was laughter throughout the pub then, some of

it nervous, as women didn't generally swear a lot on the Outer Hebrides. But Edeen Dougal was a force unto herself and they knew enough to accept it when she did.

Angus Dougal pushed through the crowd and came to stand before her. On the table, Edeen stood a half foot above her brother's mass of brown hair. She glared down at him, daring him to say something. He dared. "Edeen, get yerself down from there an' don't interfere—"

"Och, shut up, Angus. Ye're no' me da'." She made a dismissive gesture toward her older brother and rolled her eyes. "Awa' with ye an' bile yer heid." She jumped down from the table and sauntered toward the front door, tossing a lock of her blond hair over her shoulder as she did so. "I'll no' take part in this; I'll have nothin' of it." She turned and addressed the patrons of the pub, in general. "Ye're all a wee bit childish, don't ye think?"

Her friends joined her at the front door a moment later, one pulling her jacket on over her sweater, the other adjusting the strap of her purse. Both looked highly amused and a touch embarrassed. But they were obviously used to Edeen's shenanigans.

With one more farewell nod to the pub owner and bartender, who nodded back with a knowing smile, Edeen Dougal and her companions left the pub.

Gabriel could have wept with relief.

"Ye're saved, Black." Stuart grinned, shaking his head admonishingly. "And by a girl, no less."

"Aye." Gabriel raised his glass, a lopsided smile on his handsome face. "God bless the womenfolk."

CHAPTER TWO

"What do you think the other archesses will look like?" Eleanore was seated on Uriel's lap, her finger idly twirling a lock of her long blue-black hair as she stared into the fireplace in the massive living room of the archangels' mansion.

"I don't know. But you look exactly how I'd always imagined you," Uriel said. "So probably they'll look like whatever my brothers have in mind."

Eleanore turned to face her mate. Uriel was as handsome as ever with his jade green eyes and mass of dark brown wavy hair, but she frowned at him nonetheless, unable to hide her irritation with what he'd just said. Why should what a woman looked like be dependent upon what a man wanted?

As if he could sense her irritation, Uriel smiled one of his devastating smiles and chuckled softly. "Of course, it's also possible that it's the other way around," he said. "What you look like could very well determine what we want and expect."

She liked the sound of that a little better and offered Uriel a smile that said as much. She took in his thick hair and the impossibly handsome lines of his chiseled face and then peered into the green of his gorgeous eyes. She'd never said so, but he was her idea of perfection, too. He had been since the first time she'd seen him in a movie poster for *Comeuppance*, in which he played the main character, a vampire named Jonathan Brakes. Like Gabriel, all the brothers maintained a human identity, some more visible than others. Uriel went by the name of Christopher Daniels, an A-list Hollywood actor.

Slowly, she cupped the side of his stubble-shadowed face and ran her thumb over his strong cheekbone. He narrowed his gaze questioningly. "You know, one thing I'll always miss about that vampire curse Sam put on me is the ability to read your mind," he said softly. "Penny for your thoughts?"

Eleanore laughed and shook her head. "No deal. I know you can make gold out of anything in this room. Pennies won't cut it, young man."

He laughed, too. "I'm anything but young, Ellie."

It was true. She reasoned that, by all rights, he was more ancient than time itself. He had been on Earth for two thousand years, as had his brothers, but he'd existed as an archangel in another realm before that.

"Well?" he hedged. "You gonna share?" His green eyes twinkled. "Or do I have to torture it out of you?" His hand slipped under the hem of her shirt and his fingers brushed teasingly—threateningly—against the lace of her underwire bra.

Ellie's heartbeat kicked up a notch, her temperature rose a few degrees, and her lips parted as she watched her husband's pupils expand in hunger. As if he could sense her response, his smile turned dark, spreading to a dangerous grin.

She decided to prolong the torture. "I was just think-ing that with the Adarians out there and Sam watching over everything, it'll be war for the others," she admitted truthfully. She *had* been worried about the other archesses. She, herself, hadn't had an easy life. She'd run from the Adarians since she was a little girl and their leader had spied her healing another child. The other archesses were one of the main reasons she had decided to stay on Earth with Uriel after their souls had united and they'd literally earned their wings four months ago. They'd had a choice then—they could have left Earth and returned to Uriel's realm, or they could remain behind. They'd chosen the latter.

Uriel's smile stayed put; he clearly knew she was turned on and teasing him. "The other archesses?" He played along.

Eleanore nodded. There were supposed to be three more women out there, somewhere in the world: three more like her. Each one would be gifted with supernatural abilities and each one was fated to become the soul mate of one of the four favored archangels. But it hadn't been easy for her and Uriel. The Adarians, twelve very powerful archangels who were cast to Earth by the Old Man, were dead set on obtaining an archess of their own in the hopes of somehow absorbing the archess's ability to heal. And Samael . . .

With that thought, some of Ellie's mounting desire slipped away. "What do you think Sam's plan is?" she asked softly. Samael was an enigma. He was an archangel who had once been the Old Man's favorite but who was displaced by Michael. He was also the thirteenth Adarian, but unlike the other twelve, he had not been discarded by the Old Man and sent to Earth all those years ago. For some reason the Old Man had kept him in their realm. He'd left only when the four favored left, in order to track down the archesses himself. Or at least that was the assumption.

The truth was, nobody knew what Samael's motivation or plans were.

He was certainly more powerful than the four favored, a fact he made more painfully clear as time passed. And he made life hell for them at every given opportunity. Four months ago, Sam had tricked Uriel into signing a contract that indirectly caused him to become the very same vampire he played in Hollywood. The curse had nearly torn him and Ellie apart at a time when they had just found each other and should have been focusing on growing closer.

Why had Samael done this? they had wondered. He claimed that he wanted an archess of his own—for his own reasons. But in the end, true to his enigmatic ways, Samael had turned the other cheek and shown a different side of himself by helping Ellie and the brothers defeat the Adarians in a harrowing battle in Texas. He was mysterious and dangerous in equal measures. Well, perhaps not quite equal measures.

He was very, very dangerous.

"Who knows?" Uriel said in answer to Ellie's question. He sighed heavily, obviously disappointed in the turn of conversation. Then he slid his well-muscled arms around Ellie's waist and pulled her back with him as he sank farther into the cushions of the couch. "But I'm starting to believe he exists for no other reason than to tempt me to kill him."

Ellie cocked her head to one side and narrowed her gaze on her lover. "Oh?" She noted the tightness in his jaw and the unconscious possessiveness in his flexed muscles. He was irritated that she was bringing Sam into the conversation just then. Samael was a distraction Uriel didn't want Ellie to have at that moment. "Jealous?" she asked.

A hint of Uriel's smile was back. His hand slid beneath the wire of her bra. "Always."

General Kevin Trenton was a tall, well-muscled man with blue-black shoulder-length hair and ice-blue eyes. He was also known as Abraxos, the leader of the Adarian race, the first archangels created by the Old Man and

consequently discarded to Earth due to their frighteningly immense powers. Over the years, he'd changed his
name many times and now most of his men simply referred to him as General.

At the moment, Kevin stood in front of the mirror
above the sink in one of the many rooms in the Adarian
headquarters in Texas. In the mirror's reflection, he saw
the tall, strong form of one of his men fill the space in his
doorway. "Come in, Ely."

Elyon was a black man and one of Kevin's best fight-
ers. As with all the Adarians, Elyon's name had naturally
been shortened over the last few millennia. His Adarian
abilities had long ago proved themselves to be of the
nastier, more potent variety. Among other things, with a
single touch, Ely could wither a person's body around its
skeleton, sapping it of the water it needed to fill out its
human cells. After a few seconds, Ely's victim would fall
at his feet, lifeless and crumpled as weathered parchment.

Ely nodded once and entered, but Kevin did not fail
to notice the quick, nervous glance the Adarian shot toward the bound victim in the corner of the room.

The human male had been cuffed to a chair and apparently drugged. His eyes were unfocused and half-
closed. He had put up a struggle when Kevin's men
brought him in, and his clothes were torn in places.
Where the rips in the material of his pants rested against
his skin, blood soaked it a fresh, wet red. His button-
down dress shirt had been equally mistreated, but it was
the sort that had once been worn beneath a suit coat and
tie.

"Pay him no heed," Kevin told the soldier. He turned
and retrieved the razor blade he'd set on the counter
alongside a basin of water and a clear drinking glass. He
picked up the glass, then turned back to face the Adarian.

Ely's amber-colored eyes were shot through with a sudden strain of apprehension at the sight of the blade, but his dark, handsome face managed to maintain a semblance of impassivity that Kevin was admittedly impressed with. Ely had always been an incredibly strong man, even among Adarians. That was why Kevin had chosen him for this test.

"Bare your wrist, Ely."

Ely hesitated for a mere heartbeat before he raised his arm, rolled up his sleeve, and offered his right wrist to his general. Kevin lowered the razor blade to the inside of the man's wrist and Ely's body became a statue, unbreathing, unmoving.

The blade sliced swift and clean and the blood welled up at once. Kevin caught it with the glass as it escaped from the wound and ran down Ely's wrist in a thick, crimson tributary. As the glass began to fill, Ely's gaze wavered. He looked away from his wrist and focused on the wall. And then, eventually, he closed his eyes and swallowed hard.

"You look a tad pale, Ely," Kevin joked, as it was actually difficult for Ely to look pale at all. Ashen at most, perhaps.

Ely said nothing. He was clearly not amused and knew better than to say anything unless he could say something nice.

When the glass was three-quarters full, Kevin set it down and retrieved the gauze bandaging from the counter. He wrapped this around Ely's wrist and pressed hard on the wound until the red on the gauze stopped spreading.

"Get yourself some protein," Kevin told him calmly. "And then return."

Ely was very obviously confused and more than likely curious as to what the hell his general planned on doing with his blood. But he had been trained to follow orders and he'd done so for the last several thousand years. Now was no different; he nodded, said, "Yes sir," and left the room, softly closing the General's door behind him.

Kevin turned toward the bound, seated man and approached him. "If you have any final prayers, I suggest you utter them now. Not that anyone is listening."

The man made no attempt to speak behind his gag. He only looked up at Kevin and let his heavy head drop back onto the top of the chair.

Kevin raised the glass of Adarian blood to his lips, closed his eyes, and began to drink. He swallowed tentatively at first. He was uncertain, after all. This was just a hunch, an experiment. And blood tasted terrible, whether it was angel blood or not.

But after the first few swallows, he felt able to drink more readily. He finished off the glass and left it, stained burgundy, on the counter above the man's head. Then he leaned over the bound man and pressed his hand to the human's chest.

He searched for the new ability within himself the way he always called forth his own abilities, and attempted to open that familiar channel inside that would allow the power to arc through his body and out into the world—out into the man before him.

He knew what he wanted to do.

Nothing happened right away, but the passage of inordinate amounts of time had taught Kevin nothing if not patience. He waited, ever determined, and left his hand where it was. The man's eyes opened and focused on Kevin, his expression both lackluster and confused and yet filled with hatred. Kevin ignored him.

And then the man's eyes filled with something else. It was pain, easily recognizable. He tried to scream behind his gag, but the sound was muffled and weak. Kevin smiled, instinctively pressing his hand harder against the man's chest. The man bucked beneath the touch, shrieking into the gag and trying to get away despite the drug running through his system.

But he wasn't going anywhere. And Kevin could see that his experiment was working when the man's skin turned slightly green. Then gray. It was drying, cracking and flaking around the hairline. The cracking spread, crisscrossing his flesh, until the man stopped screaming and sat still as his body was leeched of every last drop of moisture within it.

When the foul deed was completed, Kevin extracted his hand with a strange crackling and sucking sound and stepped back. The corpse tied to his chair was nothing more than a mummy's remains and Kevin had the sudden sensation that if he was to touch it again, it would crumble to dust.

He looked down at his hand and pondered what had just happened.

For centuries, Kevin had been searching for some means with which to give himself and his men the power to heal. The Adarians had been on Earth for thousands of years, and in that time, they had seen battle with many foes, almost all of them of a supernatural nature. The Old Man had used Earth as a trash heap for the creatures he created for eons. Most were in hiding now, having learned that fighting one another was only seeing them to extinction. For the most part, they stayed in the shadows, often passing themselves off as human, and left one another alone. But for many, many years, this wasn't the case, and Kevin and his men had collectively sustained more injuries than they could count. The ability to heal was the one ability they lacked, and it was invaluable. The Adarians were hard to kill in that human, mortal wounds did not destroy them. However, the wounds healed painfully slowly, nearly at a human rate.

Over the course of thousands of years, many wounds

are sustained by a single individual. It amounts to vast amounts of pain.

One day, not two decades ago, Kevin happened upon a little girl who displayed the ability to heal with no more than a touch. For twenty years, he followed her. She grew into an extraordinarily beautiful young woman with lustrous black hair and striking blue eyes. Her name was Eleanore. And she was an archess.

Kevin had had it all planned out. He would introduce himself, earn her trust, and she would join him and his men, willingly offering up her healing power to them for their use. One of his abilities was the power to change forms. He did so, appearing to Eleanore as a teenage version of himself when she was a mere fifteen years old. He could tell that she was falling for him, but before he could get close enough, she and her family caught the scent of danger on the wind and disappeared. The Grangers disappeared again and again over the years, always moving from one place to the next in order to protect Eleanore and her amazing abilities. It was the greatest frustration of Kevin's painfully long existence, because as time passed, he found himself desiring Eleanore not only for her abilities—but for herself.

Eventually, and unfortunately, despite all of Kevin's careful watching and planning, Uriel happened upon Eleanore as well—and recognized her as his. The ensuing struggle to secure the archess eventually culminated in a terrible battle on a turbine field in Texas, ending in the Adarians' defeat.

In Dallas, where that battle had taken place several months ago, Uriel had proved himself at a distinct advantage by sinking his fangs into the throats of Kevin's men and draining them. In doing so, he temporarily absorbed their powers and was able to use them against the Adarians.

Since that telling battle, Kevin and his men had lain

low. They'd recuperated, regrouped, and reassessed their goals. Or Kevin had. He had also never stopped thinking about what Uriel had accomplished.

Nor had he stopped thinking about the *fifth* archangel. At least, that was what Kevin assumed the man was. He'd been unstoppable . . . and oddly familiar to Kevin.

Uriel's transformation and the stranger's unexpected appearance had been troubling enough to warrant several months of idle planning before attempting anything further on the archangels or their precious, irreplaceable archesses.

But at the moment, Kevin was touching upon something that might amount to a real plan. This little experiment had proved his suspicions.

Just as Uriel had been able to do, Kevin was capable of absorbing the power of another Adarian by drinking his blood. Already, he could feel the power he'd taken from Ely waning. *It's temporary,* he thought. That made sense; Ely was the true owner of the ability and Ely was still alive. The power did not reproduce but was lent through the taking of Ely's blood. *And now that I've used it once, it has returned to its rightful owner,* he realized.

Kevin turned his hand over and looked up at the door through which Ely had disappeared. Three of his Adarians had died on the turbine field in Texas. But nine remained, including himself. Eight of them waited for him beyond that door. Kevin pondered their individual powers and the implications of what he'd just learned. And he wondered. . . .

He pulled a tarp over the prisoner's withered body and stepped back. In a moment, Ely returned and Kevin approached him. "Bring Xathaniel to me."

Ely nodded again and left once more. Xathaniel, also known as Daniel among the Adarians, was what Kevin would consider the weakest member of their group. His only power was the power of invisibility.

While invisibility certainly had its uses from time to time, Kevin was more interested in offensive powers that could be used in battle, and that one didn't cut it. However, it wasn't unworthy of consideration for what Kevin had in mind.

If he was able to absorb an Adarian's power temporarily through the taking of his blood, what would happen should he drain the Adarian dry? What if he killed the man he drank from? Would the power he absorbed remain his?

"Sir, Daniel is not in his room. He seems to have left the complex."

Kevin turned to face Ely, whose large frame was once more eating up the space in the doorway. "Oh?" He pondered this a moment. Daniel may have stepped out for coffee or a beer or even to get laid. His men had needs, after all. "Bring him to me when he returns."

Ely nodded and left.

Kevin considered Xathaniel and his invisibility. If his little experiment worked, that invisibility would soon belong to Kevin permanently—and Daniel would be dead.

Samuel Lambent was a man of many secrets, not the smallest of which was the fact that "Samuel" was not his real name, and being the richest, most powerful media mogul in the world was not his full-time job.

Samuel Lambent was actually Samael, the incredibly tall and handsome, ash-blond archangel with charcoal gray eyes, known to a select few as the Fallen One. Right now, the notorious archangel was staring at a photograph that had been given to him months ago by one of the many "men" he employed around the world. It was a photograph of Juliette Anderson, the second archess. She was bent over the unconscious form of a man who had just been pulled from the sea after a surfing accident. She'd had no idea that she was being caught on film. She was dangerously unaware that her little secret could so easily fall into the wrong hands.

The archess was beyond precious, able to heal with no more than a touch, control the weather, influence fire, and move objects with her mind. However, it was unclear whether Juliette was aware of the extent of her powers.

Samael had thought long and hard about what he planned to do with little Juliette. The five-foot-three archess posed several options to Samael. It all depended upon which direction he wanted to go from here.

He could take her. He could make her his. It wouldn't be difficult; it never was for him. Plus, she was innocent— and he had something he could offer her. Juliette Anderson's bank account was on the shallow end of the pool, and always had been. Her parents were professors, but in fields that paid inadequately, and they squandered their money on travel, backpacking trips, camping expeditions, and the like. Neither of them knew how to save anything, and Juliette had learned long ago not to ask them for financial assistance. They would give it, but they couldn't afford to, and it was hard on Juliette's ego.

Oh, he had something he could offer. Sam had walked among the human race for a good while. And he knew well that, of money and sex, money was the more powerful lure. It truly was the root of all evil.

Anderson was gorgeous. There was a smoothness to her healthy, tanned complexion that normal humans did not possess; her archess's soul was hard to hide, just as it had been for Eleanore Granger. Juliette's hazel eyes shifted from light brown to stark green with the slightest provocation, if Samael's photographs were any indication. Her lips were full and pink, her teeth straight and bright white, her thick shining hair a mass of fantastic waves the likes of which Sam had only ever seen once before. On the first archess.

Juliette was beautiful, and as of yet, the four favorites were unaware of her existence. Making her his would forever deny at least one of them his match. That, in and of itself, was an incredibly tempting proposition. The warmth and pleasure he imagined he would feel with her in his bed made the idea of claiming her himself nothing short of a blissful win-win situation.

But . . . *no*.

Sam had other plans. *Broader* plans—that, thus far, were coming to delightful fruition. Of course, it helped that he was able to so easily manipulate events from behind the scenes. Strictly speaking, Juliette Anderson wasn't the one Sam was after at the moment. But if she somehow wound up in his bed anyway, the universe would get no complaints from him.

CHAPTER THREE

"Great." Juliette scowled at the darkening sky through her windshield. "*Juuust* great." She pursed her lips and clutched the steering wheel until she was white-knuckled. It was hard enough gauging the distance between the tires and the side of the road when you were seated on the right side. But the traffic was bumper-to-bumper and the car felt like moldy plastic around her, and she hated the fact that she was even sitting *down* again, much less stuck on a foreign road with no hope of reaching her hotel anytime soon.

Should she even be able to find it. Luckily, she had a GPS on the dash to help her with at least that much. And it had the most wonderful British voice to tell her she was going the wrong way.

Again, Juliette chanced a glance up and was a little surprised to see lightning spiderweb across the sky. The peal of thunder followed two seconds later.

Personally, Juliette enjoyed a good storm. But what it did to traffic was never a good thing. The roads sucked enough as it was; there were strange signs everywhere, the streets were basically shoulder-width narrow, parking was parallel or nothing, and there were simply too many vehicles that needed accommodation on a road system that had been built a thousand years ago. Throw in wet conditions and what you had was a big fat slow-moving mess.

It would be hours before she got to the Radisson Blu. She was suddenly grateful that British cars got about a thousand miles to the gallon. She hadn't seen a gas station anywhere along the road since she'd left the airport.

Christ, you're in a good mood, Jules, she told herself as she took a minute to rub her eyes while the cars in front of her came to a full stop once again. *Lighten up. You landed safe and sound. Everything else is trivial.* But the stupid airline had lost her luggage, and her right butt cheek was numb from sitting, and she was terrified that she was going to get into a wreck and wind up in a foreign jail before the end of the day.

The car behind her began honking. Juliette looked up and peered at the driver through her rearview mirror. Past her own honey-brown-haired, hazel-eyed reflection, she caught sight of the man in the BMW behind her. The man was middle-aged, from what she could tell. Gold wristwatch? Maybe silver; hard to tell in this light. Balding with glasses. He had a cell phone to his right ear.

Juliette frowned. What the hell was he honking at?

Up ahead, traffic began to crawl forward once more. Jules reached a good five miles per hour, before it once again slowed to a halt and she sighed.

The driver in the BMW behind Juliette leaned on his horn. Jules glanced up, caught him in the rearview mirror, and shot him a dirty look. In response, he palmed the horn and kept it down. *What the hell?* she thought. *Does he think I can make the three hundred cars in front of me move faster? Does he actually think I can go anywhere?*

Thunder rolled across the highway, rumbling the windows in their panes and temporarily drowning out the sound of the BMW's horn. Lightning crashed to the right of Juliette's car, somewhere not too far away, and when she began to count the seconds, she didn't even reach the number one before the sky erupted with a bellow of sound.

She jumped a little and ducked instinctively. Somewhere over the green hill, in the neighborhood of the suburbs, car alarms went off.

Juliette turned on her car radio and got nothing but static on every station. She tried to swallow and found her throat a little dry. Her head was aching now as tension rode up through her arms and into her neck.

Her car was presently stuck underneath an overpass and the damp gray cement had been decorated by no fewer than ten different gangs. Juliette frowned at the visual cacophony of paint as a man dressed in shabby clothing came slowly lumbering around the corner of one of the overpass's support columns. His shoes had no toes and he was holding a hat. There were a few coins in the hat, not much paper. However, in Britain, the coins tended to be worth a lot more than they were in the US, so that wasn't necessarily telling.

Juliette automatically began rummaging in the backpack beside her in the passenger seat of the rental car. She knew she had some two-pound coins in one of the outer pockets. She checked ahead as she dug around; the traffic still wasn't moving, so she was safe. Once she found the coins, she rolled down her window and called out to him. At first, he didn't seem to hear her. Thunder once more rolled over the traffic jam, making it harder for her to gain his attention. She tried again and again, and on the third attempt, he looked up, his blue eyes stark against his ruddy face and stubbled chin.

Juliette waved him over and the man hobbled to her window. She handed him every coin she had and the man took them gently in his stained fingers as his weathered lips cracked a grateful smile.

Behind her, Mr. BMW laid into his horn a third time. Juliette's eyes widened. She raised her head to look at him through her rearview mirror. He glared at her and her blood began to roar through her eardrums. She slowly narrowed her gaze, glaring back at him. She was normally a nonconfrontational person, but this guy was pushing the envelope with her.

In response, he flipped her the British rendition of the bird: a backward peace sign.

And then the hood of his car erupted into white sparks and flame as a bolt of lightning shot through it like a massive white-light tree trunk. Juliette saw the strike as if in slow motion. Time slowed down, allowing her to witness the billions of minuscule tributaries of electricity that shot off the massive main column of the bolt. It reminded her of one of those glass balls that you put your hand on and the static electricity shoots from the ball toward the center of your palm.

But the sound was deafening. There was a blast, like a bomb, and then a high-pitched ringing and little else. Juliette knew that somewhere, just outside this little bubble of reality that the lightning bolt had affected, even more alarms were going off, horns were being honked, and people might be getting out of their cars now.

But for her, there was only time, slow and impossible — and the man behind her, who now literally could not let go of his cell phone as the electricity from the bolt shot through his car and into the cabin, zapping his glasses until they singed his eyebrows and nose, and melting his wristwatch onto his arm.

I did that, she thought suddenly. Mr. BMW was screaming now, but there was no sound. Only the ringing and a muffled reality. He clutched his arm and fumbled for the door handle and Juliette could only watch, in stunned realization.

She knew it in the core of who she was. It was a certainty, like the knowledge that the sun would rise in the east and that thinking took place in the brain. *She* had called the lightning on that man's car.

That was me.

Reality freezes at points in a person's life. Time is like everything else—relative. It took years for the man in the BMW behind Juliette to come to his senses and feel for his slightly melted door handle, open it, and scramble out into the street to topple over. It took another year for her to open her own door and rush out into the street after him.

With guilt heavy on her shoulders, she propelled herself forward, through the waning gale to the unconscious man's side. She saw her fingers at his throat, checking for a pulse. A century later, she was leaning over him, hoping to feel his breath against her ear.

When she did, she sat back on her heels and looked down at his melted watch and scorch marks. Then, without premeditation, she placed her hand to his chest and closed her eyes.

It was what she had done in Australia. But she didn't have time to contemplate the madness of it. Her body was acting of its own accord.

All around her were the sounds of people stirring. Someone was yelling about calling ambulances and someone else was yelling back that an ambulance would never make it through anyway. There was still thunder, but it had settled a bit. There was the crackling of a fire and Juliette knew that it was the interior of the BMW she was listening to as it smoldered and popped itself into oblivion. A thrum of hard fear rushed through her at the sound. She didn't mind fires when they were contained, and even enjoyed a warm blaze in a hearth, but fires on their own were ravenous, unpredictable forces that belched poison and consumed everything in their paths.

She heard rain falling, though, and also knew the fire

would soon be put out. She was soaked through and growing cold just as the familiar heat gathered beneath her palm, spread up her arm, and seeped into the sleeping body of the man beside her.

This isn't happening, she thought, as weakness stole into her body while the man stirred in front of her and his burn marks melted away. *I can heal . . . and I can call lightning from the skies.* It was a floating realization, a faint voice whispering in the halls of her conscious mind. It was a verity, though, real enough that it couldn't be ignored.

She opened her eyes to find the man she'd given money to standing across from her, watching her silently. Her heart thudded hard in her chest and she froze, feeling as paralyzed as a deer in headlights.

Beneath the light touch of her palm, the injured man rolled over a bit, turned his head, and opened his eyes. Juliette glanced down at him, blinked, and then hurriedly removed her hand and slid back a few inches.

She felt tired, more weary than she should have. She now recalled feeling the same way after healing the surfer in Australia. *This is real. What I did in Australia was real. Not a breakdown. It was real.*

The man looked up at her, blinked when rain fell into his eyes, and threw his arm over his face. Then he frowned. *"You,"* he said, his features filled with disdain. "Are you robbin' me or somethin'?" he asked in a heavy Scottish accent.

Juliette was taken aback, despite the impossibility of the situation. But she was not one to be mistreated. His words instantly got her ire up. Once she recalled the rudeness he'd displayed only minutes ago, she recovered and met his look of disdain with one of her own. "You *fainted,*" she told him, "like a little girl. I was only trying to help you out."

He blinked again, this time not from the rain, and

then glanced at his burning car. Black smoke curled up from the shattered sunroof and billowed above the street before the rain and clouds ate it up.

The man looked back up at Juliette. And then, in a most unexpected move, his face broke a broad smile and he began to laugh. It was a pleasant laugh: a chuckle, deep and true. "Figures," he said. "I finally get somethin' worth a shite out o' me divorce and God goes an' takes it away again. He really does like me ex-wife better than me." He sat up, and because Juliette was there in front of him, she found herself helping him.

Once he was upright, he looked at her again. "You look like her, you do," he said. "When she was a younger lass." He ran his hand over his bald head, washing away a bit of the rain, and then sighed. "She was too good for me. She knew it—I should've." He shook his head. "I'm sorrae I'm such an ass."

Juliette blinked. That was why he had honked at her and flipped her off? *Wow,* she thought. *Must have been a rough divorce.* She licked her lips and tasted rain. "It's okay?" What was there to say to that? She was trembling, but she managed a small smile.

He shrugged helplessly. "You *really* look like her now that I don' have me glasses. Everythin's blurry." He glanced around at the ground and, not finding them, seemed to give up. "The name's Albert." He held out his hand.

Juliette hesitated briefly and then grasped it firmly, never one to give a limp handshake, no matter what the circumstances. "I'm Juliette," she replied. Then she glanced at the cars around them. Sirens could now be heard in the distance. Someone was arguing over a fender bender about twenty cars down. Juliette and the BMW guy were starting to acquire an audience.

"Oy! Are you okay, there?" A pair of teenage boys was peeking tentatively around the car behind the smoldering BMW. They appeared genuinely concerned.

"Do we need the paramedics?" one asked.

"One's already on the way, James. Can you no' hear it?"

Their conversation continued and Juliette ignored them. She leaned a little closer to Albert. "Can you stand?"

"I think so. I thought the lightnin' had done me in bu'" — he looked at his arms and felt his face — "I guess I was wrong. Me ears are no' even ringin' or anythin'."

Juliette knew why. As the storm quieted around her, reflecting her own emotions, that truth stomped its foot and banged on the door of her consciousness, asserting itself blatantly. Albert had been *plenty* hurt by the lightning and she'd been the reason for that damage, not any deity. She was also the reason he wasn't hurt now. *That* was the truth.

However, what she said was, "Maybe God doesn't like your ex-wife better than you, after all."

Albert met her wry smile with a lopsided grin of his own and she helped him stand.

Twenty minutes later, the police arrived and managed to get everyone back into their cars — except of course for Albert, whom they forced into an ambulance on the sheer principle that he'd been inside of a car struck by lightning.

Juliette caught his good-bye nod, returned it, and got back into her own car at the behest of the police. As she settled, still shaking, into the driver's seat and looked over the steering wheel, her gaze met one of stark blue.

It was the man that she'd given money to. She'd forgotten about him. He'd watched her heal Albert.

Juliette swallowed hard and peered into the man's eyes. Slowly, he lifted the coins she had given him for her to see. Then he nodded once, slowly and surely, as if to say *I understand*, and *Thank you*. And then he put the coins back into his hat, turned around, and walked away. She lost sight of him as he rounded the corner beneath the overpass.

A few seconds later, Juliette followed the car in front of her as traffic began its slow crawl back to life. The rain had all but stopped and the sun peeked through the clouds up above. And Juliette was no longer uncertain of her sanity. Now she was uncertain of just about everything else.

Daniel knew he was on borrowed time. His plan had taken him from the Adarian complex and across the Atlantic to where the second archess had just landed. It was a risky plan and it wouldn't be easy to execute.

But his life depended on it.

Abraxos was going to kill one of his men. The tall and handsome, raven-black-haired, blue-eyed Adarian General had been the first archangel in existence. He was the leader of the Adarian army, which had been tossed out by the Old Man eons ago and had been forced to scratch out an existence on this trash heap of a world the humans called Earth.

And now, because the General knew of the existence of the archesses and their inherent healing power, the Adarian leader was evolving a horrid plan. That plan involved kidnapping every one of the archesses and murdering them so that the General, and a few select Adarians, could live out the remainder of their immortal lives enjoying the healing power of their archess blood.

Only a few would be chosen to receive the blood. Daniel knew he was not to be one of them. In fact, he knew that if he had remained behind, he would have been killed outright. That much had been painfully clear. The General believed that Daniel's ability to become invisible was the only power Daniel possessed, and that apparently wasn't enough to keep Daniel alive. The General needed a guinea pig—and he'd chosen Daniel for the mortal task.

However, the General was mistaken. Daniel also had

the power of prophecy, of divination: the ability to see into the future.

He'd always kept this second ability a secret from the General because the power of prophecy wasn't an easy one to use, no matter how valuable it was. It *hurt* him to use it. Every time he performed a divination, it left him sick and weakened and in vast amounts of agony. No amount of morphine was capable of ridding him of this pain. It was a supernatural suffering, without recourse.

As long as these side effects were not his own to suffer, Abraxos would not have cared how horrible they were, and he would have forced Daniel to use that power with great frequency to locate the other archesses or supernatural beings. The advantages to knowing your opponent's next moves before they did were enormous. So Daniel had hidden his prophecy power from his leader, and only his ability to turn himself invisible had been of any use to Abraxos—that was all the General knew Daniel had to offer.

Several days ago, Daniel had performed a divination. He didn't normally do so, again because of the pain, but he'd been riddled with a foreboding feeling and wanted to know why. So, he decided to put up with the pain long enough to satisfy the niggling sense that the prophecy was necessary. He performed the divination and had seen within it something wholly disconcerting: the General and his plan to kill Daniel by ingesting all of his blood. The entire scene unfolded before Daniel's mind, along with the General's reasons for doing so.

Whether Abraxos's plan made sense or not was another question entirely. As far as Daniel was concerned, it was an impossible dream that the Adarians would ever successfully get their hands on even one of the archesses, much less all of them. As far as Daniel was concerned, Abraxos was going mad and that plan alone proved it. But that was beside the point. The General would carry out the worst part of his plan no matter what, and kill Daniel whether the rest of the design made sense or not.

Daniel wondered whether the General had chosen another Adarian to die in his stead now that Daniel had escaped. Maybe he had—and that soldier was already dead. If that was the case, he wondered who it might be. And he wondered if it had worked. Had Abraxos been capable of absorbing the Adarian's power?

If so . . . would he decide he wanted more abilities? Would the General now go after any of the other men for their powers? Where would it stop?

Daniel knew that he'd been originally singled out by the General because all he seemed to offer was his invisibility. But if Daniel could prove that he had more to offer, it might just ensure that the General never turned on him and decided to take his power as his own. Abraxos would not want to suffer the agony that came with using the divination ability himself, so Daniel highly doubted that his leader would take such a power from him. But the General *would* allow Daniel to live as long as *Daniel* was the one to suffer the pain—and as long as Daniel delivered a prophecy whenever the General wanted him to.

Even if it promised a life of agony, it was better to Daniel to use his divination ability whenever his leader saw fit rather than face the gruesome death he had foreseen in that terrible glimpse into the future. It was his only hope. He could never leave the Adarians; he could never disappear entirely. He didn't belong anywhere else and knew of nowhere to go—and it didn't matter. No matter where Daniel went, the General would find him eventually. There was no escape from him. And the Adarians were the only family Daniel had ever known.

He had nothing else. This plan had to work.

All he needed was Juliette Anderson. She was his proof. Other than Eleanore Granger—who was now not only married to one of the archangels but very much in the public eye as the wife of a famous actor, and hence virtually untouchable—Juliette Anderson was the only archess known to exist. And thus far, Daniel was fairly certain that only *he* knew she existed. The archangels themselves were clueless.

If Daniel acted fast enough, he would gain the upper hand on every player on the board, archangel or Adarian. He would have Anderson in his possession and he could use her as the evidence he needed to prove to Abraxos that he was a valuable member of the team.

That was why he was here, in this hotel room in Scotland. It was why he now tossed Juliette Anderson's stolen suitcase on the hotel bed and unzipped it, pulling the lid up and over to let it drop against the comforter. It had been ridiculously easy for him to steal from the baggage car on the tarmac, as any nonliving item he was carrying also turned invisible when he used that power. He wondered what she must have thought when her suitcase never came down the chute onto the baggage claim carousel. He let his eyes graze over the contents, slowly taking it all in. The first thing he noticed was the plush elephant in the center of the cushion of clothing. It looked a tad worn, its stitching weathered, its dark gray color faded in spots. Around its neck was a makeshift collar sewn out of scraps of velvet. Lettering on the collar read, "Nessie."

Daniel grinned, unable to help himself, and lifted the animal out of its nest. "Nessie, huh?" he said to no one. Juliette was sure to miss the stuffed animal. It had a distinctly personal feel to it, and for a moment, Daniel felt a touch guilty for the theft. But it was fleeting and passed quickly. Out of curiosity, he placed it to his nose and inhaled. It smelled like Parma Violets. It was a distinct candy-flower scent and surprised him in its rarity. Gently, he laid the elephant on the quilt and returned to the contents of the suitcase.

There were a few trade paperbacks on the subjects of archaeology and Caledonia. Among the books was one on the interpretation of dreams. Daniel frowned at it, wondering at the oddball subject, and then tossed it aside. After a few minutes of sorting through decidedly delicious undergarments and petite-sized clothing, he found what he was hoping to find. He pulled it out of the suitcase and held it to the light.

A USB memory stick.

With a smile, Daniel tucked the memory stick into his pocket, then lifted a soft white pair of cotton panties from the pile of messed-up clothes. This, too, he shoved into his pocket before he pulled on his Belstaff jacket and headed toward the door. Divinations regarding a certain individual were more easily performed when he possessed something that belonged to the person he was divining about.

As Daniel passed the bathroom, he glanced at the man reflected in the mirror. The blond stood six feet three with broad shoulders, a strong chin, and ice green eyes possessing deep, dark pupils like inky black pools. Daniel stopped and smiled at his twin, noting the cruel tilt to his lips. It was a reflection he'd seen millions upon millions of times and yet it gave him pause for the simple reason that it was there. When your most valuable Adarian power was invisibility, it felt reassuring to know you became solid once again at the end of it all.

The lobby was grandly decorated, sporting marble flooring, gold-veined mirrors, and vase upon vase of real, live orchids. Daniel made his way past several hotel workers, nodding at the women who openly ogled him, and slipped into the business center where the hotel kept several desktop computers for guests to use.

The room was empty, which was fortunate. Daniel sat at the computer farthest from the door and slipped the small memory stick into the drive slot on the computer's tower.

The smile on his lips spread as he opened the drive and began perusing the titles of the files within it. There were several working papers on the drive, old articles, and even a few electronic books. But what interested him most was the file labeled "Journal, 2000–present."

With the slow deliberation of one who not only needs to absorb what he is learning but enjoys it immensely, Daniel clicked the file open and sat back to read.

CHAPTER FOUR

She had to tell someone. She had to confide in someone or she was going to . . . she was going to . . . "I'm
going mad," she whispered in frustration, as she ran a
shaking hand through her hair and then held on to it,
fisting it in agitation.

The hotel's Internet connection was down, so going
online and using chat or e-mail to talk to Sophie wouldn't
work. And though it would give her time to sort through
her thoughts as she wrote them down, it was way too im-
personal for what she had to share. She'd have to call her
best friend, but even that seemed wrong for what she
wanted to say. What if Sophie just hung up on her? Not
that she ever would. Soph wasn't like that. The girl had
gone through so much in her own life, it had left her mind
wide open to the eccentricities and "impossibilities" of
the world.

But what Juliette had to tell her was so unbelievable, Sophie would at least think she was joking. Unless Juliette could sit Soph down and stare into her
friend's beautiful gold eyes as she told her the truth,
there was no way Soph would recognize her seriousness. She would have no real reason to believe that
Juliette could not only heal people but control the
weather as well.

There was no doubt remaining in her mind about these supernatural powers now. Once Juliette had made it to the nearest grocery store after the lightning bolt incident, she had pulled into the lot and parked the car in order to steady her nerves and catch her breath. She checked her location on the map against what the navigation system on the dashboard was telling her.

The storm had more or less stopped where she was and only a few errant raindrops splattered against her windshield.

Juliette had decided to conduct a little experiment. She gazed out the windshield and paid close attention to the patterns of the waning storm. There was a house next to the grocery store and in the yard in the back was a large tree with a wooden swing.

She had closed her eyes and imagined a strong wind blowing the wooden swing. When she'd opened her eyes again, the swing was rocking wildly back and forth in a sudden and isolated wind.

After that, she tried calling a single rain cloud. It reminded her of that Winnie the Pooh song "Little Black Rain Cloud" as she imagined it, but when she had finished, there it was, hovering right above the car. It drenched her rental and every patron unlucky enough to choose that moment to leave the store.

At last, Juliette had attempted one final test. She wanted to know whether the lightning, in particular, had really been her fault. Squeezing her hands into painful fists in her lap, she imagined a single bolt of lightning shooting from cloud to cloud above her. She was very careful not to imagine the bolt coming anywhere near the ground or its buildings or treetops. A split second later, a boom of thunder rocked her vehicle, set off several car alarms, and surprised a dog down the street, who began barking furiously.

So, now she knew. It was official. She was a weather-controlling freak of nature, with the ability to heal the injuries caused by her horrid meteorological mistakes.

Juliette's teeth clenched as she continued to briskly pace the same path that she'd already carved across the hotel room's carpet. Her cell phone was clutched tightly in her hand; she just didn't know whom to call.

And then it rang, vibrating weakly in Juliette's death grip. She stopped in her tracks and stared down at the instrument. The LCD screen read "Dad."

Juliette took a deep, steadying breath, then flipped open her phone and placed it to her ear. "Hi, Dad!" She tried her best to hide her mounting unease behind faked excitement.

"Hi, sweetie, how was the flight?"

"Long," she answered easily. That much was true.

"I bet. Did everything go well? Do you have your luggage?"

Another easy one. "No, the luggage is MIA, but I'm fine. I just got to the hotel."

"Ah, good. Sorry about the luggage, sweetie. With as much as you travel, it was bound to happen eventually. How is the jet lag treating you?"

"Like a war prisoner," she replied. That was true, too. She'd only just gotten over the jet lag from Australia before she'd had to fly to Scotland. Her body was confused, to say the least.

Her father laughed. "I bet."

"How's Mom?" Juliette asked, desperately wanting to talk about something that would take her mind off her present predicament.

"On another bicycle tour. She's been gone six days. She'll be back before you leave, though, and when she checks in tomorrow, I'll let her know you're safe. We're not that far away now; maybe you can hop a train and come see us sometime soon?" Her parents taught at the university in Gmunden, Austria.

"I'd love to, Dad." She really would. She could tell her parents about her new abilities. They would believe her—wouldn't they? A hard shiver went through Juliette and she had to close her eyes. "Let me get some things squared away here first and I'll let you know," she told her father.

"Okay, sounds good. Love you, sweetie. Get some sleep now. Bye-bye."

"Love you, too." Juliette hung up, feeling strangely bereft on top of the fear and anxiousness she was already suffering. The silence in the hotel room sounded hollow and gave her the sensation of cold. She was probably overly tired, she knew; she felt gritty from all the travel, and the promise of more of it didn't help matters.

But her *secret* hung over her just like Pooh's little black rain cloud, and it wasn't going to go away. She knew that. It wasn't so much the abilities, themselves, that had her worried. It was the fact that she *had* them in the first place.

Why? Why did she have these abilities? Why were they cropping up now? What was next? Did she have some sort of brain tumor or something? Like a main character in a science fiction novel who discovers superpowers right before he has an aneurysm and croaks?

She wanted to tell her dad. She really did. It just wasn't doable. She could just imagine the conversation: "That's great about you getting tenure, Dad, but you know what really trumps that? I can heal people! That's right, just like Jesus!"

No, no.

Talking it out with Soph would help. But not here, and not on the phone. She was going to have to wait until she returned to the States.

Juliette fell onto the hard wooden chair at the desk in her hotel room and sighed heavily. She only hoped she could survive holding it in that long.

*   *   *

Gabriel finished hammering the board into place and then stepped back to survey his work. As he did, he was slammed into from behind by a small but determined body that then proceeded to wrap itself around the bottom half of his leg.

"Go now!" came a small cry from below. Gabriel smiled and looked down into the eager, bright face of one of the children who would be living in the home once Gabe and the other men finished constructing it. "Go on, now, ye promised!" the boy insisted, his broad five-year-old's smile devoid of two front teeth.

Tristan was a wiry, strong little towheaded boy with bright blue eyes and a slight sprinkling of freckles across his nose. He was forever growing out of what clothes the town could supply him with, not because they were slow to clothe him, but because Tristan was too quick to grow. His twin sister, Beth, was a hand shorter and had slightly darker hair but slightly lighter eyes. In the frame of her pale face, they looked like ice, cold and clear and older than her years.

Gabriel set down his hammer on a nearby pile of rocks and put his hands on his hips. "Aye, Tristan," he admitted. "I did tell you I'd give you a ride, did I no'?"

Tristan nodded emphatically.

"Well, where's your bonnie sister, then?" Gabriel asked, referring to Tristan's twin.

"I'm here!" came an exuberant cry. A moment later, a second small body slammed into Gabriel, drawing a deep laugh from within his chest. Beth quickly seated herself on Gabriel's other boot and wrapped herself tightly around his leg.

"Go now! Go!" the two cried.

Gabriel shook his head and began making a show of lifting their tiny weights as he lumbered around the kirk-yard that bordered the small plot of land where they were building the children's home. The siblings giggled and squealed and held on for dear life as he picked up the pace and trotted in between the gravestones of men and women he had actually known while they were alive—all those years ago.

He knew the other men were watching him and judging him. In their eyes, he was a newcomer, having arrived on Hebridean soil only a few months ago. He was the "son of Duncan Black," a man whom many of the older inhabitants of the Western Isles had come to trust and call friend. Would his son fit in as well?

Gabriel knew that he would. He always did. And at the moment, their opinions were but faint worries as little Beth giggled in that way that was completely contagious, drawing laughter from Gabriel as easily as one drew water from a well.

Tristan and Beth were two of nineteen children who had been recently displaced in the economy's downturn. Their orphanage in Luskentyre needed so many repairs that it had been virtually falling down around them. Gabriel had decided that instead of turning a few of the mansion's items into gold to fund repairs that would amount to no more than Band-Aids, he would simply pay for the building of a new home.

It was easier to pull such a trick on the Western Isles than it would have been on the mainland. The people in Harris and Lewis were tight-knit and down-to-earth. They were well accustomed to doing whatever had to be done in order to help one another get through. So, when Gabriel Black, son of Duncan Black, arrived on the islands several months ago with a certain amount in "savings" and stated that he wanted to use it to help the community get back on its feet, not one of them blinked an eye before offering to lend a hand. The new children's home was one of several projects he had helped get started across the Hebrides, but to him, it was the most important.

Early mornings, Gabriel sailed out with Stuart Burns on his fishing boats in Ardvey. In the afternoons, he traveled to Luskentyre, picked up a hammer and a pack of nails, and got to work building the future of the land he had long ago decided to call his home. And that was what he was doing now, on this Friday afternoon.

Sundays in Harris were sacred and kept with strict adherence. Nothing was open on Sundays, so Gabriel spent those days with the children as well. Beth and Tristan tended to monopolize that time; the two had taken to him like glue. He didn't mind at all. He was quite fond of them as well.

He would have adopted them long ago—along with all the other children at the home—if it weren't for the fact that he didn't age. It was a hard supernatural truth that there were no easy ways to skirt around. He would remain young forever to watch his children grow old and die.

On Gabriel's left leg, Tristan issued a challenge to his sister, claiming that he would beat her to the next headstone. Beth excitedly took the challenge, but not before she turned in her perch on Gabe's right leg and studied the distance between herself and the MacDonald headstone twenty paces away.

"Ye're goin' tae lose, Trist!" she shot back at him, her smile broadening. She, too, was missing teeth. "I'll get there before yae do!"

Gabriel tried not to encourage them. He simply took the steps to the headstone, and of course, Beth was right. Gabe's right leg was the first to close the distance, much to Tristan's chagrin. But Tristan got over it quickly; he was used to his sister winning. Beth was a very smart five-year-old.

"Black!"

Gabriel turned to see one of the workmen striding toward him across the kirkyard. There was a worried frown on his face. Gabe bent and patted the children on their backs. "Off with you, now," he whispered. "An' stay away from the bogs, do y'hear?"

The twins nodded and though Tristan made a very disappointed face, they both stood, releasing Gabriel's legs. Then Tristan issued another challenge to his sister, and the two were off like lights, running helter-skelter across the cemetery.

"Timothy," Gabriel greeted the man who hurriedly approached him. "Wha' is it, then?"

"Black, someone's got tae speak with the debtors on the mainland," Timothy told him, somewhat out of breath. "People are beginnin' tae ask questions. They want tae know about yer money an' . . . taxes an' all that." Timothy gave a helpless shrug, took off his hat, and then nervously glanced behind him.

Gabriel followed his flick of a gaze to a tall, broad-shouldered man standing against the wall of a nearby building, his thick arms crossed over his chest. Angus Dougal.

"And wha' people exactly would these be, Timothy?" Gabriel asked, not taking his eyes off Dougal's watchful form.

Timothy didn't answer, which told Gabriel everything he needed to know. Dougal had been asking questions about him. The townspeople knew that he'd been a fire-fighter in New York because that was the story he'd given them upon arrival. Dougal no doubt wondered how a firefighter could afford the things Gabriel was paying for. Not that he couldn't handle anything the man threw his way, but it was irritating, to say the least. Gabriel would have to set things right now, quiet people down, and cover a few things up. After all, Dougal was a smart man—and the money had come from a strange source, indeed. Gabriel was a firefighter in New York City and as such, he didn't make a millionaire's living.

The money he had donated for the rebuilding projects had come from his ability to take any item in the world and turn it into gold. He was an archangel; it was only one of his many powers.

Dougal was on to him.

Gabriel gazed across the distance, his silver eyes locked with Angus's emerald glare. He wished he didn't have to have this trouble with a fellow clansman. Dougal was a good man and a good cop. His soul was clean, but there was an aura of bitterness around it these days. Gabriel could guess as to what that was all about.

Angus and his longtime girlfriend had recently split up. Unfortunately, right after that event, Gabriel had slept with Dougal's sister, Edeen. The compounded situation had ignited a would-be hatred in Angus for the former Messenger Archangel.

Gabriel sighed. He would have to travel to Glasgow now and might even need his guardian, Max Gillihan, to help set the records straight and wipe memories. With a set jaw and clenched teeth, Gabriel nodded at Angus Dougal.

Angus nodded back.

General Kevin Trenton slowly paced around the small metal-lined chamber, his hands clasped calmly behind his back, his stark blue eyes knowledgeably surveying the faces of his men with an inscrutable expression.

Three of his men were gathered within the secure chamber, and three alone. They had been selected and separated by careful consideration—and for good reason. Each possessed powers or abilities that were unaccountably useful and irreplaceable, powers that the Adarians could not continue to survive without. They had earned their place in that room, for those gathered were about to have a very great gift bestowed upon them.

They were the Chosen.

In one corner of the small room, a strangely humanoid-shaped bundle was hidden beneath a simple white sheet. Its identity was unknown to the men and the shape did not move.

"I'll get straight to the point, gentlemen," Kevin began, turning his back to his men as he glanced once at the barred metal door. "We have been searching for thousands of years for the means with which to prevent the suffering that time inflicts upon our race." He paused and turned to face them once more in order to measure the understanding on their faces. "We can't heal ourselves," he stated simply, placing his hands on the back of a metal chair before leaning on it. He looked each of his men in the eye, one after another. "We take on wound after wound and suffer the slow healing process of a human, unable to die no matter how grave the injury. The only thing that sets us apart from mortals in that respect is our lack of scars. We can't heal ourselves," he repeated. And then he added quietly, "Not on our own, anyway."

At this, they seemed to straighten in their seats, their interest piqued.

"Eleanore Granger represented a chance for us that we'd never before possessed." The men were silent, but he knew what they were thinking. Even if they'd managed to abduct Granger, there had been no promise that her ability to heal could have successfully been transferred to the Adarians.

However, for him, that uncertainty was laid to rest the moment he took Ely's blood and absorbed his withering power.

"Ely," Kevin addressed the large black Adarian personally.

The Adarian stood, gracefully and fluidly, and nodded in respect at his general. "Yes, sir."

"I know you have been wondering why I took your

blood earlier. I will tell you now." Kevin released the chair and began pacing once more. "Quite frankly, men, I drank what I took from Elyon. I absorbed it into my own body." Here he paused, glanced at them, and continued. "And in doing so, I absorbed his power as well."

With one clean pull, he yanked the sheet off the mystery form in the corner of the room, revealing the dried corpse of the man he had killed during his experiment that morning.

The surprise was clearly evident on his men's faces. None of them spoke for some time, their eyes wide, their postures now hyperalert. They looked from the corpse to him and understanding dawned on their handsome features.

Elyon, who was still standing, now smiled a slow, knowing smile. "Sir," he said, flashing bright white teeth. "You did a better job than I normally do."

Kevin flashed his own winning smile and then nodded for Ely to sit. The Adarian obeyed and Kevin moved away from the withered corpse. "Unfortunately, the effects are temporary. I tried the experiment a second time on a fresh prisoner, but failed." He stopped and faced them. "Because only a few hours have passed since I absorbed Ely's blood, I am assuming that it was not time that caused the power to dissipate. Instead, it is most likely the case that the ability can only be used once before needing to be replenished."

"Sir." One of the soldiers, a blond man with light blue eyes, nodded at his general, gaining Kevin's attention. Kevin waited for him to continue. "What exactly does this mean for Eleanore Granger?"

Kevin's smile was back. "I'm glad you asked, Luke." Luke's Adarian name was Laoth and his given abilities allowed him to hypnotize the mortal minds of his victims. He could also call darkness upon a certain area, silence it, and send anyone without the will to resist him into a deep sleep. Once they were asleep, Luke could enter their dreams at will, forming them and molding them to his specifications. His abilities had been incredibly useful on many, many occasions.

"I believe Granger is the first of what will soon be the revelation of all of the archesses," Kevin told them. "And I believe each one will possess the ability to heal— among other talents."

"How many will there be?" asked a dark-haired soldier by the Adarian name of Morael. He went by "Mitchell" now and had for some time. His powers allowed him to change the molecular structure of an item, move the very earth beneath their feet, and control the temperature of the air around them. He also possessed the ability to read minds, though he had never been successful at reading Kevin's.

"Four." Kevin paused a moment, frowned, and then added, "I could be wrong. But it would make sense. This is why I have chosen the three of you to receive their blood. I, myself, will drink from Granger."

Again, the group fell into silence and Kevin could just imagine the implications that were undoubtedly spinning in their heads. After a few moments of somewhat stunned quiet, Kevin went on. "Of course, we will take a small amount at first in order to test our theory. But if the biological makeup of an archess is anything like that of an Adarian, this should work. And if it does, then our wisest step would be to carry out the final act quickly and completely and take the power their blood gives us."

Mitchell focused his dark eyes upon his general and frowned. "Are you saying what I think you're saying, sir?"

Without missing a beat, Kevin replied, "I am," and accompanied it with a very serious nod. He could feel the tension in the room thicken then; it almost crackled with foreboding intensity. What he was suggesting would most likely be regarded as insane at first. They would balk at the idea, which he could plainly see was happening before his eyes. Kill an archess? And not just one archess—but *all* of them?

These women were not only special; they were nearly sacred. What kinds of repercussions would causing their deaths bring down upon the already cursed Adarians? Their knee-jerk reaction was understandably one of terror.

But in a few minutes, it would settle in and they would realize that he was right. They had no choice. If Kevin and his men were actually fortunate enough to be able to locate and capture every one of the archesses, they couldn't afford to risk that the women would be taken away, along with their powers, once more.

The women had to die.

"Sir . . ." Elyon shifted in his seat, glanced at his fellow Adarians, then looked back at his general. "There is nothing more dangerous than a man who has nothing left to lose. And an *archangel* in that position? They won't stop coming after us until we're all dead."

"I know," Kevin told him. He wasn't about to share with them the fact that he, himself, had killed another Adarian and drained him of all his blood in order to see whether this plan would indeed work. Instead, he simply expected Elyon to trust him. After all, he had never led them astray before. Not in thousands upon thousands of years. "Either way, men, the archangels will have to die as well."

Now the men before him sat in stunned silence, obviously trying to absorb all this new information—and failing. Kevin took a deep breath and crossed his arms over his chest. "For the moment, trust that I am working on a few plans," he said. "You'll be briefed when the time is right. In the meantime, the information I have shared with you is not to leave this room. Am I understood?"

His men nodded. "Yes, sir," they replied in unison.

With that, he dismissed them, and when he was alone, he sat down in the metal chair he'd been leaning on. He ran his tongue over his straight, white teeth and the gums that ached above them. He frowned and stared at the blank white wall, his thoughts turned toward a woman with jet-black hair and gorgeous blue eyes.

CHAPTER FIVE

How many times he had taken this very same ferry across from Ullapool to Stornoway, he couldn't count. Gabriel was older than the ship. He was older than the ferry system itself. For a hundred years, the ancestor of each ship had seen and felt him mount its planks, climb its stairs, and watch the cold gray sea through its salt-stained windows.

Yet, every time, it was as if he were doing it for the first time. The magnetism of the water never lost its pull. It never grew un-grand or un-magnificent. It was never less than it was the time before. Gabriel felt a respect for the sea that he felt for little else in the world. It was older than he was. And just as deadly.

He liked it out here, on the open observation deck, the best. The wind was cold and cut to the bone and would probably rip the immune system of a human to shreds. But he was no human. The wind hurt, but it was a begrudging kind of pain. He put up with it, and as his reward, he was allowed to stand alone, a solitary figure in black, and gaze out across the ocean's bottomless plain.

He needed this right now. He'd felt anxious of late. He had no idea what it meant, as it happened very rarely. But every once in a long, long while, he felt restless and uncertain and his brain felt slightly fuzzy. It was how he had felt as he'd boarded the ferry in Ullapool and headed straight to the top deck. He had known that the wind would slice through his anxiety and rescue him from the fuzzy shroud that had wrapped itself around him. He was right; it hurt, but it helped.

Traveling by ferry wasn't necessary for him, of course. Anytime he wanted, he could find a door and simply open a portal to the mansion he shared with his brothers and its extra-dimensionality would transport him to any location he desired.

This time, he was on his way back from a quick trip to Glasgow to straighten things out with the banks. It hadn't taken much: a phone call to Max explaining the situation and a fast pop-in at the main office, and everything was squared away again. Gabriel and his brothers and their guardian were used to covering their tracks in this manner. Luckily for them, Max's ability to erase memories, clean files, and destroy evidence was always available to help them clean up their messes. And the four brothers weren't without recourse themselves. Michael was a cop and knew how to move through the proper channels. Uriel could bribe just about anyone to do something for him now that he was a famous actor. And Azrael was famous, too, as he was in a very popular band, but he also possessed powers beyond the scope of most people's imagination.

In fact, Gabriel could have handled the new trouble Angus Dougal had caused for him without ever leaving the Western Isles. But Scotland was old country. Its people were steeped in tradition and culture and superstition. He didn't want to raise any suspicions. He needed to appear, for all intents and purposes, as normal as inhumanly possible. So he took the ferry. It was worth it.

He smiled to himself as he watched the waves crest white over a gray blue sea. Scotland would always be worth it.

*   *   *

Juliette stared out the ferry window at the gray blue water of the deep sea beyond. It looked cold. And it looked timeless, like everything else in Scotland.

She had been in Scotland for three days: one day in Edinburgh, one in Aberdeen, and one in Glasgow. Due to various complications, Juliette had failed to obtain an Internet connection in any of the hotels. She couldn't seem to call her adviser when Dr. Larowe was actually in the office, so she had yet to check in with anyone in Pennsylvania, answer her e-mail, or even get much work done. As a result, she'd been forced to put family, friends, and school more or less out of her mind and focus on the world around her.

The first thing she'd done was go shopping to replace her lost luggage. She'd never been more grateful for the advance that Samuel Lambent had sent to her—or for Samuel Lambent, himself.

The second thing she'd done was hit the streets to take pictures, speak with locals, and get as much of a feel for Scotland as possible.

As she'd ridden the train from Inverness to Ullapool, a sobering sensation of bereavement and stark loneliness had come over Juliette. She'd gazed out the window at the craggy highlands, and realized that she had never been to a land more beautiful than Scotland. It had everything: crumbling castles; fascinating history; ancient stone ruins; black rock shorelines topped with yellow moss and green grass; bright white seagulls; aquamarine inlets; golden sandy beaches; countless tiny islands graced with abandoned monasteries, kirkyards, and keeps; rolling hills made purple with blooming heather; misty mornings; and stars that shone bright at night in an unpolluted sky. . . .

She could see where the fairy tales originated from now. She could easily spy a quick flash of red in the tall, dense, and dark evergreen forests that dotted the land-scape, and she could just as easily imagine a wolf chasing after that bit of red. She could pretend, without trying very hard, that if she gazed long enough at the mush-rooms on the grassy hill, a sprite would peek its head out from beneath one of their umbrellas. This was where the lords and ladies were born. This was where they lived still today.

Juliette had been in a strangely altered state of mind ever since landing in Edinburgh. The appearance of her new "abilities" aside, life felt surreal here. She felt as if she were stuck in one of her many haunting dreams.

There were places she passed by on the train or in the car that she would have sworn she'd seen in those dreams, in fact. Was such a thing as a genetic memory possible? Had she seen these places before—through her ancestors? Both of her parents were Scottish by her-itage. Her blood was steeped in the richness that was this land. It was why she had wanted to visit since she was nine and had decided to do her dissertation on Scottish heritage and culture.

Scotland was a part of who she was.

But there was something slightly uncomfortable in the way the ancient green land called to her. It wasn't a siren song she heard, but the eerie whispers of ghosts and spirits, echoes of voices from the past. It pulled at her like wispy skeletal arms in the shadows or the gray-ness of the fog at dawn—and at times, she found herself disturbingly close to tears.

Overhead, an intercom crackled to life and the cap-tain announced that they would be arriving at the dock in ten minutes. Juliette pushed away from the window by which she had been standing since they'd departed from Ullapool, and made her way to the stairs leading to the floor below.

*   *   *

They hadn't seen him yet, just as they had never noticed him watching them from across the street in Ullapool where they had each boarded the ferry. Daniel was very good at keeping himself hidden. It might have had something to do with his invisibility power. It was in his blood to be able to blend into his environment; most of the time he didn't need to use his powers at all. He just stood behind a bookshelf or raised the hood of his jacket or covered his face with a newspaper. And he could watch all he wanted, listen to every exchanged word, and learn everything he needed to learn in order to carry out his plan.

He had been watching Juliette Anderson very carefully when she turned in her car at the rental shop and made her way down the street to the ferry's dock. Her elflike slender form moved with enough supernatural grace that, to him, it was as if her archess nature were overtly trying to present itself to the world. Everyone noticed her and yet she seemed oblivious to the attention. She was as much a beauty as Eleanore Granger, her skin clear and poreless, her eyes unnaturally bright, her tiny nose upturned like a fairy's. Her newly purchased clothes—he had to smile at that thought—fit her like a glove, clearly outlining every one of her enticing curves.

It was dangerous to look like she did. If there was anything Daniel had learned over the thousands of years he had existed among its predators and prey, it was that the men of Earth were capable of insane selfishness and cruelty.

As for himself—if Daniel hadn't known that touching the archess in any untoward manner would be as good as signing his own death warrant, he would have acted on the dark thoughts that ran through his mind as he watched Juliette. As it was, however, time was short and she was too valuable. So he settled for watching her. He'd also been watching Gabriel Black. The archangel.

Gabriel and his archess had somehow managed to book the very same ferry and were headed to the very same place. Though Daniel wasn't exactly surprised, he was definitely disappointed. This wasn't the time and place he would have chosen to make his move on the archess.

He'd hoped for just a little more time. He'd learned by reading her files that she was going to do research on the Outer Hebrides. He could have posed as a librarian or fellow ethnographer—something to gain her trust until he could get her alone, in some secluded spot at night. He had also hoped to have enough time to make preparations for their return trip to the States. It wasn't easy to transport an unconscious or unwilling captive overseas. Not these days, anyway.

But the fates had conspired against him, and time had all but run out. With the archangel and his archess in such close proximity, there was no way they wouldn't be meeting up soon. And once they did, Daniel didn't stand a chance of getting Juliette Anderson alone—ever again.

Daniel leaned forward in his chair and sighed through his nose. If he didn't move now, it would be possible for the two to meet while disembarking. He watched a minute more while the lovely archess made her way down the stairs to the level below, her waist-length hair shimmering beneath the low lights as she moved. And then he rose from his seat, taking his black backpack with him. He'd purchased it after leaving the Adarian headquarters. It had everything in it that he would need to subdue Juliette if it came to taking her by force. He was fairly certain it would.

He moved to the stairwell and stared down into a steadily growing crowd below. He didn't see the archess anywhere. Cursing under his breath, he took the stairs at a rapid pace and searched the sea of faces that had gathered between the two stairwells. He met several pairs of female eyes as he hastily searched, but none of them belonged to Juliette. His heart rate kicked up a notch. How could he have lost her so quickly? She'd simply rounded the corner in the stairwell and slipped his grasp.

With a growing sense of unease, Daniel pushed his way through the crowd and gazed across the expanse of the deck to the stairs on the opposite side. They were the stairs that led to the observation deck outside, and as far as he knew, only Black had taken them up during this trip.

No sign of him. He must still be up top.

Daniel turned and followed the crowd down the second set of stairs to the disembarking station. His mind worked quickly. He needed to be able to follow the archess until she was somewhere alone, and he needed to guarantee that he wouldn't be seen. Daniel paused near the wall by one of the restroom doors and fiddled with his backpack. When he was certain no one was watching him, he slipped into the men's restroom, double-checked that he was alone, and became invisible.

Then he waited until another man came in, and used the open door to slip back outside once more. The crowd bottlenecked onto the outer lower deck and he expertly navigated the sea of bodies until he was able to stand apart from them and scan the crowd.

There.

Juliette broke away from the crowd and headed across the street. He knew from reading through her receipts on the memory stick that she had reserved a car to pick up here in Stornoway. That was where she was headed.

Daniel broke into a run after her and then, when he was twenty paces behind, he slowed and trailed her. There was still no sign of Black, but there were loads of other people around, too many for him to make his move without a witness.

He was feeling impatient. There was something niggling at the back of his mind. He recognized it as a holdover of his ability to divine future events. It came with the territory—this "feeling" he sometimes got. And he didn't like the way this one felt. He wondered exactly what it meant. The only real way to tell would be to divine again, and the act weakened him to a dangerous degree. He needed his strength to deal with Juliette.

The sooner, the better. Retaining his invisibility always weakened him and he wasn't certain how long he was going to have to remain as he was.

Up ahead, Juliette crossed the street to the only car rental shop on the Outer Hebrides islands. He waited, growing more impatient by the minute. His mind flicked to the other Adarians and he couldn't help but wonder what was happening with the General.

Juliette stepped inside the shop and Daniel leaned against the damp stone wall to wait. *Just a few more hours,* he told himself. *Just a few more hours and she'll be alone on the moors in the fog. Well, almost alone.* He would be with her, invisible in the backseat. It would be so easy to cover up Juliette's disappearance with an accident. The roads out here were dangerous. They were narrow and winding, lined with craggy cliffs and obstructed by sheep that meandered, sightlessly, into oncoming traffic.

"Patience, Daniel," he muttered softly.

But as he watched, the archess clearly became agitated. Juliette ran a frustrated hand through her hair. She wasn't smiling. Daniel cocked his head to one side and looked closer. The woman behind the counter who was helping Juliette was shaking her head and her expression was pained with something like guilt.

Daniel's gaze narrowed. He remained invisible and moved across the street to stand beside the glass door to the establishment. He listened.

". . . it's the festival. All cars have been booked for weeks."

"Festival?" Juliette asked, barely managing to keep her voice down.

"The music festival," the woman replied.

"Feis nan Coisir," Juliette sighed, pinching the bridge of her nose and momentarily closing her eyes. "I remember now."

"Yae've go' a fairly good accent there," the woman behind the counter admitted, her pained expression lightening a little.

"Thanks," Juliette said, clearly trying to remain cordial. She looked at the woman behind the counter. "I have a confirmation number. Just let me find it." She started fishing around in her leather backpack.

"I'm so sorrae, boot I'm afraid it won't matter," the woman told her, shaking her head and appearing truly apologetic. "The lot's emptae. There aren't any cars, whether yae've go' a number or no'."

Juliette's beautiful face turned stony and Daniel wished he could read her mind. Alas, that wasn't one of his powers. "Well, that's good because the stupid confirmation number is in my lost suitcase anyway," she said as she let her bag drop back down against her shoulder.

"There mi' be a few rooms still available here in Stornoway," the woman offered. "Yae can take a taxi to yer cottage tomorra, though I'm afraid yae'll be payin' posh prices."

Daniel ran his hand over his face as he listened to Juliette succumb to the circumstances and use the rental shop's phone to check on room availability at local hotels. His sustained invisibility was draining him. Luck was not with him in this venture. It was as if fate were conspiring against him. *Figures,* he thought. The Old Man's four favorites would always have the upper hand.

He waited until he had the name and address of the

hotel where Juliette would be staying—an older building turned tavern just around the street—and then he pushed off the wall. He needed rest. He would find a hiding place, some secluded location where he could both sleep and stash an unconscious body. And then he would take a look at Juliette's hotel.

CHAPTER SIX

Daniel was sweating; he could feel the moisture gathering at the back of his neck and soaking through the collar of his shirt. He had sustained the invisibility for too long and desperately needed to eat and possibly sleep. He'd found an ideal place to escape to with Anderson once he had her, and now he just needed to get the lay of her hotel, but the effort he was sustaining was killing him.

Still, he forced himself to ignore the burn that was starting in his muscles and concentrate on the target.

Juliette was just now entering her room down the hall. It was an old building and the key to her room was the genuine article, a skeleton key that had to be no less than a hundred years old. The archess was clearly not happy with her situation, but if the slowness of her movements and her lack of any form of negative expression or complaining were any indication, she was tired enough not to fuss over it.

He watched her enter the room and shut the door behind her. Then, still invisible, he made his way down the hall and its adjoining staircase. This entire process had taken too long. She was finally alone, but now he was too weak to take her. Archesses were not powerless individuals and Anderson was bound to be dangerous when fight or flight kicked in. He needed a few hours of sleep—no more. Just two or three. And then he could get through the difficult part of this cursed plan.

The pub downstairs was already packed; in another two or three hours it would be wall-to-wall, and if the vibe he was getting was right on, it wouldn't clear out again until two or three in the morning. If he came back then, it would give him the time he needed to rest, and he wouldn't have to deal with an accidental audience as he carried an unconscious woman down the service stairs and out into the night. And any stray onlookers would be too drunk at that point to know what was going on. Hell, they would think it was normal. If not . . . he would just have to kill them.

It was getting late and the sun set early in March. Gabriel glanced at the dim skies and considered finding a deserted doorway in order to open a portal through the mansion to his home in Harris. The mansion stood as both a magnificent living abode and a teleportation device. All the angels needed was a door—any door—and they could travel through it, through the mansion, and out the other side to any other location that also possessed a door.

He'd finished tending to the business with the money in Glasgow, and even for an archangel, financial issues were tiring. A part of him also felt strange; there was a bizarre sort of buzz in the air, as if everything were electrically charged, and it made him edgy. He longed for his fireplace, a beer, and the view of the shore outside his living room window.

But Gabriel was ever a Scotsman and if the crowds milling about were any indication, then the Feis nan Coisir was in full swing. The drink would be flowing. Gabriel had never been one to turn down an opportunity to get lost in fine music and even finer brew. It, in and of itself, could melt the stress from a man's body.

The Caorann Hotel, the only hotel directly across from the ferry's docking station, was rather ill named as a hotel, since it was the pub *beneath* the hotel's rooms, and not the rooms themselves, that attracted more guests. During festivals of any type, the Caorann pub was always packed wall-to-wall.

His clansmen would be there. The pub called to him.

Gabriel shoved his hands into the pockets of his leather jacket and made his way at a quick pace down the street. When he entered the pub, several familiar sensations hit him at once. It was warm inside, almost overly so, as the pub was indeed full of revelers and the hearth in the corner was stoked and crackling at full force. The din of conversation and drunken laughter was only slightly overshadowed by the music that was being played by an equally drunk-looking band on a platform against one wall. The smell was a combination of sweat, perfume, spilled ale, woodsmoke, and chips, or French fries, as they would have been called by Gabe's brothers.

Gabriel smiled and let the door swing shut behind him. This was just how he liked it. He stood there a moment and allowed his vision to adjust to the dim light and chaos, and as he did, someone called his name.

He turned to find Stuart's ancient and arrow-straight form heading through the crowd toward him. "Black, yae bugger, yae're back!"

Gabriel smiled at his old friend and met him halfway.

"Aye, let me buy you a drink," he told the old man. Stuart nodded and clapped him on the back, never one to turn down a free drink even though he already held a half-filled mug in his right hand. They wove their way through the undulating crowd and sidled up to the bar. The man and woman team behind the counter recognized Gabriel at once.

"Gabe! *Dè a tha thu ris?*" the man asked in Gaelic, his Hebridean accent thick. He wasted no time in topping off a fresh mug and handing it to Gabriel, who took the drink with a nod and a grateful smile.

"*Fada 'nurcomain*, Will," Gabriel replied, also in Gaelic. "It's good to see ya." Will was the barkeep at the Caorann. He was also the hotel's owner.

The woman behind the bar was Will's sister. She winked at Gabriel and he gave her an appreciative nod as well before raising his glass and downing half its contents in one long pull. It wasn't easy for an archangel to get drunk. But he'd had years of practice.

"Wha' are you doin' up here anyway, Burns?" Gabriel turned and asked his old friend. Stuart's fishing boat and cottage were in Harris, not far from Gabriel's.

"Same thing yae be doin', Black. Havin' a drink." Stuart then downed what was left in his own mug and plopped the empty container on the counter with a flourish that would have resounded loudly if it hadn't been for the noise level in the pub. "Nae pay up an' git me tha' beer yae promised."

Gabriel laughed and tossed several notes on the bar. The two refilled their mugs and made their way to a table near the hearth where many of the revelers had more or less evacuated because they were dancing and the heat from the fire was too much for them. Gabriel and Stuart sat and Gabe leaned back against his chair, taking it all in.

"I saw an angel coom in 'ere aboot twentae minutes ago, Black," Stuart said, gaining Gabriel's attention. "Yae'd've lost yer nuts if yae'd seen 'er. The wee lass was jus' what ye're always describin' as yer perfect soul mate an' wha' no'." His bright blue eyes glittered like the eyes of a man much younger and his smile was mischievous.

"Oh?" Gabriel's brow rose. "Why'd you no' buy her a drink, then?"

Stuart laughed, the sound like a pen scratching parchment. "I dinnae think she much cared for the a'mosphere."

He laughed again and shook his head. "She did 'er business with Will—Juliette, 'er name was—an' then she sho' upstairs withoo' further ado."

Gabriel considered this a moment and found that his gaze wandered to the archway that led to a stairwell and the Caorann's tavern rooms up above. *Juliette* . . . It sounded like rain in the desert. Like a warm fire on a bitter winter's night.

Gabriel's gaze darkened thoughtfully on the empty staircase. Then he raised his mug with one hand and flagged down a passing server with the other.

Juliette rolled over on the lumpy, hard mattress and glared at the ceiling. The Caorann's rooms sported paper-thin walls barely made livable by ten-year-old wallpaper that had definitely seen better days. There were three lamps in the room, one of which didn't work at all and another of which made a strange crackling noise when clicked on. There was no TV, no Internet connection to speak of—again—and the only bathroom on the second floor was shared by all six of the tavern's available rooms. And there was mold growing in the shower.

Juliette was fairly sure this was the first time in her life that she'd stayed in a half-star hotel.

She missed her Nessie. Her arms felt empty without her stuffed elephant to squeeze.

With a frustrated sound, she sat up quickly on the bed and tossed off her covers. The noise from the pubs downstairs was indescribable. She could barely discern the music the band was playing from the raucous singing of the revelers; the two were melding together in discordant strings of unintelligible lyrics and laughter. The sound was so clear, the party could be going on out in the hall.

Juliette scowled at the door that led to that hall and

thought about the peaceful, quiet cottage that was now being paid for but lay empty somewhere on the Luskentyre shore. Her stomach churned and growled; she hadn't eaten dinner. The crowd in the pub downstairs had been so thick and so cumulatively hot, she'd lost her appetite.

Now she regretted not having at least a bread roll or a small bucket of fries. Or crisps. Or chips—or whatever! She huffed more frustration and swung her legs over the side of the bed.

It occurred to her then that the conversations and traditions and culture being shared downstairs at that moment were exactly what she needed in order to write her ethnography and graduate. And it might be along the lines of the kind of dirt Samuel Lambent wanted as well.

She was just so tired. She reached for her diving watch, pressed the LCD light, and adjusted for the time difference. It was two a.m.!! And she was still jet-lagged, so for her it was even worse.

With a hand that shook a little with hunger and exhaustion, Juliette ran her fingers through her hair, combing out the knots. She did this when she was stressed; it was a habit. When things got *really* bad, her friends and family could usually find her in the bathroom, furiously running a straight iron through her locks. Nothing said good-bye to stress like ironing out all of the kinks.

After a few moments and a cringe-worthy peal of laughter from downstairs, Juliette sighed dramatically and got out of bed.

"If you can't beat 'em, join 'em," she muttered to herself as she pulled on the only new clothes she still hadn't worn. She didn't know why, but she guessed she'd been saving this outfit for some occasion. It was the nicest, and it was all she had left before she would have to hit the Laundromat.

Juliette had purchased a new pair of leather boots to match the outfit, which was something she never did. It had been a treat to herself, a celebration of sorts for getting the contract with Lambent—and a consolation for losing Nessie and the rest of her luggage.

As quietly as she could, she donned the skinny jeans, deciding to go commando so that she would still own a clean pair of underwear for the morning. With a glance at the off-the-shoulder blouse she'd purchased to go with the jeans, she opted for braless as well. What the heck? It sounded like a party down there, and probably no one would even notice someone like her. She was small enough that she usually blended right into a crowd.

The shimmering material struck a hue somewhere between peach and gray, and shifted as she moved. It was flattering in the extreme, she had to admit, drawing attention to her collarbone and tanned complexion and offsetting the hazel in her eyes.

Once she'd sat back down on the edge of the bed and pulled on the knee-high leather boots, she stood and felt a strange rush. The hotel room floor seemed so far away! The boots were platforms and must have added a good four to five inches to her height. She blinked and made her way to the mirror tacked to the outside of the wardrobe.

"Wow," she whispered. Her legs actually looked *long* in the jeans-and-boots combination. She couldn't help but smile. "*Loving* it," she whispered again, and then shook her head at her own ridiculousness. What the hell did she care how she looked? She was going to go down and sit in a corner somewhere and quietly observe the local people make drunken, debauched fools of themselves, hoping to God that she could remember half of it come morning. She had no intention of joining them in their fun. . . .

Right?

Juliette frowned at her reflection, catching the strange

shift in her own gaze. Sophie was right. There was a sadness to her eyes when they turned green.

"Fuck it," she said suddenly, and straightened a little. She rolled her shoulders back, tossed her long, shining hair over her shoulder, and then gave herself a devil-may-care smile. "Maybe just one drink."

She took the small iron skeleton key from atop the credenza beside the door and then made her way out in the hall, closing the door and locking it behind her.

At the end of the hall, a line of women were waiting to use the hotel's upstairs guest restroom. Juliette barely managed to refrain from rolling her eyes. She was lucky she didn't have to pee. This was just cruel. Surely the owners were making enough money on the booze they sold downstairs to afford putting in another bathroom somewhere?

This is so going in my thesis, she thought morosely as she sidled past them, offered up as friendly a smile as she could, and made her way down the carpeted stairs. The din grew exponentially in volume as she neared the bottom landing. She had to move to the side to allow another pair of women access to the stairwell as they no doubt headed up to stand in line with their compatriots.

Once she reached the pub, she pressed nervously against the wall and scanned the room's interior, trying to gain her bearings. For some reason, her heart was hammering. Maybe she was tired or maybe hungry or maybe it was a combination of the two, but she actually felt panicky there, plastered to the warm stone like some kind of selkie statue.

There were so many people. . . . Juliette could hear so many different conversations going on at once. The couple nearest to her were speaking in an accent so deep, she barely understood a word or two here and there in the stream of nonstop chatter between them. The smell in the room was hot and stank of perfume and liquor and the smoke from the hearth in the corner.

Juliette's eyes trailed nervously to the hearth, as if to confirm her suspicions that the fire was roaring in its stone setting. It was a little bigger than she liked a hearth fire to be, but it seemed to mirror the mood in the tavern, boisterous and fueled. People moved about in front of her, blocking and unblocking her view, but something caught her eye and she craned her neck to get a better look.

The profile of the man was arresting. He looked so tall. . . . His black hair looked like thick waves of silk and curled where it brushed the collar of his button-up black shirt. His shoulders were enticingly broad, superhero-like. She watched him raise a mug to his lips—perfect, kissable lips with a slightly cruel tilt to their corners—and take a drink. The muscle in his forearm flexed, growing taut below his rolled-up sleeve.

Juliette's mouth suddenly felt dry. She swallowed and blinked and found herself hurriedly craning her neck the other way when someone rudely stepped in her line of sight.

Again, her eyes fell upon his profile and locked on as if her life depended on it. He was sitting with an old man, listening as his white-haired friend expostulated about something humorous. The man with black hair smiled at something his companion said, flashing straight white teeth.

Again, she swallowed, almost coughing. *His eyes,* she thought. She had yet to see his eyes. She needed to see his eyes!

Why? a little voice asked dimly, as she absently licked her lips, utterly distracted by this unbelievably perfect man. *Why do I care? Why do I need to see his eyes?* She ignored herself and continued to stare.

And then he stopped laughing and froze in the middle of raising his mug once more to his lips. He seemed to stiffen in his chair, cocking his head slightly to one side. In the next moment, he was leaning forward and gracefully coming to his feet.

So . . . tall . . .

He turned to face her.

The man's platinum silver gaze speared through the space between them and pinned her to the wall behind her. He stood stock-still, a formidable study in black and gray, and in that strange moment that his eyes held hers, he seemed to nail her to the floor. His expression was unreadable but for the hint of what could only be shock that registered across his rugged, handsome features.

She was unable to move. There was a roar in her ears then that had nothing to do with the cacophony of the room around her. Her skin felt prickly. She felt dizzy.

It's him, she thought. *The angel. Those are the eyes from my dream.*

And then he was leaning down and placing his beer on the table, his gaze never leaving hers. Juliette tried to move; she really did. But she couldn't so much as budge when the man stepped around his chair and began to walk toward her. The crowd seemed to part to make way for him; he strode with nearly inhuman grace and a determined sort of purpose and Juliette wondered, for just a moment, whether she were still upstairs in her bed and only dreaming again.

And then he was standing before her and she was nearly gasping for breath.

Outside, a gale began to grow. Rain started pelting the windows and very distant lightning illuminated clouds miles away.

"I canno' believe it," he whispered. Despite the whisper, she heard him over the noise around them. The milling crowd could not diminish his presence before her in any way. His eyes trailed over her face; Juliette watched him as he seemed to take her in, from the top of her head to the tips of her boots, and his expression became more and more bewildered with each passing second. "It's you."

Juliette had no idea what to say to that.

But she was spared any words she might have muttered anyway, as in the next instant, he was moving forward, his left hand slamming against the wall to her right, his right arm snaking around her waist. She inhaled quickly, as if readying for a dive, and then was crushed against his hard body as he trapped her beneath him and claimed her lips in a kiss.

Lightning struck somewhere nearby, followed closely by a peal of thunder that effectively overrode every other sound in the pub.

Reality took a backseat in the heat of the kiss; its magic seared through her muscles and bones, boiling her blood in her veins and curling her toes in her shoes. Her hands found their way to the rock wall of his chest and she felt the bass-beat drumming of his heart as he devoured her and she melted beneath him. Time ceased to exist; she could almost hear it winding down and dying. Sound faded and her world tunneled until only she was left standing. She—and this stranger who was kissing her as if she were his wife and he had not seen her in a thousand years.

Stranger . . .

Lightning struck again and the band stopped playing. A few couples stopped trying to talk.

Reality nudged at Juliette. But she heard someone groan, helpless and wanting as the heat that had invaded her body coiled and pooled beneath her belly. And she knew that she was the one who had groaned.

He's a stranger.

He tastes good, she thought, utterly distracted. *Like licorice and mint and really dark ale . . .* She was lost, floundering in some kind of pleasure-induced labyrinth of which she had no hope of finding a way out. She had never been kissed like this. No man could kiss like this. It was the stuff of fantasy.

What am I doing?

The storm outside picked up in strength and wind began to rattle the windowpanes.

Christ, he feels good.

Reality now honked the horn in Juliette's fevered brain and the world crashed in around her. Sound was the first thing to return: the hushed music, the rolling thunder, the nervous laughter and stilted conversation that was slowly working its way back to normal. She blinked—

And then she realized where she was and jerked in the man's tight grasp. With as much force as she could muster, she shoved against his chest, catching him off guard. He moved—a little, but his arm was still a band of steel at her back as he broke the kiss enough to stare down at her once more.

She instantly missed the feel of his lips. The intensity of the impossible, molten mercury in his eyes made her feel even smaller than she normally did. She was positively tiny in his grasp. She knew damned well that if she hadn't caught him off guard with her shove, he would not have moved at all. He was a rock wall.

"What the hell do you think you're doing?" she demanded, hissing the words through lips she could feel were swollen from his kiss. Lightning struck again, drawing a nervous gasp from a woman nearby. Juliette ignored it. She had no choice.

His kiss . . . Her gaze flicked to his mouth and back again. *Sweet Jesus, his kiss . . .*

"Wha' am I doin'?" he asked, his brogue beautiful and deep and perfect. "I'm doin' wha' I've waited centuries to do," he told her. What little bit of her had not melted beneath his passionate embrace now liquefied at the sound of his voice.

But there was enough reason still making a righteous racket inside of her now to know that what he said made no sense. He was drunk. That explained the taste of ale on his tongue. He was drunk and he was taking advantage of her in the worst possible way.

"Get off of me," she told him firmly. "And step back."

He smiled an utterly roguish smile, making Juliette's breath catch. *Omigod, he's beautiful.* Another flash of lightning lit up the darkness beyond the tavern's windows and thunder made the lights flicker.

"Aye? And wha' will you do, lass, if I don' step back?" *I'll die. . . .*

"Please," she added, a little too softly for her own liking. She'd tried appealing to his rougher side, but it hadn't worked. Maybe good manners would get him.

No such luck. He stayed where he was and the silver in his eyes darkened as if sheltering storms. "Is that wha' you really want, then, luv?" he asked softly as his hand spread where it grasped her waist. She felt his thumb slide beneath the filmy material of her blouse to caress a bare strip of her flesh.

She was trembling now. She could feel it in her legs; her knees were growing weak.

This is ridiculous, she thought. *I can't let him do this to me.*

"I said get off of me!" She hauled back then and balled her hand into as tight a fist as she could make. If her shove hadn't taken him by surprise enough to move him, the punch she landed on the side of his face just then sure as hell did.

A bolt of lightning sent the pub's electricity into recession, causing the lights to flicker and die as the man's head snapped to the side and his grip on her waist slackened slightly. She used the momentum to shove at his sculpted marble chest once more, affording her a precious half foot of space. It was enough.

Instantly, she was dodging to the side and racing for the staircase she had just come down. She could barely see it in the temporary darkness, but its outline was clear enough.

Well, that went well! she berated herself as she took the stairs two at a time, a feat made possible only by the extra inches her boots gave her. By the time she reached her floor, an emergency generator had kicked on and the lights were back. Juliette kept running and didn't stop until she was standing before her door and fumbling for her key. She'd never let someone scare her like that before.

"Jesus H. Christ, Jules," she muttered, her voice shaking as badly as her hand, which was also feeling more tender by the moment. She'd never punched anyone before; she'd probably broken a knuckle. She focused on the key and tried desperately to slide it into the lock without scratching off all the paint on the sides. "You're a piece of work."

The electric wiring in the building crackled through the walls, fizzling for several seconds before it once more went dead just as Juliette wrenched the door open and flew inside.

CHAPTER SEVEN

Daniel watched the meeting of the archangel and his archess through narrowed, angry eyes. This was why he'd felt so nervous, so wrong, all afternoon. It was this. In the back of his mind, he must have known it would happen.

He shouldn't have taken the time to rest. But then again, even if he hadn't, it wouldn't have mattered. There would have been no way for him to get Juliette Anderson's unconscious body out of the hotel without being seen.

This couldn't be helped. And the fates truly did hate him.

He would never have believed that he would enter the tavern and turn around to find the archess pinned against the wall, stuck between hard rock and an archangel. Even the sudden storm, which he knew must be the archess's unwitting doing, matched the mood that had come over him in that moment. It was all so dramatically perfect—and perfectly horrible.

Gabriel had kissed her. He'd barely spoken a word to her—and then he'd simply moved in, as if for the kill.

Daniel's vision was now tinted ever so slightly red. Of all the nerve. Of all the shitty luck. The anger that coursed through his veins like lava was taxing him. It wasn't helping with his invisibility. He'd rested, but he hadn't yet eaten, and though he'd regained some of his strength, he was not at all certain how much longer he could maintain a body seemingly without substance.

With gritted teeth and a mind bent on murder, Daniel watched the archess fly up the darkened stairs, leaving a stunned Gabriel Black rubbing his jaw and looking after her.

Daniel pushed off the wall on which he'd been leaning and silently slid past several revelers to race up the stairs after her. As he passed by Black, a strange vibration thrummed across his skin. It was power, raw and awakened, and the sixth-sense part of him recognized its source. Black had found his archess.

Time had officially run out.

Gabriel couldn't believe what he was feeling. What he was seeing—what he'd just done. He felt stuck in a dream. Maybe he'd had too much to drink and passed out in front of the fire. Maybe this was a fevered nightmare brought on by one of those damned Adarians Uriel had told him about who could control dreams and visions. Maybe ... maybe it was a thousand things that it wasn't. Because it was actually something else.

It was real.

"Well, it seems yae found 'er after all, Black," came a scratchy voice behind him. Gabriel turned slightly as Stuart approached, the old man grinning ear to ear. "What did I tell yae? An angel, isn't she?"

Gabriel felt his sore jaw drop open. "Tha' was her?" That was the girl Stuart had been talking about earlier?

"Aye." Burns nodded and slapped a hand on Gabriel's back and shook his head. "She's go' a good arm on 'er for such a wee lass." He chuckled to himself and looked up toward the tavern's roof. "Och, I'm glad Will go' that generator, bu' 'e could've at least made sure it wouldnae blow the power all tae hell. Ruddy weather'll turn on yae like a Campbell, it will." He turned to head to the bar for another drink.

Gabriel let him go. He was still in shock; he couldn't really move.

Parma Violets . . . She'd tasted like flowers and candy. *Juliette,* he thought next. Burns had said her name was Juliette.

He had never felt as he did in that moment. He'd been sitting by the fire, one moment feeling nothing but slight boredom. And then, suddenly, he'd felt feverish and the air around him was filled with a strange tension that arrested his breath. And then he'd stood up—and turned around to find her staring at him across the room.

A thousand thoughts had raced through his mind in that moment. A thousand thoughts—and none. There was nothing but a roar and a silence as time both sped up and stood still.

Two thousand years. Twenty centuries. It was a long time to search for something. When he'd looked up and met her green brown gaze and beheld, in the flesh, the image he had dreamed of for the last seven hundred thousand nights, he knew at once that his searching was over. He couldn't let her go. Especially not when she'd walked into his bar wearing those painted-on jeans and leather boots and that shirt that exposed the creamy flesh of her shoulders . . . *Och, hell no,* he thought. There was no way he was going to lose her again.

Gabriel frowned at the sudden friction in the air around him and turned back to face the staircase. It was empty.

His archess had run from him. He couldn't blame her. She most likely thought he was a callous, drunken rake. And rightly so.

But he wasn't going to let that stop him.

"Yae plan on goin' up there, don' ya?" Stuart asked.

He'd returned from the bar with a fresh mug of something darker than the last drink.

"Aye," Gabriel said.

"Might want tae apologize, then," Burns warned. "Yae scared the hell out of 'er, yae did."

Gabriel already knew this. The sudden appearance of his archess had thrown him for a loop. Kissing her had all but driven every last sane thought from his brain. He was no stranger to the ladies, but he'd never wanted to bed one so badly nor so quickly before in his very long life. He wasn't at all sure he could trust himself around her at that moment, and God knew he didn't need any help further messing things up.

"I'm aware," he said, still gazing steadfastly up the stairs.

"An' one more thing, Black," Stuart continued, his tone low. Gabe glanced at him as the old man swigged a big swallow and lowered his mug again. "Ye're wastin' precious time."

Gabriel gave the old man a devil-may-care smile and shot up the stairs like a light.

Juliette slammed the door shut behind her and leaned up against it, trying to catch her breath.

"I can't believe what just happened." She shook her head, ran her shaking hand over her face, and stopped at her lips, her quivering fingers rubbing the sensitive, puffy flesh. "I just got kissed by the most gorgeous man ever to walk the face of the earth."

Juliette closed her eyes and let her head drop back. Her body felt as if it were humming around her soul. She recalled that he'd said something to her, but as she tried to think back on it, all she could remember was the kiss and the heat it awakened within her. And his eyes . . . those molten silver eyes. The eyes of the angel in her dream.

Juliette frowned when she felt a sudden stirring of the air in front of her. She opened her eyes and gasped. She had only enough time to give a short scream before the man who had not been there a second before was upon her.

The stranger rushed her like a dark blanket, smothering her with his hard presence as he twisted her around. He wrapped his arms around her and pinned her back to his chest. At the same time, his hand slammed down upon her mouth, bruising her already swollen lips. She felt cloth over her nose and mouth and was hit with an acrid stench and knew, instinctively, that he was trying to poison her.

She couldn't even breathe. Her thundering heart demanded oxygen, but if she dared inhale, she would take in the chloroform and it would be over. She had never felt this afraid. Now she knew what real fear felt like.

Through the haze of her terror, Juliette noticed that the objects in the room had begun to rattle. The lamp shook on the tabletop. Juliette's brand-new hardback suitcase slid along the wooden floor. The doors of the wardrobe opened and closed. Her already wide eyes widened farther. A phantasmal nightmare had been unleashed inside of the hotel room, and the lightning that crashed just outside her window only lent credence to its monstrosity.

But Juliette had no time to consider the impossibility of what was happening in the room—she was dying for air. Her body felt bruised, and the world was tunneling around her. The insidious power of the chloroform was seeping into her body, despite her lack of breath. She fought uselessly in the man's grip as he lowered his lips to her ear. "Relax, sweetheart. It'll all be over soon."

And then the man was ducking behind her and cursing and his hand was sliding away from her mouth as the hardback suitcase rose from the ground and flew toward his head. As soon as her mouth was free of the poisoned rag, Juliette dragged air into her lungs, furiously fighting the weakening effects of what little chloroform she had absorbed. With what strength she had, she sharply elbowed the man in the gut, trying to wriggle out of his grasp.

He grunted and wrestled with her, but his progress was once again interrupted when the door to the wardrobe swung open on him, slamming its corner into the base of his skull. Juliette felt dizzy, not only from the poison, but from disbelief. What was happening? Was there a poltergeist in the room?

He dropped the rag in his struggle, but managed to wrap his arms around her once more and then drag her against him and into the shadows of the wardrobe as the door to her room came crashing in.

Gabriel froze on the top landing when a high-pitched scream sliced through the softer din that surrounded the small crowd outside the women's restroom. The scream was cut short, but had come from down the hall. The women in the hall turned to peer down the length of the corridor, but it was empty on that end.

All the hair stood up on the back of Gabriel's neck and he broke into a run, shoving the women aside as gently but as quickly as he could. There were five rooms and he'd forgotten to ask Will which one belonged to the angel.

But the sound of a struggle from beyond door number three marked his destination and Gabriel wasted no time in turning the knob. The door was locked from the inside. Gabriel reared back, raised his leg, and shoved his boot against the door just below the handle.

The door splintered in its frame and swung open as shards of wood went flying in all directions. The room was dark beyond, and suddenly it was all too quiet.

Thunder rolled outside the windows and lightning momentarily illuminated the room's interior. Gabriel's heart hammered painfully in his chest. It had never done that before. The metallic tang of fear was sour on his tongue as he pushed the door open the rest of the way and stepped into the room.

A muffled sound greeted his ears, somewhere off to his left. He turned toward the wardrobe and searched its surrounding shadows.

There.

And then the lamp on top of the bedside table lifted off its surface and went careening across the room. Gabriel watched it through another flash of lightning and barely managed to duck in time as it sailed past him to hit the wall beside the wardrobe. The old glass shattered violently, drawing a string of distinctly male curses from the faintly outlined silhouette of the man beside it.

Gabriel shot forward, reaching for the man's neck when lightning detailed him once more. The stranger had Gabriel's archess trapped in his arms; Gabe caught the sharp, alcoholic stench of chloroform and knew, instantly, what was going down.

Somehow, the stranger had failed to knock her out as he'd no doubt planned. And now it was too late, for Gabriel's grip found the man's throat and the archess was thrown to the floor. She landed hard on her side and Gabe heard the air knocked from her lungs. She slid a little across the wooden planks and then scrambled to her feet.

"Get out now!" he growled through clenched teeth as he and the Adarian struggled. Gabriel recognized the sensations he was receiving from the man. Fighting with an Adarian felt like struggling with a bolt of static. The power that ran through archangels and Adarians acted like negative and positive ions; they were abrasive against each other. It was like fighting through sandpaper air.

The Adarian growled low in his throat, animalistic and determined, and Gabriel grunted as the man's fist found his kidney. He recovered quickly, though, renewing his efforts as, through the corner of his eye, he saw the archess bolt for the door and race out into the hall beyond.

Juliette shot out into the hall as if the devil were on her heels. She couldn't understand what was happening. She could barely make sense of where she was and the fact that she had just been attacked and was now escaping—escaping what, she didn't know. She knew she needed to get out of the room, though. *Out of the hotel—go somewhere safe. Send for the cops. . . .*

The hall beyond her rented room was strangely empty, and its walls echoed with the rolling thunder that rumbled through their foundations. Juliette glanced quickly toward the stairs that led to the bar below, and for some reason, she spun on her heels and headed in the opposite direction. It was a spur-of-the-moment decision, lacking in any clear logic. Instead, she headed toward the end of the hall, where a small wooden door at the very end bore no lock. Juliette turned the knob and pried it open to reveal a servants' stairwell. Without thinking, she shot down into the darkness.

The exit door was warped from the moisture in the air, but when Juliette put her weight against it, it gave and she made it out into the cold, wet alley. The night was dark and windy and the rain bit into Juliette's skin like teeth.

She no longer felt her muscles or bones and her legs moved of their own accord. She was growing numb from the inside out. She wondered at her spreading weakness. *It has to be the chloroform.* She was a small woman, and the stranger had no doubt used a lot on the rag. But this felt like something else. Chloroform was supposed to feel like a drug, a blanket of sleep that smothered you from the outside in. This was different. It was a familiar, deeper sort of weakness. She felt as if strength had been pulled from her muscle and bone, as opposed to feeling as though sleep had been draped over her. She felt the same way that she had the two times that she'd healed someone close to death.

Juliette blinked as she rounded a corner and continued down the street, running blind. *It's the storm,* she realized. *The storm is my fault. And the flying luggage,* she thought, recalling the way the items had flown around her room as if animated by a poltergeist. *It's no ghost,* she thought. *It's all me.*

I won't last, Juliette thought. She knew she was going to give out. She only hoped she could get far enough away from the danger behind her before it happened. She came to the end of an alley, turned a corner, and ran down another blind street. The cobblestone road was shrouded in mist and the streetlamps were dim. It suddenly seemed as if the entire world had retired, leaving her alone, a sole figure racing madly through a deserted planet.

Her boots clicked loudly on the smooth, weathered stone, adding to the eerie cast of her surroundings. Juliette's breathing was harshly loud in the thick, ominous silence. She turned another corner, ran half a block, and then paused to rest against the storefront of a shop that sold Harris Tweed.

Juliette bent to catch her breath and a wave of horrid dizziness washed over her, bringing her to her knees. She hit hard, but barely felt it. Her legs had gone numb. It was then that she realized she was really in trouble. She had no idea where to go or what to do, and wouldn't be able to stand back up even if she did. She had no phone, she didn't know where she was, and it was two in the morning. Every window was dark.

She really was alone. No one was there to help her. And as the mist that surrounded her grew thicker and clouded her tunneling vision, she realized that she was going to pass out right there, on that empty sidewalk, without another soul in sight.

CHAPTER EIGHT

Gabriel watched the archess leave the room out of the corner of his eye and then returned his full attention to his opponent. He remembered now how hard it was to fight an Adarian. Those fated first archangels had been kicked out of their realm and thrown to Earth for a reason. The Old Man had made them too powerful, too strong, and then he'd grown wary of their strength and gotten rid of them.

Fighting this Adarian now was like fighting Superman. Gabriel could see the man was struggling; sweat beaded his brow and soaked the collar of his shirt. And yet, he wasn't losing either.

With a great deal more effort than it should have taken, Gabriel grabbed the front of the man's shirt and shoved him back up against the wall. The room shook from the impact and the Adarian merely gritted his teeth. Gabriel leaned in and hissed across the man's lips. "Where the fuck is Abraxos?" he asked, assuming the leader of the Adarians must be nearby. He must have sent this soldier in after the archess; Abraxos had wanted to get his hands on an archess for years; he wanted their healing ability for his own.

But the Adarian merely smiled then, his cruel and handsome face breaking into a truly nasty grin. He shook his head. "You're clueless, Gabriel." His laughter was out of breath and vindictive. "You have no *idea* what's going on."

With that, the Adarian reared his head back, then jerked it forward, smashing his forehead against Gabriel's nose. Pain exploded before his eyes, a red blossom of confusing agony that caught him off guard enough for the Adarian to shove him away from the wall.

He stumbled back, blinded, and tumbled over the edge of the nearest bed. As he spun to catch himself, the doorway to the hall filled with shadows and the sounds of footfalls and raised voices.

Gabriel braced himself against the mattress, shoved himself back to his feet, and spun around. The Adarian was gone. A flashlight beam momentarily blinded him, and Gabriel realized the power must be out again. He hadn't noticed the darkness until someone was shining a flashlight in his face. He ignored the spearing light and frantically searched the shadows of the room for the man he had been sparring with only seconds earlier. There was no sign of him.

Invisibility . . .

"Well, wha' 'ave we here?"

Gabriel turned back to the doorway and shielded his eyes once more as the man behind the familiar voice continued to point the flashlight directly at his face.

"Gabriel Black," the voice taunted, *tsk*ing him reprimandingly. Gabriel knew that voice. It was Angus Dougal—Edeen's brother . . . and chief inspector for the Western Isles command team police force.

Christ, he thought. He wasn't surprised. The women in the hall had seen him break the door down. They'd heard someone inside scream. One of them must have made the call. *This isn't good.* He could go through Dougal in a heartbeat and take care of his men as nothing more than an afterthought. Then he could go after the archess.

But he might hurt the man in the process. He might even kill him.

And the hall was full of onlookers. Everyone would witness his actions—and everyone had a cell phone these days.

Max might not catch everything in the cleanup. And then what?

He almost didn't care. But the fact of the matter was, even if he took down all these men and went after Juliette himself, chances were he wouldn't find her. Not alone. There were Adarians out there. He needed help. He needed to call Max.

In the hall, the police turned to get the crowd to stand back, but it was too late. Gabriel and the mess he was in had been noticed by too many people.

"Turn around, Black," Angus commanded calmly. Gabriel thought furiously and tried not to glare at the man. His archess had caused the storm; of that he had no doubt. She'd thrown things around the room with telekinesis. She would be weak.

She was fodder for the General at that moment and the last thing Gabriel needed was to have to deal with Angus Dougal and his minions.

He slowly turned in place and waited with his hands splayed at his sides as Dougal's flashlight beam made its way around the room. *I need to get ahold of Max.* He would get a phone call once he was arrested. It was the best way to go about things. It was easier than erasing the memories of a hundred revelers and possibly burying innocent bystanders. But impatience burned his blood. *Get it over with, Dougal.*

"Where is the girl who rented this room?" Angus asked, a hard edge to his voice.

"I'm no' answerin' any of your questions, Angus. If you're goin' to arrest me, do it an' shu' the hell up."

There was a brief period of silence as Dougal and his

men no doubt absorbed his comment. And then Angus was behind him, a body as hard and tall as his own, and his wrists were being cuffed none too gently. "Have it yer way, Black," Dougal hissed behind his right ear. "Ye're in for a long night."

"Uriel, you need to stop staring at your wife and pay attention." Max waved a hand in front of Uriel's face, then snapped his fingers.

Uriel blinked. "Get your fingers out of my face, Max. I'm fine."

Max rolled his eyes. "So is Eleanore. Now pay attention."

Max was a tall, slim man who appeared to be in his late thirties. He had brown hair and brown eyes, wore spectacles, and had an undeniable preference for three-piece suits. Also brown. He was Uriel's agent. He was also the guardian to Uriel and his brothers, and had been sent by the Old Man to help the four favored in any way he could. Max's abilities were not as flashy as theirs, but he served a very real purpose and the abilities he did have luckily reflected as much. Anytime the archangels caused enough trouble to be "noticed" by the world, in general, Max was there to erase minds, destroy evidence, and turn everything right again.

Uriel shot Max a dirty look, then sighed. "Do they have to stand so close to her?"

Max turned to glance at the bodyguards who stood around Eleanore. She seemed oblivious to them; she was reading something on her electronic reader. She was fond of vampire romance stories written in a much darker tune than *Comeuppance*. Lots of erotica.

In a way, it was good that Eleanore was less shy about her sexual preferences now. Being with Uriel had opened up her self-esteem and truly brought out the power of her sensuality. On the other hand, she was an archess and already attractive enough. Add the new sensuality to that beauty and she was a veritable magnet for men. Including the bodyguards that Uriel, himself, had assigned to her.

"You hired them." Max smiled wryly. "Maybe you should specify that you want eunuchs next time." He shrugged and turned around. "Besides," he added with a lilting, sardonic tone, "*Christopher Daniels's* fans get a lot closer to *him*."

Uriel had the good grace to look the slightest bit chagrined. But it didn't last long. His gaze once more cut to the black-haired beauty sitting on a crate against the back wall of the backstage area, and as if sensing that he was watching her, she looked up. She gave him a coy, teasing look—then winked.

Max watched as Uriel's eyes widened slightly, and it wasn't until Max's grip on his upper arm tightened painfully that the archangel realized he had begun striding toward her.

Uriel looked down at Max's hand and then back up at Eleanore. She was laughing, her gorgeous blue eyes glittering merrily under the backstage lights. Uriel's gaze narrowed, but he returned the smile. Max knew he couldn't help but do so. She was everything to him and Max could understand his protective streak. It was a mile long and twice as wide.

"Mr. Daniels, we're on in two minutes." A young man with a headset waved, got a nod from Uriel and Max, then disappeared back into one of the wings of the set. It was nearly nine o'clock and Jacqueline Rain's show would begin any minute. She'd become so popular, she'd gone from a daytime talk show to nighttime entertainment, where her tendency to prefer guests in more notoriously gothic movie roles admittedly fit in a little better.

"You know, Ellie's more than capable of protecting herself," Max said then, speaking under his breath so that the conversation included only him and Uriel. "And if she can't protect herself," he continued, gesturing toward the two guards standing beside her, "they're not going to do any good."

"I'm aware," Uriel said. Then he sighed and looked guilty. "They're meat shields," he admitted, which meant that if they were attacked by someone who could actually harm Eleanore—such as the Adarians—then the men around her would slow the enemy down long enough for Uriel to get to her. Hopefully.

"Ah." Max smiled. Then he grinned. "I knew that already. But I'm proud of you for admitting it."

"One minute!" someone called.

"Jacqueline Rain really loves it when you come on," Max mused. "You increased their ratings by twenty percent with your last stunt." The last time Uriel had gone on Rain's show, he had asked Eleanore to go out with him on national television. Eleanore hadn't been pleased, but the public had eaten it up. And the fact that Christopher Daniels was now a married man hadn't seemed to deter their affections any. In fact, they'd taken to calling Christopher and Eleanore "Christellie," and that amalgamated word had found itself on the front cover of dozens of magazines and newspapers across the nation.

"How is Gabe?" Uriel asked suddenly, changing the subject completely. Gabriel had gone back to Scotland four months ago and they rarely saw him these days, even though it would have been easy for him to call a portal into the mansion and pop in to say hello. Gabriel liked heading off on his own. He was rather brooding and preferred solitude more than the others. It was just how he'd been created.

Max knew Uriel was probably a little worried about his brother, especially now that he'd found his archess and his brothers had not. So, he took the change of subject in stride and considered how to reply to the question. "He's holding his own, as usual. But—" He broke off as his cell phone rang. It was Gabriel's unique ring, one that they had chosen a year ago when they'd signed on with the phone company. Max had actually never heard Gabriel's ring go off before.

At once, he and Uriel froze and both of them looked down at the breast pocket of Max's suit, where the cell phone was hidden. This couldn't be good. Gabriel never called him. Max pulled the phone out of the inner pocket and flipped it open before placing it to his ear. "Gabriel. We were just talking about you."

Then he fell quiet. He silently absorbed Gabriel's words while Uriel looked on. In his peripheral vision, Max saw the stagehands waving at him and could make out the muffled, staticky sound of someone communicating through headsets. But it became background noise to him, at once trivial compared with the man speaking to him on the other end of the line.

"I understand." Max closed his phone and pocketed it. Then he turned to Michael, who had just walked backstage and had made his way to Uriel and Max. The former Warrior Archangel stood tall and strong and proud. His thick blond curls and sapphire eyes were striking, his jaw strong, and his morals stronger. He was a police officer for the NYPD, currently off duty.

Michael arched a brow at Max to convey his interest as he prepared to pull off his jacket. Underneath would be a double shoulder holster, two police-issue firearms, and a badge tucked into the waistband of his jeans.

"That was Gabriel," Max told them both. "He's found his archess."

Michael froze, the jacket half-off. "Come again?"

"Gabriel has found his archess," Max repeated, more slowly this time.

Michael shrugged his jacket back on and put his

hands on his hips. "No shit." His blue eyes glittered beneath the recessed lighting.

"You're kidding me," Uriel added. Beside him, Eleanore nudged her way in to be part of the conversation.

"Spill," she said, obviously having heard enough. "Is she okay? What's her name? Is she in Scotland? Does he need our help?"

The men blinked, absorbing her questions; then Max braced himself. "He thinks her name is Juliette," he said, "but he doesn't have a last name. Right now, the fact of the matter is that she might be in trouble. He was speaking in our tongue, which can only mean one thing. He told me that the archess ran out into the night with an Adarian hot on her tail. He's currently in police custody."

"What?" the men all asked at once.

Max grimaced. "He was calling from a jail cell in Lewis."

"Then Lewis is where we will go," came another voice, this one deeper and more melodic than the others. The men turned to see an extremely tall man dressed in black boots and jeans, a black button-up shirt, a black leather vest, and a black sport coat coming down the hall that led from the backstage to an exit into the alley behind the studio. His shimmering jet-black hair was straight and shoulder length, his mesmerizing eyes were starkly amber-colored, and his features harshly beautiful. His presence was frankly stunning—which was fitting. He was the former Angel of Death, Azrael.

The sun had set two hours ago and Az had no doubt just finished feeding. Unlike his brothers', Azrael's transformation upon reaching Earth two thousand years ago had taken a rather dark turn. Max was sure Azrael's past had something to do with it: that the inherent tenebrousness of what he had done for so long somehow warped his essence. Unlike his brothers, Azrael was not merely a displaced archangel. He was a vampire. He'd been the first of his kind.

"What time is it there right now?" Michael asked, obviously concerned about Azrael and the sun. Direct sunlight was out of the question.

Max looked at his watch, did a mental calculation, and said, "Roughly three in the morning. We have a few more safe hours."

"Ellie." Uriel turned to Eleanore and took her gently by the upper arms. "Please do me the favor of staying here."

Ellie instantly stiffened and it was clear that she wanted to argue. But Uriel was asking nicely; he knew he couldn't make her stay if she chose not to.

"You might need me," she reminded him, raising her hands as if to show him her healing devices.

Uriel nodded and Max was impressed with the archangel's learned patience. "I know, baby, but wait until we know for sure that we need you there. I don't want you walking into a trap or something."

Ellie seemed to consider that a moment. She lowered her head, closed her eyes, and nodded. "Fine, go fast. I'll be here if you need me."

Uriel kissed her on the forehead—and then kissed her on the lips. And then he and his brothers and Max turned and made their way across the backstage area. None of them mentioned Jacqueline Rain or the show they were missing as they came to the stage's exit. This was more important. It was the reason they were there on Earth to begin with.

Azrael easily dealt with the minds of the humans around them, hypnotizing them into stunned acquiescence as he moved past them. At the same time, he used another of his powers to scramble the electrical field in the building. The lights went out as the group reached the exit and pushed through the metal door. Chaos ensued behind them, but they ignored it.

Max closed the exit door and stepped to the side. Azrael was already raising his arm toward the very same door. As they watched, a portal swirled to life around the exit, expanding to reveal the foggy darkness of the Scotland night beyond.

Gabriel got up from the bench in the small cell and walked to the bars. There, he held out the phone he'd been given and Constable Fields, a young Englishman who had turned Scot when he'd fallen in love with the nation in his teens, took it back with a nod.

Then, as was expected of him, Gabriel turned and allowed the officer to cuff him through the bars once more, on Dougal's orders. It was useless, of course, but humans wouldn't know that.

Gabriel made his way back to the bench and sat down. Then he took a very slow, very deep breath and let it out through his tender nose. It was still healing from the Adarian's assault. He glanced up and surveyed the room. There were three guards beyond the bars to his cell: one doing paperwork, another taking a phone call, and a third drinking coffee as he carefully watched the prisoner, which his chief inspector had told him was top priority.

Even if Gabriel had possessed the use of his hands in that moment, he would not have been able to call a portal to the mansion. There were too many witnesses and that was something the archangels had decided on preventing at all costs long ago.

Angus Dougal had left promptly after delivering Gabriel to the jail. He'd said he was going after the girl who had rented the hotel room. She was a witness in this affair.

Though Gabe had made a call to Max, he'd had to be covert about the details, using the language they'd spoken before coming to Earth two thousand years ago. He only hoped Max would remember enough of it to understand what was really going on and respond to the urgency of the situation. He was almost positive he would, but *almost* positive wasn't good enough to quell his fears.

Juliette.

He closed his eyes and spoke the word softly, a whisper only he could hear. It felt like a promise across his tongue, sweet and smooth and perfect. It was such a beautiful name. Gabriel had fallen in love with the character from Shakespeare's play immediately upon reading the work more than four hundred years ago. There had been something ethereal and yet strong about her. William had captured it sublimely.

"Comfy, Black?"

Gabriel opened his eyes again and stared out at the man on the other side of the bars. Jake Campbell was a sergeant in the constabulary and the kind of man who thoroughly enjoyed pulling his rank as often as possible. Even Angus Dougal wasn't overly fond of the sergeant; Campbell's pale face and somewhat watery eyes reminded Gabriel of the sticky, slithering features of a cave creature, trapped without light for too many years. As if to make up for an appearance he knew was less than perfect, Campbell used steroids and worked out at the local gymnasium nearly every day of the week. As a result, he was a walking combination of resentment and testosterone wrapped in the skin of a fish.

"Sod off," Gabriel muttered, all but ignoring the man.

Keys instantly jangled in the lock of the cell, and Gabriel knew well what was coming. It wasn't anything he couldn't handle. Over the past two millennia, he'd been through much, much worse.

Still, it was irritating to know that he couldn't knock the rat unconscious. He certainly couldn't kill anyone—that went without saying. Maintaining a normal profile and hiding his archangel heritage aside, it was essential to appear all but human if you planned on returning to the same locale century after century. He'd managed it so far. He didn't want to screw it up now.

Then again.

Juliette was out there in the cold and she was his archess, and a man reached a point in his life when he both knew what he wanted and *had* it, and if he didn't hold on with tooth and nail in that moment, he could lose it forever. He could so easily break out of here. He could use any number of his powers to either melt the bars or send objects flying around the room with telekinesis or open a portal through the jailhouse door into the mansion.

And Max would be obligated to clean the mess up. That was what he was there for. He could wipe the memories of these officers, clear records, and destroy footage and no one would be the wiser.

So. Easy.

Just as he was making up his mind to do it, the sergeant entered the cell like a righteous storm and pulled the truncheon from his belt. Gabriel stood and broke the cuffs behind his back.

There was a scuffling sound beyond the bars of Gabriel's cell and he knew that the other men were mobilizing. Someone rushed forward to pull Campbell backward, away from Gabriel, and Gabe looked up toward the doorway behind them in time to see a Colt .45 materialize out of thin air a split second before the invisible Adarian used it on one of the officers.

In the blink of an eye, the weapon was fired at Fields as the confused constable turned a stunned look on the floating firearm over Campbell's shoulder. The Adarian pulled the trigger twice and Fields jerked backward, releasing Campbell to land on the desk behind him, then roll over it.

Gabriel rushed toward the Adarian, but was knocked

viciously backward as the gun was turned on him and a bullet sliced through the air. The impact took him by enough surprise that he had to catch himself on the bars of the cell to keep from falling.

A few feet away, Campbell stared at the floating weapon, horror shaping his features. The weapon was then turned back on him and fired three more times.

Gabriel ignored the pain in his jaw and shoved himself away from the bars. He was on top of the Adarian then. There was a flicker, a blinding flash of light, and the Adarian was solid again.

His green eyes flashed malignantly. "How will you explain this one, Gabe?" he hissed as Gabriel tried to wrestle the weapon out of the man's hand. "You've attacked two officers and escaped from your cell." He *tsk*ed reproachingly, gritted his teeth, and then roared with rage as he grabbed Gabriel by the front of his shirt and spun with him until he could slam him up against the wall.

Gabriel hit the wall hard and heard the plaster crack beneath the impact. "It'll be easy with your dead body as evidence," he hissed back, taking one from the Adarian's book and slamming his forehead into his opponent's nose.

The blond man reared back, eyes closed, and dropped the gun as he covered his nose with his hand. Gabriel took the opportunity to lunge at him, ready to end this fight once and for all.

And that was when the Adarian reached his free hand behind his back, took the shard gun from the waistband of his jeans, and aimed it at Gabriel's head. It happened so fast, Gabriel found himself literally skidding to a halt, his breathing ragged, his eyes burning in his face. He knew they must be glowing.

He hated shard guns. They were an Adarian invention, and evil to the core. Their bullets—if they could be called that—solidified flesh into stone upon contact, and the horrible poison of their effect spread until it encompassed a good portion of a victim's body. The pain was immense and unrelenting, and being healed from such a wound was nearly worse. He should know. He'd been shot with the infernal weapons numerous times.

"Do you have any idea," the Adarian asked as he wiped the blood from his nose on the back of his hand and cocked his weapon, "what it's like to have all the power in the world but the one you need most?" With this, he quickly swung the gun down at Gabriel's left leg and pulled the trigger twice. The gun flashed, the air warped, and Gabriel's lower body was wrapped in horrid, solidifying pain.

He fell to his knees.

"Hurts, doesn't it? Imagine you had no one to heal you from that pain," the Adarian sneered, his green eyes glowing now as well. "No Michael, the fucking blessed. But someone out there *could* help you. And she was destined to be with someone *else*." This time, he swung the gun to his left, put two shard blasts in Gabriel's right leg, and again leveled the weapon on Gabriel's head.

Gabriel's heart hammered behind his ribs; he could hear the flow of blood through his eardrums. *This isn't happening,* he thought. *Az!* he called out, wondering whether Max and his brothers were close enough yet for Azrael to hear him with his vampiric mind-reading ability. *Azrael!* He was in so much pain. There were no words for this kind of pain. Flesh was not meant to be petrified. . . . *Az, for fuck's sake! People are dying!*

We're here, came the calm reply. *We're coming.*

And then the Adarian pulled the trigger again and Gabriel knew it was coming. There was a split second of warning in his opponent's green eyes—it was enough. Gabriel lunged to the right and took the shard blast in the shoulder as he went down, hit the ground, and rolled to a stunned, heavy stop a few feet away.

"You're a bloody coward," Gabriel told him with as much calm as he could maintain. Agony was warping his senses, but on the sidelines of his consciousness, he knew human lives were fading. Hearts were slowing and blood was going stagnant in emptying veins. What the hell was taking Max so long? These men needed Michael!

"And you're a selfish bastard," the Adarian hissed in return. "You have everything." He shook his head and something strange flickered in his eyes. His sneer softened and his expression took on a faint poignant cast. "And I have nearly nothing left to lose."

The door to the jailhouse slammed open as the Adarian weapon went off a final time. The bullet whizzed past Gabriel and blackened the plaster wall behind him as a red-gold mist cascaded into the room on a hurricane wind.

The Adarian cried out as the gun was knocked from his hand, and his body was picked up and tossed across the room. He hit the opposite wall with tremendous force and slid down its length, knocking a corkboard and various wanted posters to the ground beneath him.

At once, he was invisible again, vanishing from sight even as Azrael's mist coalesced and solidified into his tall, strong form.

"Don' let 'im get away!" Gabriel shouted, knowing the Adarian would make a break for it, slip past them, and be gone without a trace. But the warning was useless. Even as Azrael lunged forward with that impossible kind of speed only a vampire archangel could exhibit, it was clear the Adarian was already gone.

So, Azrael let him go and focused on Gabriel.

Gabe watched as his brother gracefully knelt beside him and surveyed the damage. "You're fortunate he missed your vitals," he said calmly, even while Gabriel just wanted to curl his fingers into fists in the black material of Azrael's sport coat.

"Where's Michael?" Gabriel asked, his words hissing shakily through clenched teeth. *Eleanore would work, too,* he added mentally, knowing Azrael could hear his thoughts.

"He's coming," Az replied, setting a gentle hand on Gabriel's untouched shoulder. And then the vampire turned to glance over his own shoulder at the fallen officers behind them, and his expression became very grim. "He can't heal all of you." *We'll need to get Ellie up here, after all.*

Over Uriel's dead body, Gabriel thought. He knew the former Angel of Vengeance would never allow his wife to get involved in something like this. Then again, Eleanore wasn't the kind of woman to be denied something when she really wanted it. And she would claw through anyone and anything who kept her from healing someone in need.

If necessary. Azrael smiled, his own projected thought reflecting Gabriel's internal reasoning.

CHAPTER NINE

"What the—"

Azrael stood as Uriel and Michael came through the doorway, Max behind them. Michael surveyed the damage; his gaze fell upon the injured men, and at once he was at the constable's side, his hand pressed tightly to Gerald Fields's bleeding chest.

"Michael, save some of that," Max warned softly, his worried tone drawing Michael's attention even as the wounds in the man beneath him began to close up. Michael met Max's gaze and Max nodded toward Gabriel.

Gabriel tried not to let his expression show how much pain he was in. His wounds were not life-threatening. The humans, however, would most certainly die without Michael's immediate attention.

"Get Ellie," Michael commanded calmly.

Gabriel glanced at Uriel to see the archangel run a rough hand over his face. He obviously had an objection to this. He also obviously knew they had no choice in the matter. Uriel waited two seconds more and then opened a portal to the mansion through the office door.

When he'd disappeared, Gabriel closed his eyes, unable to keep from succumbing to the pain any longer. The wound in his cheek and jaw smarted. Shard guns were an Adarian invention, and Adarian enemies were never human. The guns were made to defeat supernatural beings—*archangels*. And that, they did perfectly. At that moment, Gabriel felt as if he had three appendages with third-degree burns all the way down to the bone. A burning, throbbing, insistent, and horribly wrong kind of pain—that was as close a comparison as he could summon.

He heard scuffling and shuffling across the room and knew that Michael had moved to tend to the other officer. He also knew that healing mortal wounds was horribly draining for an angel. He wondered how his brother was feeling at that moment.

"Hang in there, bro," came the sudden reply as Michael knelt over him and Gabriel opened his eyes.

Michael's sapphire blue irises were glowing with stunning, unnatural light. He was pulling his strength from deep within at the moment. Gabriel could see that sweat was just beginning to dampen his thick blond waves.

"Ellie's coming," Gabriel gritted out. "Don' bother."

"Let me try."

"Suit your bloody self," Gabriel growled, letting his head fall back on his arm and closing his eyes. He felt Michael's hand on his chest then, hot like a brand, and his teeth clenched so tight, he thought they might break.

What remained of Michael's power seeped through the archangel's palm and into Gabriel's body, spreading across the muscles of his chest until it had enveloped his entire upper torso. From there, it traveled across his petrified shoulder and Gabriel felt a tingling. He sensed the healing power as if from far off, through too many layers.

It was too weak.

"I can do your arm, but then I'm tapped," Michael told him, slightly out of breath. Just as he'd said, Gabriel felt Michael's magic de-solidifying his arm; it crackled and popped as it melted back into living flesh, and Gabriel put his good wrist between his teeth to keep from bellowing with the agony.

When it was done, Michael sat back on his heels and ran a slightly shaky hand through his damp hair. Gabriel peered up at him through blurring vision. The pain was getting the best of him and he wasn't even one-third of the way mended.

Behind Michael, Gabriel could see the air begin to warp and swirl. "Sorry, Gabe," Michael said, glancing at Gabriel's petrified legs.

"It's okay, Mike. I'm here," came a female voice from behind Michael. Gabriel watched Eleanore step through the widening portal and hurriedly make her way to his side. "Take a breather," she told Michael, who slowly stood and stepped away.

Uriel was by Eleanore's side. Max and Azrael moved closer as well; Az had picked up the shard gun and was holding it ready in his right hand. It was the first time they'd managed to obtain an Adarian weapon; Gabriel imagined Max would want a good look at it later.

"Christ," Ellie whispered, surveying the damage. "How many were there?"

"One," Az told her. She glanced up at him as she knelt and placed her hands on Gabriel's chest. Then she turned back to face him and closed her eyes. Gabriel shut his as well when her magic began pouring into his body. It was different from Michael's. He was probably one of very few people who would ever be privy to this particular realization. But her magic felt smoother — like a beer instead of Scotch. It went down a little easier, but it worked a little slower.

Despite her magic's gentler touch, as Ellie worked, Gabriel jammed his forearm between his teeth once more to keep from screaming.

What felt like ten years later, she was finally done. Gabe opened his eyes and sat up in time to see Uriel catch her as she wobbled on her knees and fell slightly backward.

"How . . ." She closed her eyes, shook her head a bit, and began again. "How many times did he shoot you?"

"Five," Gabriel replied. "Twice in each leg, once in the shoulder." The men in the room seemed to still at the slightly stunning news. But Gabriel didn't stop there. "He was aimin' for my head on tha' last shot."

"He didn't hold back," Max stated, his expression deeply troubled. He stared at the floor, obviously deep in thought, and then took off his glasses, wiped them down with a cloth he kept in an inside pocket of his suit, and then replaced them on his nose. "He really hates you, it would seem. You saw no other Adarians with him?"

Gabriel shook his head. "He was alone. An' he told me I had no idea wha' was goin' on." Gabriel tested his legs and looked past his brothers to where the officers still lay unconscious. Max had most likely already wiped their memories and Az was probably keeping them under until the situation could be contained.

"Strange," Max said. "I should think we were quite clear on what was going on. He wants you dead."

"Any idea what the hell he was after?" Michael asked. "Other than your imminent demise, I mean?"

"Yes," Gabriel said, coming to his feet. "He's after Juliette."

Juliette's body felt so heavy and weak, it was nearly delicious. There was no pain, just a slow, peaceful thickness that enveloped her form like a warm, soft blanket.

Wait a minute. . . . Juliette frowned and rubbed her hand over the front of her torso. It *was* a blanket. Fleece, from what she could tell. She tried opening her eyes, but her lids were heavy. She tried again, managing to blink slowly, languidly, allowing light to suffuse her senses.

She was lying on a couch in a well-appointed living room. There was a fire blazing in the hearth across the room. A glass of water rested on the coffee table beside her.

A man sat in the love seat across from the couch. "How're yae feelin'?" he asked softly.

Juliette didn't answer. Alarm kicked off a fresh injection of adrenaline into her veins. She looked the man up and down, appraising him quickly. He was very tall—as tall as the man at the inn. The one who had kissed her and then saved her life. But instead of silver eyes, this man had green, and his hair was many shades lighter, at a sable brown. He was dressed in jeans and a thermal shirt and jacket. She could see leather straps running taut across his well-developed pecs. *Shoulder holster straps,* she thought. But in Scotland?

The man smiled a friendly, dashing smile, and as if he knew what she was thinking, he glanced down at the shoulder holster. He shrugged off his overcoat, revealing the holsters and their weapons.

"My name is Angus Dougal," he told her softly, his brogue at once warming Juliette's blood. "I'm the chief inspector in Lewis." His smile broadened, flashing straight white teeth. "I promise I won' shoot yae."

"What am I doing here?" Juliette asked, deciding for now just to believe he was who he said he was. She was so tired.

"Well, I was goin' tae take yae to the hospital, boot I happen tae know the nurse on dutae tonight, an' fer yer own good, I brought yae here instead. This is ma home."

Angus Dougal chuckled; his green eyes were sparkling. Juliette's mouth went a little dry. Slowly, she rested back against the pillow once more. Her head was spinning. This man was a cop. She was in his house. Some other man had broken into her room in the inn and tried to chloroform her. The man who had kissed her had suddenly come in and saved her.

Juliette's eyes widened at a sudden thought. "What happened to the stranger?" she asked, her voice still softer than she would have liked.

"The one who attacked yae?" Dougal asked, his eyes pinning her with sudden stark attention.

Juliette swallowed hard. There was something in his green eyes that left her feeling suddenly unnerved.

"Gabriel Black has been taken intae custody. Yae're safe from his advances fer the time bein.'"

Juliette blinked. "What?"

"The man who attacked yae—his name is Gabriel Black. Black hair, gray eyes—ring a bell?"

"What?" Juliette repeated, feeling at once confused and angry. The man Dougal was describing was the one who had kissed her in the bar—the one who had saved her from the blond stranger. *Gabriel Black,* she thought. She liked the name. It suited him.

Angus Dougal's gaze narrowed. He watched Juliette like a hawk and seemed to carefully consider her reaction.

Juliette sat up again. "Black wasn't the one who attacked me," she said, finding enough strength to defend the man who had saved her life. But her mouth was still dry, so she took the glass of water and downed several swallows before returning it and swinging her legs over the edge of the couch.

"Gabriel Black saved me," she told him. "It was another man who attacked me. Black pulled him off of me and gave me time to get out of the room."

Dougal considered this a moment more, his expression unreadable. And then he sat back on the couch and draped his arms over the cushions. "Oh?" he asked quietly. "That's real interestin' seein' as how Black was the onlae man in the room when my men and I arrived."

Juliette frowned and tried to digest this. She looked down at the glass of water—the coffee table—the couch.

And then she looked back up at the inspector. "Was he okay?" she asked, finding that she truly wanted to know.

At this, Dougal cocked his head to one side and regarded her with renewed interest. She realized, at that moment, that in the space of half a second, she'd gone from being the victim to being a suspect. In what, she had no idea.

Angus Dougal chewed on the inside of his cheek a moment and then stood, coming to a very impressive six feet and three or four inches. Juliette's mouth went a little drier.

Dougal stepped around the coffee table and closed the distance between himself and Juliette. And then, just when she was beginning to feel a little dizzy from staring up into his green eyes, the man sat on the coffee table in front of her.

"Miss Anderson," he said, his brogue gentle and deep, "yae've been through a lot tonight. When we found Black, he was in yer room, alone an' more or less unharmed." He let this sink in a moment and then leaned forward, folding his fingers together in front of him as he pinned Juliette to the seat with a hard, searching gaze. "Are yae sure yae saw wha' yae thought yae did, lass?"

Juliette could have groaned with the amount of foreboding she felt in that moment. She had no idea what was going on. Why Black would be alone. Who the stranger was who had just suddenly . . . *appeared* in her room. Something was happening that wasn't supposed to happen. Something with a clearly supernatural bent.

Juliette swallowed hard and fumbled with the warm blanket she'd kicked off beside her. When she didn't answer right away, the inspector leaned back a bit, his gaze sharp and penetrating.

"From wha' I hear, Miss Anderson, Gabriel Black assaulted yae in the pub downstairs before comin' to yer room an' kickin' the door in."

Oh Christ, thought Juliette. *The kiss.*

"Um," she mumbled, feeling her cheeks grow pink. "He kissed me."

Angus Dougal's mouth curved into a knowing smile at this and he leaned forward once more. "Yae hit evera man who kisses yae, then?" he asked softly.

Juliette felt her blush deepen and became distinctly uncomfortable beneath the inspector's keen gaze. She was all too aware in that moment of how handsome a man he was. And of the fact that she was sitting on his couch in his home. Alone.

She cleared her throat. "Inspector," she said, "is Gabriel Black in custody right now?"

"Aye," he said. "There be a fine amount o' damage done tae the room, an' by all accounts, yae were attacked." He stopped there, as if waiting for her to contest his words.

She did so. "But he's innocent," she told him steadfastly. "I was being attacked by another man. He was blond and very large and very strong. Gabriel Black may have been a little drunk and maybe he shouldn't have kissed me downstairs, but he did save me from the man who attacked me."

The inspector studied Juliette closely for a moment in that ultraobservant way of his, and Juliette tried her best to stare unflinchingly back. And then Dougal shook his head. "We found no evidence of anyone else in the room, Miss Anderson." He paused and his gaze narrowed. "Exactly wha' did this other man attack yae with?"

"Well, for one thing, he was using chloroform." If the cops hadn't found evidence of anyone else in the room, then that meant that they hadn't found the rag with the chloroform on it. The act had been completely covered up and Juliette didn't know why. But whatever the reason, it couldn't be good.

Dougal considered this in silence as well, his green

eyes never wavering from Juliette's face. And then he sighed. "Miss Anderson, there was a lo' of damage done tae tha' room. Yer belongin's were scattered everae-where an' the lamps are all shattered. Do yae mean tae tell me tha' one man with a rag an' a bottle o' chloroform did all tha'? I cannae see why, tae be honest. Yae're no' a big lass, if yae'll permit me sayin'. A verra large an' verra strong man would no' have sae much trouble as that, noo, would he?"

Juliette blinked. She found her throat felt tight and tried to swallow; it was hard. He raised a good point. The man who attacked her hadn't broken the lamps and thrown her things around the room. *She* had. Telekineti-cally. And she was still trying to accept the fact that this new power of hers had surfaced; there was no way she could share it with Angus Dougal, the chief inspector.

So, she remained quiet. After a long while, Dougal nodded. "Verra well," he said, coming to his booted feet.

He's so tall, thought Juliette. But then, most men were tall compared with her. She also took note of the way his muscles flexed enticingly beneath the material of his thermal shirt.

Jesus, she thought. *What's wrong with me? I've got skin on the brain.*

This, too, did not go unnoticed by the inspector, whose green eyes flashed with something equally enticing as he looked down at her. "It's clear tae me tha' yae've go' somethin' under wraps aboot this case. I suppose I've nae choice but tae keep yae under house arrest until we have more information tae go on."

He waited, his gaze locked on hers, as this statement settled in. When her jaw dropped open and she stood, it was clear he'd gotten the reaction he was hoping for. Ju-liette couldn't believe this. Could the police do this? Keep witnesses locked up? Especially when no real crime had been committed? Vaguely, she recalled something about people being guilty until proven innocent in the UK and her stomach began to feel strange.

"For what crime?" she asked.

"Disturbin' the peace an' destruction of public property," he told her calmly. "If Black is no' responsible for the damage, as you say he's no', then I can onlae assume yae were in on it with him." His gaze traveled across her face to her neck and collarbone and back up again. His voice lowered a bit. "Which means, yae're responsible yaerself, Miss Anderson." He smiled a *gotcha* smile and added, "Of course, yae can always pay for the damages an' be on yaer way."

CHAPTER TEN

General Kevin Trenton ran his tongue along the edges of his teeth for the thousandth time that afternoon and frowned.

"You look troubled."

He turned to find Ely standing in the doorway, leaning against the wall. The Adarian was studying him closely. Kevin wondered how much the big man had noticed.

"I have to orchestrate the killing of four very beautiful women," Kevin told him, his tongue feeling strange against the new sharpness in his mouth. "I *should* look troubled."

Ely said nothing, but he continued to stare at his leader a moment before his gaze slid to the shut blinds at the window behind Kevin. "Is the sun bothering you again, sir?"

To this, Kevin said nothing. He didn't have to answer. He was the General. And it didn't matter anyway; whatever he said, Ely would know the truth. He was a smart man and he'd been chosen to receive the blood of an archess for a reason.

Instead, Kevin changed the subject. "Xathaniel has not been found. If there is anything Daniel is good at, it's hiding. I suppose an inherent invisibility will create that in a man." He turned away from the window that he had just indeed shut his blinds against and walked to his desk. "I want him found."

"Sir, we've—," Ely began softly. But Kevin held up his hand and the Adarian fell silent at once.

"Change tactics, Ely. Think like he would. We can't afford to allow him to leak information about our organization. Think on it for a moment." He cocked his head to one side and pinned Ely with a hard stare. "Going to the press or the American government would be one thing. But that's not what he would do. He would go to the archangels." He paused, allowing the information to sink in. "My job is hard enough, Ely. Understand?"

Ely straightened and cleared his throat. "Perfectly, sir." With that, the Adarian left his general's office and Kevin was once more alone. Kevin looked up at the empty doorway and took a deep breath. The last few days had been incredibly difficult.

Completely destroying an Adarian was not easy. Not by any means. The men who served under Kevin had served him for many millennia. Human beings would have no idea what kind of a bond this amount of time formed. And that bond was broken earlier that week as Kevin had chosen his victim.

The Adarian's name was Hamon. His power was slightly more impressive than Daniel's invisibility, but still expendable. Hamon was able to control the will of nonhuman animals. It was a power that might come in handy at a zoo or an establishment guarded by Dobermans, but, other than that, bore little significance.

Kevin approached Hamon when he was alone and immobilized him with a shard gun. As the soldier lay petrified on the cold slab of metal Kevin had laid him out upon, the General had proceeded to drain his strong body of every last drop of Adarian blood. He then decapitated and burned the body in the building's incinerator. The blood he then drank. As he drank, he concentrated on absorbing the power he wanted. As it had been when he'd taken Ely's blood, it was nauseating at first and Kevin had been forced to swallow his own bile in order to keep the thick red substance down.

But he'd managed. And after the second glass, the blood's consistency seemed to change as it went down. It felt thinner, cooler, less like metal. By the fourth glass, it was almost cold and nearly refreshing.

When he'd finished, he licked his lips, and as he'd suspected, all he had to do was consciously reach out for the power he'd absorbed, and it was there for his using.

Covering up the homicide wasn't easy. It had required careful planning. First, Kevin paraded around in front of his men in the guise of the Adarian he had killed. He told them he was going out for drinks. Then, a few hours later, Kevin, now dressed as himself, alerted his men to the fact that Hamon was missing and would not return Kevin's summons by cell.

Puriel, or Paul, as he went by now, was an Adarian capable of "sensing" the existence of other Adarian minds. It was only one of the man's abilities, and the far less valuable one at that, but it was the one that Kevin then called upon. He asked Paul to send out his mental feelers in order to "make sure" everything was all right with Hamon. When Paul could not feel the other man— the Adarians assumed the worst. Hamon was dead.

It was easy for them to make the next logical leap and take it for granted that one of the archangels had come across Hamon and done him in. The Adarian soldiers now wanted archangel blood more than ever.

Everything was going splendidly and according to Kevin's plans.

However, in the aftermath of the ordeal, Kevin had been hit with the reality of what he'd done. He'd killed a man loyal to him. A man he had often called a friend.

He'd then had to call his three chosen men to a meeting and declare his edict. It had been incredibly painful to look into their faces and know he had destroyed one of their own.

It had been necessary. The Adarians and the archangels were the only two beings he knew of who possessed powers above and beyond the mortal realm of understanding. It would have been perfect if one of the four favorites had been residing in the Adarian prison instead. *Uriel would have been so much fun to drain,* Kevin thought darkly. If Uriel were dead, he would never be able to touch—to kiss—Eleanore Granger again.

And as to Eleanore, absorbing the power he wanted from the archesses would be much more pleasant. If Eleanore's loveliness was any indication, each archess would be a beauty to behold. Taking their blood would be easy and pleasurable. In Ellie's case . . . well, if he decided to keep her around for a bit and enjoy other aspects of her being, it was his prerogative.

Kevin's lips curled into a smile at this thought. And then he turned toward the window and the fading light outlined by the slats that covered it.

There was still Xathaniel to deal with. He was out there somewhere, apparently far from the compound, as if he'd known exactly what had been about to go down inside its walls.

Kevin's gaze narrowed as he considered this. *Could* he have known? The skill he brought to the Adarian table had always been his invisibility. But the Adarians were incredibly powerful beings and Kevin had always felt a very strong aura around Daniel. It didn't quite seem to match his singular power, truth be told. It had always felt uneven—skewed.

The realization hit Kevin in that moment, and he felt as Dorian Gray must have felt when he'd looked upon his own image that final and fateful time. *He was holding out on me,* he thought grimly. *All this time, he was hiding his true gift.* Daniel had another power. And that power had saved him from his slaughter.

Kevin lowered his head to his chest and felt his hands curl into fists at his sides. If he'd wanted Daniel found before, it was nothing compared with how badly he wanted him now. None of the Adarians had the ability to scry on happenings elsewhere in the world. In fact, the existence of such an ability had been no more than unsubstantiated, legendary hearsay until his men had discovered that one of the archangels did indeed possess that incredible talent. Lord Azrael, as he had been called eons ago, the former Angel of Death, purportedly had the ability to find anyone he wanted anywhere on the planet as long as he knew enough about them to do the search.

The ability to scry a person's whereabouts in such a manner would have served the General very well at that moment. Unfortunately, scrying wasn't an Adarian gift.

Morael, or "Mitchell," as they called him, possessed the power of telepathy, among other abilities. Mitchell was able to read any mortal's mind, and every Adarian's mind except for Kevin's. The General assumed this had something to do with the fact that Kevin was the first archangel to have been created. His mind was decidedly different from all the others to come after his.

Mitchell's telepathy and Luke's dream-invasive abilities were as close as any of them could come to something like scrying. If they could be combined . . . Kevin frowned and pondered the possibilities. What might happen should the two powers be joined together—and focused? He had learned more about Adarian powers in the last week than he'd learned for the last several thousand years. What he had only dreamed could be possible was becoming a reality for him. So, there could be no harm in trying this one extra little experiment. After all, no one's death was necessary for this one.

Kevin took the radio off his desk and used it to call two of his men to his office. He looked up again when he heard Mitchell and Laoth on the other side of his door.

Before the men could knock, Kevin bade them to enter.

Mitchell was what a human woman would most likely refer to as tall, dark, and exceedingly handsome. He had a quintessential Italian feel to him, from his black hair to his black, star-speckled eyes and his penchant for sleek, fast cars. Laoth, or Luke, was a finely sculpted man with blond curls who had once modeled for Michelangelo, so very many years ago.

Kevin gave the two men their instructions. Like the loyal Adarian soldiers they had always been, they took their orders, nodded their consent, and left his office once more.

Kevin watched them go. And then he turned and studied the single window in his room with a mixture of curiosity and strange, cold trepidation. The sun would set any minute, but where it rested on the horizon just then, it shone bright and orange and the rays forced a bright glow to the edges of the window's blinds.

He felt threatened by it.

It was a disturbing realization. Elyon had been right. The sun was indeed bothering him of late. And that wasn't all.

As his tongue gingerly prodded the slightly longer, noticeably sharper shape of his incisors, Kevin realized there was a pulse to his thoughts now. It beat like a drum, both feeding him and starving him at once. As he had since he'd discovered her healing power, he longed for little Ellie. From the moment he'd beheld the woman that she had blossomed into at the ripe age of fifteen, that longing had taken a more personal bent.

She'd looked at him through the slats of her window blinds with those blue, blue eyes—and now he wanted her to do so again. He longed to feel her body beneath him on his bed. That was as it had been for years.

But now, underneath the hunger he felt for her flesh, for her submission, and for her power, lay something entirely new. Beyond his yearning for her body was the foreboding and very real hunger he felt for the taste of her blood.

Juliette was dreaming again. This time, she was walking down a hall both rich with rugs and tapestries and hollow with wind and crumbling walls. Again, one image overlaid itself upon another, a transparent echo of what it once was that draped the cold, stone reality of what it had become.

Voices carried through the yawning doorways, snippets of conversation in a lilting accent she could almost place. Formless, incorporeal figures moved above her, as if there had once been a ceiling and a floor where now there were only the muted grays of fog and sea mist in the open castle ruin.

She caught the scent of baking bread and cooking meat. It wafted by and was gone, replaced at once with the salt and brine scent of the North Sea. Wind whispered through her hair and caressed her neck as she rounded a set of winding stairs, and stepped through an archway into a massive chamber.

A fire crackled in the grate, blazing bright and high, but its image was transparent over the hollow hearth and black stone that had once offered warmth to the lord of the castle. This was his bedroom.

Juliette paused in the arched entry, her gaze skirting over the ghostly impressions of the master's furnishings. A writing desk, a wardrobe, a chest—a bed. Its four posters rose like spires to the cloudy sky, the faintest misting of draperies cascading from their tips to blow in the lingering breeze. The furs looked warm and soft, the wool thick and finely woven, and the blankets mussed as if the bed's owner couldn't be bothered.

She moved toward it, caught in a pull she could not understand, and heard music. It was muffled, barely audible, and yet it tore at her heartstrings. She closed her eyes as footfalls joined the tune, echoing in the chamber's outer halls, drawing nearer.

He was behind her then, and she knew he was there. His presence was the only real and solid thing in this haunted dreamscape. His touch was warm as he laid his hands upon her shoulders and drew her against his chest. She pressed into him, needing his strength, and moaned when his hand slid from her shoulder to her neck to encircle it gently, tenderly.

Anticipation thrummed through her, a drug in her bloodstream, awakening a desire she'd only ever known once before. He took her chin in his hand and turned her head, slowly, softly. She held her breath as he bent over her and whispered words across her lips. The language was old; she had understood it once, but had forgotten.

His teeth nibbled her lower lip, clasping it as he drew her nearer, tighter, and then he was claiming her with his kiss, and she couldn't have breathed if she'd wanted to.

The blankets were over her head. They were smothering her. Juliette gasped for air, rolled over, and fought with the covers until they slid in a heavy, twisted heap, off the bed. Then she sat there on the mattress, breathing heavily, as her hair acted like a curtain around her face, long and tangled beyond help.

She huffed at it and slapped it away, clearing her vision. *Where the hell am I?* she wondered, feeling disoriented and unsure. The room was dark and quiet and wind howled at a windowpane. She closed her eyes and swallowed, feeling a touch sick. She racked her brain, trying hard to recall. . . . Australia? No. She'd flown home. Pittsburgh? No. She had a night-light in her room there.

Scotland.

She opened her eyes and blinked. This was her bedroom in the cottage she was renting in Harris. A few more seconds and she recalled everything. The pub in Lewis, the dark-haired, silver-eyed Gabriel Black, and the deadly stranger who had attacked her in the hotel room.

Inspector Angus Dougal had issued a house arrest for her only minutes before he'd received a phone call from one of his men at the station house. The officer on the other end of the line suggested that new evidence had been found in the room where Juliette was attacked, and Gabriel Black had been released. Dougal's entire demeanor had gone stony, but he'd played the good cop well enough, and he even drove Juliette down to her cottage in Luskentyre and saw her inside. He also apologized for all her suffering that night and left her his cell number in case of any further emergencies.

Juliette couldn't help but wonder what the "evidence" was that the officers had apparently found. Was it chloroform? Something else? What did this mean for her? And for Gabriel Black?

If he'd been released, where was he now?

Juliette suddenly found herself imagining Black in his bed. It would be a big bed. With four posters and a canopy? Her mind trailed off. Would he sleep in the nude?

She swallowed hard, found her throat had gone dry, and then violently shook her head. Her heart felt racy and strange. Beads of sweat had broken out along her brow. Sleep would be a long time coming.

With a heavy sigh, she pushed herself off the bed and put out her arms like a blind person so that she wouldn't bump into anything. She found the light switch, flicked it—backward, as all the switches ran backward in Scotland—and light flooded the room. In a few moments, she'd donned some leggings, sheepskin boots, and a huge pullover sweatshirt.

Then she grabbed her laptop from the bedside table and made her way into the cottage's living room. The connection here was a dial-up, which meant that when she could hop on, it would be slow as Christmas, and that she would have to compete for computer time with anyone else staying in the cottages or the main house. But it was the middle of the night, it was better than nothing, and she'd been dying to reconnect and touch base with people.

Juliette plugged in her laptop, turned it on, and waited for it to boot up. While she waited, she raided the kitchen for crumpets and black currant jam and Scottish cheese and oatcakes with hazelnut spread and lots of tea. She would lose sleep, but she'd make up for it by eating twice as much.

Once the connection was up and running, Juliette opened her e-mail and gave a small gasp when she found that she had 172 messages, 31 of them from her adviser.

Juliette's blood pressure shot through the roof. Fearing the worst, she opened the latest e-mail from Dr. Larowe first and braced herself.

> Juliette, where in God's name are you?? Lambent's already on his way over there; I got a call from his assistant this morning!! I just wanted to give you a heads-up. He's decided he wants to meet with you himself, so be ready! And be NICE!! Please, please let me know you've gotten these messages. Just a quick pong to my pings! Love you, kiddo.
>
> —Tony

Juliette stared at the screen, utterly confused. "Lambent is coming here?" she whispered out loud. *Where, here?* she thought. *Is he coming to Harris?*

With a sinking feeling in her gut, Juliette glanced at the date stamp of the e-mail. It had been sent the day before yesterday. She groaned, ran a frustrated hand through her knotted hair, and sat back on the couch with another dramatic sigh. In the tumult of recent events, she'd all but forgotten about her contract with Samuel Lambent. She was required to meet with one of his representatives once a week. And it looked as though she'd missed her last meeting without even realizing it. Now Lambent was most likely worried.

This wasn't good. Juliette was going to have to call her adviser. Or she'd have to call Lambent's office and find out where he was staying.

It looked like she'd be drinking her tea cold.

CHAPTER ELEVEN

It was easier than she'd thought it was going to be to get a train ticket from Ullapool to Inverness. It was a tribute to Scotland that its people were almost universally friendly and helpful; travelers in the station had directed her through the entire process from beginning to end. And now she sat in her own booth with her own table, and her carry-on was perched safely in the stowaway bin above her. Once she reached Inverness, she would switch trains and take another into Glasgow, where Samuel Lambent was planning to meet with her.

It was early Sunday morning and not a high-travel time; her car was empty but for her. She felt like Harry Potter when the trolley came by with teas and soups and biscuits for sale. There were no Bertie Botts Every Flavor Beans, but with a little effort it was easy to imagine that when she turned around and looked out the window, she would see the towering spires of Hogwarts rising over the hills in the distance. It was enough to take her mind off the attack she'd suffered and her burgeoning powers and what the hell they could possibly mean. At least for a little while.

But the sense of bereavement and haunted remembrance she experienced while traveling across Scotland was stronger on the train than it had been in the car.

Perhaps it was because she had nothing to do but stare out the window at the passing countryside and its crumbling castle walls. Whatever the reason, though, Juliette remained nearly motionless as the world passed her by, and memories she knew she couldn't have had assaulted her mind.

A flash of an ancient church, and a chill ran down her spine. A shadow across a painted red door, and Juliette felt sad. A path beckoned into the darkness through a tall wood, and Juliette had the sudden urge to jump off the train and run down the trail. It was almost frustrating the way the land made her want to remember.

"I see you feel a kinship with our bonnie Caledonia," came a deep brogue from behind her.

Juliette jumped just a little, and turned in her seat to find herself staring up at the man who had kissed her in the pub. The man who had saved her from the stranger. The man who had, until only a few hours ago, been in police custody.

Gabriel Black. True to his name, he was dressed in head-to-toe pitch, his wavy, raven locks blending in with the leather collar of his jacket. His silver eyes sparkled with secrets as they locked on to hers.

Juliette's jaw grew slack, and her tongue found itself knotted, useless and mute. She caught a whiff of him, a scent like sandalwood and cedar and hearth-fire smoke, and images of her dream flashed before her mind's eye. Her fingers went limp on the tabletop; her legs pressed themselves together self-consciously, and her bottom lip began to tremble.

"B-Black," she whispered.

Gabriel smiled and then, without being asked, he lowered himself into the empty space on the seat beside her.

His solid nearness washed over her like a blanket of intoxicating sexuality, and Juliette hurriedly scooted back a bit on the seat. She could go no farther when her left arm pressed against the cold metal beneath the coach window.

Gabriel watched her retreat, his eyes sparkling with amusement. "We need to talk, lass," he said, his accent so much more broguish than that of most of the people on the Western Isles. By and large, Hebrideans sounded Irish and Gaelic. Black, however, sounded as if he'd come from all over Scotland; it was the timbre and lilt of his tone that bespoke the land.

"A-about what?" Juliette asked. *The kiss? The man in my room? The fact that you were arrested?*

Gabriel's smile broadened, his silver gaze flicking to her lips and back again. Casually, he turned toward her, caging her with the hard mass of his body as he reached across the table and picked up her cup of tea. It was still steaming. Without taking his eyes off her, he placed it to his lips and took a sip. "You've go' good taste," he said as he put the cup back down. "Bu' then, you're a Scottish lass by blood, so I'm no' surprised."

"Look," she said, feeling a little dizzy. "I'm grateful to you for saving me from whoever it was that came into my room last night, but . . ." She lost track of what she was going to say when he reached over and nonchalantly took a lock of her long, thick hair in his hands and began rubbing it between his thumb and forefinger. "But . . ." She licked her lips, utterly distracted by the scent and sound and feel of him so close. The air around her felt too thick, too charged.

Somewhere in the distance thunder rolled, barely audible over the rhythmic sound of the train on the tracks. But Black's eyes cut from the hair in his hand to Juliette's eyes once more, and he cocked his head to one side. He said nothing, as if waiting for her to continue.

"But I don't know you and you're . . ." She trailed off again.

"I'm wha', Juliette?" he asked softly.

He knows my name, she thought. For some reason, she wasn't surprised. He seemed unreal, sitting there only inches from her, more solid than a sable-draped statue of bronze. He seemed impossible, like a super-hero. Like a dream. *You're scaring me.*

Thunder boomed closer to the train, the storm obviously having moved in, as it was easier to hear over the metal slide of the rails. Something strange flashed in the light gray depths of Gabriel's eyes. He gently released her hair and leaned in a bit, closing the space between them. "You'll want to control that, luv." He smiled a decidedly dark smile. "Let it rage an' it'll drain your strength." He leaned in even farther so that Juliette's head bumped the wall behind her. "An' then how will you fight me off, lass?"

Juliette could barely breathe now. Her mind fought to process what he had just said, even as her body fought with itself over the effect he was having on her. Enough of his words got through that her blood pressure shot through the roof, and adrenaline poured into her bloodstream. "Control what?" she asked, her voice barely more than a whisper.

"The storm, Juliette," he replied. "It's one of your powers as an archess, is it no'? An' from the way it's growin' stronger by the moment, I'd wager it's a fairly new one to you."

Terror thrummed its way through Juliette's body, instantly chilling most of the heat Black's nearness had awakened. Her stomach turned to lead in her middle, and her heart hammered bruisingly against the inside of her rib cage. "What are you talking about?"

Gabriel's smile never wavered. The pupils of his eyes were expanding, like those of a predator singling out its prey. "You know verra well, luv. An' I do, too. I know because I've been searchin' for you for so long, I've lost track o' the time."

The world blurred around them and melted into slow motion as Gabriel slowly raised his hand and cupped her cheek. At the contact, Juliette felt trapped and possessed and wanted and cherished and more beautiful than she had ever felt in her life. Even through the fear, her body was responding to his as if it wanted him more than it wanted life itself. His hand held her as if she were a delicate treasure; she felt a tremble in his fingers, despite the apparent calm of his tone, and it echoed the chaotic beat of her heart—and the growing storm outside the train windows.

She wanted to close her eyes as he leaned a little closer, so close now, his next words whispered across her lips, a breath of mint and Parma Violets. . . . She loved Parma Violets. "You were made for me, Juliette," he said. His thumb brushed possessively, enticingly, across her full lower lip. His gaze flicked to her mouth and back again; the silver in his eyes had become mercury: liquid lightning that reflected the gale building beyond the window. "How else would I know wha' I know aboot you?"

Juliette kept her gaze locked on his as she shook her head. "I don't know what you're talking about," she insisted stubbornly. He couldn't know. This was insane. She barely knew about her powers herself. "Please back off," she added, almost desperate now for him to either kiss her or disappear. One or the other—or she would pass out.

"Och, no, I canno' do that, luv," he told her with a single shake of his head. His thumb brushed across her lower lip again, and she shivered. "There are men after you, if you'll recall. The one who attacked you last night was no' the first of his kind to come after an archess. An' he won' be the last. You're no' safe alone, an' there's no' anythin' I won' do to keep you safe."

Juliette's gaze narrowed. "How do I know you didn't set up that entire scene last night?" she asked him.

"Scumbags sometimes work in teams, one to play the bad guy—the other to 'save' the victim." She gritted her teeth, trying to believe her own words enough to deliver them with some conviction. "I'm not stupid."

"No, lass, that you're no." He shook his head, clearly agreeing with her. His eyes still twinkled with some secret merriment and it made him so handsome, she had never felt so close to losing control. She'd never thought herself the kind of woman who could lose her composure around a man simply because he was beautiful. Gorgeous. Godlike. But she may have been wrong. Because at that moment she wanted to kiss him—and do other things with him—so badly, her body was aching in the most embarrassing places.

As if her own need were a signal of surrender for the predator in him, Black's pupils ate up the silver in his eyes and the sight of it made Juliette weak from the neck down. Before she could react, he was moving in for the kill, his lips slanting over hers even as his hands framed her face, claiming her for his.

God, yes . . . She was lost now; there was no coming back from this. Nothing else in life would ever feel so good. Juliette was instantly on fire, her heart hammering, her body melting, her core throbbing as wetness wantonly gathered between her legs and her breath left her lungs. Her hands came up of their own accord and clutched at the thick black leather of his jacket, her fingers curling into the material as if holding on for dear life.

He was an expert kisser; he did everything right. He knew how to surround her, how to open her up and delve deep. He possessed her with that kiss, taking and tasting and destroying her defenses as if they were tissue paper. And then, suddenly, he went still above her. His body tensed, his hands slid to her hair and tightened their grip, and very, very slowly, he pulled away.

The moment his lips left hers, Juliette experienced

such cold and emptiness, she actually shivered. It was like tasting despair, this abrupt separation. It *hurt*. But she retained enough control over herself to release his jacket and open her eyes.

When she did, she almost gasped at the change she saw in Black's expression. The lust and need were still there in that handsome face, but there was anger there now as well, stark and dangerous. His own gaze had narrowed, and lightning reflected in the molten silver of his eyes. His stubbled chin was set with hard determination. "Do no' move from here, lass. Stay in this seat until I return," he told her firmly.

Juliette was too stunned to react in any way. He must have taken it for acquiescence, because with that, he pulled back, and in one fluid, graceful movement, he stood in the aisle on the opposite end of the table. Juliette sat up a little straighter in the seat as reality slowly flooded her world like a cold shower. She watched his tall, dark form take a step back, and in that brief moment of space and clarity, she entertained a hundred different thoughts. *He's crazy. This is nuts. He's dangerous. He knows. I have to get out of here. Wait until he's gone—*

As if he knew what was going through her head, Gabriel came forward again to brace his hands on the surface of the table and lean in toward her once more. "Know this, lass. There is nowhere you can go where I will no' find you. Leave here an' I promise you'll no' get far." His eyes speared her like silver daggers.

She swallowed hard. He waited a moment more, trapping her in his metal gaze, and then he straightened and turned to stride down the aisle of the otherwise deserted coach. The automatic door opened before him. He stopped, turned to look at her over his broad shoulder, and captured her gaze with his. There was a world of meaning in the look he gave her. It was a brand of a look, hot and searing.

Then he turned back around and stepped through the plastic sliding doors and out of her line of sight. Juliette sat there in the seat, just as he had told her to, for several long moments. She couldn't help it. It wasn't that she was obeying his order; she simply couldn't move.

The first time he had kissed her had been heaven. He'd torn down her walls and breached her world with seemingly no effort at all. The second time he'd kissed her, he'd marched right into her castle and claimed it as king. She was ruined now. No man in the world would ever kiss her like that again.

Slowly, Juliette raised her fingers to her lips. She touched the swollen, sensitive flesh and closed her eyes. No matter how perfect the man was, he claimed to know about her ability to control the storm—which was throwing as big a fit as ever outside the windows now. He had called her something strange—an archess. And now that she'd said it out loud, the possibility that he had collaborated with the blond in her room to set up that kidnapping attempt just so that he could rescue her seemed much more likely.

She didn't trust Gabriel Black. She didn't trust anything about him—not his tall, hard body or his piercing silver eyes or his incredibly handsome face or his accent, which melted her bones in her body. She didn't trust the graceful way he moved or the sexy way he smelled or the subjugating perfection of his damnable kiss.

Definitely, she didn't trust the kiss.

Juliette's fingers trembled on her lower lip. "I have to get out of here," she whispered to no one.

As if the train had heard her and decided to become her partner in this venture, it slowed as the next station drew closer. Juliette lowered her hand and scooted to the end of the seat to peer down the length of the aisle. The doors on both ends were shut tight, and though she detected movement beyond them, it was blurred and

on her shoulders. She would run. He'd seen the thoughts in her eyes as he'd left her. He could threaten and try to scare her all he wanted, but it wouldn't work. In the end, she would flee.

At least there was nowhere she could go on a moving train. She was too smart to try to jump off it, and the doors wouldn't open in that fashion while the train was moving anyway. For the moment, she was stuck, giving him the time he needed to track down the Adarian.

What was confusing Gabe, however, was the apparent absence of any of the other Adarians. Where was the General? Why hadn't Abraxos made his infernal appearance yet? What the bloody hell was going on?

Gabriel strode through the aisles of the train, honing his senses for that familiar spark of negativity that would tell him the Adarian was near. He cursed his luck that just as he was finding the woman he had searched two thousand years for, his enemy had found her as well. At least he didn't have to deal with Samael the way Uriel had when he'd found his archess months ago. Small blessings.

Nonetheless, witnessing the Adarian's intrusion was like watching the Roman army lay siege to Gabriel's homeland. She was his—and *only* his. It was time to deal with the intruder once and for all.

Gabriel ignored the stares he got as he passed through the compartments. He was too focused to pay them any heed. But the farther down the train's length he got, the more agitated he became. The air was clean of the feel of the Adarian. There was no static, no thickness, no wrongness—not like there had been in Juliette's cabin. Where had the intruder gone?

And then something niggled at the back of Gabriel's brain—and the train began to slow. *No.*

Gabriel stopped in the aisle and turned to face the direction from which he'd come. The LCD screen at the end of the car read "Muir of Ord," and a few people were grabbing for their luggage. Gabriel broke into a near run, brushing rudely by the people who had claimed space in the aisle. The doors opened for him as he neared them and he shot on through.

But by the time he reached Juliette's car, the train had been stopped completely for several seconds and his fears were confirmed.

She was gone.

CHAPTER TWELVE

"Mitchell, tell me what you hear," Ely instructed as his dark eyes scanned the faces of the passengers disembarking from the train.

Beside him, the tall Greek Adarian nodded his assent and began scanning the faces as well. The dark of his eyes sparked with what looked like stars in a night sky as he concentrated. Ely glanced at him, noting the change. He'd always been fascinated by his fellow Adarian's ability.

But Mitchell fell silent as he worked, and Ely began to feel anxious. He was tired; the flight had been long, and he'd never dealt well with idleness in the first place. He, Luke, and Mitchell had traveled to Scotland as soon as Luke and Mitchell had managed to combine their powers in order to perform a makeshift scry on Daniel.

The fact that it had worked was shocking enough. The fact that no one had thought of trying such a thing until now was even more stunning. The possibilities it opened up were potentially endless. All it required was the consumption of blood.

Blood. In the end, it always seemed to boil down to blood.

"I don't hear him," Mitchell spoke beside him. Ely and Luke turned to face him. "But I do hear something interesting." He nodded toward a car at the front of the train, and Ely looked to see a stunningly beautiful petite woman disembark. She stood around five feet and two or three inches and was as slender as a dancer. Her skin was flawless and tanned a light gold, her features delicate, her green-brown eyes large and bright in her lovely face. She was in a hurry, her long thick waves fanning out behind her as she moved quickly and purposefully through the crowd.

Ely wasn't a fool. There were attractive people in the world, and every now and then a true natural beauty came along. But this woman was different. She had an aura around her that Ely instantly recognized. It was too pure, too magnetic. She didn't even notice the men stop to stare as she passed them by.

"Let me guess," he said, his low voice rumbling as he watched the woman turn a corner and disappear from sight. He turned to face Mitchell again, and the dark-haired man flashed him a smile. "Daniel's been holding out on us."

Luke chuckled darkly beside them. "An archess. And a lovely little lass at that."

"We're in Scotland, so if I had to place a bet, I'd say she's Gabriel's," Mitchell said as he dug into the inside pocket of his sport coat and pulled out a pack of cigarettes. He always did this after scanning people's minds. Either he would smoke, or he would drink. Ely had asked him about it once, and Mitchell shook his head and said, "Believe me, you would, too."

"Nice try, Mitchell," Ely said. "I would be impressed if it weren't for the fact that you just read her mind. She's got the archangel on her brain, hasn't she?"

Mitchell smiled again, put his cigarette between his lips, and then ignited his lighter. "She has a beautiful mind," he said. "Open and honest."

"And I bet that just turns you on like mad, doesn't it?"

Ely asked. He knew how Mitchell felt about honesty. It was as refreshing to the Adarian mind reader as water in a desert. He could tell already that Mitchell was going to claim *this* archess as his own.

Mitchell didn't bother replying to the insinuation, but he didn't have to. His secret smile was response enough. "She's afraid of him," Mitchell continued. He spoke around the butt as he lit the cigarette and repocketed his lighter. "She plans to hide in the women's restroom until the train takes off, and then hitch a ride into Inverness." He took the cigarette out of his mouth, blew a cloud of smoke, and then replaced it. His dark eyes were shining.

"Gabriel is here, then," Luke deduced, his light blue eyes suddenly flashing with hyperawareness as he scanned the faces of the passengers with renewed interest. The other two men turned to join him, and as if on cue, a sable-haired man dressed in black stepped off the train and onto the platform.

"And we have visual," Luke muttered.

As one, the three men stepped back and into the shadows of the alley between the train station and its neighboring houses. Once they were safely sequestered in the relative darkness, Ely turned up the collar of his coat. "Daniel's here somewhere; I can feel him. He can see us and we can't see him, so pinning him down won't be easy."

"It'll be easy if we take the archess. He'll follow her like a fly to honey," said Luke.

"Luke's right. She's our bargaining chip. And the General wants her, anyway," agreed Mitchell.

Ely nodded. "My thoughts exactly."

Mitchell chuckled darkly, flicking his cigarette into the nearest trash receptacle. "I know."

Daniel watched through narrowed green eyes as the Adarians slipped into the alley. He could follow them and listen to what they had to say, but he'd already pressed his luck enough just being within close proximity. It was sheer fortune that Mitchell hadn't managed to catch his thoughts. It was like a dart game with that man; sometimes he nailed you and sometimes he didn't. This time, he'd missed, but if Daniel didn't get out of there soon, Mitchell would have him pinpointed and everything Daniel had planned would be obsolete.

As would his life.

Silently cursing his luck, Daniel slipped behind the train and followed the tracks a few hundred yards. How the hell had they found him? He'd left no indication of where he was going. And none of the Adarians could scry or divine as he could. What the hell was going on?

A harsh vibration in the air scraped across his skin and he paused. Black was nearby. Daniel bent and peered beneath the tracks to the space on the opposite side. Sure enough, a pair of black motorcycle boots stared back at him. But within a few seconds, they turned and began striding away.

Daniel swore softly and ran his hand over his face. He needed to get to the archess before Gabriel did. Before Ely and the others did. He had seen her heading around the building to where she no doubt intended to hide in the women's restroom, so he had a jump on the archangel. But Mitchell could read minds; he might have the same information, stolen directly from Juliette's brain.

This was a royal fucking mess.

Daniel's mind spun as he attempted to come up with a makeshift plan. Quickly, he glanced at his watch and then glanced up toward the conductor's seat. The train would take off again in another four minutes.

Daniel made up his mind and broke into a run.

Juliette was about to duck into the restroom when she caught sight of something out of the corner of her eye.

She stopped and did a double take. It was a taxi. Sitting right there at the curb, its light on, its cab empty. The taxi driver leaned over in his seat and gave her a wave.

Juliette couldn't believe her luck. But she wasn't about to waste time questioning it. With but a second's pause, she waved back at the taxi driver and raced to his car. He got out and made his way around to her side, ready to take her carry-on bag, despite its small size. "Where ye headed?"

"Can you take me all the way to Inverness?"

The man's eyes widened as he set her bag in the trunk. Then his face contorted a bit while Juliette imagined he tried to hide a mile-wide smile, and finally he nodded. "Aye, boot it'll cost yae a posh pound or tae," he replied.

"Do you take credit cards?"

"Aye." He nodded, opening her door for her. Juliette glanced once over her shoulder and then slid into the back of the car. No sign of Gabriel yet. While the driver got behind the wheel on the right side of the car, Juliette fingered the credit card, license, and folded wad of pounds she had placed into her zip-up hoodie before she'd left the cottage. As long as she could get away with using the credit card, she would, so that she had receipts to show to Lambent's office. Besides, you never knew when you would need cash.

The taxi pulled away from the curb a few seconds later, and Juliette glanced once more out the rear window. She stifled a gasp as Gabriel Black stepped into the sunlight on the sidewalk beside the women's restroom. She was at once caught by the arresting profile of his tall figure.

Juliette quickly slid down in the seat and ducked her head. He was either dangerous or insane and possibly both. This was her one hope at escaping him. On instinct, she closed her eyes and held her breath.

After a few seconds, she sat up again and looked

around. The taxi had pulled away from the station and was on one of the main roads. Safe for the time being, Juliette exhaled and ran her hand over her face.

"Are ye here on business or pleasure?" the taxi driver asked.

Juliette glanced up and caught his reflection in the mirror. He looked to be a middle-aged man, but as with so many people in Britain his complexion was on the pale side, which kept the wrinkles at bay. His eyes were blue; it was the most common color she'd come across thus far.

"A bit of both, I guess," she replied, noting a slight tremble in her tone.

The man in the mirror smiled a strange smile, his blue eyes turning more intense. "An' which would yae be hidin' from, there? The business or the pleasure?"

Juliette felt the heat rise up her neck and into her cheeks. *He noticed me hiding from Black,* she thought. Of course he noticed. She was being a conspicuous idiot. She wasn't exactly giving Americans a good name with her behavior.

She tried a smile, but it came out lopsided. So she shrugged instead. *Pleasure,* she thought, unable to keep the memory of his kisses from her mind. "Neither," she lied. Hoping that he would get the hint, Juliette turned to gaze out the window, hiding her blush as best she could.

The taxi driver must have caught on that she didn't want to talk, because he said nothing further and the car was almost painfully silent for the remainder of the trip. When they reached Inverness, he drove her to a car rental shop and let her off.

She tipped the driver well and continued to count her blessings when the rental shop had available vehicles. She chose the cheapest, and then rented a navigation system to go with it. A quick stop at a convenience store for a Diet Sprite and a Wispa bar, and she was on her way once more.

It was late on Sunday night when she finally pulled into the parking garage adjacent to her hotel in Glasgow. This was the hotel in which Samuel Lambent had apparently booked her a room. As uncomfortable as it made her feel to be beholden to someone for a place to stay for the night, at that moment Juliette was enormously grateful that she wouldn't have to go through the booking process and cross her fingers for a room. The drive had been hard, the day trying, and she was very tired. She just wanted to get into her room, take a long, hot shower, and curl up in bed with a bunch of junk food and the Syfy channel.

When she checked in at the front desk, the woman behind the counter gave her a big smile. She had thick, shining brown hair, flawless skin, and bottomless dark eyes. She welcomed Juliette and very quickly and efficiently logged her into the system. She then handed her the key card to one of the hotel's four top-floor corner suites. Juliette stared at the card, blinked a few times, and then frowned. "Are you sure you have that right? A luxury suite? I'm just one person—"

"Yes, Miss Anderson," the woman said with a smile. She was foreign, as far as Scotland was concerned, because she had no trace of a Scottish accent. She sounded more American than anything else. The name tag on the woman's vest read LILY.

"Mr. Lambent has secured the room for you for the next week and has placed a deposit on it so that if you wish to continue your stay, you may, at his expense."

Juliette stared at the woman. She ran Lily's words once more through her brain to make sure she had processed them correctly. "A week?" Juliette asked softly. This was a very nice hotel. And the suite had to cost a fortune for one night alone. The last thing she wanted to do was wear out her welcome with the man who was funding her burgeoning dream by taking advantage of him and his money.

"Yes," Lily said, nodding reassuringly. Her natural, friendly smile was still in place. "And he has left this message for you as well," she then added, taking a beige envelope from a slot behind the desk and handing it to Juliette.

Juliette turned the envelope over. On the cover was her name, scrawled in black ink with what looked like a calligraphy pen. On the seam on the back was a wax seal, deep charcoal gray. It was a pair of angel wings.

"One last thing, Miss Anderson." The woman drew her attention once more and Juliette glanced up. "Your meals are to be on Mr. Lambent as well. You can order anything you wish from room service and the cost will be added to his tab." Lily held out Juliette's receipt and a second key card for her, but it took a moment for Juliette's body to move properly. She was still getting over the fact that Lambent had given her the luxury suite for a week. Free meals were yet another shock on her tired brain.

As if Lily understood what was going through her head, she smiled sympathetically and true kindness touched the darkness of her pretty eyes. "If you need anything, Miss Anderson, my name is Lily. Don't hesitate to call the front desk and ask for me. I'll be happy to help in any way that I can."

Juliette managed to nod and return the smile, though she knew that her surprise clearly showed through. She took the things from Lily's hand and said, "Thank you."

"My pleasure," Lily said. "You'll want to take the South elevator. It will ascend straight to your room."

Juliette headed toward the elevator with her small carry-on bag. Once inside, she stared warily at the dozens of round numbers on the panel and chewed on her bottom lip.

"Up we go," she whispered as she pressed the button for the top floor and then slid her hotel card into the slot when the red pass-code light came on. Apparently, not just anyone could get to the top floor; you had to have a key. It was the first time she had ever stayed in a location so exclusive. And though it made her feel somewhat like a phony, on the upside, she felt safer. She doubted anyone with chloroform was going to be waiting in her room in *this* hotel.

The ride up was much quicker than she would have expected. The elevator never once stopped for the other floors. It just shot straight to the top, and Juliette felt as she always felt on "lifts" like these: as if her stomach had taken up residence in her shoes.

Once it reached the top and stopped, the doors dinged open and Juliette found herself facing an elegant foyer. The floors were marble and the walls were painted in tasteful murals. Gold-gilded mirrors graced the entryway. Everything shone.

"I think the elevator went too far," she muttered as she stepped off the lift and her boots clicked on the marble floor. The stone had gold and silver veins in it, polished to perfection. "It's dropped me off in heaven."

Distractedly, she stepped forward so that the elevator could close behind her. The doors dinged shut and the lift descended without her.

Juliette turned to face the entryway to her suite once more. Massive double doors, also gilded, beckoned to her. *I don't deserve this,* she thought. She'd been in Scotland a week already and had yet to do any real, hard research for Lambent's show. To say nothing of the research she'd planned on doing for her own thesis.

In all fairness, her world had been turned upside down of late. First the healing, then the storms. And then she found out she had telekinesis. How was any of this possible? Why her? And why now? And then there was

Gabriel Black and the stranger who had attacked her in Stornoway. It was all too much and her lapse in focus was logically forgivable. She'd gone from town to town so fast and so furiously, her mind wrapped up in the chaos of the moment, that any kind of quality work on her part had been all but impossible to undertake. But Lambent wouldn't know that.

Juliette stood there in the entryway and rubbed her eyes. Her right hand still clutched the envelope that Lily, the woman at the front desk, had given her. Juliette glanced down at the envelope and sighed. Then she opened the double doors and stepped into the suite beyond.

It was everything she had feared it was going to be. Plush white rugs covered the marble floor in elegant disarray, the leather couches wore throws of cashmere and silk, and there were three different rooms—each with its own bathroom. Each bathroom possessed a jet tub, also constructed of marble. Each bed was draped in Egyptian cotton. And the honor bar carried a full bottle of Grande Siècle champagne.

Once she'd been through the entire suite, Juliette stood at the center of the massive hotel room and spun in a slow circle. Then she sat down on the couch and opened the envelope from Samuel Lambent.

She pulled out the folded document and read it carefully. And then she groaned and fell back against the thick cushions of the expensive leather sofa.

"Tomorrow. He wants to meet tomorrow," she muttered to herself. "Figures." She'd hoped she would have at least one extra day to actually do some research and concoct a halfway decent report by the time she met with her benefactor. But no such luck.

She didn't even have the option of staying up all night to "study." It was Sunday night and everything in the civilized world shut down early on Sundays. She hated

Sundays for that reason, alone. She could always go online; the Trinity Hotel had an excellent Internet connection. But anyone could go online to research something and Juliette had a feeling that Samuel Lambent, the incredibly wealthy and intelligent *media mogul*, would know online research from the real deal.

"Christ," she swore, as a feeling of dread sank heavily over her. "I am so screwed."

Samael leaned back in the large leather chair and thoughtfully placed his fingers against his lips. His charcoal gray eyes watched the screen before him carefully as his mouth curled into the slightest of smiles.

"Welcome, Juliette," he spoke softly.

The woman on the screen nervously clutched an envelope in her hand as the elevator she rode in sped upward through the many floors of the hotel. She was priceless—a treasure. And the fact that she was finally under his roof, within his reach, sequestered from the others who sought her, was fair consolation for the trouble that he had gone to in order to get her there.

His smile broadened as he watched her step off the elevator to stare, wide-eyed, at the double doors that led to her suite beyond. He chuckled softly at her innocent indecision. She was feeling guilty, no doubt. Unworthy.

As if.

She had no idea how precious she was. Samael had been forced to send one of his own men into the fray of her pursuers at the Muir of Ord train station in order to extract the archess before one of the others could get to her. She'd become the unwitting prey in a feeding frenzy of sharks. They'd scented blood in the water.

Juliette Anderson was painfully vulnerable at this stage. She'd only recently discovered her ability to heal. Her other powers were bombarding her all at once now, one after another, leaving her breathless beneath their supernatural onslaught. Naturally, she had no idea what was happening to her or why.

She was confused and lost and alone.

Again Samael chuckled, the sound as dark and sexy as the distant rumble of a Harley's engine. "Don't worry, little one," he said as he watched Juliette finally step through the double doors and disappear into the suite beyond. "I'm right here." *And I'm going to make it all better.*

CHAPTER THIRTEEN

Juliette had been told that Mr. Lambent wished to meet her in the hotel's restaurant for lunch at one on Monday. So she spent Sunday night researching online until she could no longer stay awake. Then she shut her laptop down and began going through the meager belongings in her carry-on bag.

She soon realized that she hadn't been thinking clearly when she'd hurriedly packed for the train ride the day before. She had no idea what people wore to fancy business lunches, but she was guessing it wasn't the same kind of clothing a PhD student wore on campus.

If she woke up early enough, she might get lucky and find a shop nearby that sold suits or business-casual clothing. Otherwise she was going to end up meeting the world's most powerful media mogul in jeans and a bulky sweater.

Juliette was literally too exhausted to worry properly about it. She set her alarm for six a.m. and crawled into bed still dressed.

The next morning, after a hot shower and several hot cups of coffee, she was a little more clearheaded. She took the elevator to the concierge's desk and asked for Lily. When the girl at the desk went in the back room to see whether Lily was working that day, an incredibly striking young man came out.

He was tall and slim, with dark brown hair and stark blue eyes. The name tag on his crisp, dark blue suit read JASON. He smiled warmly at Juliette and took her hand to introduce himself. Apparently Lily wasn't working that morning, but Jason was the concierge; he clasped her hand between both of his, and assured her that if there was anything at all she needed, he would be able to get it for her.

Juliette was more than a little self-conscious about asking him about shopping. She didn't want to admit that she didn't have the right clothing to meet Samuel Lambent. But before she could explain why she was asking, Jason was smiling and waving her concerns away. "Not to worry," he told her confidently. "I know exactly what it is you need."

It turned out that he wasn't exaggerating. He sent her into the hotel's café, instructing her to get anything she wanted for breakfast, and assured her he would take care of everything.

Two hours later, the bellhop arrived at her door with several enormous clothing boxes. Jason was a godsend. He'd managed to track down a formfitting skirt and jacket in lilac pin-striped silk, and a gorgeous white lace bustier to match. The color was incredibly flattering against her gold tan, and the shoes he'd purchased to match were a leather of the same lilac color with a high but firm heel and a rounded toe.

In a separate box were a small purple and gold handbag, a lavender-scented silk scarf, and a single amethyst-encrusted hairpin in what honestly looked like gold.

Juliette gingerly fingered the items for several minutes before taking them out of their boxes and laying them on the bed. Then she donned the clothing with an almost ritualistic kind of care. The material was so expensive, so soft, she was terrified of ever seeing the bill, which she was certain Jason would happily tack on to her credit card.

Except ... that she hadn't given them her credit card. They had Lambent's instead.

Oh my God, she thought as she stared at herself in the mirror. She was gorgeous. In fact, she couldn't remember the last time she had looked so good. The suit fit her like a glove, accentuating everything in a way that she'd never experienced. She felt like she was looking at a newer model of herself—one that was taller, sexier, and more confident. She looked radiant.

I have to make sure Lambent doesn't pay for these things, she thought to herself. She made up her mind to talk to him about it at lunch. But despite her trepidation over the bill, for the remainder of the morning, every time she passed a mirror in her suite, she would find herself smiling. It had been a while since she'd smiled so much. Amazing what a good set of rags could do for a girl.

When twelve forty-five rolled around, Juliette headed for the elevator. She got off on the third floor and made her way across a massive open area replete with fountains and a pianist. The restaurant's giant double doors were wide open, and a maître d' stood ready behind his reservation podium.

Several yards away, Juliette paused and took a deep breath. She was trembling. *I can't do this,* she thought. *What if I blow it? What if I say something stupid? What if he's pissed at me for not having anything substantial yet? What if I trip all over myself before I even reach the table?*

"Miss Anderson?"

Juliette turned to see the concierge that had helped her earlier coming toward her from a door in the wall to her right. She instantly blushed, knowing he was now seeing her in the very clothes he had chosen for her.

"Well, how do I look?" she asked, deciding to own it. She knew her cheeks were pink, but it couldn't be helped.

Jason's smile told her everything she'd wanted to hear, and that admiration was matched by the twinkle in his blue eyes. "You look stunning," he said as he reached for her elbow and gently took it with his hand. "Why are you waiting out here?"

She returned the smile and shrugged nervously. "Just trying to pump myself up."

Jason nodded his understanding, then leaned over to whisper in her ear. "So long as you don't psych yourself out." With that, he led her to the restaurant's doors and the maître d' came out from behind his podium. "Miss Anderson is here for lunch with Mr. Lambent," Jason announced softly.

The maître d' nodded knowingly and turned to gesture toward the restaurant's interior. "This way, Miss Anderson," he said with a smile.

Juliette allowed him to take her inside, and tried with all her might not to stare openmouthed at her surroundings as she was led through more amazingly rich architecture. Finally, Juliette's attention was pulled from the beauty of the decor as she neared the back of the restaurant and the private tables.

She turned to see where it was exactly that the maître d' was taking her, and found herself pointed in the direction of an incredibly elegant table with two incredibly gorgeous men seated at it. Juliette stared at them and felt her legs grow heavy.

No . . . way . . .

One of the men she recognized instantly. He was the wickedly handsome actor who had played the evil vampire on the movie *Comeuppance*, opposite Christopher Daniels. His name was Lawrence McNabb, known by his adoring public as simply "Law." The blond-haired, violet-eyed movie star was only slightly less drool-worthy than Daniels himself.

But more impressive yet was the man seated across from the movie star. Juliette had never seen anyone like him. She recognized him, of course, as Samuel Lambent, because she had seen vague, blurry profile photos of the man in newspapers over the years. But to say that they didn't do him justice would be a gross understatement.

He looked like some superhero figure or manga drawing: an impossible representation of the ideal male. His hair was thick and so blond it was white, like the down of a dove. His stature was incredibly tall and well built, filling out what she could see of his expensive dark gray suit with delicious perfection. His bone structure was that of a model; he was nearly so handsome, he was uncomfortable to gaze upon.

And she hadn't even seen his eyes.

And then the maître d' was bringing her up to his table and both men were looking up at her. She thought she would die right there as two sets of eyes fell upon her face and she became the sudden object of both men's attention.

"Mr. Lambent, may I present Miss Juliette Anderson."

Samuel Lambent had charcoal gray eyes that seemed lit from within, as if statically charged with lightning. Juliette's breath caught in her throat as those eyes trapped her in their thrall and Lambent gracefully stood. McNabb stood as well.

"Juliette. We meet at last." Samuel's voice was beautiful, smooth, and deep and reminded her of chocolate. She was right about him being tall. He was as tall as Gabriel Black, if not taller.

Black . . . For the briefest of instants, Gabriel's face flashed before her mind's eye and her mouth watered at the memory of his kiss.

And then Samuel was coming around the table and taking the place of the maître d' beside Juliette. As he drew nearer, the air around Juliette heated up. It was a familiar sensation, charged, electric, and heavy.

Lambent took the back of her chair and pulled it out for her, his smile warm and inviting. It was a killer smile. "I'm so glad you were able to meet with me," he said, his voice continuing to pour over her like satin. "I know how busy you must be."

Juliette smiled back at him and took the seat as gracefully as she could. She was so nervous, so self-conscious, that she was afraid she would make some horrible mistake just by sheer power of suggestion.

"Please allow me to introduce one of my clients," he continued as he returned to his seat and sat down, smoothing his tie as he did so. Everything he did was practiced and easy. It was like watching a well-choreographed dance. "This gentleman is Lawrence McNabb, a very talented actor. I do hope you don't mind that I've asked him to join us today."

"N-no, not at all," Juliette stammered, feeling her cheeks grow pink again. McNabb seemed to notice, but instead of thinking ill of her for her nervousness, he seemed to be charmed by it. His strange, violet eyes glittered and his lips curled into a sincerely amused smile. She was almost surprised, and admittedly a touch disappointed, not to see fangs peeking out from behind his lips. "I know who you are, Mr. McNabb—"

"It's just 'Law,' please," he chuckled, leaning forward conversationally. "And I know who you are, too. Mr. Lambent has been telling me all about you. He was quite impressed with your knowledge of the history of Scotland."

Juliette blinked, felt herself tremble with shock, and chanced a glance at Lambent. His storm gray gaze was too powerful. She saw admiration in its charcoal depths, but to look closely almost hurt; it was too intense. She felt as if he could read her mind—possibly her soul. She fought to cover up her fumbling thoughts. "Mr. Lambent is too kind."

"Not at all," Samuel insisted calmly. Something dark flickered across his handsome face and was gone. He leaned forward, pinning her to her seat with his attention. "And please call me Sam, Juliette." His tone had lowered, and his words wrapped around her like a silk cord, binding her before him. For several seconds it felt as if they were the only two in the room.

"I have to admit, though," McNabb continued, breaking the spell, "that Sam didn't tell me how lovely you were. I was expecting a spinster in black with a graying bob."

Juliette somehow managed to pull her eyes from Samuel's long enough to meet McNabb's gaze again. "I already wore all of my black clothes this week," she softly joked. When the actor chuckled, she cleared her throat. "But thank you." She found herself looking down at the tablecloth, distinctly uncomfortable beneath their scrutiny.

"Juliette, may I get you something to drink?" Sam asked as he waved the waiter over.

Double Scotch, she thought recklessly. "Yes, please," she said. "I am a little thirsty." In truth, her mouth had gone dry with apprehension. Samuel ordered a bottle of wine for the table and water for each of them and then he focused on Juliette once more.

"How are you liking Scotland?" Sam asked, folding his hands neatly before him.

Juliette thought of the castles and the moors and the forests, and she smiled. "I love it. It's everything I thought it would be and more."

"I'm glad to hear you say that," Sam told her, matching her smile with one that made Juliette's insides melt a little. "I do hope that you haven't done too much research already on the folklore of Caledonia, because I have some ideas about the show that I would very much like you to hear."

A wave of relief washed over Juliette at those words. She tried to hide it, but was unsuccessful. Her smile broadened and she relaxed a little in her chair. "Not too much," she said.

"Fantastic." Sam nodded. The wine and water came and conversation was put on pause for a few seconds. Juliette hurriedly grabbed her glass and swallowed several long pulls of ice-cold water. When she set it back down again, Samuel was filling her wineglass with a wine so dark it looked like blood.

"I understand that you most likely already have a strong sense of what you need to learn for your thesis while you are here," he told her as he set the wineglass down in front of her. "However, as far as your work for me is concerned, I would like to narrow the field a bit."

"Oh?" she asked, eyeing the wine warily. She wanted to drink it; it would burn going down and settle her nerves and temporarily clear her mind. But it was still relatively early in the day, and if she drank it now, she'd be hungover by six.

"There is a specific legend in Scotland that originated on the Western Isles, where your family is from," Sam told her. Juliette glanced up at him, a little surprised that he knew so much about her family. But then, her adviser had most likely filled him in over the last few weeks. "It has always intrigued me," said Sam.

"The legend tells of a warlock who walked this land two thousand years ago," McNabb picked up, his handsome face alive with the kind of expression that only an actor could manage. "Maybe you've heard of it? The *dorcha draíodóir*: the Black Wizard."

Juliette frowned. Technically, *dorcha* would mean

"dark," but she was assuming that in this case, "dark" had been translated to "black" long ago. "I'm sorry," she admitted. "I've never heard of the Black Wizard. But your Gaelic pronunciation is amazing."

McNabb grinned, obviously pleased that she'd noticed.

"As legend would have it," Sam continued, "this wizard achieved long life by absorbing the powers of young women through . . . a certain ritualistic behavior."

Juliette's blush was back. Her attention, however, was rapt.

"He would take them into his bed and by morning, the woman would be dead—and he would be twice as powerful as before," McNabb went on. "He only chose certain women, apparently. They had to be special."

"These women were referred to by villagers as archesses," Samuel explained.

Juliette's blood ran cold. Her heartbeat pounded in her eardrums and her vision tunneled ever so slightly.

As if he didn't notice, Samuel continued. "They were purported to possess certain abilities, not the least of which was the ability to heal." Sam shrugged then, lifted his glass of wine, and casually took a drink.

Juliette watched him with waning sight. Everything had gone blurry. Her chest hurt and her mouth was once more dry. She couldn't believe what she was hearing. It wasn't possible.

"This legend of the *dorcha draíodóir* is too good to pass up," Sam said. "I've decided to take the story and turn it into a miniseries, which is why Law has joined us for lunch." He nodded toward the actor. McNabb's grin stayed put. "He will be playing the part of the wizard on the show, and I felt it important that he be in touch with you personally so that he can get a good feel for what the part entails."

Juliette heard herself talking and wasn't even sure

how she'd formed the words. It was as if she were watching herself in a dream. "You want me to research this legend for you?"

"Absolutely." Samuel smiled. "If anyone can come up with the information, you can, Juliette."

Juliette fell silent beneath his all-seeing gaze. She was suddenly afraid she might faint.

"I can't wait to get started," McNabb admitted as he, too, took a drink of his wine. "Of course, I don't look anything like the wizard was supposed to look. Apparently, he had black hair and his eyes were a different color, but that's what makeup artists are for."

"Gabe, have a seat, man. You're making me nervous with all that pacing." It was late Monday afternoon and Michael was lounging on one of the three sofas in the mansion's living room, his blue eyes locked on Gabriel's tall figure as the former Messenger Archangel moved restlessly around the room.

"He can't, Mike. Believe me, you'd be doing the same thing." Uriel spoke up from where he sat at the dining room table through the open archway.

Gabriel stopped and turned to glance at Uriel. It was no secret that the two archangels didn't always get along. But now there was a knowledge in Uriel's green eyes that was separate and new. He understood what Gabriel was going through at that moment. He'd gone through the same with Eleanore.

Gabriel gave him a slight nod. It was enough.

"Well, you were right," said Max as he came from the hallway that led to the other wings of the mansion. He was pocketing his cell phone, and his expression was grim. "Sam is involved. He's the reason she disappeared so readily from the train station."

Gabriel's vision flashed red. "Bloody son of a—"

"How the hell did *Sam* get involved in this?" Michael

asked as he came to his feet, his blue eyes sparkling like sapphires. "She isn't even in the US!"

Max sighed heavily, took off his glasses, and pinched the bridge of his nose. "I never used to get headaches."

"Max," Michael growled, obviously wanting answers as badly as Gabriel did.

"I just got off the phone with Lilith," Max began, replacing his glasses and moving to the liquor cabinet. "Christ, I never used to drink either," he muttered under his breath.

"Max!" Gabriel barked. Lilith worked for Samael—more or less. She was as old as the archangels, and in fact older. Eons ago, the Old Man had created her and then tossed her to Earth to be punished for the crime of wanting to live a free life. Since then, she had attached herself to Samael, in a way, and also managed to aid the archangels here and there. She was the softer side of Samael, and their relationship was a strange and complicated one.

"I'm getting to it," Max assured him with a hard glance. He unstopped a bottle, poured himself a drink, then took a big swig. "Apparently, Samael has known of Juliette's existence for some time. Lilith couldn't give me details." He shrugged, his brown eyes reflecting something private and painful. Gabe guessed it had something to do with Max's love for Lilith and his silent, desperate desire for the woman to stop working for Samael. "But she did say Juliette is staying in a luxury suite in the Glasgow Trinity Hotel and that no one could get to her there."

Gabriel's teeth clenched together.

"The only way we wouldn't be able to get to her would be if she was inside of Samael's fortress," Uriel said, also coming to his feet and placing his hands on his waist. "But she's in a hotel in Glasgow and Sam's fortress is in the top half of the Sears Tower in Chicago."

"Former Sears Tower," Max corrected before swigging a drink. "It's the Willis Tower now."

"Not to anyone in Chicago, it's not," Michael muttered.

"Besides the point," Uriel continued. "Max, what's going on? What else about Samael don't we know?"

"Obviously, his fortress shares properties akin to the mansion's," Max guessed. "His territory may cover a lot more ground than we thought. And there are a lot of things about Samael that we don't know, Uriel." Max took another drink from his glass of liquor and looked at Uriel thoughtfully. "Speaking of things we don't know, where is Eleanore?"

"With her parents," Uriel replied. "They went out to dinner."

"I think you should bring her back and keep her and her parents at the mansion until we have a better handle on this," Max said.

"What aboot the Adarians?" Gabriel finally spoke up. His entire body felt like one rigid, electrified mass. His muscles wouldn't relax and his heart rate wouldn't calm. Juliette was with Samael. It was Uriel's nightmare all over again.

"You were right about them, too. There is more than one involved. Apparently there were several waiting for her at the train station," Max supplied.

"I assume Lilith filled you in on this as well?" Michael asked.

Max nodded.

"Well, tha's fucking grand," Gabriel ground out through gritted teeth. "The entire bloody supernatural world knows aboot her." She was a wanted woman in every sense of the word, and to make things worse, Juliette didn't trust him. He knew he had gotten to her with that kiss; he'd seen it in her eyes and felt it in the way she melted beneath him. But she'd run from him. And his power over her wouldn't do him any good if she was firmly in Samael's grasp. The bastard was probably adding to the misgivings she already had about Gabriel.

"Gabe, you look kinda scary right now," Michael said.

"We have to get her out of there," Uriel said.

"I'm having déjà vu," said Michael. Gabe and the others watched him as he made his way to the window, pulled the curtain aside, and glanced up at the setting sun.

He was right. The entire scenario was too familiar. When Eleanore had been discovered by Uriel, she hadn't trusted him either. And why would she have trusted him? She had powers to hide and had been running from the Adarians all her life. She'd been seduced by Samael's lies and it hadn't been easy for Uriel to win her faith. Just when he *had* more or less managed to win her over, Sam had stepped in again and turned Uriel into a vampire, complicating things to a painful degree and making their lives a living hell for a while.

Michael let the curtains drop and turned to face them once more. "Az will be up soon."

"And you think he can get her out of Sam's fortress?" Uriel asked.

"We certainly stand a better chance with him than without him," Max said.

"Seriously, guys," Uriel muttered. "You don't honestly think Sam is just going to let her walk out on him and go anywhere she wants alone, do you?"

"I don't have a clue as to what Sam is or is not going to do," Max said testily. "None of us does. But Juliette is an archess and from Gabriel's description of her, she is a smart, independent woman. She isn't going to take well to being shadowed by him."

"And wha' makes you think he's goin' to give her the choice?" Gabriel asked.

Everyone fell silent. No one had an answer to that one.

They were all well aware that Samael was more powerful than they were. If it came down to it, he was probably capable of forcing Juliette's surrender. He might hypnotize her, wipe her memory, or even go the old-fashioned route and lock her up in his dungeon.

Or in his bedroom.

Gabriel felt a pain in his right palm. He glanced down with faint surprise to see that he'd fisted his hand so tight, his fingernails had broken the skin over his lifeline. Thin crescent moons of blood were appearing across his palm.

"You'll want to control that," came a deep voice from across the room. Gabriel glanced up to meet a glowing gold gaze as Azrael stepped out of the shadows of the hall that led to his wing of the mansion. The sun had gone down—and the vampire had risen.

Is that not what you told her? came Az's voice again, this time in Gabriel's mind. Gabriel swallowed hard. Azrael could easily read other people's memories, but Gabe didn't need his brother's help remembering what he had said to Juliette. *"You'll want to control that, luv. Let it rage an' it'll drain your strength. An' then how will you fight me off, lass?"*

Gabriel had cornered her with his knowledge of her power right off the bat. And then, to make things worse, he'd threatened her. He'd told her there was nowhere she could hide that he couldn't find her. Gabriel closed his eyes and swore softly. He'd done irreparable harm. Juliette would never want to speak with him again.

Not necessarily true, said Az. *And remember, Eleanore was furious with Uriel after his televised announcement about her.* Gabriel could hear the smile in Azrael's voice at that. *She forgave him in the end.*

"Are you two finished having your nice private conversation?" Max asked, his voice tight. Gabriel looked up to see that Uriel, Michael, and Max were all watching him and Azrael expectantly.

Gabriel glared back. Az simply smiled, flashing fangs.

"So, once Ellie's back here, what's the plan?" Uriel asked, ignoring Gabriel's look.

"Actually, I might have an idea," Michael said. Everyone turned to face him and he turned to Max. "How many floors does the Trinity Hotel have?"

"Roughly forty," Max said.

"Okay." Michael put his hands on his hips and looked at the floor, clearly ruminating on something. Then he looked back up and continued. "The mansion can open anywhere there's a door," he explained. "Granted, the Trinity is a lot smaller than the Sears Tower, but it's a tall public building, just the same. Assuming Sam has treated it as he has the Tower, then he'll probably only have control of the upper floors and possibly the ground-floor entrances."

"Assumin'," Gabriel muttered. That was a big assumption.

"It's all I've got," Michael shot back.

"Even so," Uriel said, "his men'll be stationed all over the building. If you're thinking we'll get by them unseen, you're wrong."

"That's not what I'm thinking," Michael told him. "I'm thinking that we should open a portal from the mansion directly into the Trinity Hotel. Preferably as close to the top suites as possible."

Once again, everyone was silent. What Michael was suggesting was not only a really good idea—it was a plausible one.

"We wouldn't have to wait for Juliette to leave the hotel," Uriel said.

"Nope," Michael continued. "All we would need is for her to get on the elevator."

"You're thinking of opening the mansion's portal directly onto the elevator?" Max asked, his eyes a little wide behind his spectacles.

"Into the shaft, to be more precise." Michael nodded. "Gabriel's been in enough elevator shafts while working as a firefighter to know how they work. Once we're in, we can shut the elevator down. From there, it's just a matter of redirecting traffic—and isolating Juliette."

"And I've been in enough five-star hotels to tell you that they all have more than one elevator," Uriel interrupted. "In fact, wouldn't the suites have their own dedicated elevator?"

"Not in this one," Max supplied. "You get to the suites with a key card."

"So, we shut down all of the elevators. One at a time." Michael shrugged.

"We would have to work tremendously fast," Max said. "Before Samael figured out what was going on and put a stop to it."

"That we can do," Azrael stated calmly. The others turned to look at him. Archangels were fast by nature—freakishly fast. But Azrael was a vampire on top of it all and could move with such speed that his form actually appeared to blur to everyone around him.

The brothers were quiet for several long seconds. And then Max swigged the remainder of his glass and replaced it on the liquor table with a thunk. "Well, then what are we waiting for?"

CHAPTER FOURTEEN

Daniel knew what he was going to have to do. Once he'd managed to escape from the other Adarians, he'd had a lot of time to himself to think.

He'd gotten away from Mitchell and the others by racing along the tracks and into the forest where the tracks led. He continued running until he was a good half mile away from them, well out of Mitchell's psychic reach. Then when the train came by, he simply used his Adarian speed to hop it. He'd ridden the line straight into Glasgow.

Those moments at the train station had changed everything. The fact that Ely, Luke, and Mitchell were there meant that they had somehow figured out he would be there—or that the archess would. Either way they had an ability they hadn't had before. Maybe they could scry now. Or perhaps they could even divine. He had no idea how or when this had happened, but it altered the course of just about everything as far as he was concerned.

Subduing and kidnapping the archess in order to present her to the General wasn't going to work now. Kevin wouldn't care that Daniel could divine the future whereabouts of the archesses. Daniel was going to have to do better than that now. He needed to take matters into his own hands.

If the powers of an archess—or an Adarian, for that matter—could be absorbed through their blood, then there was no reason why Daniel couldn't absorb Juliette's powers as easily as the General could. If he drained her entirely, the powers he took from her might be permanent. He might be able to heal wounds on his own.

If there was one power in the world that General Kevin Trenton found indispensably valuable, it was the ability to heal. There was a good chance that if Daniel could absorb this power on a permanent basis, that, combined with his other abilities, could make him enough of a boon to the General that it would buy him his life back among the Adarians. Juliette was still Daniel's ticket to safety, but the role she played would now be different.

And shorter.

Juliette leaned heavily on the brass bar in the elevator as it shot through the floors toward the top of the hotel. She'd had the wine after all. And boy was it strong.

But it was either down the wine or pass out from shock in front of two gorgeous strangers. When they'd started talking about the "Black Wizard," her world had begun spinning. The warlock had possessed black hair and silver eyes? He'd gone after women he called "archesses"? He'd seduced them into his bed? It was too much. It was too close to be coincidence.

I would sleep with him in a heartbeat, she thought hazardously. *Gabriel Black is sex with a Scottish brogue. He kisses like an angel. . . .* Juliette momentarily closed her eyes and the memory of his kiss washed over her, eliciting from her a careless moan.

Fuck, I'm drunk, she thought. She'd had only the one glass of wine. But it had been so dark . . . so red . . . and it had burned all the way down, just as she'd thought it would. Three sips, and she'd felt some of her fear drift away like so much dust on the wind. And when the fear went, she started thinking about what Lambent and McNabb were saying.

And wondering whether the legend could be true—and whether Gabriel Black could be the wizard.

And she, the archess.

But it couldn't be true, could it? It had to be coincidence, didn't it? People didn't live for two thousand years, and there were no such things as warlocks or wizards. And whatever the hell an archess was, it had nothing to do with her, one way or another. "Archess" must just be a word from some other language that meant something in particular—like virgin or woman or something.

Then again . . . Juliette could heal people. And control the weather. And use telekinesis. And people weren't supposed to be able to do any of those things either. "God, what is happening to my life?" she asked herself, as she ran her hand over her face. She felt hot; the alcohol was burning through her veins like a fossil fuel. She almost never drank. This wasn't like her.

Without warning, Juliette's legs gave out and her body slid down along the wall in the elevator. She sat on the floor, bending her knees and pulling them to her chest. She knew that she would be the only one on the lift until she reached the top floor; once she slipped her key card into the slot, the elevator wouldn't stop until it reached the suites. And she was too stunned to stand. Because it hit her then, in that instant. It *really* hit her—everything that was happening to her. She had become a superhero. A figure from fantasy.

And in the last week, she had met far too many handsome men. Men like this didn't really walk the Earth, and definitely not unattached. And this legend . . . it was the straw that broke the camel's back. She was floating in a soup of nonsense now. *Drowning* in it. She was trapped in a fairy story with no way out. It was like being caught up in a dream from which you never woke. Was that what was happening? Was she in some sort of coma somewhere? Had she hit her head on coral while trying to pull that surfer out of the water and now she was lying in a hospital bed somewhere imagining all of this?

That thought scared her more than anything. It was something no person ever wanted to be—trapped between life and death, her parents and friends sitting in a hospital chair beside her, tired and giving up hope. She wanted to wake up.

But there was a part of Juliette, deep down, that knew it couldn't be a dream. If it was, then she had had dreams within dreams. And she never felt pain in her dreams. This was different. It was all too real—even as it was all too unbelievable.

"Somebody save me," she whispered, feeling close to tears.

Suddenly the elevator jerked around her, and it was fortunate that she was sitting or she would have fallen. It screeched loudly as it slowed and then jammed noisily to a halt. Juliette's heart rate kicked up and her eyes widened. The LCD readout on the wall told her that she was somewhere between floors thirty-four and thirty-five.

She grabbed the brass bar above her and hauled herself to her feet. She was about to slam her hand down on the red emergency button when another screeching noise sounded from above her. She looked up to see the brass ceiling of the elevator warping.

And then it split—and peeled away.

Juliette's mouth went dry. Her legs went numb again and she slumped against the bar, temporarily incapable of coherent thought. She watched in stunned silence as the roof of the elevator was completely ripped off, revealing a yawning chasm of darkness that stretched beyond.

For a single second, Juliette stared into that darkness, unseeing, unknowing. And then a tall outline of a man stepped into the elevator's light and knelt on the edge of the roof. Juliette gazed up at the man. He was incredibly tall—he had several inches more than a foot on her. His hair was a little longer than shoulder length, layered, and jet-black, and his eyes glowed like twin golden suns. He looked at Juliette, seemed to study her as deeply as Samuel Lambent had, and then he smiled, sporting straight, bright white teeth—and fangs. He was a vision out of some combination of a nightmare and a gothic wet dream.

Beautiful. Deadly. Impossible.

Juliette wanted to scream. She really did. But the man quickly stood and then leapt down into the elevator, landing lightly on his booted feet with supernatural grace. Juliette backed into the bar behind her until she felt it bruising her bones.

She had been right about his height. He towered over her.

"Juliette," the man spoke, saying her name as if it were a piece of candy he wanted to savor upon his tongue. "I won't hurt you," he promised softly. "You need to come with me, though," he continued. "And I won't ask you twice."

All of my powers, Juliette thought wildly, *and not a single one will help me now.* There were no clouds to call lightning from, no objects to throw with her telekinesis, and it didn't bloody well matter that she could heal. What she needed to do was *harm.* And then fly away.

"Wh-who are you?" she asked, her voice no more than a whisper. Her hands gripped the bar behind her painfully; her fingers had gone numb.

"My name is Azrael," he said. "I am Gabriel's brother."

Gabriel Black, she thought, knowing that her face reflected the recognition and heightened fear his name produced in her. *Samuel was right. Black is a wizard— and his brother is a fucking vampire!* It was a senseless assessment, but it was one of those spur-of-the-moment assessments that happened when fear completely took control of a person's brain.

Juliette had no idea what to do when the vampire who called himself Azrael took another step toward her. But her body did. She felt it searching for her powers before she realized what it was doing. It was this inward pull and then an outward yank and she was suddenly spinning in place and rewrapping her hands around the brass bar in the elevator.

A split second of hard concentration and the brass bar came away from the wall with a rush of telekinesis, and Juliette wasted no time in turning with it, intent on slamming its shiny metal against Azrael's handsome skull.

But the vampire did not move or even duck as she swung the bar around. Instead, he simply raised his right hand and caught the weapon, halting its progress completely. Juliette gazed into his eyes, terror taking trepidation's place inside of her.

The bar began to grow cold in Juliette's hand—colder than it should have been. She glanced down at it to see ice crystals forming along the metal. And then steam rising. And then her hands were stinging and she was forced to let go.

She released it and stepped back, once more trapped against the elevator's wall.

"I'm sorry, Juliette," the vampire said calmly. "I don't want to frighten you. But I told you I would not ask you again. I'm afraid there's no time."

With that, he dropped the brass bar and rushed forward, his form blurring before her as he closed the distance between them. Juliette tried to scream again, but as she inhaled sharply to take that breath, she was caught up in a pair of strong arms and spun around to be pulled back against a hard chest. At the same time, an alien sense of deep calm washed over her, melting the tension from her body even as it clouded her mind.

She felt instantly fuzzy and relaxed, and she lost the will to fight.

The vampire pushed off the floor of the elevator even as, beyond its stuck doors, Juliette began to hear the sound of men shouting. But in a moment, the shouts were all but inaudible, and Juliette and the vampire were airborne.

The flight was a short one, however. Azrael's right arm held Juliette securely against him as they shot up the elevator shaft toward a set of doors farther up that were glowing. She had no more strength to wonder about the glowing doors—it was simply yet another supernatural novelty in a world that no longer made any logical sense.

Instead, she focused on them as they neared them and she let her mind go. She had no choice. She felt drugged, peaceful, and incapable of anger or escape.

The vampire stopped as they came to float before the doors, and he raised his free hand. The doors began to warp and then to spin. Out of the blurred mass of metal, a portal yawned open. Beyond the portal, Juliette could see what looked like a living room with leather sofas and chairs and a crackling fireplace.

And there were men there, waiting for them. She recognized two of them. One was Christopher Daniels, the famous movie actor.

The other was Gabriel Black.

Before Juliette could fully comprehend what was happening, the vampire was moving forward, through the portal, and time and space were warping around them. It was an extremely bizarre sensation, and she would not have been able to describe it had someone asked her.

But her relaxed state took it in stride as they came out the other side and the portal door closed behind them.

Azrael set her down gently, and she wobbled a little. Immediately Gabriel was at her side, steadying her with a tender but firm grip on her upper arms.

"Juliette," he said softly. "Look a' me, luv."

Juliette realized that she'd been staring at the ground, trying to get a sense of its firmness; she felt disconnected from reality and incapable of speech. She forced herself to look up at Black, but still said nothing.

"Wha' did you do to her?" Gabriel asked, glancing up to meet Azrael's gaze. It was no longer glowing. The vampire's eyes were now a beautiful amber color with veins of gold, stark and gorgeous.

"She's in his thrall," came a female voice. Juliette blinked and looked around, trying to locate the woman speaking. The woman stepped around Christopher Daniels and gave Juliette a warm smile. She had long blue-black hair and light blue eyes. She was singularly lovely.

Gabriel shot the vampire a withering look.

Azrael was unfazed. "It was necessary. She has a lot of fire in her, even though Samael did his best to get her drunk." A slight smile curved his lips, revealing a hint of fang. "She pulled the railing off the wall in the elevator and tried to attack me with it. There was no time to reason with her. Samael knew what was happening seconds into the attempt. If I hadn't performed a scry to find her exact location before we'd begun, we would have failed. As it was, his men were outside the elevator doors as I brought her through the portal."

Juliette was having a hard time following their conversation. She looked at the windows in the posh living room and was surprised to see that it was nighttime outside. Hadn't it been only around three in the afternoon just seconds ago?

"He was probably watching her through the elevator's camera," another man said. He had thick, wavy blond hair and sapphire blue eyes. He was tall and muscular, like the others. He wore blue jeans, a long-sleeved thermal shirt, and a double shoulder holster; both holsters bore guns. A folded wallet with an NYPD badge was tucked into the front of his jeans. Juliette couldn't help but think that if she'd ever been pulled over by a cop who looked like that, she would have gone out of her way to break the law again just to have him on her tail once more.

"She's completely out of it," said a man with brown hair and glasses. He was dressed in a conservative but expensively tailored brown suit. The man came to stand before Juliette, gently nudging Gabriel aside. He pulled off his glasses and peered into her eyes. "You don't mess around, do you, Az?"

Azrael said nothing to that. He was still as a statue clothed in shadows.

Juliette closed her eyes and shook her head gently. She didn't feel bad—not at all. She just felt as if nothing mattered, and everything was fine, and there was no danger. None. Despite the ridiculous evidence to the contrary all around her.

"Let 'er go," Gabriel commanded then, pulling Juliette behind him so that he stood between her and Azrael. She craned her neck to peer around him.

The vampire cocked his head to one side and narrowed his gold gaze. "Are you certain that's what you wish?"

Gabriel said nothing. Juliette couldn't see his face, but she could imagine the look he was giving the vampire. *His brother.*

"Very well," said Azrael. He turned away from them then, and made his way to the double glass doors that led out onto what looked like a balcony. "I'm going to eat. But before I do, you should know," he said as he glanced at Gabriel over his broad shoulder, "Sam's been in her head."

The double doors swung open as he neared them, and when he stepped through and disappeared into the darkness, Juliette felt the blanket of calm that had been draped over her lift. Her thoughts were no longer fuzzy. She was no longer relaxed. A hard, sharp anxiety spiked through her blood, heavily laden with cortisol and adrenaline. Her stomach roiled with what felt like a sudden hangover and she felt nauseated. Her head ached.

She stepped back from Gabriel, who turned to peer down at her. Unsteadily, she looked around the room as if seeing everything for the first time. There was a cop, a famous actor, a beautiful woman she didn't know, a man in a brown suit and glasses, and, seconds ago, there had been a vampire.

Her stomach lurched and she swallowed down bile. She'd just been ripped out of an elevator, mentally controlled, and taken through some kind of portal through space and time.

Her heart hammered hard, increasing her nausea and her headache. She'd just had lunch with Samuel Lambent and another famous actor, and they'd all but told her that Gabriel Black was an evil warlock who wanted to have sex with her to steal her powers, and then kill her.

"I think I'm—" She couldn't finish the sentence. Reality was bent on sending her lunch back to where it had come from. She slapped her hand over her mouth and fell to her knees.

Out of the corners of her eyes, she could see the cop and the woman with black hair racing toward her. She could do nothing to stop them as they both knelt before her and the woman pressed her hand to Juliette's chest. That nearly did it—the food almost came up.

But then, miraculously, the nausea was ebbing. It felt

like heaven—that cessation of what Juliette considered the worst kind of pain. She closed her eyes and moaned softly. The pain in her head lifted next, leaving with an almost crackling relief.

After a few moments, the woman removed her hand and Juliette raised her head and opened her eyes. "Feel better?" the woman asked softly. Her light blue eyes reflected a kindness and an empathy Juliette had rarely seen in another human being.

Juliette nodded. "Thank you."

The woman shrugged. "It was nothing. You could have done it yourself if you hadn't been so overwhelmed." She and the cop stood back up, and Gabriel was back at her side then, offering her his hand. Juliette glanced down at the hand and trepidation flooded her. She stood on her own, ignoring his offer of help, and Gabriel took a deep breath through his nose.

"Who are all of you?" Juliette asked, taking several steps back from them to give herself space. She felt immensely better physically, but her mind was still spinning. The man in glasses came toward her, but Juliette held up her hand. "Please. Don't come any closer. Just answer my question."

Thunder rumbled in the distance, drawing everyone's attention to the windows. The flash of lightning could be seen illuminating the curtains. Juliette knew it was her fault. The storm was reflecting her emotions.

"Well, here we are again," mumbled the cop as he ran a hand through his wavy blond hair. "Ellie, can you help her with that?" he asked the black-haired woman, gesturing toward the windows and the storm beyond.

The woman shook her head. "Sorry." Then she turned back to face Juliette. "I'm Ellie," she said kindly. "That's Uriel, my husband. Azrael is the one who brought you here, this is Max, and this is Michael." She introduced the party one at a time. "I know you're confused, and I don't blame you for thinking this is insane. But I promise that no one in this room would ever harm you in any way."

Juliette looked at their faces, trying to memorize their names. The woman had introduced Christopher Daniels as Uriel. Maybe she was wrong about him. Maybe this wasn't the actor after all, just some look-alike. "What do you want?" she asked the room.

"We just want to help you," Max said, replacing his glasses and gesturing beseechingly with his open hands. "We know you're going through a lot right now, and you probably don't understand any of it. That's why we're here."

Juliette thought of the way she'd dropped to the floor in the elevator and pleaded for someone to save her. Had the fates heard her? Had the gods sent her a hero? If so, they were rather unlikely heroes . . . a movie star look-alike? A vampire? And a man who might be a warlock who wanted her dead so that he could continue to be immortal?

At least there's the cop, she thought, desperately wanting to believe that a badge automatically made a good man. Even while she knew it wasn't true.

Lightning struck closer this time, and they caught the sound of a tree being felled. It crackled harshly in the night and crashed to the ground.

"We need to talk, little one." Gabriel came to stand before her again, and this time she didn't back away. Her attention was instantly arrested by him. His nearness subjugated her with memories. His kiss. His scent. The silver of his eyes.

"That's what you said on the train," she told him.

"Aye," he said. "Bu' we have yet to speak of anything." He gave her a small smile and Juliette felt her gaze narrow.

"I don't trust you," she told him flatly.

Lightning struck just outside the window and a few in the room found themselves ducking out of instinct.

"Lass, you need to control that," Gabriel told her with a wary glance toward the windows.

"Why? Because if I don't, it'll drain me and I won't be able to fight you off?" Juliette asked. "Isn't that what you told me? And why would I have to fight you off, Black? Can you tell me that?" Her bottom lip was trembling; in fact, she could feel a tremble begin to thrum through her entire body. She might be healed of her hangover, but her temper was taking over now.

"I'm heading out for my shift," said Michael, the cop. Gabriel turned to glance at him and something unspoken passed between them. "I'm in the middle of a nasty case involving a serial rapist," he said as he pulled a brown leather bomber jacket on over his shoulder holster and guns. "Give me a call if you need me."

"Thank you, Michael," Max said.

Michael picked up a black duffel bag, gave Juliette a nod of farewell, and headed toward the mansion's front door. Juliette watched him go and fought the urge to call him back. He was a cop—he was the good guy here.

When he was gone, Max again came toward Juliette and Gabriel. "Miss Anderson, we haven't handled this properly at all. I'm so sorry. But what Eleanore says is true. We would never harm you. You are more important to us than you can know." He took off his glasses and pocketed them and then gently took Juliette's elbow in his hand. "Please, won't you at least come and sit down?"

Juliette allowed him to lead her to the nearest couch. She decided that pulling away from him would accomplish little. If she needed to escape them, she could use telekinesis to slam something into someone's head or call lightning through the window. And anyway ... Eleanore had actually healed her.

Juliette chanced a glance at the dark-haired woman.

Was she like Juliette? Could she control the weather and use telekinesis as well?

Max sat her down and pulled a throw from the back of it to drape over her shoulders. The warmth was definitely welcome.

"I'll make you some tea," said Eleanore as she hastily made her way across the living room toward one of many archways that led to halls across the room.

"Wait!" Juliette hurriedly stood from the couch, at once apprehensive. Eleanore was the only one in this mass of people that Juliette had any reason to trust. The others were . . . strangers to her. And Gabriel Black was too close. Juliette's eyes cut to him. He was watching her so intently, his head lowered, his silver gaze cutting through her as if he couldn't wait to get her alone.

She swallowed hard, confused by the warmth that gathered between her legs at that thought. Then she looked back at Eleanore, who had stopped and turned to face her. "Please don't leave," Juliette said.

"Ellie, you stay here with Juliette, and I'll get the tea," said Max. He nodded at Eleanore and she nodded back, taking his place beside Juliette.

"All right," she said with a warm smile. "Sit with me, Jules." She sat down on the couch beside Juliette and patted the cushions, indicating that Juliette should do the same. Juliette stared down at her hand and thought of the way she'd just referred to her as "Jules." Only Sophie, Juliette's best friend, had ever called her that. Even her parents used her full name. And yet, somehow it sounded right coming from this woman. It sounded natural, in fact.

Juliette found herself sitting down and even feeling a bit calmer as she did so.

But then Gabriel was coming toward her again, and Juliette's body once more went on high alert. He knelt before her and she caught a whiff of his cologne. It washed over her like a drug and her mouth watered. As he knelt, he placed his hands on the cushions of the couch on either side of her legs, and she was painfully aware of the nearness of his fingers to the skin of her thighs.

Juliette steadfastly stared at the coffee table. She couldn't bring herself to look into his eyes. She knew if she did, she would be lost.

"Look a' me, luv," he told her softly. His brogue was like fingers through her hair, a hot breath on her nipples. It seduced her as little else could. She closed her eyes and shook her head.

"Ah, lass," he breathed. "I mean you no harm. Can you no' see that?"

"What are you people?" Juliette asked, her eyes still shut tight.

"They're archangels," said Eleanore. "And we're archesses."

Juliette's eyes flew open at that. She looked over at Eleanore, meeting her blue-eyed gaze. "What did you say?"

"Archesses," Eleanore repeated patiently, her smile genuine. "I'm an archess—a female angel made as a mate to one of the four favorite archangels," she explained. "And so are you."

CHAPTER FIFTEEN

Lilith warily glanced upward when the overhead lights began to flicker. She wasn't surprised; she'd been here before. The air in the room was thick with pent-up power, and it licked out at the world with white-hot electric fingers. At the center of this barely kept tumult stood Samael, gazing steadily out over the cityscape of Chicago below.

Jason stood opposite Lilith on the other side of the room. As usual, the man was wearing a blue suit and blue tie that matched the blue of his eyes. He watched his employer—his master—with an expression that spoke of both trepidation and thrill. He was enjoying this. It was in his nature.

Jason was not a normal man. Once long ago, he had walked the Earth as a human, and in that state he had committed monstrosities against the human race. As punishment, Uriel, the Angel of Vengeance, had been sent after him. The battle between the two was woefully short, and of course, Jason lost.

His spirit was trapped, as all such spirits are, in a place that no mortal spoke of—because no mortal knew it existed. Thousands of years later, Jason's spirit had been pulled from its waiting place and put to work.

For Samael.

Only Samael could control the spirits of that realm—no one claimed to know why—but control them he did. Jason was his assistant, but there were other not-so-human minions in Samael's employ. Some could not hide their otherworldly natures, such as his Dark Riders, black-armor-clad humanoids atop sable steeds with burning eyes. Others, however ... others looked utterly human and walked among the mortals of Earth without detection.

Her gaze flicked to the violet-eyed man standing on the opposite side of the room to Jason. Lawrence McNabb watched Samael with an unreadable expression. Lilith's skin prickled.

"Gabriel and his brothers are more reckless than I imagined," Samael finally said. His tone was low, his voice so quiet it was almost a whisper. "Azrael could have harmed Juliette in his methods."

"But he didn't," Lilith quietly insisted. "He knew what he was doing."

Samael looked away from the window to glance at her. His storm gray eyes were glowing as if lit by the very lightning she could see in their depths. "No doubt," he said simply. "They all did."

Sam turned from the windows and paced slowly to his desk. His expression was introspective. The quiet tension coming from him was wholly unnerving. Lilith would almost have been happier if he'd have let loose with his emotions, so that she would at least know where she stood with him.

There was a manila folder on his desk, among other documents. Samael slowly picked it up and flipped it open.

Apparently unable to stand the tension any longer, Jason spoke up. "Will we be going after her, sir?"

Samael allowed the question to linger on the air unanswered for several long seconds. Jason swallowed hard; Lilith could hear it. And then Samael plopped the folder, still open, back onto his desktop. "No," he said simply. "There's no need."

A mixture of relief and worry coursed through Lilith. She glanced down at the open file, wondering what it held. All she could see of it, however, was illegible, type-written text and a pair of lines at the bottom, each bearing a signature. She frowned; one of the signatures was readily recognizable.

Lilith's eyes widened. It hit her. "That's Juliette's contract," she said. It wasn't a question—just a statement of realization. Sam glanced over at her. The hint of a smile, cold and calculative, curled the corners of his mouth.

And that was when Lilith's heart sank. She knew what he had done. History had a way of repeating itself and contracts were Samael's specialty. She glanced over at McNabb, as if for confirmation.

His steady, knowing gaze said it all.

Young, eager Juliette Anderson had no doubt signed her agreement without hesitation. Not that it mattered. No one but Sam could unravel the spells he wove within his contracts. Well, no one but Sam and possibly Max. But it wasn't easy for the guardian to do so.

Max had been forced to unravel one such contract four months ago, when Uriel had signed an agreement with Samael over the "acquisition" of his archess, Elea-nore Granger. It hadn't gone well for Uriel.

"It's a simple nondisclosure agreement, Lily," said Sam, using the nickname that only he ever used with her. His smile broadened. "More or less."

Gabriel was certain that this must be the kind of apprehension one experienced right before heart surgery. Or before giving birth. Or negotiating a hostage crisis involving a school bus full of small children.

Because as he watched the expression on Juliette's

face change as she took everything in, he felt a growing sense of unease. Something wasn't right.

Thus far, he, Max, Uriel, and Eleanore had all painstakingly explained the situation to Juliette. They'd taken great care to go easy on the shock factor of her powers and their being archangels, and go heavy on the empathy so that she would know she wasn't alone.

Through the course of the night, Eleanore had been an angel in every sense of the word. She'd been so patient and kind. She'd actually managed to win Juliette's trust, from what Gabriel could tell, and for that alone he could have kissed her. If Uriel wouldn't have killed him for it.

But despite their efforts, something wasn't sitting well with Juliette. He could see it in the wariness of her hazel eyes, which at the moment were a strange light green-gray-brown color that seemed to glow in the frame of her perfect face.

He could tell she wanted to leave. He could even sense that she wanted to run. He felt like a wolf staring down a fawn; she was all caution and barely contained panic, frozen in some sort of cosmic headlight. Of course, allowing her to leave was out of the question. Samael was out there and he was bad enough. The Adarians were fast proving themselves to be far worse. She was a sitting duck, and there was no way in hell he was going to let her out of his sight.

At the same time however, he knew he'd messed up on the train when he'd told her she would never be able to escape him. He knew he needed to make up for that. He wanted to calm her fears, let her know that she would be all right. It was painfully important to him that she not fear him—that she trust him. This was not some Saturday night fling. This wasn't a comely wench on a rainy night in the dark of a tavern's hallway. This was his archess and as difficult as her nearness was making things for him, he had to rein himself in and take it slowly.

At the moment Juliette sat curled up on one of the living room's two leather sofas, a chenille throw draped over her legs. Gabriel stood leaning beside the fireplace, his thick arms crossed casually over his broad chest. He couldn't take his eyes off her. Every now and then, it hit him that she was really there—that she was real and not a dream—and he simply couldn't believe it.

He had to touch her to be sure. So despite his silent oath to take things slow with Juliette, his manipulative side shoved its way to the fore and took over. Once, he pretended to head to the kitchen for more tea, and on the way he allowed the backs of his fingers to brush along her upper arm. She shivered at his touch, warm and supple beneath his fingertips, and a new and different kind of tension thrummed to life between them.

A few times over the past few hours, he'd been more devious. At one point, he used telekinesis to will her blanket to the floor. It slipped from her body, revealing her bare legs beneath the lavender silk suit she still wore, and Gabriel was forced to exercise immense control over his all-too-male body.

She bent to lift the blanket again, but he never gave her the chance. He moved forward and knelt before her, picking it up before she could do so. Then, as his eyes caught hers and held them, he proceeded to lay the throw over her once more. She pulled her gaze from him and stiffened as his hands tucked the soft material around her hips and over her legs. But he continued to watch her closely, noting the pinkening of her cheeks, the parting of her lips, and the way her pupils expanded beneath her lowered lids and long lashes. "There, now, lass. All tucked in."

She thanked him, although begrudgingly. No matter

how she might pretend, he could tell he was getting to her. This was an oddly ambivalent position for Gabriel to be in. On the one hand, he had never had to try to win a woman's trust or affections before. And God knew there had been plenty of women. On the other hand, however, whenever he looked at Juliette, he didn't feel like himself. He felt like a fledgling man, new and uncertain and in utter fascination of the female before him. And he hated it.

And he adored it.

It was like being in love. *Being in love...* Gabriel rolled the idea around in his head as he watched his archess play with the stitching on the edge of the throw. Her profile was intensely feminine. Her long, thick hair fell in lustrous waves down her back to her tiny waist and her long, slim fingers fidgeted nervously—delicately. He'd never been in love before, of course. No archangel had ever experienced love until Eleanore came along and claimed Uriel's heart.

But there was a stirring of something wholly different inside of Gabriel. It was like a gentle hand in some ways—it forced the animal in him to heel. But it was also more vicious. Because while he had never had trouble letting a woman go before, he knew in his heart that if it came right down to it, Gabriel would die rather than let go of Juliette.

She's mine. Gabriel's eyes widened. *Och, Christ,* he thought suddenly, as he ran a hand through his thick black hair. It was a thunderstorm of a realization—loud and blustery inside of his head. It shook the rafters of his spirit, drenched his soul, and left him quivering in its aftermath.

I love her.

"Samuel Lambent," Juliette suddenly said. She hadn't spoken for a while, but someone had obviously just asked her a question. And the name she'd replied with cut through the fog of Gabriel's inner musings like a shark fin through water.

"What?" he asked, unable to stop himself.

Uriel looked up at him, green eyes narrowed questioningly. Everyone was watching him now. They'd been talking among one another, but he'd gotten so wrapped up in his own dawning realizations, he'd lost track of what they were saying.

That feeling of something being wrong washed over Gabriel again. He wanted to know why Juliette had just said, "Samuel Lambent."

"I said, Samuel Lambent is the one funding my research," Juliette told them, as if she could read his mind.

Uriel spoke before Gabe could. "Lambent is paying you to conduct your PhD thesis research? Is that why you were meeting with him in Glasgow?"

Juliette looked nervous. She ducked her head in something akin to righteous embarrassment and nodded. "Well, yes," she said. "And no. He's creating a miniseries on the legends and cultures of ancient Caledonia and I'm supposed to supply him with the information he needs to make sure it's accurate." At that, she looked up at Gabriel and something secret flickered in the depths of her hazel eyes. For just a moment they turned more green. And then they darkened once more. "However, the fact that you ripped up his elevator is probably going to put a thorn in his side. I doubt he'll continue to fund me now."

Gabriel's teeth pressed against each other, his jaw tightening as she went on.

"Somehow, he found out that I was doing the same kind of thing for my dissertation that he would need for his show, and he contacted my adviser. I guess he wanted to save himself the hassle of hiring someone else to do it."

She was growing angrier as she spoke, and Gabriel

was bewildered by the outrageousness of it all. Samael had fooled her completely. She'd fallen for his lie hook, line, and sinker. She thought she had a right to be angry with them for saving her from the Fallen One? She had no idea. The man was without scruples, and Juliette was far too innocent. And yet she was on the defensive with Gabriel and his brothers and trusted Samael completely.

Well, you did threaten her, he reminded himself. *I doubt Sam threatened her. And then Az, the bogging red-eyed vampire, ripped her out of an elevator and whisked her through a fecking portal. Can you bloody well blame the lass for not trusting you?*

But he'd also saved her as well. He'd taken on the Adarian in her room for her. Did that not win him any trust points with her at all?

She glanced up at him, once more as if able to read his thoughts. This time, he caught her gaze and held it, unwilling to let go just yet. But she didn't back down. "He'll most likely go with someone else to do the research now anyway, I suspect," she said. "Contract or no contract."

Gabriel felt his rage spike and knew it had been visible in the quicksilver of his eyes when Juliette leaned back a little, her expression suddenly a tad more wary than it had been a second before. "You signed a bloody contract with Samuel Lambent?" he asked.

She hesitantly nodded. "Of course," she said, obviously unsure as to whether she should be admitting as much. But then, true to her Scottish heritage, she seemed to steel herself against him. "That's how these things are done," she told him, her eyes hard.

"Aye, lass, it is," he said. "An' no one knows it as well as Samuel Lambent." He almost spit the name; he was so disgusted. "Wha' was in that contract?"

"None of your business," she retorted hotly. She was a true thistle, both beautiful and painful to hold.

Gabriel's ire was now sharply rising, but he wasn't angry with Juliette. Not really. It was Samael and his infernal mechanics that were boiling Gabriel's blood. "You have no idea wha' that man is capable of, Juliette," he told her. "He's no' wha' you think he is."

Juliette came to her feet as thunder rumbled overhead. "And what about you, Gabriel Black? Are *you* what I think you are?"

Gabriel cocked his head and narrowed his gaze. "Well, now, that depends, lass," he said, his teeth gritted tight. "Wha' exactly do you think I am?"

Juliette's icy glare matched his. "You don't want to know."

"Wha' horse shite has Lambent been puttin' in your head, Juliette?" he asked, moving forward to close the distance between them. To her credit, the archess stayed right where she was, glaring up at him despite the fact that he had a good foot of height on her. The teacups on the coffee table began rattling against their saucers. He heard it, but ignored it.

"Uh, Gabriel—" Eleanore tried to say something, but Juliette cut her off.

"Lambent has been nothing but kind to me. You, on the other hand, have assaulted me, kidnapped me, and threatened me," she told him, her tone as icy as his own. Gabriel could see green sparks shooting off in the depths of her eyes. "Lambent could tell me you're a saint and I wouldn't believe him," she said. "And you want me to believe you're an *angel*?" She shook her head.

Max was suddenly between them, filling a space that Gabriel hadn't thought a single breath could fit into. The guardian's hand was on Gabriel's chest, shoving persistently back, putting more room between Gabriel and his archess.

Gabriel tore his gaze from Juliette's to look at Max. The expression on his guardian's face was one of warning, stark and angry. Gabriel wasn't sure Max had ever looked at him that way before. He forced himself to take a step back and try to calm down.

Max turned to Juliette. He took a deep breath and, though Gabriel couldn't see his face, he imagined Max was giving Juliette a much more understanding look than he had given Gabriel.

"Admittedly, Gabriel has behaved rashly," Max said in a gentle, placating tone. "I won't deny that a bit. But you haven't given us much of a chance to prove ourselves to you. We've told you no lies. Samuel Lambent, on the other hand, is nothing *but* lies."

Now Juliette's narrowed gaze was on Max. "How so?" she asked, her tone still chilled.

"Well, Gabriel's right," Max said. "He's not who he pretends to be; that's for certain."

"Who exactly is he, then?" she asked.

"His real name isn't Samuel Lambent," Max said. "It's Sama—"

There was an intense flash, white and hot and sudden, and everyone in the room shielded their eyes. Gabriel felt a tug and pull in the air, a sort of sucking from all around him, and it was impossible for him to breathe for just a moment. And then the flash faded, the air was clear, and he was lowering his arm from his face.

And Juliette was gone.

CHAPTER SIXTEEN

Juliette cried out as her body jerked into open space and her surroundings blurred around her as if she were jumping into hyperdrive. And then she was hovering, absolutely nowhere, surrounded by streamers of rainbow light and darkness, and for a half second she couldn't breathe.

Then time kicked in once more, grinding to life around her and pulling the stars and planets back into shape. She took another breath, if only to scream, but there was a pop and a flash—and she was floating two inches above the overstuffed couch in her rented Luskentyre cottage. Juliette gazed down at it with wide eyes as she was gently lowered onto the cushions and released.

She was still in a sitting position. She sat there for a moment, stunned and a little breathless, and gazed around her at the cottage's interior. It was still and dark in the early morning. Nothing moved and the air was cold.

"What the hell—" Her voice shook. A tremble had started in, deep and horrible. *What just happened?* She felt frozen and exposed and alone and the world was yawning around her, its maw gaping and threatening. She desperately wanted something to hold and missed her Nessie elephant more than ever.

Juliette lay down on the couch and curled her legs up to her chest.

And then the peat-burning stove against the opposite wall burst into fiery life. Juliette bolted upright, her heart in her throat. But she was all out of screams. She stared at the perfect fire and the warmth that was already emanating from it and the glow it gave off that was chasing away the shadows. For several long seconds, she expected something else to happen and her senses were on high alert.

But all else was still. That was when she noticed a small gray box, wrapped with a charcoal-colored silk bow, sitting on the floor beside the stove. It had been revealed by the fire's light; she hadn't noticed it before.

Juliette pushed herself off the couch onto jellylike legs. She hobbled toward the stove and fell to her knees beside the box. With shaking fingers, she pulled the bow free and slid the top off. Inside was a gray piece of folded parchment—and her lost plush elephant.

"Nessie," she whispered as she ignored the note and pulled the stuffed animal out of its resting place. She had no idea where it had gone to or where it had come from, but it felt real and soft and squishy when she pulled it against her chest and squeezed. A few seconds later, she took a deep, shaky breath and put Nessie in her lap. She turned her attention to the note.

With fingers that no longer trembled, she unfolded the paper and read the beautiful, scrolling script.

> *Juliette—*
> *I have never been one for shadows either.*
> *I hope that this will help chase them away.*
> *Until we meet again,*
> *Sam*

"S-Sam?" she whispered. How was this possible? How

had he managed to find Nessie, let alone get him to her cottage? Especially when she wasn't there herself?

But Juliette knew the answer. The fact that the fire had burst to life on its own was evidence enough. Her mind was simply rebelling at the proof—the confirmation that Samuel Lambent was so much more than he seemed to be. The verification that Gabriel and his "brothers" had been right.

Juliette pushed every coherent thought in her mind into the shadowy recesses of her brain and hugged her elephant to her chest.

Two hours later, she turned off the water in the shower, wrapped herself in thick, warm towels, and headed to her room. She'd had some time to think, and though she still felt rather numb and shocked about everything that was happening in her life, she had been able to put it more or less in perspective.

"Okay," she said out loud, just to put force behind her thoughts. She picked up Nessie from the bed and fingered his button eye. "It doesn't make sense, strictly speaking and as far as human knowledge is concerned." She turned and looked out the window at the Luskentyre shoreline. It was early morning and the sea beyond the pristine strip of beach beside the cottage was still indigo with waning night. "But what do humans know?" She thought of the endless multiverse beyond her planet and all its dark matter secrets and shook her head. "We know nothing," she muttered, looking down at Nessie once again.

So all of this might really be true, she thought. *I have these superpowers and I don't know why, unless I believe Gabriel Black and Eleanore Granger and Uriel, the Christopher Daniels look-alike who actually turned out to be Christopher Daniels.*

If what they said was true, then she was an archess, a female angel created as a mate for an archangel. And not just any archangel, but one of the four favorite archangels.

Specifically, Gabriel.

Juliette moved into the living room and sat back down on the couch, still wrapped in her towels. The fire in the peat stove still burned bright and warm and she hadn't had to replace any of the fuel. It was obviously there by some supernatural means, and at this point, she was no longer terribly shocked by the idea.

By the fact that it should have been impossible for him to procure and leave the stuffed animal in her cottage, Juliette was guessing one of two things. Either Sam had been the one to hijack her luggage in the first place, which seemed extreme and unnecessary—or Sam wasn't human, after all. In the latter case, Gabriel and his companions had been right—Samuel Lambent was more than he seemed to be. And by the proximity of his gift to the ever-burning flames in the stove, she was also guessing Sam's possible superhuman nature had something to do with the fire. Chasing away shadows . . .

Juliette sat back in the sofa and looked down at the stuffed elephant he had returned to her. It was as if he'd known exactly when she would need him the most. He had good timing. Just like Gabriel and his timely interruption when she'd been attacked by the Adarian.

Juliette thought of Gabriel Black. It wasn't hard. His tall, broad form and silver eyes and killer kisses rushed in from the gates, flooding her thoughts, the moment she considered allowing them in. She tried to think past it all, to the man who was *behind* the kisses and the liquid metal eyes. He'd cornered her in the tavern's bar, but in all honesty, that hadn't been a bad experience. Quite the opposite. And she *had* punched him for it. And then he'd saved her from the man who attacked her in her room. And, again, if what he and his companions said was true, then the man who attacked her had been an Adarian—definitely *not* Gabriel's partner in crime.

Juliette turned to stare out the tall sliding glass doors at the rising tide. She couldn't really claim to believe any longer that Gabriel had planned that attack. As little as she knew about him, it still felt wrong. Gabriel really had saved her.

He really was an angel.

Barring the fact that she'd always assumed angels to be cherubic figures with tiny, flittering dove wings and bows and arrows, the scenario made sense. In a sick sort of way. It explained so much. It explained her powers. It explained why she had been so fascinated with Gabriel's profile in that tavern bar before he had even turned around and she'd seen his face. It explained the impossible sexual hunger he awakened within her with no more than a glance. And his kisses?

"Christ," she mumbled, closing her eyes once more. *"It explains everything."*

Juliette pushed off the couch and headed back to her room to get dressed. Halfway there, she stopped and shook her head, smiling a wry smile. She'd forgotten to do a load of laundry and all her clothes were dirty. She would also probably have to put some money into the generator in order to work up enough power to get the washing machine going. Electricity was like that in Scotland, and especially in highly remote places such as Luskentyre on the Western Isles.

Juliette opened the door to her room and again stopped dead. Her suitcase was lying open and inside were all her clothes—and more—freshly folded, except her dresses, which were lying out across the bed.

Without missing a beat, Juliette knew it was Sam again. Whatever he was, he was powerful. And very considerate.

She moved to the bed and gazed down at the clothes

lying across it. They were gorgeous but also looked warm and comfortable. They were exactly the kinds of clothes she would purchase for herself if she had enough money to shop the Burberry, Gucci, Hilfiger, or Kors lines. Samuel had known exactly what her tastes were.

Juliette ran her hand along the leather and fleece aviator's jacket from Burberry and experienced a shiver of pure, hard delight. Was it even right to accept such a thing from someone? Then again, she'd already accepted so much from him. . . . What did it matter to add to it now? It was probably horrible reasoning, but she was a bit emotionally drained at the moment. She was also cold. The clothing looked warm. And she'd always admired Burberry.

Without giving it further thought, Juliette dressed in a new pair of jeans, a warm long-sleeved shirt, a pair of boots, and the Burberry jacket. Then she headed back to the kitchen to put the teakettle on.

She jumped a good two inches when there was a knock on the door in front of her. Her eyes flew to the sliding door and stared through the glass at the woman standing outside. She was dressed in a floor-length parka, which looked warm, but perhaps a bit much for Scotland at that time of year. She also looked familiar. The woman raised her hand and gave a little wave.

"Lily?" Juliette asked, realizing that it was the woman from the hotel. She worked for Samuel Lambent. Another shiver wracked through Juliette's petite frame, but this one wasn't so pleasant. She looked down at herself and the new clothes she wore and then she looked back up at Lily. The woman smiled sheepishly and shrugged, mouthing the word "Sorry."

Juliette made her way to the door, unlocking it to slide it open. "Lily?" she asked, bracing herself against the wind and chill that instantly struck her exposed face. The rest of her was cozy warm.

"I'm sorry, Miss Anderson," Lily said urgently. "But I really felt that we needed to talk. My name isn't Lily," she said. "It's Lilith. And I need to speak with you about Samuel Lambent."

"I'm gonna kill him," Gabriel growled.

"Good luck with that," said Uriel.

"Wow, this week is a déjà vu train wreck," said Michael, running a hand through his thick blond curls. "We've been here before, people. I can't believe you're surprised by this anymore. Sam is a bastard. He's also very smart. We really should learn to expect this kind of thing, don't you think?"

"Michael's right," said Max. "He may have helped us on the battlefield outside of Texas a few months ago, but I'd chalk that up to his way of confusing the hell out of us and call it good."

"You could have warned me." Gabriel turned on Azrael, who was leaning against the fireplace in his stone chamber of a room, his arms crossed casually over his broad chest. He'd returned from feeding twenty minutes ago. The vampire just stared at Gabriel, his expression unreadable. But his gold eyes began to glow.

"Don't go there, Gabe," warned Michael. "Whether Az could have told you about the contract or not, you never gave him the chance. Lay off."

"And you say I'm the hotheaded one," muttered Uriel as he lifted himself up onto the stone altar upon which Azrael normally slept. He looked down at the stone slab and then around the room. "This brings back memories."

"Boys, we need to focus." Ellie crossed her arms over her chest and turned in place, eyeing each of the archangels with impatience. "Speaking from experience, Samael isn't going to hurt Juliette, and we know that it was Sam's doing that she disappeared. So, she's probably safe."

"You're working under the assumption that he still wants an archess for himself," Max told her.

"No, I'm working under the assumption that Sam isn't that kind of person. He's not violent toward women. It's not his style." Ellie shrugged and looked at the ground. "I don't know how else to tell you. I just know that Sam doesn't want to hurt us. He may be sneaky and conniving and underhanded, but he was always a gentleman with me. He has something else in mind."

"Like what?" Michael asked.

"I have no idea." Ellie shook her head helplessly. "But the thing we should be focusing on right now is where Jules may have gone. I wouldn't automatically assume that Sam would yank her back to him."

"Why not?" Uriel asked.

"Because," Max butted in, "she'll be on the defensive, and Sam's not stupid. He doesn't want her to think ill of him. He'll send her somewhere else to calm down for a while."

"Right," Ellie agreed. "As long as you've received the message loud and clear that you're not allowed to bad-mouth Sam in front of the new archess, nothing else will really matter to him."

"He's very touchy about his little secrets, isn't he?" Uriel muttered, clearly reliving his own experience of attempting to disclose Samael's true identity to his archess.

Gabriel watched them all for a moment, his mind spinning at a thousand RPMs. He figured they were probably right and Juliette had come to no harm. Sam was a lot of dangerous things, but an outwardly aggressive individual he had never been.

So Juliette was safe. And hopefully he and his brothers had managed to fill her head with enough of the truth about what she was and about what they were that it would simmer for a while, and she might even come around to believing them. He hated that he hadn't had more time with her, but he'd been a fool not to expect this. Like Michael had said—they needed to be on their toes with Samael. They were learning.

Gabriel wanted to ask Azrael to perform a scry and find out just where in the bloody hell Juliette actually *was* at that moment, but he figured that he probably wasn't on the vampire archangel's good side just then. Admittedly, Gabe wasn't behaving like himself. He was picking a fight with the entire world. This whole affair was getting to him. Two thousand years and he'd always managed to remain relatively cool in a crisis. He'd had no idea that someone as small and unassuming as his little archess would wind up tossing every last ounce of his sanity out the window.

"I'll do it," Az said suddenly, straightening from where he'd been leaning against the hearth. "And then I must rest."

Gabriel didn't know what to say, so he said nothing. He was more grateful than words most likely would have expressed anyway.

Max looked questioningly from Az to Gabriel, as did Michael and Uriel. But Eleanore didn't seem surprised. She'd probably been thinking the same thing Gabriel had. She was a smart girl. Uriel was a lucky archangel.

The others figured out relatively quickly what he was going to do when Azrael gracefully sat down on the rug-covered stone floor in front of the fireplace and began to gaze into the rising flames. He didn't need something like that to stare into when performing a scry, but it seemed to help, because he preferred it.

"She's in Luskentyre," he said a few seconds later. "In the cottage she rented."

He stood then, in one fluid, unnatural movement, and extinguished the fire with a wave of his hand. At the same time, the torches in their sconces along the wall burst to fiery life. "Now leave. It's past my bedtime." He smiled, flashing fangs.

Gabriel watched Max and the others leave. He slowly followed behind them. But before stepping out into the stone corridor that would lead him to the rest of the mansion up above, he turned and looked back at Azrael.

The vampire was watching him steadily.

"Thank you," Gabriel said.

"You're welcome," Azrael replied. "And I should probably also tell you this," he added. Gabriel waited, tensing up as he expected the worst. "Sam's been very busy on the enticement front."

"Wha's that supposed to mean?" Gabriel asked, gaze narrowed.

"She doesn't hate him," Az replied simply. "She's also not alone at the moment. Lilith is with her."

Gabriel frowned. Lilith was with Juliette? Why?

Obviously reading his mind, Az shrugged and leapt, very vampirelike, on top of the stone slab upon which he would be sleeping. "Lilith may work with Samael, but her loyalty to him runs through a strange and secret vein," he said as he lay down and closed his eyes. "Who knows why she does what she does? But my guess is that she doesn't wish the archess to be alone while the Adarians are yet at large."

Gabriel felt very torn. He liked Lilith. All the archangels did, and everyone knew that Max had fallen head over heels for her at least a thousand bloody years ago. Gabe was grateful that Juliette wouldn't be alone right now.

But where did that leave him? Where did he go from here? What was he supposed to do now?

"There's always the old-fashioned way," Az said. His eyes were still closed, but a smile was curling the corners of his handsome mouth. "You could make amends. You could *woo* her," he said before his smile broke into a full-fledged grin, fangs pronounced and gleaming in the torchlight.

"As if that'll work after wha' I've already pu' her through," Gabriel said.

"Women are amazing creatures, Gabriel," Azrael said as his smile slipped from his face and his features relaxed. He was sliding into sleep. "Give them the credit they're due. Juliette may surprise you."

Juliette had never liked Tuesdays. They were worse than Mondays as far as she was concerned. On Monday it sucked because you had the entire week ahead of you, and you were relentlessly bombarded with all the crap that everyone was able to think up over the weekend. But Tuesdays were brutal because you were already tired from Monday, and you still had four long-ass days ahead of you, and it was a safe bet that you didn't get half of the stuff you had to do on Monday finished anyway.

But this Tuesday was different. It wasn't harried or frantic—it was surreal. And if it and the Monday preceding it were any indication of what the rest of the week would be like, she was going to have to take up drinking. Or sniffing glue.

"Okay," Juliette said, placing her hands palms down on her lap and taking a deep breath. "Let me see if I've got this straight."

Lily, or "Lilith," as she'd told Juliette her real name was, had been in the rental cottage for the last four hours, telling Jules the truth about Samuel Lambent—also known as Samael—and his very tricky contracts. She had also filled Juliette in on the other archangels and the Adarians. And so far, everything but the news about Samael had been a repeat of what the archangels had already told her.

"The Old Man made me for Gabriel—and then

tossed me down to Earth to protect me. And this was two thousand years ago?" Lilith nodded. She raised her teacup to her lips and took a sip. Juliette frowned. "Where have I been for the last two thousand years, then?"

Lilith put her cup in the saucer in her hand and tilted her head to one side. She studied Juliette closely, and not for the first time, Jules was struck by the way Lilith looked so young, though her black eyes looked ancient. "I think that's a very good question, Juliette."

"What do you mean?"

"Well." Lilith shrugged slightly and turned to look out the window at the turquoise water at the shore. "Where do you feel like you've been?" she asked without looking at Juliette.

"Nowhere," Jules answered without thinking. It was a weird question. There couldn't be a correct answer for it.

But Lilith turned away from the windows and pinned her with that dark gaze once more. "Are you sure about that?"

Juliette blinked several times. And then she looked away, picked up her own teacup, and hurriedly brought it to her lips. The truth was, *no* — she didn't feel as if she'd been nowhere. For years she had been haunted by dreams filled with images of crumbling castles overlaid with the transparent impressions of what the buildings had looked like thousands of years ago. She'd dreamed of cemeteries both old and new, streets made of cobblestones and yet paved in asphalt.

She'd always wondered why she had these dreams. She wondered why, when she picked up a book with a photograph or painting of the past, it felt familiar to her. It was the reason she had focused on history and ethnography in school, and it was why she spent so much of her free time in libraries or online, browsing books and maps and pictures of what had been long ago.

She didn't feel as if she had never been anywhere. She felt as if she'd been *everywhere*. Or, at least, every*when*.

"What about Eleanore Granger?" she asked, wanting to take the attention off herself. "Why wasn't she found before now? If what you all tell me is true, then archesses are coming out of the woodwork after two thousand years. Why?"

"That's a good question, too," Lilith said, smiling a strange, secret smile. "But I'm afraid I don't have an answer I can share with you."

Juliette mulled that over, wondering whether it meant that Lily didn't have an answer at all—or just wasn't going to share the one she did have. Finally, she changed the subject entirely and asked, "If Samuel Lambent is actually Samael, is this deal he made with me even real? Do I still need to collect this information for his show?"

"Oh, it's real," Lilith said, setting both her cup and saucer on the coffee table in front of them. "He is a media mogul, after all. He may not be human, but he's lived amongst them for thousands of years. One thing he's always been good at is multitasking." At this, Lilith chuckled softly. "He might be turning the world upside down with one hand, but at the same time, he'll be making money with the other."

"So this miniseries he wants is on the level? It wasn't just a ruse to get me to meet with him?"

Lilith considered her words carefully. "He will definitely follow through with the miniseries, and most likely, it will get great ratings. Everything he creates does. But he's not opposed to killing two birds with one stone, and yes, he did initially use the proposal to bring you to him." She stopped and considered something else, and then shrugged. "Not that he couldn't simply meet you whenever he wanted to without any kind of scheme."

Juliette put her teacup down on the table. "But the business about the warlock . . . that's all a lie, isn't it?"

Lilith shook her head. "Every untruth has at least the tiniest amount of truth to it," she said. "For all intents and purposes, archesses do possess a special kind of magic. And there is another being of immense power out there who wishes to take that magic from you."

"But it isn't Gabriel, is it?" It wasn't really a question. Juliette already knew the answer. Lawrence McNabb had said the warlock had black hair—and eyes of a different color. He hadn't come out and said those eyes were silver. According to Gabriel and his brothers, Abraxos, the leader of the Adarians, had black hair and blue eyes. It was the Adarian General who wanted Juliette's power. He was the warlock—not Gabriel.

Lilith shook her head, her eyes twinkling. "No. I think it's safe to say that Gabriel wants something entirely different from you, Juliette."

A rush of warmth thrummed through Juliette at those words. It was akin to a best friend telling you in high school that your crush is crushing right back. But this was stronger. She ducked her head, rubbed her hands on her jeans, and changed the subject again. "Lilith . . ." She trailed off as she thought about how best to put forth her next question. "Gabriel and the others . . . they dislike Sam greatly. Is Samael a bad man? Is he that dangerous? He's never been anything but kind to me. And if he was talking about the Adarians when he made up that warlock story—then he was in fact warning me, wasn't he?"

Lilith straightened in her seat and gazed steadily at Juliette. The look in her dark, dark eyes was suddenly so intense, Juliette felt uncomfortable there beneath it.

"Good and evil are subjective, Juliette," Lilith said, her tone much more serious than it had been a moment ago. "But as to whether or not Samael is dangerous . . . let's just say I wouldn't take him lightly." She paused a moment, then added, "Ever."

CHAPTER SEVENTEEN

L ilith stayed with Juliette until a few hours later, when there was a second knock on the door. Angus Dougal stood on the doorstep, his hands on his hips, his green eyes turned out to sea.

"Ah, the chief inspector," said Lilith as she stood from the dining room table, where she and Juliette had just finished sharing a light Scottish brunch. "Quite a few women in Harris and Lewis have their eye on that one. Unfortunately, he's still pining over the lovely young woman he'd been dating until a month ago. She broke his heart."

She moved around the table as she told Juliette all of this and Juliette could only listen in faint surprise. How the hell did Lilith know all of this?

Juliette got up and joined her then, walking to the edge of the kitchen. At that point, Dougal turned and looked through the glass doors. Juliette met his gaze.

Lilith leaned in and whispered, "I'd imagine that entertaining such a guest would make Gabriel's blood boil." She straightened, an enigmatic smile on her lovely face. And then she winked, pulled on her humongous parka, and headed to the glass doors, Juliette on her heels.

Juliette opened the door and Angus nodded at her.

Something flattering flickered clearly in the depths of his jade green eyes. She took a deep breath and asked the chief inspector in. At the same time, Lilith nodded her good-bye and saw herself out. Juliette shut the door and wondered where the woman was going. Would she take a car? Or simply pop out of existence? Come to think of it, Juliette had never asked Lilith what *her* story was. Why did she work for Sam? And as what?

"Miss Anderson, I'm sorrae tae intrude on yae without notice," said Angus, his deep voice heavy with accent. "But I was in the area and saw yer lights on and wanted tae check up on yae."

Juliette turned to face him and felt dwarfed. He was as tall as Gabriel, and as broad as well, and she had to crane her neck a little to look up at him. "I'm fine, Inspector," Juliette said. "Can I get you some tea?"

"Please." He smiled a friendly smile that gave him a pair of dimples and softened his otherwise hard expression. "It's a wee bit nippy with the wind as it is." He began to shrug off his jacket, once more revealing his shoulder holster and the guns it held. "Oh, sorrae." He looked embarrassed for a moment. "Do yae mind if I—"

"Not at all," Juliette assured him, gesturing to the coatrack in one corner. He nodded and strode to the rack, his long legs eating up the distance in a meager three steps. Once he'd hung his coat, he turned to regard the peat fire in the stove. After a moment, he nodded, seemingly satisfied that it was burning well, and then turned an appreciative gaze on Juliette again.

"Ye've built a nice fire," he told her as the firelight reflected in his eyes. "Ye'd do well livin' here, if I may say so."

Juliette had nothing to say to that. She ducked her head, a touch ashamed that she hadn't, in fact, built the fire at all. But she wasn't about to tell the inspector that the blaze had leapt to life of its own accord. "Your tea," she said, holding out the cup she'd poured for him. "Cream or sugar?"

"Nae." He shook his head, his thick wavy hair brushing the collar of his shirt and curling on his forehead like Superman's. "Thank yae. It's fine as is." He strode back across the room and gently took the mug from her. Then he took a sip and cocked his head to one side, studying her carefully. "Have yae had any more trouble with Black?" he asked. His green gaze was penetrating as he waited for her reply. She remembered that look—the inspector was very observant. He wasn't missing anything in that moment.

Juliette wasn't sure she could hide the thoughts she was thinking, so she ducked her head and turned to regard the view beyond the sliding glass doors. "No," she said. "I haven't had any more trouble from him." It both felt and sounded like a lie and there was nothing in the world she could do about it.

"I see," Dougal said softly. Juliette could feel his presence behind her. She felt like a specimen beneath a microscope; the heat from the lens was burning a hole through the back of her neck. "That's good tae know, Juliette," he said, using her first name this time.

She turned to face him and was struck with a hard, green gaze that pinned her to the spot. The corners of his mouth turned up ever so slightly as he continued. "Because we've learned a few things aboot Black lately that tend to the troublin' side."

Juliette swallowed hard and squared her shoulders. "Like what?" she asked, trying to sound as carefree as possible.

Dougal's smile never wavered. He turned away from her and made his way to one of the couches. He took another sip of his tea, then leaned over and placed the mug on the coffee table. "Gabriel Black is the benefactor for qui' a few charitable projects goin' on in Harris a' the moment," he told her, taking a seat and draping his thick arms over the back of the sofa.

"Funds from 'is account are buildin' a new children's home, among other things. The thing is, this account of 'is seems to have nae backin'. There's nae trail to tell us where this money's comin' from," he said. "Black's job as a firefighter in New York can no' accoont for the lo' of it. An' though 'e's go' the Glasgow banks in 'is pocket, we're dubious." He leaned forward on the couch then and rested his elbows on his knees. "A man doosn't hide his past without good reason, Juliette. Charity is a cover for many a criminal. Black may be a verrae dangerous man."

You have no idea, Juliette thought. Her heart was hammering. Her head was beginning to pound. She knew that Angus Dougal had no doubt come to her cottage that day in order to convince her to stay well away from Gabriel Black. He had some kind of problem with Gabriel. She was willing to bet it was personal. But she knew where Gabriel's money came from and it wasn't what Dougal thought. She knew that Black could take any object in the world and turn it into solid gold. It had been one of the demonstrations he and his brothers had given her back at his mansion last night and early that morning.

His wealth didn't surprise her.

What took her breath away was that Gabriel Black was using that money to help homeless children. Beneath the hard edges and angles of the black-clad archangel, there appeared to be a genuinely good man. And she'd most likely misjudged him in the worst possible way. *She*—judging *him*. An archangel, of all things.

"What else?" she asked suddenly.

Dougal frowned, tilting his head a little, clearly not understanding the question.

Juliette swallowed hard and cleared her throat. "I mean, what else is he funding? You said he was funding several charitable operations."

Dougal's gaze slowly narrowed. His body was stock-still as he replied, "Black's money has restored several crofts across Harris an' Lewis."

Juliette thought of the peat bogs she'd seen on her drive from Stornoway into Luskentyre. She knew a lot about them; she'd done her homework. Their winding lines carved the landscape of the Western Isles and much of the mainland as well. They were quintessential Scotland; people on the Outer Hebrides had been making their living that way for centuries. But peat crofting and sheep raising were a failing way of life as well. Crofters were a dying breed. It was an incredibly hard living and the younger generations more often than not opted out of it. They would head to Glasgow for other work, leaving behind generations of history. Eventually, the family land and home were sold or left to rot—empty and useless reminders of what once was.

Gabriel Black was trying to change that. He was trying to preserve a piece of history and save Scotland's way of life. Juliette's heart melted a little in that moment. She was very fond of Scotland; she felt a kinship to it and its people somewhere deep, deep inside. Gabriel was using his gifts to give its children a better life and save what was left of its legacy. What had his brother Uriel done with his gifts? Become a famous movie star.

There was a depth to Gabriel that others didn't have. And up to that moment, she'd all but missed it.

On the couch, Angus Dougal straightened, his expression dark. He stood and picked up his mug and moved around the coffee table to approach the kitchen. Juliette watched him rinse out the mug and place it in the sink. Then he turned, leaned against the sink, and crossed his muscular arms over his chest. He cut a handsome figure and Juliette was reminded of Lilith's parting words.

To take the heat of the subject off Gabriel—and because Juliette really was curious—she asked, "I've been told that you're unattached at the moment. Is this true?"

Angus's eyebrow shot up and he went very still where he stood. It was clear that he wasn't sure whether to entertain the question at first. But then he uncrossed his arms and placed his hands palm down on the counter. His gaze left hers and settled on the floor. "It is."

"Did you break up with her or did she break up with you?"

It was a long while before Dougal replied to this one. He was no doubt wondering how much Juliette had heard about him. And from whom.

"She left me," he said then. Juliette could hear the pain in his voice. She also recognized that he was trying very hard to hide it.

She paused for a respectful amount of time and then quietly asked, "What happened?" She knew she was crossing a line, but she didn't care.

Surprisingly, Angus didn't seem to care either. He looked back up at her. "She wanted bairns bu' could no' have them. She's unable."

Juliette frowned. That made no sense. Why would a woman leave a man because she was unable to have children?

"I never cared," he continued as if he could see the confusion in her expression and didn't mind clarifying. "Bu' she thou' I did. An' it scared her. I know she felt she could never make me happy."

"So she ran away." Juliette put two and two together then.

Angus nodded. Another long moment of silence passed between them. And then he straightened again. "Yae're a kind lass, Juliette," he said. "A trustin' lass. An' tha's wha' scares me." He strode out of the kitchen to the coatrack, then pulled his coat down and shrugged it on.

All the while, Juliette watched the muscles flex and ripple beneath the material of his clothing.

She imagined Angus Dougal could have his choice of women in the Western Isles. That he wasn't currently attached must mean that he cared for his ex-girlfriend a great deal.

Dougal turned to face her again. "Juliette, I'll give yae fair warnin'," he said. "Gabriel Black has made 'is forsaken way through many a woman on these isles." He shook his head slowly. "There are no consequences for tha' man, lass. I don' trust Black an' I don' think yae should be trustin' him either." With that, he brushed past her, and a gentle wave of aftershave wafted over her. The inspector made it to the door and opened it himself. "Good day, Miss Anderson," he said, reverting at once to formality. He stepped through and began to close the door behind him. But before he shut it all the way, he stopped and turned to glance at her over his shoulder. "An' please be careful."

Juliette watched as he shut the door and descended the stairs from her cottage, turning around the corner on the first floor and disappearing from sight.

When he was gone, she leaned back against the wall behind her and closed her eyes. "What do I do now?" she asked softly. Gabriel Black was confusing the crap out of her. He was a tomcat and a rake and he kissed like he'd kissed ten thousand women for practice. But he was also kind. She had Angus Dougal to thank for showing her that much. But it wasn't just that. Juliette's entire world had been turned upside down. Gabriel and the other archangels aside, Juliette had more mundane and real-life issues to consider as well.

Did she fly home now? Throw in the towel? Run back to Pittsburgh and move in with Sophie for a while? Did she call it quits with her career and forget about her PhD because she'd just learned that she was an "archess"?

"No," she whispered to herself, putting her hand to her forehead. She wasn't ready to give up on all of that. She loved history. She loved Scotland and its past. She had wanted this so badly for so many years, she could taste it.

She was in danger. The Adarians were out there somewhere looking for her, and they'd found her once already. Going home wouldn't ensure they didn't find her again. They could track her down in the US as easily as they could here. And if she was with Sophie . . . she could put her best friend in danger.

"I'll stay," she told herself. She would remain in Scotland—at least for the time being. But if she was going to stay there, do her research, and write her thesis to graduate, she would need to take safety measures. Remaining in that cottage might not be so wise. It was too remote in Luskentyre; she was too alone. She needed to move somewhere with more people—surround herself with protection.

Juliette pushed off the wall and ran a hand through her long, thick hair. "All right," she said. "Time to pack."

It was late afternoon and Juliette was just finishing packing everything she could get to fit into her suitcase. She was still wearing the Burberry jacket. She was indoors, but the aviator's coat was so beautiful, she found she couldn't take it off.

Juliette's head cocked to one side when she heard a motorcycle's engine draw closer outside. She paused in her work and listened. The roar of the bike didn't die down; it got louder as it approached, obviously turning onto the side street that ran to her cottage.

And then it shut down altogether and she froze in the following silence. *Someone's here.* Cortisol and adrenaline flooded her blood system, putting her stomach in her throat and momentarily causing her heart to race.

Footfalls, determined and certain, made their way across the gravel driveway to the sidewalk. Juliette swallowed hard and looked toward the small windows of the cottage bedroom. But she was on the second floor and they would show her nothing.

She thought fast. There were no weapons in the cottage. In fact, other than the two guns she'd seen on Chief Inspector Angus Dougal, Britain gave the impression of being firearm free. An entire bloody kingdom and not one weapon.

Juliette's heart was hammering. She turned to the door as the footfalls made their way up the outdoor flight of stairs and came to stand on the threshold on the second floor. There was a hard rapping on the sliding glass doors.

Juliette ran her palms along her jeans; they'd begun to sweat in her fear. Was this an Adarian? It wasn't the inspector. He drove a car. It wasn't Lilith. She hadn't made any sound at all after she'd left, and had probably just used some sort of magic.

The rapping at the door came again, a touch more insistent this time. Juliette had no idea what the emergency number in Scotland was. Not knowing what else to do, she picked up her cell phone, dialed the cell phone number that Angus Dougal had given to her, and left her thumb hovering over the "talk" key. Then she stepped through the door of the bedroom and into the living room beyond.

Gabriel Black stood on the other side of the glass doors. His pitch-black, wavy hair looked wind tossed. He wore motorcycle boots, black jeans, and a tight black sweater beneath a black leather jacket. He stood tall and dark and his eyes were hidden behind a pair of mirrored sunglasses.

The sudden image of him there, only a few feet away, with that touchably messed-up hair and all that leather had a strange effect on Juliette. She stopped in the living room and watched him warily, even as her stomach warmed and her legs grew wobbly. Gabriel reached up with a gloved hand, and as his perfect lips curled into some secret sort of smile, he pulled off his shades.

Quicksilver, Juliette thought. His mercury gaze shot through the glass doors to nail her to the spot. His smile broadened and she heard his chuckle through the thickness of the glass. It was a delicious sound.

Before she knew what she was doing, Juliette found herself walking across the living room to the doors. She hesitated only a moment, glanced up at him as he continued to smile down at her, then unlatched the door and slid it open.

"Good day, lass," Gabriel drawled, his eyes sparkling like diamonds. "May I come in?"

"You're not a vampire like your brother, are you?" Juliette found herself asking. She wasn't sure why she said it. It was broad daylight, after all. It just spilled out.

Gabriel's gorgeous eyes widened and then he threw back his head and laughed, the sound warm and deep and intoxicating on several levels. "No' bloody likely," he chuckled. "Bu' you're lucky you did no' meet my family two months ago," he continued. "When I had two brothers that were vampires."

Now it was Juliette's turn to have wide eyes.

"It's a long story, little one," he said then, quieting down a bit. His gaze softened, his pupils expanding as he looked down at her. "I'd be happy to share it with you over dinner."

Juliette tried to think of everything she'd learned about Gabriel—and about her messed-up life—in the last forty-eight hours. But none of it would present itself to her in an orderly fashion. All she could really think of at that moment was the man before her; he filled her senses. Made her feel warm—breathless.

She looked at the clock on the wall. "It's four in the afternoon," she told him.

"Aye, bu' it'll take a while to get where I'd like to take you," he said, his smile as bright and beautiful as ever. He raised one well-muscled arm and braced it on the doorframe beside him. The scent of his soap and aftershave drifted toward her on a breeze and Juliette's mouth went dry. "I know you'd enjoy the ride, luv," he said softly. "Wha' do you say?"

She looked up into those silver eyes that were glittering like diamonds, and any anger she felt over the way he'd previously treated her began to melt rapidly away. "Angus Dougal said that you're a playboy," she accused. There was no real vehemence in her tone, however, and she found that her gaze kept slipping to his lips.

Thinking of his kiss.

"Did he, now?" Gabriel looked amused—and entirely unabashed. He leaned in then and something dark flickered in the silver depths of his eyes. "An' why would such a man be sayin' such things to you? I wonder."

"Maybe he's trying to warn me."

Gabriel's brow shot up. "Warn you?" His gaze narrowed. "Away from me?"

"He's a good man," Juliette insisted. "And he seems to think that you're *not*."

Gabriel stared down at her for a good few seconds. Again, that something dark flickered in his stormy eyes. "An' wha' do *you* think, lass?" he asked, his voice now barely more than a whisper. "Am I no' a good man?"

Juliette gazed up at him and felt time slow down. The sound of the cold surf on the shore below was a gentle roar in the background. Seagulls cried. The wind was sharp and smelled like salt; she could see that saltiness in Gabriel's hair. He seemed a part of the land in that moment, rugged, hard, uncompromising. His piercing, stark eyes were ancient. There were stories there by the thousands.

What did she think of him? She could barely think at all.

"I . . . ," she started to reply, but when she realized she didn't know what she was going to say, she fell silent again. Her chest felt strangely tight, her stomach warm. It was his eyes—they were doing odd things to her. His tall, strong body caged her in, towered over her. Everything about him begged to be touched—tested.

How gentle would Scotland be with her? Would he bend for her? Or would he break her?

There was a blur before Juliette's eyes, and before she realized what was happening, Gabriel moved forward, bent, and lifted her, throwing her over his broad shoulder. She landed gently on the hard plane of his muscle; he seemed to be careful in that respect. But she was still too shocked to do anything but gasp and then cry out.

"Sorry, luv," Gabriel said as he reached out and closed her cottage door and then turned and began descending the steps to the driveway. "Bu' we need some time an' I'm no' gonna wait for you to decide you trust me."

"Gabriel!" Juliette gasped, her fists curling into the hard leather of his jacket. "Jesus, put me down!"

And then, suddenly, he did. In one swift movement, Gabriel was lifting her and setting her down on her surprised feet. She wobbled a bit and he steadied her with one hand, gesturing to the bike they stood beside with the other. "Get on, lass."

Juliette stared at the bike—a Triumph of all black and chrome. "Absolutely not!" she breathed, still somewhat shocked.

Gabriel ignored her refusal and mounted the bike, his body moving with fluid and controlled grace. She felt herself flush when he started the engine, twisted the throttle, and then cut his silver gaze to her once more. "Juliette," he said, somehow managing to make his brogue sound perfectly clear over the engine. "There's nothin' to be afraid of." He shook his head, his smile horribly charming. "I promise you'll be safe with me."

"I don't even know how!" Juliette insisted, hugging herself. She'd never ridden a motorcycle before. Not once. How did she even get on such a thing?

"Give me your hand, lass," he said, offering her his. She looked down at it and then back up at his eyes. Again, time slowed.

She took his hand.

CHAPTER EIGHTEEN

"That's it," Gabriel said as he helped her swing her leg over the back of the bike. She straddled the seat and, because it was angled forward, she slid down until her body was pressed tightly against Gabriel's.

Heat rushed through her; he was solid and warm and the curve of his neck above the leather collar of his jacket was enticing in the extreme. Juliette was incredibly grateful that he couldn't see her face when she was seated behind him, because she was flushing furiously.

The bike itself was a strangely erotic experience for Juliette; the motorcycle vibrated between her legs and the leather was hard enough that it didn't mute the sensation. The combination of the metal horse beneath her and the hard man in front of her was wreaking havoc on her senses.

"You all right, then, lass?" he asked her over his shoulder.

Juliette's voice cracked as she replied, "I'm fine!"

"Good," he said, smiling broadly. "Now hold on to me," he instructed.

Juliette's eyes went wide. She looked down at his waist and knew he wanted her to wrap her arms around him. But that would mean touching him—closely. And she didn't trust herself to do that just now.

In front of her, Gabriel chuckled. He turned slightly and grabbed her left arm with his left hand. She tried not to pull away when he wrapped her left arm around his waist and pressed the fingers of her hand into his ridged abdomen.

"Oh Christ," she muttered under her breath.

"Wha' was that, luv?" he asked, turning the other way now. His smile and the wicked twinkle in his silver eyes told her he knew damn well what he was doing to her. But that didn't stop him from grabbing her other hand and doing the same thing with it.

In the next moment, she had her arms wrapped securely around his waist and he was holding both of her hands with one of his, pressing them into his body. "Don't let go, lass. Do you understand? Wha'ever happens, do no' let go."

He turned back around then and twisted the throttle, kicking up the stand. The Triumph's tires skidded a little on the gravel and then caught once more as the bike left the driveway and headed toward the road.

Juliette found herself instinctively holding on for dear life as the wheels bumped onto the asphalt and the bike rocketed down the street. But a few seconds later, the planes smoothed out and Gabriel began to carve around the curves, expertly operating the motorcycle with practiced ease. And Juliette began to relax.

The Scottish air was cold and clean and the sky was relatively clear. It was a gorgeous afternoon, warm for March, and Juliette couldn't help but feel as if she were flying along only a few feet from the speeding ground. It was liberating. The closest she'd ever come to such a feeling was when she'd ridden her bicycle as a child, making her way laboriously to the top of the hill so that she could sail down it with the wind in her hair.

That wind whipped through her long hair now, tangling it hopelessly. And she didn't care. Several minutes into the ride, Juliette found that she was smiling—no, grinning. All sound was drowned out beneath the steady drone of the motorcycle's engine. Her aviator's jacket and boots kept her warm against the early-spring air, and Gabriel's body in front of her felt like a protective shield.

She settled into him, even going so far as to close her eyes as the feel of him wrapped around her. She lost track of the time, but as she straightened and opened her eyes to once more look out over the rolling land around them, a fog rolled in across the moors. It rose over the hills like a giant white beast and slid down the slopes like an avalanche, draping the landscape in cotton until it began to creep across the road and Gabriel slowed the bike.

He had perfect timing. Just as the mist was beginning to block out the stretch of black in front of them, he was turning off the road and onto a gravel drive. He pulled the bike up to a wooden stop for a parking space and shut it down. Then he helped Juliette off. She felt a bit unsteady on her legs at first; the lack of vibration left her feeling slightly used. But it passed quickly and she looked around.

There were a few other vehicles in the drive, but not many. The gravel gave way to a wooden pier overlooking a small port. There were fishing trolleys in the water, their mooring ringing out through the fog as if they were speaking their own language. They were easier to hear than see, but every once in a while a small mast tilted through the mist to reveal its slick surface. Seagulls cried in the distance.

At the other end of the drive stood a small cabin. Gabriel gently took Juliette's hand and smiled down at her, leading her toward the wood-beamed building. Their boots crunched the stones beneath them as they approached the door and Gabriel led them inside.

The air was instantly warm and filled with delicious

aromas. Juliette stood on the threshold and slowly inhaled. The smell of cooking wafted over and through her, chasing away the chill and welcoming her like a hug. The cabin was a small two-room restaurant, divided neatly between a bar with stools and a strong stock of Scotch and a formal seating area surrounded by floor-to-ceiling windows overlooking the sea.

It was beautiful and cozy and perfect. It was exactly the kind of place Juliette had always wanted to escape to. She caught the sound of crackling and glanced toward the end of the restaurant to find a massive stone hearth merrily ablaze in the formal area.

"Come with me, luv." Gabriel led her through the bar area and into the formal dining area. The restaurant was deserted but for them.

Where is everyone? Juliette wondered.

Candles had been set out on all the tables, but at one table, right beside the windows that sported the best view, the candles were actually lit. Place settings had been laid out, and a steaming pot of tea was waiting on the table's surface. Gabriel led her directly to that table and Juliette stared at the wisps of steam rising from the kettle.

Then her eyes drifted to the windows and the foggy scenery beyond. She imagined it would have been a gorgeous twilight view if it hadn't been for the fog. Not that she minded fog at all—in fact, she had always been rather fond of foggy days. They made her feel as if she were being transported to some magical land and as soon as the fog lifted, she would find herself in Willy Wonka's chocolate room or something similar.

But how often did one get to gaze out over the sea like this?

"No one will notice, lass."

Juliette looked up at Gabriel to find him staring at her knowingly. He looked from her to the window and nodded. "Go on, then."

Juliette needed no further encouragement. She already knew that Gabriel was well aware of her powers—that definitely wasn't an issue any longer. And they seemed to be alone at the moment. And ... well, she didn't need any other reasons.

Juliette concentrated on the thick blanket of fog and imagined it receding like a tidal wave in reverse. She felt the familiar, if rather new, magic swell within her and then escape with an almost *whooshing* sensation; the candles flickered—and the fog began to roil outside the restaurant windows. Juliette's eyes widened as it spun, swirled, and then pushed itself from the shore, gathering cloud upon cloud until it had retreated a good half mile out to sea.

"That's my girl," Gabriel said softly. She looked up at him to find him smiling out at the pier and the water beyond, a proud expression on his handsome features.

"Aye, that's a nice bit o' view yae've go' there, isn't it?"

Juliette blinked and spun to face the source of the new voice. An ancient-looking man stood a few feet away, his thick white hair flyaway, his rail-thin figure standing straight as an arrow despite his age. He was smiling broadly, his expression mysterious, his stark blue eyes glittering with vast intelligence.

Beside her, Gabriel chuckled softly and turned to face him as well. *"Stuart, ciamar a tha thu?"* He moved forward and the men each patted each other on the chest in greeting. Juliette could only stare at them in confusion and wonder. And a little fear ... Had this man, Stuart, seen her pushing the fog back?

"Ah, Juliette," Gabriel said, turning back to face her. "You need no' worry about Stuart, lass. Burns is the one man in the world who knows our secret—an' he'd fight to the death to protect it." He nodded at Stuart and Juliette digested the information.

Stuart smiled as tender a smile as his proud, rugged features would allow, and gave a hard nod in agreement.

"Aye, lass," he said. "Though I have tae admit, Gabriel dinnae tell mae yae could move the verra clouds. Tha' could come well in handy some fishin' days." He chuckled and it sounded like the rustling of ancient parchment. "Yae enjoy yer meal, noo." He turned then and headed back across the bar area and through a set of double doors that presumably led to the kitchens.

"Burns owns this restaurant," Gabriel said, taking off her jacket while she was still too stunned to say anything. He placed it on the back of her chair and turned back to her. "He fishes most mornings; his boat is out there with the others. His father left him this building an' he and his wife live in the back rooms."

"And he's a friend of yours?" Juliette asked.

"Aye, that he is. An old friend." He pulled her chair out for her and waited patiently behind it, his silver eyes shining bright. "I saved him from drowning off the bow of a fishing trolley when he was a lad. My secret slipped out, an' he kept it — an' we became close mates."

Juliette pulled herself out of her surprised state and sat down, allowing him to tuck her in. He then sat across from her. "Did you enjoy the ride, lass?" he asked as he poured her a cup of tea. Juliette stared at his strong hands, his broad shoulders, and the way the low light outside gave his hair blue highlights. She swallowed hard and nodded.

He looked up, just catching the nod, and smiled, flashing those white teeth. "Well, then, are you hungry yet?" he asked, almost chuckling.

She nodded again. She really was a bit hungry. The wind had been cold on her face during the ride. And controlling the weather to make the fog recede had sapped her just enough that the combination of the two had given her an appetite.

"Good," he said, and looked over toward the double doors. At once, they opened and several waiters came pouring out of the kitchen. Each one was dressed in the finest serving attire, black-and-white with white gloves, and each carried a steaming platter in his hands.

Juliette froze in her chair as the waiters began to set the dishes down in front of them on the table. She gazed up at them, catching pleasant, friendly smiles on faces that looked remarkably like Stuart Burns's. *They're his sons,* she realized as the table quickly became overrun with food that looked and smelled so good, she was instantly reminded of Thanksgiving. *Oh my God,* she thought, as the realization of what the platters carried hit her. *These are all of my favorite foods!* She had expected some kind of fish or maybe even lobster, not that there was anything wrong with either of those. But this was an incredibly unexpected surprise!

And how—*how*—had he known she loved these things? It was as if he'd pulled the favorites from the stores of her mind!

Maybe he did, she thought. *His brother is a vampire— maybe he read my mind!*

There was enough food to feed ten people before her, and from so many different ethnicities, it was like a cornucopia melting pot. Yet, she and Gabriel were the only two customers in the restaurant. There was no way they could finish it all!

The waiters finished arranging everything to perfection and the one who was obviously the eldest deftly refilled Juliette's teacup. Then the lot of them were heading back toward the kitchen doors. She watched them go. When she finally looked back up at Gabriel, he was positively beaming.

"Who cooked all of this?" she asked, her voice breathless with shock.

"Stuart an' his wife," Gabriel replied, still smiling brightly. It was such a beautiful smile. . . . "She's a bonnie lass, she is. Can make a meal fit for kings."

"Or angels," Juliette murmured, her gaze sliding over the vast assortment of foods before her. *I can barely cook toast.*

"Aye," Gabriel agreed, his tone dropping a little. "Your mouth is open, lass," he teased her softly, picking up a fresh piece of sourdough bread and dipping it into a bit of gravy. "Let me fill it for you." He put the bread to her lips.

She blushed furiously—and after a few seconds, she took a bite.

Kevin Trenton stepped through the hatchway of his private jet and descended the stairs to the tarmac below. His boots touched down with a decided finality. "Ah, bonnie Caledonia," he said, affecting a Scottish accent as his blue gaze took in their twilit surroundings. It had been a while since he'd been to this part of the world.

Ely, Luke, and Mitchell were standing beside a black SUV a hundred yards away. The vehicle's shining paint job was sleek beneath the tall lamps that illuminated the strip. The men nodded at him and made their way across the lot to join him at the base of the stairs.

"How was your flight?" Ely asked as he took off a pair of mirrored shades to reveal his stark amber eyes.

"Uneventful," Kevin replied. He let his gaze slip from his first chosen to the thick blanket of clouds that hung low over the land around them. Fog curled across the tarmac in white, wispy fingers that clawed and receded, leaving the black ground damp and glistening. Beside him, he saw Ely and the others turn to glance around them as well.

"At least you won't have to contend with the sun much, sir," Ely said softly. Kevin smiled at that, revealing a new set of gleaming white fangs.

His three chosen were aware of the change that had come over him now. At the Adarian headquarters, Kevin had managed to hide his body's alterations from the remaining Adarians because much of the facility was underground. And though it took Kevin a while to learn how to retract his new pronounced canines, he'd simply refrained from smiling or speaking directly to anyone in the interim. They assumed he was upset over Hamon's murder, and he didn't bother to deny the assumption. Problem solved.

However, when Ely had called him to check in, Kevin had decided to brief him on the apparent consequences of ingesting an archangel's blood to the point of death. Full disclosure had been necessary. Ely, Luke, and Mitchell were aware that their general had been the one to kill Hamon. And like the good soldiers they were, they possessed a loyalty that forced their understanding and quieted their tongues. After all, they were the chosen three. Whatever sacrifices had to be made to their beneficial ends were worth making.

Kevin wanted Ely to know what he, Mitchell, and Luke were in for should Kevin's plan to abduct and drain the archesses come to fruition. Such consequences being, namely, the transformation from Adarian to vampire. The archesses were for all intents and purposes archangels by their own rights. Therefore, if draining and ingesting their blood worked the same way that it had for the unfortunate Hamon, then there would be the same consequences to contend with.

Kevin still possessed all his original abilities. What was more, he now possessed Hamon's abilities as well. Furthermore, his vampiric transformation had blessed him with an even greater strength and speed than he'd known before. And he suspected that other abilities would be burgeoning in time. After all, the archangel Azrael was formidably powerful, and he was also a vampire. Kevin almost looked forward to his continued transformation.

However, his powers were tempered with the weaknesses of his new vampirism. The blinds on the jet had been drawn tight against the deadly rays of the sun, and he'd been forced to sleep during most of the day, as even being awake during daylight hours had become incredibly draining for him.

He was also . . . hungry.

He'd had a few days to contend with the rapid conversion his body underwent, but it still caught him somewhat by surprise. Kevin had tried to satisfy his hunger with various foods, but had found himself unable to ingest the bulk of them—and sick from the few he'd managed to get down. In the end, he had simply given in and allowed his body to dictate his actions.

He'd hunted. Killing humans had always been unnecessary and a little sad. They were so unable to defend themselves, even against one another. For an Adarian, they made pathetic targets, equating to no more than sheep, and for the most part, Adarians steered clear of human matters. But for a vampiric Adarian, a human was quite simply a meal. And that made the kill unpleasant on a whole new level.

Apparently, however, it was absolutely necessary, and it was something he needed to do *every night*. Because the hunger was back and it was strong.

Kevin was taller than most of his men, but he stood eye to eye with Ely. He turned to face his second-in-command now and pinned him with what he could feel was a more potent gaze than it had ever been. Ely was a brave man; he tried not to flinch. "We're going out tonight, Ely," Kevin said, allowing his smile to remain in place. "I'm hungry. And I want to show you what you have to look forward to."

CHAPTER NINETEEN

Juliette followed dutifully as Gabriel led her toward the back of Burns's wood-cabin restaurant. "Mind your step," he told her softly, helping her over a few outcroppings and stones as they made their way around the building.

Dinner had been amazing. Stuart's sons had disappeared as quickly as they'd appeared, leaving the former Messenger Archangel alone with Juliette. But Gabriel had filled the silence with the adept skill of a two-thousand-year-old storyteller. Juliette, the ethnographer with the background steeped in Caledonia, had hung on every word, soaking up the stories as if they were as life-giving as the food set before her. Gabriel's deep voice and lilting brogue had coaxed her into some altered state where the past came alive and her body hummed and every bite of food and drink of tea she took tasted like history.

She honestly couldn't remember a time in her life when she'd enjoyed herself more. By the time they'd finished eating, she was in heaven. She remained in that passive, eager state as she and Gabriel came to stand before the locked back door of Stuart's cabin. Juliette stepped back behind Gabriel as he raised his right arm toward the door and it began to melt away. In its place a portal swirled to life. Juliette recognized the formation now; she'd been sucked through one before.

But beyond the swirling portal, the night winds skated across a mist-laden field and parted to reveal the ruins of a mighty castle overlooking the sea.

Juliette gasped. "Slains Castle!" she exclaimed softly, feeling her toes tingle. "That's Cruden Bay!" She'd wanted to visit Slains Castle while she was in Scotland, but life had gotten crazy since she'd arrived and Slains was out of the way. She'd more or less given up on it. Slains Castle was the castle that had reputedly inspired Bram Stoker to write his incredibly famous novel, *Dracula*. She'd heard and read so much about it over the years while doing her research, she had always planned to make it a stop in her travels.

And now there it was, resting like a stone giant, magnificent and poignant against a backdrop of fog and shore and full moon. "It can't be real," she found herself whispering.

Gabriel lowered his lips to her ear and she shivered. She hadn't seen him move to stand behind her. She'd been too caught up in Slains. "That was wha' I thought when I first laid eyes upon you, lass," he whispered. "Bu' you feel real enough to me," he continued, and his hands found her arms, "an' that castle has been waitin' for you for centuries."

He nudged her then, directing her toward the portal's opening. Juliette was no longer afraid. Gabriel's whispered brogue, heated touch, and dark promise had all but chased away any doubts she had ever had about anything in her life. She boldly stepped toward the portal and moved through.

The world tilted around her and she closed her eyes. Gabriel's strong presence at her back guided her, gentle but firm. A few more steps and she felt the world return to normal. She heard the seagulls again and felt the kiss of fog upon her cheek. The feel of dirt and grass beneath her boots assured her that she had come all the way through.

She opened her eyes and turned around to see a tiny red car sitting alone on a small shoulder beside the road. A sign a few feet away read PASSING PLACE.

She looked back down at the car. Max, the archangels' guardian, had explained to her early that morning that the archangels could open a portal through the mansion as long as there was a door nearby. Any door. Even a car door would work. Now, as she stared at the little vehicle in the lot, she could only assume that Gabriel had just proved that fact.

"Whose car?" she asked, somewhat breathlessly.

"A rental," Gabriel chuckled. "Bu' the wee thing's seen a lo' of action tonight."

Juliette turned and blinked up at him. *What does he mean by that?* But his expression was mischievously guarded and his silver eyes flashed in the moonlit darkness. Whatever he meant, he wasn't sharing.

"Come, lass." He took her hand and began leading her down the long trail that wound around the massive meadow outside Slains Castle. The castle itself stood pale and beige against the dark background of the endless North Sea beyond. It beckoned like a beacon, a proud rising of stone amid a flat, endless field of grass.

The walk to the castle was long and surreal for Juliette. Gabriel didn't speak beside her; all she could hear was the sound of her own breathing, the cries of the gulls, the crashing of the surf on the rocks, and the crunching of their boots on the gravel that had been laid out over the trail to prevent it from drowning in mud.

This night had provided one new experience after another for her. Now she was about to approach the edifice of a long-awaited dream. She was about to step foot into a stone skeleton of history. She almost felt as if she were going to do something wrong. Was it still sacrilege to trample the fossils of memory if you had as much respect for them as Juliette did?

As she walked, her eyes remained glued to the looming fortress. Its empty windows yawned, broken and crumbling. She felt as if they were watching her, eyes of a weathered and put-upon beast, frozen in place and time as the world continued to bustle around it.

At last, they were turning the last bend and approaching the rusted iron gates that failed to protect the crumbling keep from tourists as lovelorn with the past as Juliette. The gate hung open, its lock cracked long ago. Gabriel gently pushed it aside and led her through.

For a moment, Juliette could not breathe. Twenty feet ahead was the foundation of Slains Castle, a monument to everything that she held spiritually dear. And, strangely enough, it even seemed to be glowing.

Juliette stopped in her tracks and frowned. The interior of the ruins appeared to be emitting a kind of light, as if the heart of the castle were alive somehow.

"What—"

"Come with me, Juliette," Gabriel commanded softly, bending to whisper the words in her ear. His grip on her hand tightened, still gentle, but now firm. The wind picked up around the castle and Juliette blinked when she thought she caught the faintest hint of the edge of a gauzy curtain. It blew into her line of sight—and then was gone.

Her lips parted, her heart beating harder now. Faster. Her legs felt strangely heavy and Gabriel began to tug her across the ancient grounds, closer and closer to the first archway that would lead into the cavernous corridors of the castle's interior.

"I'm sure you know all of this already," Gabriel said, as if he weren't pulling her inexorably toward the subject of her ambivalent awe. "Bu' Slains did no' have to be a ruin. In 1925, the family that owned the castle could no' pay its fees and had the roof removed to avoid the cost of keepin' it up."

He was right. Juliette did know the story. "It was owned by Sir John Ellerman—after the Hay family," she supplied automatically as her head tilted back and her neck craned. She gazed adoringly up at the wall of brick and stone and mortar before her and experienced a bewildering pang of fear. They'd come to the threshold—another step and she would be inside. This was an old side entrance, long ago made hollow by the destruction and pilfering of anything removable.

Beyond the stone archway lay a long, dark hallway. However, beyond the hallway, from someplace within the labyrinth of stone that she still could not see, there yet emanated a light. It was a gentle glow, warm and inviting.

Again, the wind sailed past her, wrapping around her, and she caught the sound of something that sounded like material rustling—flapping in the breeze. Water crashed upon the shore at the bottom of the notoriously dangerous cliffs that dropped a mere few feet from the castle's face. Juliette's head snapped to the side, her hazel eyes searching the darkness of the cliffs. Gabriel was still beside her, allowing her this moment.

What am I looking for? The air tasted like salt, fresh and cold and clean. But she also tasted iron on her tongue.

The wind died back down, leaving the landscape at once quiet. A crackling and popping sound snagged Juliette's attention. She turned back to the castle's interior. The glow coming from inside seemed to flicker. She frowned, straining to see.

She took a step forward, breaching the boundary of

the castle's walls. Gabriel moved beside her, steady and slow. As she drew closer, the glow became brighter and the crackling revealed its source to be a fire. Curiosity blossomed within Juliette; her steps quickened. A breeze brushed past, revealing the long filmy line of a gauzy curtain as it once more peeked from around a crumbling wall. *I knew it,* she thought. Now curiosity hummed through Juliette's blood, speeding her heart rate and widening her eyes.

She moved faster still, her attention focused solely on the inner rooms ahead. The crackling grew louder, the light brighter, and finally she was turning the corner, rounding a worn stone wall to come face-to-face with the innermost sanctum of Slains Castle.

The courtyard had once held a chapel, hidden deep inside the castle in order to protect the keep's inhabitants from the deadly bigotry of opposing religious factions. However, the chapel had been laid to waste long ago and the courtyard's gardens had fallen to seed a hundred years past. All that remained of a once quaint and kept sanctuary were the tread-upon trails made by tourists through the tall grasses—and a spiral staircase.

Juliette glanced at the spiral staircase and then tilted her head, following the strange crackling glow until she was staring up at what was once the castle's second story. The floor should have been gone, the wooden beams torn down or crumpled in for decades. However, new wooden beams crisscrossed neatly above her, forming a platform of hardwood that should not have existed.

Juliette stared with wide eyes. A four-poster bed rested atop the wooden platform, draped in silks and satins and warm, soft fleece. Rugs covered the wooden beams. A fire danced invitingly in a massive stone hearth. And curtains of gauzy white billowed from empty window frames high above, their long lean lines cascading from the second floor to the ground. It was something out of a dream.

A dream . . .

It was the master's chamber. Juliette could not help but recognize it. It was as if she had been here before. She didn't bother fighting the pull it had on her body; she made her way to the staircase and began to climb, painfully aware of Gabriel's steady presence behind her. The air grew warmer as she rose. It should have been frigid; the wind should have cut right through the hollow eye sockets of the castle's ancient rooms. But as she reached the top landing and stepped out into the chamber, the warmth from the fire wrapped around her like an embrace.

Torches had been lit and placed in sconces along the ancient ramparts. Tapestries depicting archangels with swords and shields clung to rods along the broken walls. The curtains billowed and popped and the bed waited . . . empty and alluring.

"How is this possible?" she whispered, feeling numb and warm and tingly all at once.

Gabriel bent and whispered in her ear, "We're angels, lass." He chuckled softly, his hard body pressed against her back. Juliette's breath caught when his hand came around to gently cup her chin. He turned her head and leaned over her so that they were eye to eye. "Does it please you?" he asked.

Juliette gazed up into the flashing silver of his eyes and saw storms brewing there. Lightning. His pupils were expanding and the fire in the hearth was rising. *Does it please me?* Her mind murmured the words and they floated through her consciousness like the sparks of ash that escaped the fireplace. *My God,* she thought. *He turned back time for me.* Her breath was shaking, her legs felt like jelly, and there wasn't an ounce of her any longer that was cold. Gabriel and his world had scorched her being from the inside out. It was now unrecognizable—beautifully, thrillingly, poignantly unrecognizable.

She couldn't even reply.

But she didn't have to. Gabriel gazed down into her eyes, knowing her in a way that no other human ever had. Slowly, he came around her until they were facing each other. He never released her chin. He never put more than an inch of space between them. His nearness was becoming as warm as the crackling flames in the stone hearth.

Juliette closed her eyes as Gabriel leaned down; she saw his shadow cross before the moon and then there was darkness and heat and a hint of cinnamon as his lips brushed against hers, his words an incantation of magic that sparked a fire in her veins.

"Mo sheacht míle grá thú," he whispered, and she understood. Somewhere, deep inside, she understood. He kissed her gently, tenderly, a mere hint of heaven before he kissed the corner of her mouth and then her cheek. His lips hovered near her ear and his body closed the distance between them. She could feel the heat radiating off him. The wind mirrored his moves; the waves hushed on the shore; the seagulls fell silent. He was darkness and ancient power so intricately tied with the land on which he stood, it followed his unspoken command and closed in around her, hypnotizing her—mesmerizing her with its magic.

"Mo ghrá thú," he whispered. His breath sent a shiver through her, delicious and promising. He groaned and his hand gently fisted in her hair. *"Mo ghrá thú,"* he said again. This time it was nearly harsh, choked with emotion he could no longer hold at bay.

You are my love, her mind translated. The words floated through her like an aphrodisiac, a potion too powerful to ignore. *I love you....*

And then his mouth closed over hers. Her breath caught in her throat, her heart leapt as if it would tear from her chest, and a moan worked its way up from somewhere deep inside. Instant fire raced through her veins, burning her from the inside out as Gabriel pulled her fiercely against his body, crushing her with a need that barely mirrored her own.

CHAPTER TWENTY

A zrael had told him that she had a particular fond-
ness for Slains. The vampire had shamelessly pil-
fered her mind as he'd stolen her from the elevator shaft
in Sam's hotel. When Az had suggested wooing Juliette,
Gabriel had forced the vampire to share everything he
knew about her before he slipped into his vampire sleep.
And Gabriel had run with the information. He and his
brothers had worked quickly to re-create just one room
in the castle; he'd wanted to give her a piece of the past
that she loved so much.

He'd wanted only to show her something special. To
see her smile. But when she had gone still before him
and he had moved around her to look down into her
eyes, she had besieged him. Her thankfulness was too
great, too poignant, her understanding far too deep. He'd
found himself drowning in the bottomless gratification
in her beautiful eyes, and he was done for.

So many things Gabriel had said to women over the
years—so many words he had whispered. But never
these. These were for his archess, and her alone. And
when they finally—*finally*—made their way to freedom
past the confines of his lips and heart, he was nearly
overcome with emotion. A whitewash mixture of relief,
heart-wrenching fear, and overwhelming joy swirled

within him, blotting out every sense he possessed save the ones that were occupied by Juliette.

He knew only the feel of her lips against his, the smell of her skin, the taste of dessert on her tongue, and the heat radiating from her tiny form as he held her to him—unable to get close enough. He wanted to devour her. He needed to be closer, but physics denied him. His heart was cracking open, his soul was unfolding to life, and the world was crumbling to bits all around him. None of it mattered any longer.

Somewhere in the back of his mind, he was infinitely grateful that he'd chosen the master chamber to rebuild. With a quick bend, Gabriel was lifting her into his arms. He didn't allow her to break the kiss; he needed her too badly. If she pulled away even a little, he would surely shatter.

But Juliette didn't pull away. She didn't seem to notice that he lifted and carried her toward the master bed. Her lips parted for him, her tongue tentatively explored, and her body melted into his, offering up the sweetest surrender. She was tiny in his arms, precious and tender and fragile, and he wanted her so badly in that moment, he was afraid he would break her.

Two thousand years of searching, of hunting, and of needing came rushing forward as he leaned into the bed, following her down until he was pressing her into the mattress. Still, he didn't break the kiss. And he couldn't hold back.

His kiss deepened, demanding that she open for him. His hands found her neck and gripped lightly—so small. And then he found her jacket and the clothes she wore underneath and all he could feel for them was loathing because they separated her from him. Desperate yearning ripped through him and he growled as he broke their kiss.

"Forgive me," he said. He meant it for so many things.

For what he had put her through, for the way he had treated her, even for the situation she now found herself in. He wanted her forgiveness—needed it. Because he couldn't hold back.

Her eyes were glassy, her lips red and parted, her breathing shallow. Her lids were heavy, lashes lowered, cheeks flushed.

My God, he thought. *Have mercy.* "Forgive me," he repeated, choking the words through a constricted throat and gritted teeth. He was begging her this time, beseeching—he needed to know.

Juliette smiled an impious smile that was gone almost as quickly as it appeared. "Make me," she gasped.

With that, Gabriel's eyes widened, and he felt them begin to glow. He jerked her up and shoved the jacket off her shoulders. A split second later, he was tossing it to the floor. Again, he claimed her lips with his own, stealing her breath. As he drove her into the mattress with his kiss, his hand slid up under her long-sleeved shirt. Her skin was so soft, so warm; he growled against her lips. He felt the ridges of her ribs and then his fingertips brushed the bottom of her bra. A part of him—the human, the archangel, the man—wanted to rip the garment off her and destroy it for keeping him at bay.

But there was another part of him yawning to life now. It was what was left when everything else was blown away and the soul was laid bare before the one it loved. That part of him could never do anything to hurt Juliette. So, with a gentle patience he could not believe he possessed, Gabriel slid his hands along her rib cage and across her back. As he did, he luxuriated in the feel of her, like silk and satin, warm and precious and tender.

The fingers of both of his hands curled over the clasp of her bra and he fought with himself. This time he lost. He tugged and the metal clasp broke. Then he took both bra and shirt and shoved them up her arms, forcing her to raise her arms over her head. There, he gently trapped her wrists above her on the bed, binding them in his desperate grasp.

"Forgive me?" he asked. His tone was filled with some kind of warning now. He easily held her arms with one hand as his other trailed back down her now bare arm and to the swell of her perfect breasts.

He reared up above her, knowing he must look strange to her. He knew his silver eyes were burning like liquid lightning, stark in the tanned skin of his face. He knew his pupils had expanded. He had no control over it. He looked down at her, exposed and helpless beneath him, and knew once and for all that a demon existed within everyone. Angel or not.

Juliette arched beneath him as she halfheartedly tried to pull her arms free. Her lips were swollen from his kiss, parted and perfect. Her cheeks were flushed and her porcelain skin was bathed in moonlight, nearly luminescent.

Gabriel watched the color of her eyes change, becoming starkly green. He saw her own pupils expand and couldn't look away. He had become her prisoner as much as she had his. He gazed, transfixed, wanting to see every exquisite expression that crossed her lovely face as his hand moved farther down to very slowly trail along the outside of one creamy breast.

She stilled beneath him, her breath held, her eyes caught in his, as his thumb brushed tauntingly across her nipple and she arched in response, the smallest gasp escaping her throat. She pressed her flesh into his palm and he exhaled harshly at the feel of it. Slowly, she lowered back down onto the mattress, her breathing now ragged. He leaned in and put his lips to her ear.

"Wha' do you say, luv?" His voice had become guttural, constricted with lust. Her tenderness beneath him was clawing at him. He needed to get closer.

Again, he brushed his thumb across her nipple, this time pressing ever so slightly on her hard peak before moving on. He watched the side of her face, noting how she closed her eyes and her long, thick lashes brushed across the top of her cheek. She moaned softly, such small and innocent prey, and he reveled in it. "Forgive me yet?"

He placed his lips to her cheek, kissing her tenderly. She didn't reply. His hand moved lower, sliding across the flat plane of her stomach until he was riding the swell of her hip bones. He paused, releasing a shaky breath. Juliette's power was overwhelming him. The feel of her flesh beneath his fingers was like an electric buzz humming through his hand and up his arm. She sighed and he heard music. He closed his eyes, lost in her. Somewhere in the back of his mind, he was aware that his fingers were curling beneath the band of her jeans and the underwear beneath. A flick, a pull, and her clothes were sliding down over her lean legs.

A wave of warmth washed over him; her skin radiated heat. The soft scent of soap wafted across the bed, enveloping him in its femininity. He breathed deeply, wanting to fill himself with it.

His breath caught and he stilled when he felt Juliette's fingertips lightly brush the sides of his neck. He hadn't even realized he'd released her. She was so tentative. *Och, lass* . . . He wanted more. *Touch me.*

As if she could read his mind, Juliette's fingers ran through the sable black curls of his hair, grasping them lightly as he moved over her body, covering her with his still-clothed form.

She shuddered beneath him and moaned when he snaked one arm under her to wrap it around her waist as his other hand ran along her silky, exposed body. He rose onto his knees, pulling her up with him until she was seated beneath him and he was stealing her lips with his kiss once more.

A century passed between them and he let it go. And another. He opened her up, delving past her gates and subjugating her mouth as he let the years slip away, one by one. Twenty decades and then a hundred—until two thousand years were sliding off his shoulders, and he began to feel as light as the air around them.

The wind breezed into the master's chamber, brushing her long beautiful hair around her bare shoulders and across her back. Gabriel's hands fisted in the silken lengths. He couldn't let her go, and when he felt her fingers curling beneath the edges of his sweater, he had to fight between his need to hold her to him—and his desire to feel his own skin against hers.

He growled against her lips and again lost the battle when he felt her hands on his bare waist, warm and soft and innocent. He pulled away, yanked his sweater and shirt over his head, and tossed them aside.

Juliette's green eyes widened, her gaze trailing boldly across the muscles of his chest and midsection. He wanted to let her look. He wanted to be everything she had ever dreamed of—as she was to him. But she was so small and so beautiful before him, her skin glowing radiantly, her waist trim, her collarbone inviting, her breasts small and round and utterly perfect. She raised her hands and placed them hesitantly to his chest, and Gabriel's silver, glowing eyes closed once more.

Heat sparked across his skin, sinking through the muscle and bone beneath until he felt something ignite somewhere deep, deep inside. She was consuming him with her ripe vulnerability.

"Juliette," he whispered, growled, gasped. "My love . . ." She was his archess. And he needed to be closer. *By God*, he needed to be closer.

The rest of his clothes, he simply flashed away with no more than a supernatural thought. He had officially run out of willpower. He was hard and hot and heavy and as he laid himself bare before her, he again took them down into the mattress, one hand curled into a fist in her hair, the other pressed into the sheet beneath them. His hand fisted the sheet with stark impatience, with craving, and with pain. The feel of her warm and soft against his rigid need was nearly unbearable.

Her legs bent beneath him, unwittingly opening her up to him. She gasped, suddenly feeling him there, taunting, tempting, brushing against her with red-hot warning. A monster leapt to life within him, narrowing his silver gaze, subjugating his body. He had never lost control before—but he was losing it now.

His hands skimmed her waist, trailing up to cup her supple breasts as she writhed beneath him, daring him to take what was his. She was playing with fire. He squeezed gently, brushing his thumbs against her taut nipples. They hardened under his manipulations and her head tossed to the side, her eyes shut tight. He moved in to press his lips to her throat and then trailed them along her collarbone to her shoulder.

He continued to tease her nipples and she tried to arch away, the sensation clearly too much for her. But he would not relent. His teeth raked gently against the skin on her shoulder and then he once more captured her hands in his and held them to the bed as he moved lower, until his tongue flicked out across the sensitive bud that rose so taut and tempting in the air.

Juliette gasped loudly, arching once more beneath him. He rode her momentum, expertly easing himself over her until the tip of his shaft parted her silken, moist lips. Now she cried out beneath him. "Gabriel!"

"Yes, luv?" He speared her with a hard, sultry look, his voice no more than a harsh whisper before he took his teeth to the nipple his tongue had just teased. Again, Juliette cried out, and he relished the sound. His tall form was taut as a bowstring now, strong and hard and barely contained, as his archess continued to torment him with her beauty.

"I . . ." She tried to speak, but moaned again when Gabriel used his teeth to pull on her nipple and her back followed him up, arching beautifully to relieve the quick, mild pain that melted into pleasure as he flicked it expertly with his tongue. She nearly sobbed beneath him, and he released her hands. They instantly dove through his hair, fisting tightly, gripping him with a hunger that was beginning to mirror his own.

"I forgive you!" she finally called out, curving her body into his, her skin begging to be tasted, her body begging to be taken.

Gabriel felt his eyes flash, saw something white flicker in his peripheral vision, and heard a rumble in his own chest. Her movement urged him on and he drove slowly forward, slipping exquisitely past her outer barriers and into her warm tightness.

She enveloped him, gripping him firmly, and he groaned in velveteen bliss. Thoughts scattered like bits of paper on a hurricane wind. Somewhere in the distance, he heard thunder roll and couldn't care. Slowly, he eased deeper, relishing every millimeter of hot, unyielding tightness her small body offered. She moaned again and Gabriel swallowed it, taking her mouth with renewed hunger.

She tried to meet him halfway, rising up off the sheet, but he stilled her with a firm hand on her waist and continued to take his time entering her. He never wanted this moment to end. It was maddening and delicious to the point of danger, but it was his. *She* was his. And he had waited too long for this.

Inch by inch, he delved past her defenses, sinking into her body with a slow, lascivious determination. She was so small and so tight and he was so large at points she squeezed him with a near agony—and he was in heaven.

Juliette shuddered in his arms, her hands slipping from his hair to his chest, where her nails threatened the taut skin over his hard muscles. She gasped for breath between his kisses, panting against his lips.

At last, he was completely within her, having driven deeper and more fully than he had thought possible. She trembled beneath him and he shuddered in response. Slowly, he ended their kiss and raised himself above her, bracing his weight on his hands against the mattress.

He gazed down at the woman he now claimed as his own. Her long, rich brown hair cascaded over the white blankets beneath her like a shimmering, tigereye waterfall. Her green eyes smoldered beneath heavy lids, her long, thick lashes demurely brushing against the tops of her flushed cheeks. Her lips, bruised by his kisses, were parted and panting.

Her hands on his chest slid to his shoulders as if to hang on. She had good instincts, because he lowered his head, his silver gaze stark through the tops of his eyes as his body tensed and he pulled back—just a little.

Uncertainty flickered in her beautiful green eyes. Anticipation.

He drove back in, shoving into his angel with hard strength, knowing only that he wanted to be deeper. Closer.

Juliette arched beneath him, crying out in both surprise and ecstasy. He didn't give her time to adjust. He pulled back again—and drove forward once more as he bent over her, running his hand into her hair and yanking her head gently back to expose her throat to his teeth. Her cries became gasps, and then moans, and the small sounds of helpless delight that escaped her pink lips filled Gabriel with intense triumph.

He kissed her neck, and then bit it gently, allowing his teeth to graze across her taut flesh until he reached the top of her shoulder. There, he sucked hard, leaving a mark. She gasped at the small attack and he chuckled against her, rearing back to drive ruthlessly forward, silencing her outcry with a loud gasp of pleasure.

He took her like this, mercilessly and tenderly, forcing himself into her over and over again, claiming her body with firm conviction. And she grasped at his shoulders and curled her nails into his back as if to hold on for dear life.

Gabriel slid his hand between them as he rode her and pressed his fingers into her soft mound of curls, parting them with knowing resolve. A harsh sob of bliss escaped her throat when he found the hood of her clitoris and pressed inward and downward, driving himself into her at the same time. The sharp sensation stole Juliette's breath, and again, Gabriel smiled against her throat, his body humming deliciously as she responded to his tiny tortures.

She tried to say his name, but lost the sound when he pressed again, moving in a slow circle that hardened her button and made her shake in his grasp. He could feel himself swelling within her, her tightness a gluttonous kind of friction that was sure to drive him mad.

His gaze raked across her body, her rising and falling breasts, her expanding rib cage that protected a racing heart. Juliette panted and mumbled incoherently. He pressed deeper and she writhed. He flicked his thumb across her bud and she moaned low and long. He placed his lips to the pulse in the side of her throat and felt it speeding rapidly. His tongue flicked out across it. He sensed her time coming and compelled her on.

"You're mine, lass. Now and forever," he told her, as his fingers continued to wreak havoc on her senses. He parted his fingers between them, surrounding her sensitive nub, and then gently squeezed. She bucked in his grasp and he pressed on, forcing her over that precipice.

Juliette's head flew back, her eyes squeezed shut, her

white teeth bared, as waves of orgasmic pleasure rushed through her. He could feel her wringing him tightly, yanking a growl from deep within his chest. He rose above her, and propelled himself forward, taking her now as he had wanted to since he'd first seen her in that tavern several nights ago.

Her small body moved beneath him, her head thrown back and her nails finding painful purchase in the muscle of his back. He gritted his teeth, torn wide open by the colossal, intense sensation she was awakening within him.

Lightning crashed out over the sea and thunder rolled over them as he took Juliette. He took her hard and fast and howled into the night when he felt himself explode within her. It was too strong, too severe, and it was the answer to his prayers. He jerked against her, overrun with passion. She cried out as his hot seed began to spill within her, searing her from the inside.

Lightning crashed again, closer this time, and Gabriel let Juliette go to fist his hands once more in the sheet on either side of her. It stretched taut beneath his death grip, its seams splitting as he threw back his head and roared with the sweet, perfect agony of his peak.

It seemed to last forever. And he never wanted it to end.

An eternity later, the pulsing stopped, the throbbing ended, and Gabriel slowly lowered his head. Juliette gazed up at him with half-closed eyes, her breathing once more steadying, her grip on his back easing up. As he was an archangel, any marks she made on him would heal quickly. And for that small moment, he wished he were only human so that he could wear the scars with pride.

She was so beautiful. Gabriel stared down at her, struck dumb again by what he was seeing. Never, in his long existence, had he beheld such a wonderful creature.

It was bewildering. She was everything he had ever loved—she was the most beautiful woman in Caledonia. She *was* Caledonia.

His bonnie Juliette . . . "Och, lass, wha' will I do with you?" he whispered, suddenly overtaken with emotion.

Juliette didn't answer. But when he moved to lie down beside her, rolling her over so that he remained within her, her eyes widened. He had yet to go soft inside of her. Her very nearness was keeping him from doing so.

"Gabriel," she gasped. "How can you—"

He cut off her question with a kiss, cupping her lovely face in his hands. And because he was a glutton for punishment, he moved within her, pressing against her with a desire that was already hardening him with a vengeance. She moaned in response, a helpless sound of reawakening lust.

He broke the kiss long enough to gaze into her still-green eyes. "Get used to it, luv."

CHAPTER TWENTY-ONE

I t was all around her again: the past. All her life, these
dreams had been draped in the cloth of memory, as
gauzy and faint as the curtains Gabriel had hung. But
now the past was solid, tangible, and nontransparent.
There were no overlapping images, no hint of the present in the form of crumbling castle walls.

Instead, there was a castle as it once had been, in all
its glory. The halls were lit with torches and decorated
with tapestries. The smell of a large dinner meal was
heavy in the air. The sounds of a household in full swing
were everywhere. Servants bustled by Juliette, nodding
politely as they went.

Juliette nodded back and continued to make her way
down the hall. She was heading for the kitchens. She
reached the massive archway that led to the kitchens and
the cooking aromas intensified a hundredfold. There
were white feathers on the stone floor, someone was
pulling bread out of a massive stone oven, and an old
woman sat beside a glassless window peeling potatoes.

Juliette moved past them and out the back door. The
night was coming on them quick, but when Juliette
looked left, toward the treacherous cliffs that protected
the east face of the castle, the glow from a swinging light
caught her attention. She stopped in her tracks and

squinted through the gathering darkness and creeping fog. The lamplight hovered above the edge of the cliff—and then disappeared, ducking down beneath the rocks that plummeted to the sea a hundred feet below.

Alarm shot through her. Juliette gathered her skirts and began to run. She tripped over a patch of thistle, barely caught herself in time, and continued to run, lifting her legs higher this time. But the light was fading, and at once, she realized she couldn't see the dividing line between cliff—and sky.

She slowed her steps, skidding a bit as loose gravel crumbled beneath her boots and went tripping over the cliff's rocky ledge to disappear below. Juliette was breathing hard; her heart hammered. Something was wrong. Something niggled at the back of her mind, making her fingers tingle and her legs grow weak

She quieted her breath and listened. When the crashing waves receded and grew fainter, she could make out the sound of men's voices—down below. Carefully, she got down onto her hands and knees and then lowered herself onto her stomach. Deftly, she pulled herself to the ledge and peeked one eye over the black rocks.

She had been right. It was a lantern she'd seen. There was a rowboat in the tiny cove and there were half a dozen men milling about on the wet rocks. *Smugglers,* Juliette thought. The authorities of Cruden Bay had recently been out to the castle, looking for signs of them.

The smugglers were carrying crates full of bottles. Though netting and cloth covered most of the boxes, Juliette could see the outline of several of the bottles sticking out beneath the full moon. The men were setting these boxes into the small caves that had been formed over time by the rising and lowering water. The tide was moving in with the coming night and the men seemed to know it; they were working quickly. Juliette wondered what was in the bottles.

And then one of the men looked up. Juliette scooted back, her breath caught in her throat, her heart leaping painfully. There was a shout from below and she knew she'd been seen.

Quickly, she shoved herself up and spun around. But as she did, her skirts got caught beneath her boot. The rocks crumbled once more, slip-sliding down the face of the cliffs. She had just enough time to realize she was falling, to feel the open air around her and the lack of gravity, before her body was wrenched violently in several directions at once.

"Juliette!"

The wrenching continued, but it was gentler now. Confusion danced around Juliette in colorful motes and darkness. She tried to blink them away, but chaos lingered, making up down and down up, and her fingers clutched something warm and hard as she desperately tried to hold on.

I'm falling. . . .

"Shh, lass, I'm here," crooned a deep, accented voice. She knew that voice. She clung to it, closing her eyes to let it wrap around her in place of the torment that had tried to pull her apart.

Gabriel . . . His arms were wrapped around her, tight and secure. His warm, strong body was pressed against hers, instantly chasing away her chill, keeping the distress of her dream at bay. *My dream,* she thought. *No. It was more than that.*

My memory . . . my death.

"Lass, wha' were you dreamin'?" Gabriel asked, his tone infinitely concerned. His words whispered across the top of her head, his fingers deftly, gently brushing her long hair out of her eyes. She kept them shut, willing the rest of the world away. She couldn't answer him. Her heart was still beating too hard and she felt a little sick.

"All right, little one," he whispered, slowly rocking her back and forth. "It's all right."

It wasn't until several minutes of rocking, comforting silence had passed that Juliette found the will to open her eyes. She saw the bed first, then the crumbling castle walls with their tapestries and the open windows with their white curtains billowing in the breeze—and then she looked up at Gabriel. The full moon hung ominously low over his broad shoulder, reflecting the flashing silver in his eyes. His expression was starkly concerned.

"Och, lass, you're shakin'," he said softly, curling his fingers beneath her chin as if to get a better look at her.

I remember it, she thought. *God, I remember it all. . . .*

"Wha's hauntin' you?" he asked, leaning forward to gently place a kiss on her forehead. Juliette closed her eyes and absorbed it, allowing it to chase away a bit more of her memory. His thumb tenderly brushed along her cheekbone. She opened her eyes. "Tell me," he urged softly.

"I've been here before," she said then. Her tone was flat, her voice strange. She kept going. "I've been to Slains Castle."

Gabriel frowned, shaking his head slightly. "When, lass?"

"That's just it," she said, choking as a sob worked its way up her throat from her chest. She shoved it back down and shook her head, shrugging. "I don't know. But . . . it was a long time ago."

Gabriel looked down at her for a long time. His eyes searched her face, her eyes, almost looking through her. Finally, he cocked his head to one side and took her by her upper arms, squeezing gently. "*How* long ago?"

Juliette steeled herself. She swallowed hard and went still in his grasp. "It was another lifetime, Gabriel," she whispered. A wave crashed onto the shore beneath the cliffs and then receded again. Juliette stared into Gabriel's eyes and forced the words past her lips. "I died here."

*   *   *

Daniel knew the archangel wouldn't be able to sense him at this distance, especially with the wind picking up the way it was. It looked as though a storm was on the way, building just out over the water beyond the cliffs of Cruden Bay. He was safely sequestered in the darkness behind a copse on the opposite side of the road from where Gabriel had parked his little red rental car. Out here, he didn't have to use his invisibility, which would allow him to save his strength.

He would need that strength. Gabriel's brothers had all been out there earlier in the night, each of them using their unique and strange ability to "teleport" to get here. For some reason, they had needed the car—Daniel had no idea what that was all about. He was positive that the vehicle was a rental and that there was nothing special about it.

Clearly, there was much about the Four Favored that Daniel and his brothers didn't understand. But it didn't matter right now. Gabriel's brothers were gone and had been for hours. The former Messenger was alone with his archess in that castle and Daniel knew damned well what they'd been doing.

So, he bided his time. When the full moon was high and bright in the sky, Daniel draped himself in invisibility and made his way quickly down the path, being sure to keep a wide berth of the castle. He'd lost one of his shard guns in the jailhouse when he'd attacked Gabriel, but he'd left the Adarian headquarters with two, and he still had the other.

As he approached the castle's north side, he noticed a glow from somewhere deeper within the stone structure. He wasn't surprised. It was a cold night and they had probably started a fire.

But as he drew closer still, he noticed that it was more than just the glow that was off. There were subtle details—the paths had been neatly cleared, some of the walls seemed stabilized, and he could actually catch the hint of what looked like curtains billowing in the breeze from somewhere on the second level.

Gabriel and his brothers had been busy, it seemed. How fucking romantic.

Daniel's gaze narrowed, his will resolved. The plan was simple. He was going to shoot the archangel point-blank until the damn gun was empty. Then he was going to take Juliette, knock her out, and carry her to the cute little red car that Gabriel had so conveniently placed at the end of the trail. He would drive the car a mile, trade it with his own stolen vehicle, and continue until he reached the abandoned building where he had set everything up.

Then he would drain Juliette Anderson dry and drink her blood.

At that thought, dizziness swept over Daniel and he had to stop and rub his cold hand over his hot face. He felt sick at the idea of killing such a precious creature. The archesses were . . . Daniel shook his head. It did no good to dwell on the task ahead of him. He simply needed to do it and be done with it. Once he ingested her blood, as long as he did it right, he would be able to absorb her very special healing power. And with that, he would hopefully become invaluable to his general.

Life could go on as normal. He would no longer have to be afraid that Abraxos would come after him. And he would no longer have to run. It was worth it.

Daniel took a slow, deep breath and continued toward the castle. He could now see that one of the inner rooms had been refurbished. As the rest of the castle rested in ruins, what looked like the master's chamber had been reinforced, decorated, and warmed by hearth fire.

There was a bed in the room; Daniel could see the figures atop it from where he stood outside the castle walls. The archangel Gabriel sat on the bed, his eyes closed, his archess pulled tightly to his chest. They were both undressed. Daniel wondered why the wind didn't seem to touch them and chill them to the core.

More archangel magic, he thought grimly. Or maybe it was the archess herself. He'd heard that they could control the weather. The soft sound of a sob carried to him on the next breeze and Daniel frowned. Juliette was crying. . . . What had happened? Had Gabriel hurt her during their lovemaking?

He fiercely shook his head once, forcing himself not to care. *It doesn't matter,* he thought. *This is all going to be over soon.*

He let his invisibility drop, knowing he would need all his strength and that the cloak wouldn't protect him from the archangel's ability to sense him anyway. He was close enough now; it was only a matter of time.

And then Gabriel went utterly still where he sat on the bed. His stark eyes flashed open and gazed over the top of Juliette's head. Green met silver on what was sure to become a battlefield, and Daniel pulled his gun.

Gabriel sensed him a half second before he saw him. The static, abrasive sensation was carried to him on the wind and he opened his eyes. The Adarian stood just outside the castle walls, his green eyes narrowed on the couple in the master chamber.

There was no indecision. Gabriel seemed to click into autopilot, all his defenses rising to the occasion. He moved forward on the bed, shoving Juliette behind him, and used his powers to turn the sheet over their bodies to pure gold. It became instantly heavy in his arms, but he was an archangel; such things barely mattered to his kind. He raised the sheet with no time to spare.

The shard blast struck the material, seemed to dilute, and dispersed across the makeshift shield with a crackling energy. However, part of its insidious power wrapped itself around Gabriel's hand where he held the sheet. He gritted his teeth as his fingers began to solidify.

"Gabriel!" Juliette was on her knees behind him, her hand on his shoulder a death grip.

"Stay behind me!" he commanded. The ancient doorway to the master's chamber was only a few yards away. Gabriel had never tried to open a portal through a doorway that lacked a door before. In the thousands of years that he and his brothers had used the mansion to travel around the world, it had just never occurred to any of them to try. Would it work now?

Below, the Adarian had disappeared. Whether that meant he was now moving at breakneck speed through the castle on his way to the second floor or he had actually become invisible, Gabriel had no idea. He could still feel the Adarian there. In fact, the nearly painful vibration in the air was becoming stronger.

Gabriel reached back, grabbed Juliette's arm, and hauled her out of the bed. "Sorry, luv!" he apologized, knowing he was most likely bruising her. But there was no time for gentleness—no time for anything but a rapid escape. Juliette didn't make a sound. She simply stood with him, trying her best to keep up with his strength and speed. She was a brave lass. A trouper.

Gabriel raised his half-solidified hand toward the archway that had once been a door and concentrated on opening the portal.

At once, he knew something was wrong. It didn't feel the same. The portal began to swirl to life, as he had hoped, but it was darker—denser. He had wanted to open a doorway into his own home on the shores of Harris. It had been the first place that had occurred to him. However, the image that appeared at the eye of the portal was unfamiliar to him. It was dark and draped in a thick fog. There was an archway there; he could see it as it appeared and disappeared behind the blanket of mist.

A horrid sound ripped through the air behind Gabriel, and Juliette screamed. The shard blast hit him in the back of the neck. Juliette was short enough that she'd been missed altogether. Gabriel had enough time to realize that he couldn't breathe before a second sound tore through the night, this one far louder than the first.

Lightning split the sky behind him, charging the master's chamber with white-hot might. It was as if a massive flashbulb exploded, capturing the earth in total stillness for an eternal second. All other sound became silence in the wake of the mighty roar. Gabriel couldn't turn his head, but he didn't need to. He knew what had happened. Juliette had called lightning upon the Adarian.

His stormy little angel.

I need air, he thought. The shard blast had solidified the top part of his back and lungs and seemed to have swelled his throat closed. His head began to pound, but his next thought was for Juliette. His grip on her arm was still fast. He used it to pull her after him through the portal and into the mystery that waited beyond.

His bare feet touched upon wet grass and damp dirt and he kept going, making sure they were both fully through the portal before he again concentrated on closing it. He had to turn his entire body in order to see through the swirling gateway behind him. He saw the master chamber of Slains Castle growing narrower, as if at the end of a tunnel. At its center was the Adarian, unconscious and immobile on the wooden planks he and his brothers had erected. The shard gun lay a few inches from his unmoving fingers.

Gabriel considered, for half an insane second, going back for the gun. But his vision was tunneling as quickly as the portal was closing. His heart was hammering painfully behind his rib cage. The gun would have to be left behind.

The portal closed with a strange unevenness, again

behaving differently than it had in the past. But once it disappeared entirely, Juliette was jerking her wrist out of his grasp and coming around him to stand before him. He could barely look down at her, but he felt her warm hand on his chest well enough. Her touch alone seemed to chase away some of the agony that was now ripping through his body.

And then the warmth became heat and he knew she was healing him. As it had when Eleanore and Michael had healed his body of shard blasts, it hurt when Juliette's magic invaded his system and chased the evil away. But it hurt *less*. Maybe it was simply that it was Juliette. Maybe it was something more. He couldn't have cared in that moment, because his lungs began to expand once more and his throat opened up and he went coughing to the ground. He landed on his knees, dragging in air, and pulled Juliette hard against his chest. As he clutched her to him, he felt his fingers flex and realized she had healed his hand as well.

"Are you okay, lass?" he asked. His voice was a little raspy, but otherwise all right.

Juliette nodded against him, not answering. Gabriel felt her shudder and concern arced through him. She had called lightning on the Adarian. And then she had healed him of two shard blasts. And now she was naked in the grass of a field—God only knew where.

At once, Gabriel was standing, pulling her up with him. "Hold still," he told her as he imagined her clothed in the garments she'd worn before they had made love. Slowly, he ran his healed hand over her body, hovering several inches from her tender flesh. As he moved, the clothes reappeared, wrapping her in their warmth.

"Okay . . . ," Juliette whispered, her eyes wide as she watched him work more of his magic. "That's . . . *really* cool."

When he'd finished with her heavy, plush aviator's

jacket, she closed her eyes and hugged herself, clearly pleased to have it back.

"Nice jacket," he said, offering up a lopsided smile as he began to refashion his own clothing next. When they were both fully dressed and thick, protective boots compressed the grass beneath their feet, Gabriel began to look around. The moon was full and bright and when the fog parted, he caught glimpses of stones.

They were headstones.

"Och, I canno' believe it. I know where we are," he said, shaking his head in wonder. He looked up at the stone archway above him and then looked left. As the mists parted with a new gust of wind, he caught sight of names etched into stone. They were standing in the opening of an aboveground crypt. Skull and crossbones symbols, along with Saint Andrew's crosses, were carved into the ancient rock below the names of those who had died. "Believe it or no', lass, you most likely have family buried here."

It was the kirkyard outside the St. Clement's Church in Rodel, where Alexander MacLeod, a famous war hero and clan leader, had been entombed ages ago. Its grounds bore the names of several members of the MacLeod clan and the MacDonald clan, which crisscrossed and blended through the years until it was sometimes difficult to tell them apart. The church itself was a hollowed-out stone building that had been amazingly preserved and was now fiercely protected.

Gabriel could understand why he and Juliette had been deposited here. His cottage was a mere quarter of a mile down the road and to the east, up against the Rodel shore. This was the closest location the mansion could establish that possessed, not a door, but the remains of one—an arch.

Beside him, Juliette pulled away and began walking toward the back of the crumbling crypt. She seemed still suddenly, lost or hypnotized.

"Juliette?" he asked softly. The sound of her name on his tongue was like an inner caress—a taste of chocolate or a drink of smooth Scotch. Magical. Offhandedly, he wondered if he would always feel that way. "Wha' is it, lass?"

She'd come to a stop at the back of the crypt, her eyes glued to one of the pair of names carved there. "This one," she said. She spoke so quietly, he barely heard her. Gabriel moved to her side and looked down at the name. AGATHA MACDONALD, it read. BELOVED WIFE AND DAUGHTER.

"Wha' of her, little one?" he asked, placing his hand gently at her back.

"She was my ancestor," Juliette replied. Her tone was still rather flat, distant, and cold.

"Aye?" he asked. He tried to search his memory. Had he known Agatha MacDonald? She had lived such a long time ago. Her name sounded vaguely familiar, but far away. The dates on the stone marked her as having died very young. Most likely, she had lived here during one of his twenty- or thirty-year stints away from Scotland.

"Yes," Juliette said. "And that's not all," she continued. Slowly, deftly, Juliette raised her hand and placed her fingers to the name carved into the weathered rock. Her fingertips traced the letters with reverence. "Agatha MacDonald . . . ," she said, "was me."

CHAPTER TWENTY-TWO

Juliette rested on Gabriel's couch, staring into the fire that crackled merrily in his stone hearth. His cottage was nearly right on the shore; she could hear the waves crashing outside and the gulls crying in a muted frenzy.

Gabriel hadn't wanted her to walk the short distance to his home after she had spent so much of her energy healing him—and calling lightning on the Adarian. So he'd taken her to the front door of the church and used it to open another quick portal directly into his cottage in Rodel. Once there, he had wasted no time in sitting her down, wrapping her in blankets, and making her a big mug of really strong and creamy tea. It was delicious.

And he hadn't stopped there. Her clothes he had woven through with some of his magic gold. At first, she'd thought he was "bulletproofing" her against that strange weapon she'd seen the Adarian use. The shard gun. But he'd quickly informed her that gold was caustic to Adarians. The gold, therefore, served two purposes. It might diffuse a shard blast should she get hit—and it would keep an Adarian from laying hands on her for long.

Now, as the night waned into early-morning hours, Juliette thought of all she had learned since she'd woken up in Gabriel's arms in the master chamber of Slains Castle. Her past had always haunted her in her dreams. She had never been able to make heads or tails of her fascination, both conscious and unconscious, with years gone by. History had always been so vivid to her—she saw it and felt it and heard it and smelled it as if she'd been there. And now she knew why.

It all changed with that final, telling dream. One night, hundreds of years ago, she had fallen off the cliffs of Cruden Bay and had been buried in a kirkyard beside the resting place of Alexander MacLeod. Her name had been Agatha. That life and death had marked her last—until this one.

Now they were all coming back to her, one after another. She was remembering everything. Every name, every face, every season and mode of dress, were playing itself out through her memory like a film. Only, this one she hadn't simply watched. She'd taken part in it.

A part of her—a very small part—was surprised, perhaps a little shocked, as she was probably supposed to be. But most of her felt oddly complacent. She felt as though she'd slipped the final piece of a puzzle into its slot and suddenly, everything had become so clear. At last, the picture made some sense. The mystery was solved.

She had no idea why she had lived so many lives. She was a bit numb to the fact that reincarnation was even possible. But, again, it seemed natural that she had done so. And now that she recalled the billions upon billions of footsteps she had taken over the hills and crags and moors of Caledonia, she felt more a part of it than ever before. She was perhaps even more a part of it than one tall, dark, and handsome Gabriel Black.

Juliette glanced at the silver-eyed archangel as he moved through his house. He'd left her on the couch to warm up and rest while he went about securing the home with gold reinforcements and creating weapons, also made of gold. He seemed completely unfazed by her confession concerning her past lives. He was a bit surprised at first—but then his face had taken on a look of deep contemplation, and after a few seconds, he'd simply nodded.

"It makes a lo' of sense," he'd said. And that had been that.

Gabriel, Juliette thought. He was supposed to be the former Messenger Archangel. But hadn't she read something else about him, too? Admittedly, religious studies wasn't exactly her field of expertise, but it was virtually impossible to study the past without running across a religion or two here and there.

And something about the archangel Gabriel was scratching at her memory. He wasn't just the Messenger Archangel. He was perhaps the most famous of the four favored, known not only to Judaism and Christianity but to Islam as well. And there were possibly others. He was mainly revered as the communicator between the heavenly realms and the human realms. However, he was also supposed to be associated with new births—and resurrection.

Resurrected birth, Juliette thought. Reincarnation.

And isn't he also associated with the moon? she thought. Juliette glanced out the window over the sink. The moon hung heavy and full and stark white in the early-morning sky. Everything was coming together now. Gabriel was right. It made a lot of sense.

"So, let me get this straight," she said suddenly, speaking before she even knew she was going to do so.

Gabriel stopped midway through the living room and stared down at her. "Wha', luv?"

"Because you're the archangel who deals with reincarnation, I'm the lucky archess who gets to live fifty lives—and die fifty times?" She was suddenly, shockingly angry. She thought of the way she'd fallen off that cliff and a thread of resentment unwound within her. She'd lived so many lives and in each one, she'd possessed either no powers or only one or two of her abilities. She'd never been capable of healing anyone—not until now. And, lacking that all-important ability, either she had existed as a mere human in a world where human existence was painful—or she'd been marked a witch, shunned by her village, and persecuted relentlessly. She'd been murdered. She'd been stabbed, hung, jailed, raped, and even burned at the stake.

She could remember it all now. Every terrifying, bloodcurdling moment. And the warmth from Gabriel's hearth did nearly nothing to chase away the chill that stole over her.

Gabriel gazed steadily down at her, his eyes stark in his handsome face, his expression unreadable. After a very long moment of silence, he ran a hand through his hair and closed his eyes. "You figured that out, did you?" he asked softly.

"It was all your fault, wasn't it?" Juliette asked. She didn't raise her voice. In fact, she couldn't—her breath was stolen by the realizations washing over her.

"Och, lass, you have to know it was no' my doing. I never would have put you through any of that." He opened his eyes and they were glowing. His expression was terribly beseeching. He knelt before her on the rug in front of the couch and took her hands in his. She didn't pull away. What was the point?

"Jesus, Gabriel, do you know what I've been through?" she asked, her voice cracking with the weight of her pasts. She could almost smell the smoke that had thankfully smothered her before she'd finally succumbed to the flames when she'd been tied to a stake so many years ago. She recalled the *shhhk* sensation of a knife being embedded in her chest, its long tip nicking her spinal cord as it sliced through her. She knew what it felt like to be strangled. She'd drowned once. And the diseases . . . They were so bad, she couldn't bear the reflection.

"Yes," he told her.

Juliette opened her eyes, realizing that she had closed them against her memories.

"Yes, I do," he repeated softly. There was no doubt in his voice, no indecision in his tone. He looked her deep in the eyes and held her gaze steady. "I'm so sorry, lass," he said slowly, steadily. "Humans fear nothing so much as wha' they do no' understand. And I can imagine that they did no' understand you verra well at all."

She should have been insane. Remembering your own death should make you nuts somehow. Did it get any crazier than that? And to recall such *evil* deaths—such revoltingly vile tortures and endings—surely deserved at least a hint of madness. But instead of a dawning, yawning insanity, she sensed only . . . *knowledge.* Maybe this was what wisdom was? Could she be so vain as to call it that? Did simply dying make you more aware of what the preceding life was all about?

"Gabriel," she said. "Uriel was the Angel of Vengeance. Did Eleanore suffer because of him?"

"I though' aboot that," he replied softly. "When you told me about your past lives, I wondered if that might be why Eleanore was chased all her life. The Adarians hunted her relentlessly for her power." He stopped and looked down at the floor, lost in thought. "They hounded her with a vengeance, you might say."

"Christ," Juliette muttered. It was something beyond unfair that a soul should have to suffer the consequences of another being's existence. "He wasn't even the worst, Gabriel. My *God*," she whispered as she realized something awful. "What the hell does that mean for Azrael's archess? He was the Angel of Death, for crying out loud!"

Gabriel looked back up at her and Juliette cringed at the expression on his face. It was clear that this thought, too, had occurred to him. And that he feared the worst. "I don't know, luv," he said. "I don't know."

Juliette did not voice what she was thinking then. She didn't need to. She knew that he was thinking it as well. Whatever Azrael's archess either had already been forced to endure—or would be forced to endure—death was most surely a part of it. Perhaps not her own, but death nonetheless.

"Juliette," Gabriel said suddenly, pulling away a little so that he could dig the fingers of his hand into the front pocket of his jeans. Juliette watched him pull out a thin gold band—a bracelet entwined with intricate, scrolling writing. It was incredibly beautiful.

She stared down at it and then looked back up at him.

"This isn't the first piece of jewelry I had wanted to give you," he admitted with a sorry shrug. And then he sighed and held it out for her to take. Juliette frowned, unsure of what to do.

"What is it?"

"It's one of four wreaths given to my brothers an' I two thousand years ago. It's a weapon, more or less. Don' put it on," he told her. "Just put it in your pocket. It has the power to trap a person's supernatural abilities within their body. I want you to carry it with you...." He paused, took her hand in his, turned it over, and laid the bracelet in her open palm. "Just in case."

Juliette watched as he closed her fingers over it. "Okay," she said, resigning herself to the fact that fate was going to throw one paranormal thing at her after another. "I suppose every little bit might help."

He nodded, pleased that she seemed to understand.

"Once you put it on, luv, only you can take it off. Understand?"

She nodded.

"Good. Now, lass, you need food. An' I've made some stew."

A few minutes later, Gabriel had served them both a steaming bowl of soup and coupled it with warm, fresh bread. He set the dishes and bowls down in front of her on the coffee table and joined her on the couch, pulling her up against him, where she instantly felt warm and safe.

They ate in companionable silence, both of their gazes lost in the flames of the hearth. Juliette couldn't be certain what was going through Gabriel's head as they sat there, but her own mind was spinning with the events of the last week. She'd called lightning on an archangel in the refurbished master's chamber of Slains Castle less than two hours ago. There were so many impossibilities tied up into that single event alone, it was bewildering.

"Gabriel?"

"Yes, luv?"

"What are we going to do about the Adarian?"

Gabriel fell silent beside her for a long while, and Juliette wondered what was going through his head. She put herself in his position and tried to imagine what he was thinking. What was he *supposed* to do? According to him, his brothers, Max, and even Lily—there were *many* Adarians out there, and they were always looking for ways to get to the archesses. This was nothing new. Not really.

He couldn't very well launch a hunting party for the Adarians. Where they found one, they were sure to find more. And at the moment, the archangels knew too little about the powerful warriors. There was no way to be certain that the second battle was one they would win.

And now two of the archangels had very good reasons for not wanting to die.

Juliette blinked as she realized this. Both Uriel and Gabriel had found their archesses. Their lives had renewed meaning. And she could imagine that after hunting for something for two thousand years, they wouldn't want to take any chances in losing it. They wouldn't want to pull their archesses into an unwitting battle. After all, there was no way that Juliette would agree to stay out of a fight if she knew that someone she cared about stood a chance of being injured—or killed. Her power was too valuable. And she was willing to bet that Eleanore felt the same way.

"Never mind," she said suddenly, not wanting him to have to admit that he didn't know what to do. She could feel the heat radiating off him, and along with it was a new string of tension. She knew he was angry. She knew he was even afraid. She was instantly sorry for bringing the subject up.

On impulse, Juliette reached up, cupped the side of Gabriel's face, and gently pulled his gaze to hers. His silver eyes were glowing—testament to his turbulent emotions. They were so stark in his handsome face, they momentarily took her breath away. She felt herself flush warm with the memory of how those glowing eyes had claimed her, even as his body had done the same.

There was, at once, an emotion uncurling within Juliette that she had never experienced before. It was both soft and hard and it filled her with both anticipation and fear. It was poignant. And it was promising.

Suddenly, all she wanted to do was kiss him. As if he could read her mind, Gabriel moved in, gently taking her lips with his own. The kiss was tender and sweet and mirrored the dawning realizations inside of Juliette.

The kiss slowly ended and Gabriel's arms wrapped around her once more to pull her gently into him. His delicious food in her belly and the smell of his soap on her skin and the warmth of his home protecting her began to lull her to a place where the rest of the world melted. Little by little, Juliette accepted. She relaxed—and eventually, she slept.

CHAPTER TWENTY-THREE

Juliette came awake with a slow, meandering awareness. She was enveloped in warmth and a mixture of hard and soft. She heard crackling and popping and knew there was a fire burning nearby. A moment's uncertainty shot through her, but she smelled no smoke. She caught a whiff of masculine-scented soap instead, and opened her eyes.

A simply decorated room surrounded her. The walls were wood beams woven through with gold, the window was draped in a curtain of white and gold, and the sheet over her was white with gold threading. She blinked down at it. Her body felt sore . . . but deliciously so. She tentatively moved her legs and instantly felt the resulting twinge between them. Memories flooded her and she shivered. Then, slowly, she smiled.

"Good mornin', lass," drawled a deep, rumbling voice. As always, his accent purred across her skin like a delicious promise. He was behind her, spooning her, and she was in his bed. She turned her head to look up and found him on his elbow, gazing steadily down at her.

"How long have you been watching me?" she asked.

He smiled, flashing straight white teeth. "No' long enough," he said as he gently brushed a lock of her hair from her forehead.

Slowly, she rolled over in the bed to face him. *Good God,* she thought, as she stared up at the curve of his chin, the broad plane of his shoulders, and the vast expanse of muscle across his chest and midsection. *I'm in bed with an archangel.*

"Are you hungry?" he asked, his forefinger curled beneath her chin to raise her eyes. His own eyes were twinkling with amusement and obvious pride.

She blushed, having been caught at her blatant ogling. "Yeah," she admitted. "I am."

"Good, then. I'll make you somethin' to eat."

Thirty minutes later, they were sitting at Gabriel's kitchen table, sharing a Scottish breakfast sans the blood pudding, which she admitted she just couldn't stomach the thought of. Gabriel had laughed and acquiesced.

Now they sipped strong, creamy tea and talked about their favorite subject—the history of Scotland. Juliette had never had this before. She had never known anyone who loved the land as much as she did, and she'd certainly never had a conversation with someone who knew as much about its past as she did. Now that she could actively recall aspects of the last two thousand years from a personal perspective—it gave new meaning to the subject. *Gabriel* gave it new meaning. Because even as she had experienced it, both good and bad—so had he.

Somehow, as they sat there across from each other at the round wooden table, their elbows firmly planted on the surface, their tea mugs never far from their lips, they managed to touch upon all the amusing aspects of the land's history. His stories were self-deprecating and adorable, his voice like a Scottish lullaby. She laughed and he chuckled and the morning flew by in a new and special kind of camaraderie.

"I've go' somewhere I want to take you," he told her

after they'd finished off their third cup of tea. "Are you up for a field trip?" he asked, silver eyes twinkling.

"Absolutely," she said, finding herself in a wonderful mood despite the lingering dangers associated with being an archess. What was it, exactly, that had put the smile on her face? The tea? The breakfast? The company? All of the above and more . . . "Where are we going?"

"You'll see."

They piled into his little car and Juliette had to hide her smile at seeing someone of his size fold himself the way he did in order to fit into the European vehicle. To her, all the cars in the UK looked like Matchbox toys. It was incredibly economical and it was easy to find a parking space, but she wasn't sure the engineers had men with six feet and four inches of height in mind when they'd designed them.

She, on the other hand, fit perfectly. It was a thin silver lining on the rain cloud of being small.

They wound their way through the moors and peat bogs, and she stared out the window as they drove, uncommonly easy in her peaceful, companionable silence. She gazed at the way the mists parted and retreated with the coming day. The heather was becoming greener and in late summer, it would blanket the countryside with royal purple. The sky was blue but for the faintest streamers of lingering clouds. The rolling hills beckoned, appearing impossible in their symmetry. It was enchanting.

Juliette turned from the window to glance at the man driving. His black long-sleeved sweater hugged the curves of his hard muscles and reminded her of how those muscles felt when holding her down. On a bed. As he slowly drove into her again and again . . .

Juliette's eyes widened, her breath catching, her

cheeks flushing horribly hot. The thought had overcome her with sudden ferocity. She hadn't expected her mind to go there in that manner. But now that it had . . . she was stuck in that gutter, unable to pull herself out. She couldn't stop thinking about how he had felt, how his silver eyes had been glowing like liquid lightning, how he had teased her and tormented her with gentle, expert persistence.

Juliette rolled her eyes and put her heated forehead to the glass of her window. The contact cooled her a little and helped somewhat. But he was still there, filling her senses from both the inside and out.

She could remember the words he'd whispered to her in Gaelic. . . . She'd even understood them. And now that she could recall her past lives, she knew *why* she'd understood them. They were precious words. And they confused her in a new, terrible, and wonderful way.

"Mo sheacht míle grá thú."

It didn't exactly have a literal English translation. It was more of an emotion put into the sound of words than anything else. *You are my love,* those words said. *You are my love seven thousand times over.*

You are my love.

Juliette blinked at the blurring of Caledonia as it sped by. Gabriel loved her. *He loves me,* she thought. *My God. I have the love of an archangel.*

"We're here, lass."

The car began to slow and Juliette turned in time to see Gabriel pull the vehicle off the main road and onto a smaller, winding road that led up a hill. It took her a few seconds, but as the small cabin at the top of the hill became clearer—so did the standing stones just on the other side.

Now she knew where she was. She'd been here before. Just not in this lifetime.

Gabriel glanced over at her as he maneuvered the car

into the parking lot and shut it down. His smile was soft, his eyes shiny. He reached into the backseat for his jacket, and then got out of the car and slid the garment on. Then he made his way to her side. He opened her door and offered her his gloved hand. "Come with me, luv."

She smiled up at him and took his hand, relishing the way his fingers closed so protectively over hers. She could feel the electric current of his strength even through the material of both of their gloves. He was very powerful.

And he was hers.

"I played here once," she told him softly as he led her from the car to the trail that would take them to the stones. "As a child."

"Aye, I imagine you did," he said with a smile. The wind tossed his hair and brushed the sable locks against the leather of his jacket. "I imagine you've been here many times."

They moved up the trail, their hands intertwined, and the wind kissed their cheeks, welcoming them into the past. The tops of the ancient stones appeared first, cresting the rise with monumental grace. Juliette stared at them with wide eyes as she and Gabriel approached, suitably quiet and reverent.

Clachan Calanais. These were the Callanish Stones, erected thousands upon thousands of years ago—built by a people that no one knew anything about, and for a reason that no one could discern. There were thirteen main stones in a circle that measured around thirty feet in diameter. At the center of the circle was a burial cairn that had been used over and over again by generations long past. No one knew why it had been placed there to begin with. The Callanish Stones dated to several thousand years BC. They were all tall, averaging at around ten feet, but some were taller than others. Rows of other stones extended from the main circle in long lines.

Juliette gazed out over them and remembered touching each one. At one time, she'd been a child running between them, sprinting as fast as her little legs could go, placing her tiny palm to their surfaces as if to absorb their magic. That had been several lifetimes ago.

"Do you know why I come here?" Gabriel asked softly beside her, his hand still grasping hers. She looked up at him, studying his profile as he gazed with ancient eyes out over the primordial landscape. "This place is older than I am," he told her. "I walk the Earth feelin' as though I am a livin', breathin' secret. I've seen countries come an' go, wars won an' lost. . . . Bu' here" — he paused, shaking his head — "I'm finally embraced by somethin' that knows more than I do." He looked down at her and smiled a poignant smile. "These stones keep secrets from *me*."

Juliette grew lost in that winsome expression. She was drowning in the mercury of his eyes and in the landscape around them that whispered epitaphs and promises with each breeze that sailed through the passages of stone.

She understood. Somewhere deep down, she was able to feel Gabriel's confession as if it were her own. She turned to fully face the archangel, reaching to take his other gloved hand. He cocked his head to one side, his expression at once unreadable.

And then she stood on her tiptoes, reaching to whisper something in his ear, and he bent to meet her. "I have a secret, too," she told him softly, sending the words across his skin with wicked deliberation. She saw him shiver and smiled when he pulled her closer.

"Aye, luv?" he asked softly. She could hear the smile in his voice and see the sides of his lips curled up in a smile.

"Aye," she replied, mimicking his accent. She giggled

softly and then paused, stretching the moment out. "I do," she continued. "But I'm not going to tell you what it is," she teased. "Unless you can catch me."

With that, she ripped her hands out of his and headed full speed toward the nearest stone. Grinning ear to ear, she pressed her palm to its surface, sensed the familiar buzz of antiquity, and then hurried on, moving as fast as her booted feet would carry her.

Behind her, she heard a deep laugh and it sent delicious shivers through her. She knew he was taking chase and she knew he could easily catch her if he wanted to, but she didn't care. She laughed as she ran, touching the stones as if tagging them, one after another. They seemed to laugh along with her, urging her on, giving her moral support as she raced to brush every surface before he caught her.

He was giving her a head start. It was as if he knew she needed to touch every stone. She crossed the field separating two lines of the ancient monuments and raced to the other side, pressing her palm to the nearest cold, hard surface. She spun, ran to the next one, and jumped when Gabriel came out from behind it, having moved so fast, she hadn't seen it. She laughed in surprise and bolted in the opposite direction, catching a stone here and there that she had missed.

Finally, she was nearing the end. She heard footsteps coming up behind her and she squealed, feeling his familiar heat drawing nearer. One more stone . . . she touched it—and Gabriel's arms were snaking around her, pulling her up short and lifting her. She gasped as he swung her around toward the same stone and lowered her beside it, her back pressed against the weathered rock, his own hard body locking her in. She was breathing hard as he leaned in, his smile cruel and beautiful, his eyes laughing.

"I've captured you," he told her softly, bracing his arm

against the rock by her head, caging her in before him. "Now, wha's your secret, lass?"

"Her secret is that she can heal people with no more than her touch," came a deep voice from behind Gabriel.

Gabriel spun, turning his back to Juliette, shielding her where she stood against the tall, protective stone. But she peeked around the archangel's strong body, needing to know what was happening.

Three men stood several yards away. They were tall and handsome and all of them wore black. The man who had spoken was obviously their leader. He was an African-American man, incredibly muscular, so that his clothes stretched taut across his body. His light amber eyes were stark in the frame of his face. Beside him was a man who looked Italian, with olive skin and thick black hair and deep, dark eyes. To his left was a blond man with very light blue eyes.

The men watched Gabriel carefully, not taking their gazes off him. The strange, staticlike feeling she could now sense in the air reminded her of something.

Adarians.

Her eyes widened with the realization. They made her feel the way the Adarian who had attacked her in her hotel room had made her feel. Her gaze slid from their faces to the weapons in their hands. She recognized the strange guns as the same kind that the Adarian had been carrying in Slains Castle. The shard gun. It had done horrible things to Gabriel, petrifying his body where the shots had hit home. The wounds had been very hard to heal, draining much more of her strength than she'd thought they were going to.

"The General would have been here to do this himself," the black man said, "but he's having trouble with the sun these days." He smiled a secret smile, flashing white teeth. And then he was all seriousness again. "Don't make her see you die before we take her, Gabriel." The Adarian's expression was beseeching, his amber eyes flashing in warning. "That's not how you want to say good-bye."

All three weapons were leveled on Gabriel. She could imagine the damage they would do if they went off.

There would be nothing she could do to save him then.

CHAPTER TWENTY-FOUR

She couldn't let him die. Not for her. Not like this. She would turn herself in first.

"Gabriel—"

"I know wha' you're thinkin', lass," he told her without taking his eyes off the Adarians before her. "Bu' put it out of your head, luv, because they'll kill me whether you surrender to them or no."

"Now, why did you go and tell her something like that?" the Adarian asked, shaking his head.

Juliette thought about what Gabriel had said. The truth of his words dawned on her like a horrid black plague, stealing over her in a nauseating way. They weren't going to take the chance that he would come after them. They weren't going to allow him to go back to the mansion and collect his brothers and hunt them down.

This was it. They would have what they wanted. Why allow anyone to take it away from them?

Oh dear God, she thought, feeling her chest tighten and her fingers go numb. *No, no, no* . . . She glanced at the guns they held, certain that at any moment they would pull their triggers—and that would be the end of her world.

"Juliette, we're giving you the choice," the blond man

said, leveling his icy eyes on her and filling her with what felt like an arctic chill. "Come with us and we won't kill him." His tone sounded so reasonable. But the air was so thick with tense, pent-up magic now, it was barely breathable.

"Juliette," Gabriel said tightly, drawing her attention to him. "Do. Not. Move."

They'll shoot, she thought. It was a final kind of thought, a deciding factor in fate's design. *I don't have to move,* she thought next. Conscious deliberation was slipping from her, hurriedly being overrun by instinct. Something inside was taking over. She glanced up at the blue sky and thought of lightning.

But the Adarian with the ice-blue eyes was watching her. "You can't get us all, Juliette. And those of us you miss will shoot."

She didn't like his eyes. They made her feel funny inside. Tired, even. Weak. When she stared at him, she felt as if she were falling. She shook her head, averting her eyes. "What are you?" she found herself asking, knowing full well that he was using some kind of power on her.

"Leave her alone," Gabriel growled in front of her. She could feel a ripple of power emanate from him like a whip.

I can't give myself away like that again, she scolded herself. She'd made the mistake of looking at the sky and the Adarian had guessed that she was going to try to call lightning. She licked her lips, her legs almost buckling now, her heart racing so fast, she couldn't tell one beat from the next. She considered her abilities. There was the lightning. But the Adarian was right. She couldn't get them all, could she? Then there was telekinesis. But there was nothing out here that she could move. Then she could heal. That was it. That was all she had—or that she knew of, anyway. She hugged herself, realizing that she was trembling violently. She glanced at their guns again and wondered how many more seconds she had before the world would come crashing down.

The wind brushed past them, ripping another violent shiver from Juliette. She exhaled a shaky breath and ice crystals formed in the air.

What the hell?

The temperature was dropping. Juliette frowned. It shouldn't be dropping this fast—the afternoons normally warmed up. What was happening? The cold was stealing her concentration. She glanced up at the Adarians and met the gaze of the man with the dark hair. He was watching her knowingly, noting the way she shivered. He smiled at her trembling reaction to the cold.

"You're doing this," she accused softly, her teeth chattering. He didn't bother to respond. It was clear that he was.

"I'll give you to the count of three, Juliette," the black man said. "And then this is going down one way or another."

It's now or never, she thought. If she waited any longer, they would shoot—and she would freeze. These men were beyond powerful. It had come down to do or die. And possibly both.

So, Juliette visualized a hand reaching down within herself and delving into a dark, secret abyss. From there, it ripped up something magical, something that shimmered and glowed in the otherwise stygian darkness. The hand tossed that shimmering magic hard into the air and it scattered, leaving her body and entering the real world.

In that moment, she focused the tiny motes of light, the sparkling, glittering tendrils of her power, and told them to take over. *Do what you have to do,* she thought. *Save us.*

Behind her, the ancient stone of the Callanish formation shifted. For more than five thousand years, it hadn't moved. But now the erected, weathered rock budged, moving in the earth behind her so that she gasped and lunged forward, at once terrified that she would be crushed.

Crushed.

Gabriel lunged for the biggest Adarian, the leader who was less than three feet away. A shard gun went off, its blast rippling through the air along with the sound of the earth moaning as the stone behind her continued to awaken in its ancient grave.

Juliette forced her fear for Gabriel to a back burner and continued to allow her instincts to rule. The weather she had contemplated earlier was suddenly there, racing to meet her demands. The clouds moved in at apocalyptic speed, darkening the sky above them at a frightening rate. There was a hand on her arm, its grip bruisingly tight, and she yanked hard, thinking only of escape.

But her power was still in control. She had given it free rein and it had responded with a roar of triumph. The stone behind her ripped from the earth with a horrid, monstrous sound, and the grip on her arm lessened.

Again, she yanked away, this time freeing herself from her captor's grip and stumbling sideways to tumble to the cold, hard earth. It had frosted over with rime from the Adarian's power, and ice crystals sliced into the palms of her hands and dampened the knees of her jeans. She ignored the sting, shoving herself to her booted feet in time to spin around and focus.

Him, she thought, narrowing her green gaze on the blond with blue eyes. He'd been the one to try to get into her head—to put her to sleep. He'd also been the one to grab her. He was the one she wanted to fry.

The sky responded, opening up with a vengeance as lightning crashed to the ground, cascading over the Adarian's tall form like a white-hot blanket. The sound was deafening, forcing Juliette to her knees once more.

She pressed her hands to her ears, but it was too late. A ringing followed the blast and she rocked back on her heels in time to see something dark and ominous float over their heads.

She looked up. The Callanish standing stone was no longer standing. It was hovering above them, a massive rock spaceship, heavy and menacing, a portent of certain death. *My God,* she thought numbly, knowing that it was her own power that held the ancient stone aloft.

Several yards away, one Adarian lay facedown in the grass, his body smoldering slowly, his clothes blackened by the lightning blast. Gabriel and the big Adarian were fighting in horrid, painful hand-to-hand combat. Gabriel threw the giant black man against a stone, the stone shifted ever so slightly, and the Adarian came after Gabriel in turn, grasping him around the neck.

The third Adarian stood still and somber, his black hair stirring in the crazy wind that tried futilely to balance out the heat from the lightning and the cold from the Adarian's earlier use of his power. His black eyes studied Juliette closely, carefully, his expression unreadable. Juliette glared back at him, no longer in control of her emotions or the magical mayhem they had wrought.

The Callanish stone answered her hatred, shooting forward through the sky to rush his tall form. The Adarian ducked and rolled, moving with inhuman speed so that the stone crashed to the ground in a spray of dirt and rubble that forced Juliette to shield her eyes.

A few seconds later, she lowered her arm again. The dark-haired Adarian was rolling and rising, his narrowed, angry gaze turned on Juliette. She swallowed hard, feeling the familiar, insipid weakness steal through her as her powers continued to run rampant and drain her. She glanced up at Gabriel and the Adarian he was fighting.

Where's the gun? she thought, noting that neither of them held a weapon. The Adarian must have lost it at some point during their struggle. She tried to search the icy ground for the gun, hunting for a hint of black or silver amid the white and brown. She found it lying in a patch of weeds several yards from Gabriel, but the dark-haired Adarian that she had attacked was standing now, capturing her attention once more. He got his legs beneath him and began to stride toward her.

Juliette's magic instantly responded to the renewed threat. The stone that had dropped into the earth shifted once more where it lay in the cold ground. The Adarian slowed, his dark gaze cutting to the immense slab of rock. And then she felt more of her strength rip away from her like the peeling of an onion as the stone lifted and tilted menacingly, a massive beast once more free of the bonds of gravity.

The Adarian ducked as the stone soared toward him, but Juliette knew ahead of time what he would do. Her abilities were adjusting, and so was the Callanish stone. It lowered as the Adarian did, and Juliette shut her eyes tight, unable to watch when it trapped him beneath its dense mass in a second spray of dirt and grass.

"Juliette!"

Juliette opened her eyes and spun at the sound of Gabriel's voice. "Get to the door!" he commanded harshly, gesturing to the door of the tourist shop at the top of the hill. Behind him, the Adarian he had been fighting was just pushing himself up from the ground once more as Gabriel dove third-base style for the shard gun his opponent had dropped. Before he could reach it, the Adarian lifted his right hand and the air rippled before him, a strange iridescent wave of force that draped itself over Gabriel's prone form and clearly began to crush him beneath it.

Juliette cried out in fear, unable to stop herself from rushing toward him. At the same time, she called the fallen shard gun to her, willing it into her grasp as if she were using the force. It responded, shooting up into the air and throwing itself into her hand. She gripped it hard, ignoring the sting its impact had caused, and aimed it at the Adarian. His amber eyes widened, only for a moment, and then she pulled the trigger.

Nothing happened.

She pulled it again, just as the Adarian was beginning to relax, his shocked expression melting into one of smug relief. Again, nothing happened.

The Adarian stood slowly, his amber eyes glowing, and moved toward her in easy, purposeful strides. The wind howled, and she groaned as the Adarian she had crushed with the stone began to shift beneath it, very gradually hauling the monstrous rock off himself.

Her heart hammered. She knelt beside Gabriel, but was unable to touch him; a field of hard air had wrapped itself around him, suffocating him and pressing him relentlessly into the ground.

"Let him go!" she screamed at the black man. She knew it was his magic that was doing this. "Let him go and I'll come with you!"

But the Adarian only smiled and shook his head. "It's too late for that now, little archess. You'll come with us anyway."

A roar of rage worked its way up her throat. Her body felt wrung out by the exorcism of power she'd suffered, but there was enough left there somewhere. It kept her breathing. It made her heart pump blood. It was there — and it rallied at the injustice, focusing on the large man and his ancient, horrible magic.

The sky split open a second time, the wind parted, and white-hot electricity shot through the air, filling it with the heat of a thousand suns. Juliette ducked, hiding her face as the bolt of lightning encompassed the Adarian, enveloping him in a whiteout of cacophonous rage.

She screamed when the sound ripped through her

ears and the rumble tore through her body like a cosmic thump. But her hands sank through the now-free air where they had been resting on the Adarian's force field, and she was once more touching Gabriel's jet-black hair.

"Gabriel!" she screamed, barely hearing her own voice through the numb ringing in her ears. "Gabriel!" she cried again, not knowing what else to say. But he was breathing; she could see his broad back rising and falling. He slowly heaved himself up with one arm and rolled over, gasping for air. She hurriedly brushed his hair off his forehead with the hand that didn't hold the shard gun.

She was going to ask him if he was okay, but the earth groaned again and her gaze cut to the large stone slab several yards away. The Adarian she had crushed would be free any second now.

"We have to get out of here," she said. Her voice still sounded far away, hollow and strange. And weakness was stealing over her now, nearly as potent as a drug.

A few feet away, in the opposite direction, a blond figure stirred on the ground, moaning low and then grunting in pain.

They hadn't much time.

"Get to the door," Gabriel repeated between shaky, ragged breaths. He sat up and shot her a fierce look. "Like you should have done," he reprimanded her.

Juliette ignored the scolding and rose to her feet. A wave of horrible weakness nearly took her out. Spots swam before her vision and her hand came to her forehead. She closed her eyes, wondering if she was going to faint.

But Gabriel was standing then, his presence warm and solid beside her. He bent and lifted her, grasping her firmly in his strong arms. And then he ran, carrying her swiftly over the hill toward the wooden building at the top.

She knew what he was going to do. There had been only one figure milling around behind the windows when they had arrived earlier. The salesperson would be alone inside. Gabriel was going to have to trust that the man wouldn't see him open a portal through the building's front door.

Juliette felt strange. She raised her hand to her stomach, allowing it to go limp there so that she wouldn't drop the shard gun she'd stolen from the Adarian. And then she let her head drop against Gabriel's shoulder. The world was tilting around her. She felt weightless and empty. She'd never felt like this before in her life.

As Gabriel moved them through the swirling, interdimensional doorway, Juliette closed her eyes. Blackness slipped in like an army of shadows that had been waiting to lay siege. She frowned and tried to speak. The tiniest sound escaped her lips.

And she was out.

CHAPTER TWENTY-FIVE

Gabriel's heart was aching. Juliette weighed nothing in his arms. It was like lifting a child. He couldn't believe what he had just seen—what she had just done to save them. He hadn't known she'd been capable of such immense power. The lightning bolts were impressive enough. But the stone ... *Callanish,* he thought numbly. It would never be the same.

It didn't matter. Not to him—nothing mattered but Juliette and her painful, ominous lack of substance in his arms.

"Michael!" he bellowed into the portal as it swirled before him and he raced through its kaleidoscope lights. She needed the Warrior Archangel's healing touch. Gabriel could feel her essence slipping; she'd pushed herself way too far. She'd moved the earth and altered history, and now she was fading.

"Michael!" he cried again, choking on a sob he had no power to contain. He gritted his teeth and rapidly closed the portal behind him, and even as he did, he was besieged by his brother, who had apparently heard his harsh cries.

Michael strode toward him, still dressed in the shoulder holster and guns he wore to work as a cop in New York City. The living room was otherwise empty but for

Max, who had risen from his place at a table that bore a chessboard and two mugs of what looked like fresh coffee.

"Give her to me," the blond archangel commanded, stealing Juliette's tiny, limp form from Gabriel's arms. It was everything he could do not to rip her back out of his brother's grasp and clutch her to his chest. He let her go—but it was the hardest thing he'd ever done.

"What happened?" Max asked.

Gabriel opened his mouth to answer, but he had no air in his lungs. He looked down at Juliette's still form where Michael had laid her down on the couch, and his breath was lost to him. His chest ached. He forced it open, sucked in air, and said, "The Adarians happened."

The shard gun slid off her stomach and Michael caught it, tossing it easily to Max. Then the Warrior Archangel's attention was instantly back on Juliette. "She's like Eleanore was," he muttered, placing his hand to her chest and frowning worriedly. Several months ago, Eleanore had brought herself to a similar state by healing several people at once of what would have been mortal wounds. "What the hell did she do?" Michael asked. He closed his eyes and his palm began to glow where it was pressed against her body.

Gabriel watched with wide eyes. He was shaking. He could feel the hard tremble making its way through his body like a horrible disease.

"She'll be fine," Michael whispered, obviously concentrating on his healing, but wanting to assure his brother. "She's just weak. Just like Ellie."

Suddenly Max's strong hand was on Gabriel's shoulder. "Tell me what happened."

"They attacked us at Callanish," Gabriel replied, his gaze glued to Juliette's beautiful face and her now fluttering eyelids. "Somehow, they found us. They knew we would be there." He couldn't comprehend it. He hadn't felt them arrive. He hadn't heard them. Where were they getting this new power to find the archesses and head them off without warning?

Max was quiet behind him. Juliette's pink lips parted and a soft groan escaped them. She exhaled and Michael sat back on his heels, removing his hand. Juliette's eyes fluttered open. Gabriel took her hand and leaned in. "Och, lass," he whispered softly, "you truly are an angel."

She blinked up at him for a moment and then smiled a shy smile.

"How many were there?" Max asked, moving around Gabriel to take a seat on the coffee table beside him.

"Three," Gabriel replied as Juliette tried to sit up. He pressed his hand to her abdomen and kept her down, shaking his head reprimandingly.

She blushed and shot him a frustrated look, but acquiesced, resting back against the cushions instead. He grabbed another pillow from the side of the couch and slid it under her hair. Her soft brown waves cascaded over it and the edge of the couch, nearly coming to the floor.

"There were three," he repeated softly, gazing at his archess with the pride he felt. "She moved fifteen tons of rock to save us. She worked a bloody miracle—didn't you, luv?"

"I destroyed Callanish," she said softly, her brow furrowing slightly with a frown.

"It's nothin' we can't fix," he assured her. And it was true. He and his brothers and Max could set anything right—even something as ancient and sacred as Callanish.

"The Adarians have gone too far," Michael said.

"You're right," Max conceded. "But we've been here before. Things are coming to a head."

Juliette looked from Gabriel to Michael, who was rising from the carpet now to lower himself into a love seat a few feet away. "Thank you for healing me," she said. "I wasn't feeling so hot."

Michael nodded and smiled warmly. "I imagine not. And it was my pleasure," he told her.

"What exactly happened?" Max asked, clearly wanting more detail than Gabriel had thus far provided.

"I'll tell you," Gabriel supplied, glancing over at him. "Bu' first, where are the others?"

"Uriel's filming," Max said. "And Eleanore's with him. Azrael is sleeping."

Gabriel nodded. The mansion was obviously on a similar schedule to Scotland's at that moment; it was daylight here. So Azrael would be belowground, in his private chambers. "Get Uriel back here an' find us some shade so you can wake Az up. I've go' some rather important news to share."

Thirty minutes later, Uriel and Eleanore had joined them in the mansion's massive living room. Eleanore had gone directly to the couch to sit beside Juliette and the two had been conversing quietly ever since. Max managed to shift the mansion's presence so that it resided in darkness, and now a full moon hung low in the sky outside the mansion's massive windows.

Azrael had joined them as well. His tall, dark form leaned against one of the walls, his golden eyes glowing eerily in the frame of his otherworldly, angelic face. His arms were crossed over his broad chest and his black-booted feet were crossed at the ankles. He gazed steadily at Gabriel, and Gabe could feel an unsettled vibe coming from the former Angel of Death. He was in a hard mood. They'd woken him early and he obviously hadn't had enough sleep.

Gabriel closed the blinds and turned to face his family. "Max, wha' progress have you made with the shard gun?" he asked the guardian.

Max shook his head, taking off his glasses and cleaning them on the front of his brown suit. He almost always wore a suit. He always looked like a cross between a librarian and a businessman unless he was in combat mode, and then he wore fatigues and lost the glasses. "None," he said. "I'm not surprised you want to know about that; you've been shot more than the rest of us combined with the damn things."

"How many times has he been shot?" Juliette asked.

"Thirteen, including the blasts he took while the two of you were at Slains," replied Azrael in his deep, cool voice.

Gabriel looked from Az to Juliette and found her staring at him with wide eyes.

"And the blasts hurt like nothing you've ever felt," added Uriel. Juliette's eyes widened farther.

"Shut up," Gabriel told his brother.

Uriel shot him an unapologetic look. "Being healed of the wounds is almost worse."

"I have no idea how they operate the weapons," continued Max, wisely changing the subject. "But pulling the trigger doesn't work and neither does taking it apart and putting it back together again."

"You need to be an Adarian to make it work," Gabriel said, spearing Uriel with one last hard look and then running a hand through his hair. He'd given this a lot of thought since Juliette had tried to use the Adarian's shard gun against their enemies. "Juliette tried to use one as well an' failed. None of us have go' Adarian blood running through our veins. I'm willing to bet that's the secret."

The room was silent for a long while as everyone in the room contemplated what Gabriel had just said.

Max addressed Gabriel. "Was this all that you wanted to talk to us about?" he asked, obviously catching on that the Adarian shard guns were only the tip of the iceberg that night.

"No," Gabriel replied. "No, that's no' all." Juliette's past lives were swirling through his head like a tornado. He needed to tell them about the archesses and how the circumstances of their existences were inextricably linked to the former duties of their archangels. It was an impending storm of information and it hovered on the horizon, loud and ominous. But this needed to be done.

He glanced once at Azrael and the vampire archangel straightened. He dropped his arms, coming to his full impressive height of six feet and six inches. It was clear from the way his glowing gold eyes were going from orange to red that he'd already entered Gabriel's mind and read his thoughts. And it was clear that he knew what they meant.

"It's about the archesses," Gabriel said, his gaze locked on Azrael's. "There's somethin' you all need to know."

Samael nodded at the tall, blond actor as the man stepped up to the doorway of Sam's office and prepared to knock on the open door. Sam's nod saved McNabb the trouble.

"Come in, Law."

"Sir," Law replied, falling easily once more into his role as one of Samael's . . . *employees* — and not just the actor client the rest of the world thought him to be.

"Close the door behind you," Sam instructed.

Law closed the door and came to stand before Samael's desk. Sam leaned back in his desk and steepled his fingers before him. "The Adarians are moving quickly."

"I heard," Law replied, nodding once in agreement. "Would you like me to head into the field?"

"Yes," Samael said. He leaned forward in the plush leather chair and stood gracefully, coming to his full impressive height. Then he turned away from the actor and moved to the vast windows behind him. He stood before them, sliding his hands into the pockets of his charcoal gray suit trousers. It was early evening in Chicago, and the sun had already gone down. Twilight cast a dim glow over the surface of the lake and the metal in the high-rises that made up its skyline.

"The four favored tend to throw a few wrenches into our plans every now and then," Sam said, his voice light with a touch of humor. "Still, thus far in the grand scheme of things, everything has gone according to design."

"But?" Law questioned. Samael smiled. McNabb was good at knowing what was coming next.

"However," Sam said as he turned back to face the blond man, "this last attack by the Adarians on the archess was a touch too close for my tastes. This is a pivotal moment. Everything must go exactly according to preparations." He moved around his large desk and made his way to the marble fireplace set into one wall. The fire blazed merrily, warm and inviting. Sam braced his right arm against the mantel and leaned in. His wristwatch gleamed in the crackling firelight. "The archess is very precious, Law." He said this as he felt it—with a deepness he did not fully comprehend. "They all are."

"I understand," Law said slowly. "I'll make certain she has what she needs to protect herself."

"See that you do," Sam said, still gazing into the leaping light. He pushed away from the fireplace and turned to face McNabb. "Does Uriel suspect anything of you?" he asked, changing the subject. Lawrence McNabb and the archangel Uriel had been working together for the last year and a half on the *Comeuppance* series, and so far the former Angel of Vengeance had yet to make any indication that he thought of McNabb as anything but a costar. But it didn't hurt to double-check.

"No, sir," said Law. "Your magic slides right under his

radar." Law smiled a winning smile, flashing straight white teeth in a grin that would have made many women—and men—swoon.

"Good." The last thing Sam needed was to have to recast someone in the *Comeuppance* series. His personal life might be filled with archangels and vampires and supernatural creatures galore, but he was, among many things, a very famous media mogul and he hadn't achieved that goal by being sloppy. Work did matter.

Other things just mattered more.

CHAPTER TWENTY-SIX

It was late Thursday night in Luskentyre when Gabriel once more opened a portal through the mansion to take them back to Scotland to retrieve a few things. They'd decided that staying in the mansion was the safest best for the archesses and their loved ones at this juncture. Eleanore's rather stubborn parents had finally been coerced from their cabin in the mountains and set up in one of the many guest suites.

Then Juliette accompanied Max to speak with her own parents.

She'd decided that the best way to broach the supernatural subject of what she was was to simply come right out and prove it. So, she'd put out the fire in the hearth with a wave of her hand and then floated her mother's stainless steel cookware around the kitchen. And that was more or less that.

Her parents were still shocked and they would definitely need time to adjust. But they agreed to come and live in the mansion for the time being as well, and that was where Max and Michael were at the moment—helping them move their belongings. Her father had to get someone to cover his classes. Her mother was going to take a sabbatical. They were coping.

Juliette had considered asking Gabriel whether they

could bring Sophie in as well. It was an erratic and worried thought—that something might happen to her best friend. But then she'd considered it carefully and realized she had no logical reason to fret about Soph. The girl didn't even know about Juliette's power, much less the rest of this madness. Why would she be in danger?

In the meantime, Juliette had left some important things behind in her cottage when Gabriel had whisked her off to Slains on Tuesday afternoon. She needed her laptop, wanted her clothes—and rather desperately longed for Nessie and his familiar, comforting Parma Violets smell. She also had to check in her cottage key and sign out with the owner.

The portal swirled to life before them, and by this time Juliette was used to the sight. She also had to pride herself on being used to the strange pushing-pulling sensation of walking through the portal and into her waiting cottage on the other side. They stepped through and the portal closed behind them.

The cottage was utterly still in the darkness. Gabriel waved a hand at the peat-burning stove and a fire leapt to life behind the grate. Juliette's brows raised a little at the display. She'd seen so much and he'd given her so many surprises, and yet she wondered whether she would ever get used to this new, powerful world he had introduced her to.

The next thing he did was touch his hand to the door-frame and close his eyes. Veins of gold began to appear in the wood of the cottage's walls. It spread and grew until even the curtains were laced with fine threads of the honey-colored metal.

She could only shake her head and watch.

When he'd finished, he removed his hand and opened his eyes. "Get your things, lass. I'll finish up out here."

She let out a breath and nodded. She headed to the

bedroom, where she pulled her carry-on bag out from under her bed. All the clothes that Samael had somehow whisked magically into her room and placed onto her bed a few days ago were now hanging in her closet.

More magic.

She accepted it with an ambivalent sigh and began sifting through them, picking and choosing what she would place into her bag. But as she did so, she noticed something she was certain hadn't been there before. On the shelf above the hangers was the spine of a single book. It was gilded in gold and read, *Dorcha Draíodóir*.

Juliette frowned and pulled the leather-bound book from the shelf. It was thick and heavy. She opened it to the beginning to find a handwritten note scrawled across the title page.

> *Dear Juliette:*
>   *I found this in the Stornoway library. A little light reading to get you started on that miniseries.*
>
>   *Best,*
>   *Law*

Juliette blinked down at the note, bewildered. She ran her hand over the pile of pages, noticing that one of them had been folded down. She opened the book to that page and began to read. It was written in Gaelic, but she understood. . . .

> *. . . this time, the archess was ready for the assault. She had come too far, lived too long, to allow the black wizard to drain her in this manner. So, as he began to suck her spirit from her body, she willed her magic to remain within herself. She trapped it there, deep inside, forever denying the wizard her essence. . . .*

The chapter ended there and began on the next page with an entirely different story. Juliette frowned at the small segment of story. *Trapped,* she thought. A puzzle piece slid around in her head as if searching for its mates. But it wouldn't click. Not yet.

Juliette sighed and placed the book inside her bag along with everything else. When she was finished packing, saving enough room for Nessie, she moved back to bed, took the plush elephant from his resting place on her pillow, and gave him a kiss. Then, with a soft smile, she placed him inside her bag as well and zipped it closed.

"I'm ready," she said, lifting her laptop from where it sat on her nightstand. She turned to find Gabriel leaning on the doorframe of her bedroom, watching her intently. His silver eyes were glittering in the overhead light. He smiled slowly at her, the expression sending his already handsome face into angelic perfection.

"What?" she asked, feeling a little nervous and admittedly a little treasured beneath the intense scrutiny of those searching, silver eyes.

Gabriel shook his head and pushed off the doorframe to come toward her. "You steal my breath, little one," he told her softly, closing the distance between them. His palm cupped her cheek, warm and tender, and his silver eyes flashed for a moment, sparking to supernatural life. "How can one so small be so strong—and so innocent at the same time?" He made a bewildered sound, rubbing his thumb across her cheek. "You defy reality," he told her. And then his tall form bent over her, and his lips captured hers in a tender kiss.

The soft, dry contact sent an electric current through Juliette, buzzing her nerve endings to quick, delicious life. She closed her eyes, dropped her laptop on the bed, and allowed her bag to fall to the floor. Her hands wound through his thick black hair, and she kissed him back.

Gabriel's arm snaked around her waist, drawing her up tight against his hardness, the flat of his hand palming her lower back as if he couldn't get close enough. She lost her breath as he deepened the kiss, fisting his own hand in her long curls.

But she jumped violently and drew a surprised gasp, pulling away, when there was a loud knock on the door in the living room behind them. Gabriel waited, holding her stock-still against him. The knock came again, this time a harried hammering, desperate and loud.

"Black!" came a hoarse call. "Black, come quick! Are ye there, lad? Black!"

Juliette recognized the voice. It belonged to Stuart Burns, Gabriel's good friend and the man whose wife had prepared all of Juliette's favorite foods earlier that week. He sounded terrified and out of breath and maybe even a little in pain.

Gabriel released Juliette and hurried to the door. "I'm here, Stuart," he said as he flung the door open.

Stuart Burns stood on the threshold, his cheeks blackened with what looked like soot, his white hair askew and grayed with ash. His bright blue eyes stared in at Gabriel with wide fear, and his clothes were covered in both water and cinder residue. He smelled like fire.

"Wha' happened?" Gabriel asked, concern lowering his tone and stiffening his body. Juliette saw the change come over him immediately. She moved up beside him, fear gripping her.

"The children's home, Black! It's gone up in flame! Tristan's been hurt an' we cannae find Beth!" Stuart yelled. He was out of breath. He'd obviously run from wherever the orphanage was.

Who are Beth and Tristan? Juliette remembered Angus Dougal telling her about how Gabriel was rebuilding the children's home. Was this the one he was talking about? It couldn't be, because it wasn't finished yet. No one would be living in it. It must be the old one that had caught fire—and children had been trapped inside.

Gabriel didn't hesitate. He shot past Burns like a dark blur and was ten yards away before he stopped and turned toward Juliette as she stood in the doorway. "Stay inside, Juliette! Do no' leave the house!" He didn't wait for her to respond, but spun on his heel once more and began racing at breakneck speed up the road. She had never seen a man run so fast in her life. It was both impressive and utterly inhuman.

Beside her, Burns ran a shaky hand through his hair and then began to follow after Gabriel. Juliette watched him go in nervous silence. She thought of Stuart's words. *"Tristan's been hurt...."* *Tristan must be a child,* she thought. *And he's injured.* He needed her help.

There was no way in hell she was going to hang back and be useless when there were children nearby who might need her power. Juliette turned and glanced once at the living room of her small wooden cottage. It was cozy and warm and Gabriel had laced the building materials with veins of gold to give her extra protection. In the back of her mind, she was well aware that this fire was far too convenient for the Adarians, from the timing of it—to the fact that it involved someone who might need to be healed.

She knew this might be a trap. But she was not the kind of person who could ignore pain because of unfavorable consequences. She would never feel that people had a right to sacrifice one life for the safety of a hundred. She would never believe that "free will" was an excuse for human suffering. This was not Juliette.

And so, throwing caution aside, she stepped across the threshold of her rented home and shut the door behind her. She sensed the difference in the air at once. It was heavier and fringed with smoke. She could feel the heat to it, cloying and wrong.

Juliette moved away from the doorway and came around the house to look out over the dark horizon. A glow emanated from over the moors up the road. *The fire,* she thought. Then she looked up toward the night sky. The nearly full moon gazed back at her, slightly duller now that the air was filling with ash.

They need water, she thought. And that was something she could provide. Without wasting any further time, she began to run up the street, heading toward the glow in the distance. Stuart Burns was incredibly spry for his age and had already made it well out of sight. She was alone on the road and already feeling useless. So, as she ran, she concentrated on the weather.

A burst of wind answered her call, rushing by her and throwing her hair into her face. She tasted salt on the breeze and knew it had come over the ocean. She nodded to herself. This was good. *Keep going.* She imagined clouds next. She thought of them forming over the glow that was growing brighter as she ran. She imagined them building and darkening and growing heavy with condensation.

She was getting closer now. She could actually hear what sounded like men shouting. Overriding the men's voices, however, was a growing roar. It could only be described as it sounded . . . *hot.* The air was much warmer now and Juliette was finding it harder to breathe. She could imagine that if it were daytime, the blue of the sky would be blotted out with the wisps of ash that were climbing from the blaze ahead of her.

She topped the next hill and stopped there, looking down upon the inferno below. The roar of the fire was nearly deafening. It crackled and popped and bellowed into the night. There were dozens of people running around the massive burning building, but Juliette couldn't make out their faces. They were simply dark, humanoid forms racing here and there. Two of them held a hose. Others held shovels.

In the distance, sirens wailed. Juliette looked up and out toward the road that led away on the other side of the orphanage, but she couldn't see past the blinding light of the fire. She prayed the sirens belonged to a fire truck. Maybe two.

And then she felt something wet upon her cheek. She looked up and another raindrop fell into her eye. Pushing her relief and gratitude aside, she closed her eyes and concentrated harder. *Yes,* she thought. *Rain! Rain hard! Drop buckets of the stuff!*

And the clouds listened. Almost at once, the drops doubled. And then they did so again, exponentially multiplying until Juliette lowered her head as she felt a faint familiar weakness steal over her body. For the briefest of moments, she wondered whether she would be able to heal the injured if she brought on the rain. But she ruthlessly shoved her fear away. She *would* be able to heal them. She would never fail in that—*never*. She would rather die.

After a few short moments, Juliette was drenched. She shielded her eyes and peered at the scene below, looking for signs of the injured. About a hundred feet to the left of the building was what looked like a cluster of people both standing and kneeling, their black outlines all that were visible at this distance.

Juliette lowered her arm and shot down the hill in their direction. She slid once on the slick earth as the rain pounded the ground and melted it into something akin to an oil slick. But she caught herself and continued on, reaching the group of people in seconds flat.

Their faces were drawn and she heard someone crying. She shoved past the outer layer of the circle, noting that Gabriel was not among them. It seemed to take too long, but finally, she was at the center of the cluster and looking down. There was a bent figure before her, and beneath him, a little boy lay on the ground, his eyes closed, half his body badly burned. Most of his hair had been singed off his head, and his clothes were blackened.

Juliette instantly felt like both screaming in rage and retching. But she kept both horrid emotions at bay and knelt beside who she could now see was a vicar in white collar and black attire. He looked up at her and she could see that his blue eyes were red-rimmed and swam in tears; white streams of the salty liquid had stained his cheeks despite the downpour.

She didn't waste any time or energy addressing the man. She knew that nothing she could say would make any sense anyway. Instead, she placed her hand to the boy's chest and she felt the crowd around her go still as statues, all of them suffering a volatile cocktail of emotions at her intrusion. The boy was one of theirs. She was a foreigner. What the hell was she doing?

She ignored them all and closed her eyes, concentrating fiercely. She could feel the boy's life force beneath her, faint and wispy as a tendril of smoke. It floated up and away from his body, clearly wanting free of the damaged core it had been contained in up until now.

But his heart still beat. Barely—but the pulse was there. She clung to it and willed the life back into him. She imagined him as he must have looked before. Whole. Healthy. Happy. He was a child. No child would ever die on her watch.

There would be no small coffins.

Around her, she heard gasps and exclamations amid the nearby roar of the out-of-control fire. In front of her, the vicar began to pray, speaking words of praise under his bewildered breath.

Again, she ignored them. The child's life force responded to her, as if she'd called it to play and he was peeking through the window at her now. She coaxed it further. He smiled and opened the door.

That's it, she told him. *That's a good lad.*

More weakness invaded her body, but she kept on, reaching out with the core of her being for the core of his. Beneath her hand, she felt his body stir. Juliette opened her eyes and looked down. Tristan was healed. There was no sign of the burns that had painted his body over in red and black seconds before. His clothes were still destroyed, but a thick mane of blond hair graced his head and stark blue eyes gazed out at her from a beautiful young face.

He blinked and took a shaky breath. "My sister," he said. "She's . . . Where is she?"

Juliette stood and the entire cluster of people around her stepped back like a massive ripple in a pond. The vicar crossed himself and slowly rose, his blue eyes wide in his elderly face. She looked past him at the blazing orphanage. Despite the downpour of rain she had called, the wreckage still burned bright. The fire raged as ever, seemingly unaltered by the deluge she had let down upon it.

Maybe it's too hot, she thought. *Maybe the fire is making the water evaporate before it can even reach it.* Frustration joined the weakness stealing over her. There had to be something more she could do. She just wanted the fire to die. She just wanted it to go out. She imagined Tristan's tiny sister trapped in there—in that blistering heat. . . . *Dear God, no.* Rage coursed through her. How had this happened?

"Go away!" she bellowed into the night, raising her arms at her sides, roaring her wrath at the fire that had roared at her first.

A blast of wind shot past her from behind. She stumbled with the force of it and landed on her hands and knees. *No,* she thought. It hadn't been wind. It had been something different. It had felt almost solid—like the way water would feel if it wasn't wet.

Juliette blinked up at the burning building as the wall

of hard air continued across the field. She could feel it. She could almost even see it. She watched as it struck the orphanage and the fire on the east side was smothered beneath it. The flames bowed beneath its weight, doubling in on themselves. They shrank and receded and black smoke billowed from windows she hadn't been able to see before.

She stared at the monstrously smoking windows, imagining that any second now she would see tiny arms and hands reaching through them, searching for help or a way out. More anger flared to life within her, but along with the anger came a weakness she had never felt before. This was different. It made her fingers and toes tingle. Her heart skipped in her chest, painfully fibrillating out of sequence. She closed her eyes and tried to breathe. But the wrath was solid and real and all-encompassing inside of her.

She heard a child scream. It was real and loud and full of terror and Juliette's head snapped up at the horrendous sound. *No.* Memories assaulted her—memories of a stake and a pile of wood and a mob of possessed villagers. *No!*

Another wave of hard air rushed through her and across the field. This one knocked her flat on her stomach, sapping nearly all of what was left of her strength. But she managed to keep her head up and her eyes trained on the building long enough to see the orphanage struck once again with the magical force field, its flames once more smothered beneath the weight of its power.

It's me, she thought weakly. *I'm doing this.*

She had wanted the fire to die—and now it was dying. She concentrated on what was left of the blaze's red, licking fingers, willing them away with all her might. They retreated into the inner recesses of the children's home, as if ashamed of their behavior. She glared at them and at the deadly, horrid smoke they produced, and imagined them withering. She denied the flames air. She sizzled them to death with her rain. She tore them to pieces, molecule by molecule. . . .

And then she lowered her head and closed her eyes. All around her, she heard the sounds of men shouting once more. She felt hands on her body, gently rolling her over. Voices were raised in shock and disbelief, others in praise and gratitude.

"It was her," someone said softly. She recognized the voice as belonging to the vicar. "She was sent by God," he whispered. His voice shook, but she heard it anyway. Someone touched her forehead, but she barely felt it. Her body was growing numb. Her heart felt strange in her chest. It hurt.

"Step away from her," came a deep voice.

Juliette frowned and tried to open her eyes. They wouldn't obey. She tried again and slowly, her eyelashes fluttered open. A tall blond man stood over her, a very real gun in his right hand.

"Who are you?" the vicar demanded, apparently unwilling to give her up so easily.

"I'm death, old man," the Adarian replied, flashing him an evil smile before he raised the gun and pulled back the hammer with an ominous *click*.

CHAPTER TWENTY-SEVEN

"No," Juliette whispered—begged. *"Please."* It was the faintest request, made with a voice that was fading as quickly as her body seemed to be. "No more . . ."

The Adarian glanced down at her. "You really are an amazing woman, Anderson," he told her. His green eyes flashed for a moment, revealing his paranormal nature. She stiffened where she lay there on the ground.

Then he turned his attention back to the vicar. "I said step away."

This time, the old man shook his head. "I will not."

The Adarian pulled his trigger and someone in the crowd screamed. But the gun was turned on the cluster of people then, threatening them into stillness. A few of them even stepped back.

The vicar stumbled and fell. Within a few short seconds, he was motionless on the cold, wet ground. A hundred yards away, the orphanage billowed with heavy black clouds of smoke.

The Adarian gracefully lowered himself to one knee beside Juliette. He placed his gun hand on his knee and his green eyes flashed again as he smiled what truly appeared to be a warm smile. "I knew you would save them."

"You bastard," Juliette whispered. She felt used up.

The Adarian, on the other hand, possessed not a single sign that he had been struck with lightning only a few short days ago at Slains Castle. The Adarians were frighteningly powerful archangels.

"I know," he replied easily. And with that, he reached down and grabbed hold of her arm. But as soon as his fingers wrapped around the material of her jacket, he hissed in pain and jerked back.

Juliette almost smiled. *It's the gold,* she thought. *Gabriel's gold that he wove into my clothes.*

The Adarian looked at his hand—and then lowered it and looked at her. His gaze trailed over her clothing and the gold threads woven within it. "I see," he said simply.

And then he stood and shoved the gun into the back waistband of his jeans before digging into the inner pocket of his leather jacket. He extracted a pair of black leather gloves. His cruel lips curved into a small, secret smile as he pulled on the gloves. Juliette closed her eyes in hopeless disappointment.

Once more, he bent and this time he lifted her into his arms. She wanted to fight him, but putting out the fire had taken her strength in a way that her powers never had before.

The Adarian stood, taking her with him. He was as tall as Gabriel and she felt a mile from the ground as he turned with her and strode quickly across the field, away from the orphanage and townsfolk.

"You set that fire," she accused softly. It wasn't a question.

He didn't deny it.

Speaking was strange to her in that moment. It was like being in a dream and watching your dream self talk. She couldn't feel her tongue move; she had no idea how it was working as well as it was. Her skin tingled strangely. She was cold . . . so cold.

"Are you going to kill me?" Her voice was too soft.

It took him a long while to respond. She forced her heavy eyes open and gazed up at him. He looked down into her eyes as if he was searching for something. "There's no other way," he told her.

So she had her answer. Juliette tried so hard to think. She was no match for him physically, especially as drained as she was. But did she possess any remaining power at all? Anything? A bolt of lightning? Enough telekinetic energy to lift a gravestone and send it careening into his head?

But it took strength for her to draw breath. And it was getting harder with each passing second.

I'm dying, she thought. It was a chilling realization. She wasn't even sure where the thought had come from. But she knew it to be true.

Feeling more defeated than she ever had, Juliette dropped her head onto the Adarian's shoulder. "What's ... name?" she asked with the last of her strength. She wanted to know who it was who was going to kill her.

"Daniel," he told her. He was moving over the moors with her now, carrying her with dizzying, supernatural speed through the ash-laden mists to some unknown destination.

Gabriel used his magic to create a scarf that he pulled over his nose and mouth as he shot headlong into the building. His clansmen yelled at him to stop. What he was doing was insane. But the women remained silent; there were children inside. Sacrifice was necessary and they knew it.

The first thing he did was find a doorway inside to open a portal to the mansion to get his brothers' help. But as he rushed through the portal's opening and into the mansion's main rooms, frustration gripped him. There was no one in sight, no one answered his call, and he could sense the mansion's emptiness. They were obviously dealing with the task of retrieving Juliette's and Eleanore's parents' belongings.

Gabriel bit back his anger and hurriedly opened a second portal to make his way back into the orphanage. But before he did, he used telekinesis to overturn every item in the living room and hoped that the mess, along with the lingering scent of fire he was sure would inhabit the mansion's main rooms, would tip off his brothers or Max that he needed help.

Once he was back and trapped within the hellish haze of red and heat that the children's home had become, Gabriel began using his ability to change the elements, hardening the building's flames into pillars of ice. They would melt before the building fell, destroying any evidence of supernatural activity. It was a method he used repeatedly in New York while fighting fires there.

The heat was tremendous. No human could have walked these halls and survived. The building rippled and flowed like a standing river of red and orange. His lungs felt as though they'd captured a stray cinder and caught on fire. The skin of his face and hands threatened to blister. Hurriedly, he formed gloves over his hands and exchanged the scarf he wore for a mask. He would have to get rid of it before exiting the building to assuage suspicion, but it wasn't anything he hadn't done before.

As he moved from room to room, he used his telekinetic power to shove blockages out of the way. He called out to Beth, lifting the mask to bellow her name into the smoke with fierce determination. He refused to allow the fear that sat curdling inside of him to blossom to life. It would only slow him down.

He was growing weaker. He had used so much of his power to create gold, to move objects, and to turn fire to ice. He could sense the strength within him waning and it was a terrifying feeling. He needed all his strength right now. All of it—and then some.

"Beth!" He roared into the already roaring cacophony around him, barely managing to make his archangel's voice heard over the deathly din.

A small voice finally returned his call, but it was cut off by a fit of coughing. And then there was a scream, high-pitched and childlike. Gabriel raced toward it.

He made it with no time to spare. The little girl was on her stomach beneath a bed that had just burst into fire. Its blankets were awash with fire, its pillow smoldering with the rank smoke of burning feathers. Above them, the rafters groaned and screamed—and then the roof cracked open and the ceiling fell, giving way to the second story above.

Gabriel hurled a bolt of power over the cascading timbers, willing them from fire to ice and trying to shove them away from the bed at the same time. But only part of his power returned his call this time. He felt it leave his body as if someone had ripped the skin off his soul. It peeled away from him unwillingly, leaving him stumbling into the room.

He ignored the weakness, gritting his teeth and moving on. A portion of the fire turned to ice, but the rafters continued to fall, pouring down into the room like a waterfall of flame. The ice was melted on contact and evaporated into painful steam, scalding the air around him.

Gabriel grabbed the nearest length of timber and lifted it, using his inhuman strength to toss it aside. He called out to Beth again. This time, she didn't answer. Gabriel's heart fractured in his chest and dread drove him on, infusing his body with the will to lift the second beam and throw it aside. And the third. And the fourth.

Finally, he made it to the smoking, steaming bed and it, too, he tossed aside. Beth lay pressed to the floor in her pajamas, covered in ash and unconscious. Gabriel bent beside her and lifted her into his arms. Then he stood and turned back to the doorway. He would use it to open another portal and be done with this place.

But before he could, the doorway caved in, the door splintered and buckled, and the opening crashed to the floor in a heap of hellish red fire. The hall beyond became nothing but a wall of flames. The air's heat tripled, searing his lungs even through the mask he wore. *No,* he thought. *No!* He turned back to the room. There was no wardrobe. There was no water closet or bathroom. There were no other doors. There was no way out that wouldn't kill the child. *Oh God . . .*

And then Gabriel was stumbling back, clutching the child tightly to him and bracing his leg against a smoldering trunk as a wall of hardened air rushed over him, momentarily suffocating him. He gritted his teeth and shook his head, trying to clear it as the strange wave of power passed him over and continued through the room, leaving dying flames and embers in its wake.

What the hell? he thought as he blinked at the smothered fire. The flames were shrinking and black smoke was filling the air with rapid ferocity. Gabriel rushed through the smoke and jumped over the fallen doorframe and door, into the hall beyond. Most of it had been choked by the strange force field and was clear to move through but for the insidious smoke. The hall branched off into a T section, and to the right was the orphanage's main room and the front door. He couldn't see through the black clouds that billowed all around him; however, the field of air must have stopped beyond the hall, because Gabriel could hear the flames roaring just beyond it, blocking his escape through the exit.

There were no other doors in the hall. They had all come down in the blaze. Again, he was stuck and the smoke was making him dizzy.

For the second time in as many minutes, a hard wall of air rushed into and over him like a tidal wave. Gabriel stumbled, caught himself, and straightened in time to see what was left of the hellish inferno around him sputter and shrink until all that was left was angry cinders and ash and a sky filled with smoke.

Gabriel didn't waste any precious time wondering what had happened. He took the bizarre opportunity and ran with it—literally. Clutching the little girl tightly to him, he willed away his mask and raced through the black hall toward the exit he knew was just beyond it. He couldn't see where he was going; the smoke had all but blinded him. So he sent out pulses of his power in front of him to blow everything that might trip him up out of his way.

In sheer seconds, he made it to the front door and crashed through it and into the open air beyond. Rain was pouring. He was almost instantly drenched. Twenty yards from the face of the building, he fell to his knees and was surrounded at once by clansmen and -women. He laid Beth down on the ground in front of him and pressed his fingers to her neck, searching for a pulse.

As all archangels could, he was able to feel her soul, still there and intact within her body. But he didn't know how bad the damage was. He wanted to know how much time she had.

Beth's pulse was erratic and soft, but it was there. She would live if she just got enough air now. Gabriel closed his eyes and called out to Azrael with his mind. He wanted his brothers with him. He could feel evil in the air and knew it was an Adarian who had set the orphanage blazing.

The vampire archangel was most likely an entire continent away. They were separated by an ocean. There was no way he would hear Gabriel. But he tried anyway.

Somewhere nearby, he heard sirens. There would be an ambulance. He stood and looked around at the people who had surrounded him. "See that she gets oxygen," he ordered. They nodded and crowded in around the child.

Gabriel moved out of the crowd and searched the area. There was a group of people standing about a hundred yards away, at the edge of a large clearing. Others were running back and forth from the building he had just escaped from, trying to put out what little remained of the smoldering blaze.

Gabriel frowned. The air felt strange. There was a static to it that went beyond the heat he felt from the ash and smoke. This was different. His silver eyes flashed and widened and he looked up toward the smoking building one last time. In that horrible moment, he knew what had happened.

Juliette.

She hadn't listened to him. She'd left the cottage and come after him. And she had somehow put out the fire.

His head snapped back around to the group of people standing by the field. With inhuman speed, he raced across the lot and pushed through the crowd to find himself staring down at the vicar of the nearby church. He was dead. Gabriel could sense it immediately.

"He shot him," someone in the group said. "He shot him and took the angel. The angel that put out the fire and saved the child."

Gabriel looked up at the person who had just spoken and then down at a small towheaded boy who peeked through the crowd at Gabriel. Tristan's clothes hung limply on his body, singed and scorched beyond recognition. But his skin was unmarred, his complexion was healthy, and his hair was full and blond.

The angel that saved the child . . .

"No . . ." Rage rushed through Gabriel, a powerful, insidious drug that boiled his blood and literally turned his vision red. Something inside of him snapped, cracked wide open, and lightning crashed to the ground a quarter of a mile away. He threw his head back and looked up at the heavens. The clouds roiled and churned, throwing lightning to the earth once more, closer this time.

Juliette!

His precious archess had saved them all. And an Adarian had taken her.

CHAPTER TWENTY-EIGHT

Daniel placed the archess in the passenger seat of the first car they would take and began buckling her in. She was nearly unconscious, but somehow she managed to open her eyes and stare up at him. She was incredibly stubborn, but that inner strength wouldn't be enough to save her at this point, and he needed her alive.

Daniel met her gaze, pulled a vial out of the pocket of his jacket, and placed it to her lips. "Drink this."

She shook her head—once—and turned her head away.

"It's not poison," he told her calmly, curling his finger beneath her chin so that she faced him once more. "And it's not a drug. It's glucose. You're fading on me. Now, drink or I'll inject it into you."

Juliette hesitated, then parted her lips and allowed the liquid to pour over her tongue. He could imagine it tasted saccharine sweet and slimy and even a bit salty. She swallowed, flinching a little as it made its way down her throat.

"Keep going," he ordered. She kept swallowing until the vial was empty. "Good girl." He'd given her enough to keep her awake and alive, but not enough to reinstate any real power on her part. He tossed the empty vial onto the floorboards of the car, slammed her door shut, and got in on his side.

Beside him, Juliette closed her eyes again and let her head drop back on the car seat.

It took only a few short minutes for them to get where he wanted to take them. Daniel easily steered around oncoming cars and suicidal sheep that made their way down from the moors and sauntered uncaringly into the road. Eventually he pulled over into a passing space and he parked the car. The second car he had stolen was there waiting for him in the shadows beneath a few lone trees. He got out and opened Juliette's door, leaning slightly against the frame. "Can you walk?" he asked. He was testing the waters; he wanted to know exactly how strong she was and what he might have to prepare himself for. He was hoping she wouldn't be able to stand.

She tried to stand on her own anyway, and he had to admit that he was impressed. Anderson was not a weak woman. She used her hands on the doorframe to pull herself out of the car. Daniel stepped back as she did so, pretending to give her room. But her legs almost immediately gave out and Daniel instantly lifted her into his arms. She gritted her teeth and glared up at him from the cage of his arms. Daniel couldn't help but grin back at her. He was pleased that she didn't have a lot of strength to spare. And he certainly didn't mind any excuse to hold her to him this way. He felt like he was getting away with something just by touching her. He was certain that Gabriel would see it that way.

Daniel moved her around the vehicle and made his way to the second car. This one was larger and a different model and make from the first. He opened her door with one hand, holding her aloft with the other. She was so light, it was as if she weighed nothing at all.

Again, he buckled her in, and as he did so, he could

feel Juliette tense beside him. He imagined she was trying very hard not to lash out at his face as it hovered so close to her own. The buckle's lock clicked and he turned to look down into her eyes once more.

Her normally hazel eyes were flashing green sparks at him. They were singularly lovely. He was struck, in that moment, with the perfection of her—her skin, so porcelain and perfect, her lips so pink and full, her lashes so long and thick. He felt his own green eyes flash, growing warm and beginning to glow. "You're an incredibly beautiful woman, Juliette," he told her.

"Go to hell," she hissed at him.

He was still for a long moment as he contemplated her words. He was about to destroy an archess—a perfect female being. He had little doubt that if there had been a hell, he would have earned himself a place within it. But worse than that was the knowledge that he would forever live with her blood in his veins, an eternal reminder of his hideous act. Daniel would create his very own little hell, one from which he would never escape.

She gazed up at him, no doubt wondering what he was thinking. So, he simply smiled at her and shook his head. What could he say? Then he rose again, closed her door, and got back in on his side. Once more, they began to drive and Juliette let her head drop back on the seat's rest.

"How are you going to kill me?" she asked, breaking the silence.

Of course she would wonder that. She was probably also wondering what was he waiting for. She had no idea what was going on—what was involved—and the longer he kept her alive, the greater the chance that Gabriel would catch up with them. And there was no doubt in Daniel's mind that Gabriel would come after her. This he knew with unequaled certainty. Daniel would do the same. He glanced at Juliette and her petite, precious profile and his grip on the gearshift tightened. Yes, he would do the same.

"I have to take your blood," he told her honestly. There was no point in keeping the truth from her.

She frowned at him, obviously confused. "My blood? What . . . like a vampire?" she asked softly. Her voice was still rather weak, but certainly better than it had been before he'd given her the glucose.

It was serendipitous that she mentioned the vampire relation. In Daniel's vision, what he perceived as happening to his general could very well be called vampiric. And taking another person's blood and ingesting it— what was that if not vampiric?

"Kind of," he told her, not knowing what else to say.

"You'll steal my power, then," she whispered. It wasn't a question. She was clearly simply vocalizing her thoughts and figuring things out.

"Yes," he said, glancing at her again. She looked thoughtful. Her eyes were focused on the ribbon of black ahead of them.

Daniel.

Daniel jerked slightly, blinking at the sudden invasion. There was a voice in his head, but it wasn't his own. It was deep and incredibly commanding and filled Daniel with an instant sense of dread. He looked out over the road again. A lone tall figure appeared in the cone of the vehicle's headlights and Daniel slammed on the brakes, jerking the wheel to the right.

Beside him, Juliette braced herself with her arms as the car skidded wildly, spinning around in a heart-wrenching 360. By the time the car came to a stop, Daniel already had his gun in one hand and was reaching over to pull Juliette across the car to his side. He threw open the door, his grip strong on her arm, and dragged her across both seats until she was out of the car. He supported her weight, knowing she wouldn't be able to do so on her own. The barrel of the gun was pressed threateningly to her rib cage and his eyes were on the stranger.

He was tall and trim with broad shoulders. He wore what was obviously an expensive tailored charcoal gray suit. His thick hair was so blond, it was nearly white, and his strange storm gray eyes reflected the light from the car like mirrors. *He's not human,* Daniel thought. It was an understatement really, since the man's power poured off him in thick rivulets and waves that were nearly stifling in their intensity.

The stranger gracefully unbuttoned his charcoal suit jacket and slid his hands into his pants pockets before slowly making his way down the road toward the car. When he came closer, Daniel was struck with a memory.

A man who had looked a lot like this had appeared out of nowhere on the battlefield outside Dallas four months ago during the Adarian fight with the four favored. The man had commanded a host of humanoid creatures on horseback who wielded black swords and wore black armor. The small army had turned the tide irrevocably, allowing the four favored to defeat the Adarians—killing three of them in the process. "I know you," Daniel said, his grip on Juliette tightening as anger and uncertainty stole through him. She tried to jerk away and he held her fast, ignoring her defiance. His attention was almost solely focused on the man in front of them. "You're the one who controlled the Riders during the battle with the four favored."

The stranger didn't bother denying it. His only response was to smile and glance at the ground as if in modesty.

Daniel's teeth clenched. "What do you want?" he asked, wanting to get right to the point.

"What do I want?" the stranger repeated, coming to a stop and lowering his head as if to contemplate the question. He chuckled softly and shook his head. "That's a question people have been asking me a lot lately."

Daniel wasn't feeling patient and was not at all in the mood to play games. He knew now that this was the man who had been in his head; he recognized the voice. Inhuman indeed. Daniel cocked the gun in his hand and little Juliette closed her eyes. He yanked her closer to him, pressing her right up against his side. He wasn't really planning on shooting her, but he needed to do something to make the stranger back off. "If you're here for the archess, know this," he warned. "I'll kill her before I allow anyone to take her from me."

"Oh, I know you will," the stranger replied. His dark gray eyes flashed eerily, as if lightning had struck within their swirling storms.

Daniel had barely enough time to process the words he'd muttered before the gun in his hand went off.

Juliette dropped to the ground and her eyes closed, shutting out the world.

Daniel stared down at her for a moment, lost in shock. He hadn't pulled the trigger. He hadn't. "No!" he suddenly cried, dropping to his knees beside her. "I didn't pull the trigger!" He dropped the gun, ripped off his leather gloves, and shoved up her jacket and shirt to find the wound. Dark red blood pooled at the entry site and spread quickly across her side. "No, God, no, no, no please . . . ," Daniel was muttering now. He had no control over it. His fingers were on her neck, feeling for a pulse.

"You shot her, Daniel," the stranger said calmly. The sound of his shoes echoed on the wet asphalt, drawing nearer. It was the only sound other than the harsh, quick breaths and half sobs Daniel was producing. "You've killed Gabriel's archess," the man continued. "What do you think will happen when the General finds out?"

Daniel gave a soft whimper and ran a bloody hand

through his blond hair in fierce, frantic terror. "But I didn't!" he insisted, his voice high-pitched and close to hysterics. "I didn't pull the trigger! The gun just went off. . . . It just went off. . . ." He was brushing her hair from her face now. Dark terror was flooding his system with red and black and a horrible, nauseating cold. His fingers trembled uncontrollably where they touched her. "I didn't mean it," he whispered. He didn't mean it. He hadn't wanted to destroy her in the first place — he never would have done so like this.

"Abraxos will not care whether you meant it or not, Xathaniel," the stranger continued, using his real name this time. Daniel froze at the sound. No one but the General had called him by that name for more than a thousand years. He turned to look up at the tall, enigmatic man. "You know he will kill you," the stranger said. "He will stop at nothing to do so."

Daniel thought about this. It was so hard to concentrate; his thoughts were fluttering about wildly on the hurricane winds of emotion whirling within him. But he knew the stranger was right. He had no idea how the *stranger* knew it, but there it was.

"However," the man's powerful voice continued, "I can save you from his wrath, Xathaniel. I am the only one who can."

Daniel's breath shook; he could hear it rasping in the air. "What . . . what do you want from me?" he asked, feeling desperate now.

"I want *you*, Xathaniel," the stranger told him simply. His tone was soft, but there was a finality to it that would have given Daniel a hard chill if he hadn't already been draped in abject terror. "I want your loyalty and obedience. I want you to serve me for all time."

The silence stretched, punctuated by the rolling of thunder from over the hills and the sound of fat drops of rain as they began to descend around them. Very slowly,

Daniel stood up. The stranger's shoes clicked on the asphalt once again as he calmly closed the distance between them. He stopped when he stood on the opposite side of the archess's still form.

"Who are you?" Daniel whispered, his voice shaking badly.

"Call me Sam," the man replied easily. "I need only your spoken word," Sam said, as if he had not been interrupted. Daniel could truly feel his power now; he was being draped in it, layer after layer, paralyzed beneath a force ten thousand times stronger than him. He managed to draw a shaky breath and the stranger smiled. "Oh," Sam added, as if it were an afterthought, "and your signature."

Sam slipped one hand into the inside pocket of his expensive, tailored coat and extracted a gleaming, clear fountain pen. He held up the strange pen and it shimmered in the low light provided by the car's headlights.

Daniel stared at the pen and shivered violently. Then he glanced down at the archess once again. He felt his knees bending and knelt beside her once more, pulled by her small presence and the incredible loss she represented. Impulsively, he placed two fingers to her throat, again checking for a heartbeat. Still, there was nothing. Of course there was nothing. Why would it change?

But I didn't pull the trigger, he thought manically. *I know I didn't. How did the gun go off? Why did it go off?*

"What's done is done." Sam spoke softly. Daniel looked up at him. His strange, stark gray eyes were mesmerizing. Were those actually thunderclouds in their depths? *Lightning,* he thought, as it flashed across the stranger's irises in surreal contrast. As if the world reflected the content of that phenomenally powerful gaze, thunder rolled across the fields and shook the earth beneath Daniel's feet.

"There's no ink in that pen," he found himself muttering, his gaze again dropping to the crystal-like writing utensil in the man's upturned fingers.

"It doesn't use ink," Sam said, offering him the slightest, cruelest smile. Lightning crashed again and thunder rolled closer. Daniel swallowed hard. His fingers shook horribly where they pressed to the archess's still, cold neck. He looked down at her. Her entire left side was drenched in dark, red blood. It had pooled beneath her small body, testament to the terrible, unforgivable crime that had transpired on that road that night.

She's dead, he told himself. *I'm dead now, too.* He looked back up at the stranger who waited so patiently, so silent and still, that gleaming empty pen aloft in his hand. *It's over,* he thought.

Slowly he stood, his eyes now trained on the pen. "It's a diamond, isn't it?" he whispered, tasting tears on his lips. Sam didn't answer. But he didn't need to. Daniel knew it was true. "What does it use?"

The stranger's mesmerizing gaze hardened, going from deep charcoal to nearly black as his pupils expanded and the corners of his mouth turned up slightly. Without speaking a word, he reached out for Daniel's wrist and held it up between them. Daniel felt frozen to the spot, unable—or perhaps *unwilling*—to pull away.

With the hand that still held the pen, Sam pushed back Daniel's sleeve, exposing an expanse of skin on the wrist above the ridge of his palm. He then took the shining metal tip of the fountain pen and placed it to Daniel's prominent blue vein.

There was a sharp, deep pain and Daniel winced, gritting his teeth. Fire raced up from the entry point, subjugating his arm, then his shoulder, and then his chest—until his heart felt as though it had burst into flame. He couldn't make a single sound. The pain was immense and all-encompassing. And all the while, the stranger simply gazed steadily at him as his beautiful, vile pen sucked up Daniel's blood, filling its compartment with ruby red liquid.

When the pen was filled, Sam removed the tip from Daniel's arm and released him. Daniel fell backward, barely managing to keep from falling as relief flooded over him, a cessation to the agony. Only his wrist continued to throb. He placed his other hand over the wound and watched the stranger with a new and wary respect.

"What now?" he gritted out, feeling hoarse from the pain.

Sam took a single step to the side and back, revealing behind him a tall wooden table. It was narrow and intricately carved, etched with symbols and lettering that made Daniel feel funny inside. On its small surface sat a single parchment. It was raining all around them—but the table and its document remained untouched by the wetness.

Daniel straightened and stepped around Juliette's body to come closer to the table. The paper that lay atop it was blank. He frowned in confusion.

"What is that?" he asked.

"Your contract," Sam replied. The stranger waved his right hand over the document, the expensive watch on his wrist shimmering in the car's headlights. On the paper, black scrolling letters appeared, writing themselves across the page in perfect straight lines. Daniel barely recognized some of the words—and he wasn't really certain about any of them.

He was sweating a cold sweat now, drenching himself as surely as the rain was.

The stranger held up the pen. It gleamed, ruby and wicked in the light. Daniel's gaze cut to the man who held it. *Sam,* he thought. *What is that short for?* Had he heard the name before? Something niggled at his memory, squirming under the sand. But it was as yet unrecognizable—and fear was making Daniel fuzzy. One thing was certain, however. The power he felt coming off the stranger was unlike any he'd ever experienced. If anyone could keep him safe from the General, it was Sam.

I have no choice. He took the pen with shaking fingers, the wound in his wrist throbbing painfully. And then, as two thick black lines appeared at the bottom of the parchment, Daniel bent over the table, placed the pen's tip to the first line—and signed his name.

CHAPTER TWENTY-NINE

Juliette couldn't have moved if she'd wanted to. Her body was wrapped in a cocoon of warmth and comfort that both paralyzed and soothed her. She knew the gun had gone off, but she'd felt no pain. She'd felt only a sense of calm pour over and through her, as if she were high on morphine.

Samael, she thought now, as she listened to the exchange between the two men who stood over her.

Everything had happened so quickly. Daniel had put her in the car and told her he was going to take her blood. And then—*Juliette,* a voice had spoken in her head. She would recognize it anywhere. It was deep and strong and laced with the kind of effortless sensuality that left a woman breathless. Sam was sheer potency in human form, and from the moment he brushed her mind, she'd instantly become hyperaware of him all around her.

He had chuckled, and the deep, utterly beguiling sound had echoed off the walls of her mind. She had closed her eyes, only for a moment, and when she'd opened them again, Sam was standing in the road ahead of them.

Daniel had swerved to miss him, and everything had turned to chaos around her. But Juliette felt no fear.

From the moment he'd telepathically spoken her name into her mind, she'd been draped in tranquillity. Daniel jerked her through the car and out the other side and she found the will to try to pull away. But it was a halfhearted attempt and she knew it was useless—and she didn't really care. Sam was inside of her, his charcoal gray eyes mesmerizing her, his essence filling her like a drug.

The barrel of Daniel's gun fought for room between her ribs, etching at a sharp pain. Offhandedly, she imagined the bullet chambered behind it. What would it feel like going in? It was, perhaps, the single way in which she had yet to die. Not in all her many lifetimes had Juliette Anderson ever been shot.

She had her answer then, though it hadn't been at all what she'd expected. The gun went off, but there was no pain. None at all. She wasn't in control of her own body. She hit the ground and closed her eyes before wetness spread across her side, drenching her clothes and the ground beneath her. It was Sam manipulating her. She knew it, and though it should have scared her that there existed a being who could so fully control her every action, it somehow didn't.

Everything is going to be okay, he told her.

Above her, a deal was being made. They moved away and there was a moment of silence. Then lightning flashed somewhere very close by. She wanted to cover her ears, knowing the thunder would be right on top of it, but she couldn't move. The thunder came, crashing over the road and rolling across her body, quaking the ground beneath her as it went.

It passed and Juliette lay there, her eyes closed, waiting.

There was a footfall beside her. Juliette opened her eyes to see Samael kneeling at her side. She blinked up at him, at once lost in his stormy gaze. *He's so beautiful.*

He smiled at her, using gentle fingers to brush her hair out of her face. "How do you feel?"

"Fine," she replied softly, feeling as if the world had melted into surrealism. She blinked and frowned and Sam laughed. He offered her his hand, helping her to sit up. Juliette looked down at her clothes, expecting to see them drenched in red, but they were untouched by anything other than a bit of rain.

No blood. No holes in the fabric—or in her flesh. Juliette ran her hand over her stomach, searching for the wound. It wasn't there. She exhaled a little shakily and looked back up at Sam. She didn't flinch or try to pull away when his warm hand cupped her cheek. "Did he hurt you?" he asked.

Juliette looked around at the mention of the Adarian—but she and Sam appeared to be alone beside the two cars on the deserted road. There was no sign of Daniel. She looked back at Sam and thought of Daniel and all he had done. The Adarian had set fire to an orphanage and trapped children inside, but he had never outwardly harmed her. He had given her sugar water and restored a little of her strength—quite the opposite of harming her. Apparently he hadn't even shot her, as she'd thought he had.

She shook her head. "No," she said.

"Then I will allow him to live," he said softly, his eyes flashing with some untold, very serious emotion. He once more offered her his hand and began to rise, taking her with him. She came easily to her feet, not feeling any of the weakness she had felt before. Samael had restored her strength. She didn't know how. She couldn't comprehend the last ten minutes of her life at all—but there it was.

Sam towered over her, tall and strong and draped in power. She caught a faint whiff of cologne and it reinforced the effect of his nearness, making her feel strange. He was somehow forcing other thoughts from her mind, hiding her worry from her, drowning her fears.

She gazed up at him, unsure of what it was he wanted. "Why are you here?" she found herself asking. She was just so confused.

"That's a very good question, Juliette," Samael whispered, once more cupping her cheek. "And a very big one. But if you mean why am I here on this road with you right now—let's just say that I've had my eye on a certain Adarian's abilities for a while now."

Juliette frowned. Daniel? He'd been after Daniel all this time? Was *all* of this solely so that he could get his hands on *Daniel*? Was that what he meant? She was clueless as to why he would go to so much trouble to secure an Adarian who could turn invisible. Samael seemed so much more powerful than that. And that was the crux of her perplexity right there. Samael, in general, confused the hell out of her.

"Why are you . . . here?" she asked, gesturing to the whole world around them.

"Ah." He smiled a beautiful smile. "As to that, little one, I don't have an answer to share with you."

His reply echoed Lily's earlier reply and once more, Juliette wondered whether he didn't have an answer—or simply wasn't willing to share the one he had.

"I will tell you this, however," he continued. "The world is a dangerous place. Especially for an archess." He leaned over, placed a tender kiss to her forehead, and then moved his lips to her ear. She closed her eyes, at once feeling dizzy. "Keep your wits about you, Juliette. Heed the lessons history has to teach."

With that, he pulled away, just a little, and Juliette opened her eyes once more.

"Juliette!" A man's cry caused her to jerk in Samael's gentle grip and she whirled around, turning her back to him in order to see Gabriel, Michael, and Uriel racing down a nearby hill. They moved with unnatural speed, covering the distance in seconds and leaving Juliette a little breathless. Any woman staring out across the moors to find three supernaturally handsome men running full tilt straight for her is going to have the wind knocked out of her.

Gabriel reached her first, and she found herself pulled tightly into his arms before she could react. His grip was strong and his body radiated heat. "Juliette, wha' in the bloody Christ are you doin' out here?" he asked as he took her to arm's length again and looked her over with flashing silver eyes.

Juliette's mouth opened. She blinked. She glanced over her shoulder at Sam—but Sam wasn't there. She was alone with the two cars—and three archangel brothers. She turned back to Gabriel and wondered where in the world to start.

Michael and Uriel scanned the area with glowing eyes. "When did you two get here?" she asked.

"Just now," Michael replied without looking at her. His sapphire eyes were burning a bright, beautiful blue as he searched their surroundings. "Your boyfriend left one hell of a mess in the mansion, so we came straight away and more or less followed the road." That explained how they'd found her; they probably knew that Daniel would take a car, and since they could move fast, it wasn't long before they'd caught up. But the mess in the mansion?

She looked at Gabriel. He shook his head. "Long story, luv," he said, waving the issue away. "You put out the fire."

She nodded, blushing a little. "Yeah, I guess I sort of did."

"An' you saved Tristan."

Again, she nodded, averting her gaze. His praise was making her uncomfortable. Gabriel cupped her cheek, much like Sam had done, but when Gabriel did it, it went deeper. He pulled her gaze back to his, trapping it in the silver of his soul. She felt as if she were being embraced by the land, the very earth itself. "Och, lass, bu' how?" he asked, clearly almost breathless with wonder.

"I . . . I don't know," she replied, feeling distinctly embarrassed. "Was Beth okay?" she asked, changing the subject. Tristan had been so worried about his sister. They both had. The fire had been so strong.

"Aye, luv, she's fine," he said, brushing his thumb across her cheek the way he liked to do. "Thanks to you." He leaned in then, taking her lips in a tender kiss. His heat suffused her, causing her to shudder as all traces of chill were chased away. When he finally pulled away, she was dizzy. "They said you'd been taken," he told her, whispering his words across her lips. "By the man who shot the vicar."

"I was," she told him, recalling the way Daniel had pulled his trigger on the old man. "Oh God," she said. "Did he—was he—"

"He did no' make it, little one."

A numb kind of sadness threatened inside of Juliette and she shook her head. "I was taken by the Adarian Daniel. He brought me here and was going to change cars, but then Sam came and—"

"*Sam?*" Uriel and Michael both stopped what they were doing and turned to face her, their attention at once focused on her.

"Samael was here?" Gabriel asked, his gaze narrowing, his grip on her arms tightening.

Juliette nodded. "Yes, but—"

Before she could explain further, the group was overtaken by a blast of wind so strong, it knocked Juliette and Gabriel into the car beside them. Gabriel was reacting instantly, yanking her around behind him and shielding her between himself and the source of the powerful air burst—the handful of Adarians now coming over the rise.

Uriel swore softly under his breath as he and Michael came to stand beside Gabriel, one on either side. Juliette recognized three of the Adarians. The black man, the dark-haired man, and the blond with blue eyes were the three who had attacked them at Callanish.

But there were three others there as well. All of them looked as tall and strong as their companions and Juliette's stomach was beginning to turn. She tasted sour in her mouth.

"Where is he?" whispered Uriel.

"Where's who?" Juliette asked.

"Abraxos," Michael replied, his blue eyes trained on the men staring down at them. "He's not with them."

"He's here somewhere," said Gabriel. "I can bloody well feel 'im."

Juliette gazed up at the outline of tall, strong bodies and was reminded of that scene from *The Lost Boys* as David and his "boys" gazed down at Michael from the top of a hill. They had just finished "feeding," on innocent prey. Was that what was about to happen now?

"I have to take your blood," Daniel had told her.

"Juliette, get in the car," Gabriel commanded. Juliette frowned, but when she felt the solidity of the vehicle behind her begin to waver and warp, she understood. Gabriel was opening a portal through the car door.

Just then Gabriel swore under his breath, and the world was turned upside down.

The earth began to quake, the temperature dropped fifty degrees, and Michael was struck by a stray bolt of lightning. The cacophony ripped through the atmosphere, destroying all other sound. The ground bucked beneath Juliette, shooting her forward and onto her knees as the portal behind her swirled closed once more, blocking her only exit. She looked up, shoving the hair out of her face to see that Gabriel was wrapped in a force field like plastic wrap that picked him up off the ground and tossed him into the air. She screamed, rushing forward, but was cut off as Uriel jerked her to a halt and swung her around to face him.

"Get in the car!" he bellowed. Even without the portal, he was right. It was the safest place for her right now because as soon as any of them could manage it, they could open a portal through the doors and she could slip on through.

But before she could obey him, the world was cast into utter and complete darkness. Juliette cried out as Uriel's body was simultaneously ripped away from hers and she wondered if she'd gone blind. She put her hands to her eyes, rubbed them, and then reached out around her, trying desperately not to panic. All she could feel was the car, and her fingers were quickly beginning to freeze in the unnaturally dropped temperature. On instinct, she slid down low against the car and shoved her hands into her pockets for whatever warmth they could afford. She was crying; she could feel the tears freezing into ice streams on her cheeks.

And then her fingers brushed something smooth and hard. *The bracelet,* she realized, as she recalled Gabriel giving it to her days ago. She had changed several times—but the bracelet had always somehow come back to her, taking up residence in her jacket pocket once more.

There were sounds everywhere, the earth was shaking, and the super-subfreezing temperature was causing her lungs to burn with each intake of breath. Her teeth hurt when she opened her mouth, and her nostrils were freezing shut. There was an explosion nearby and a grunt of pain and then there was a crackling sound, as if a column of ice was crashing to the ground.

"Heed the lessons history has to teach." Samael's words echoed in her mind, somehow managing to be heard in the entropy of her thoughts even over the amaz-

ing dissonance of the crumbling, crackling world around her. *What lessons?* she thought frantically. *What lessons have I ever dealt with in any of my many lifetimes that would prepare me for battle with Adarians?*

Juliette's heart was going rapid-fire behind her lungs; terror clutched at her with fingers as cold as the air around her. She ducked her head into the car door, instinctively shielding her face, when lightning struck again somewhere nearby. She could see nothing. Her existence had gone black.

I'm gonna die, she thought hysterically. *I'm gonna die and I never got my PhD. I never even did the research. The only thing I even read at all was that stupid half of a page that Law somehow slid into my cottage room closet—*

The magical, absolute darkness she had been draped in lifted then, casting her into sudden moving color that matched the sounds she'd been hearing. She unshielded her face in time to see the blond, blue-eyed Adarian who had attacked her at Callanish go sailing into the side of a peat-bog-carved hill. His back collided with the brown grass and freezing mud, sending a cascade of the muck high into the air. It had been Uriel who had tossed him into the moor—Uriel, who now sported massive black-feathered wings that allowed him to hover several dozen feet in the air above them.

Juliette's jaw dropped and she gasped, pulling frozen air deep into her lungs and searing them with cold from the inside out. She coughed violently and hugged herself, her eyes hurriedly skating over the scene, taking everything in.

Gabriel and the large black Adarian were fighting hand to hand once more. Both men were bleeding in various places and Juliette's heart ached at the sight. The blond and Uriel were going at each other, the blond apparently possessing some ability that allowed him to

move bodies around in space. Uriel landed, his giant
black wings folding behind him and then disappearing
altogether before he and the blond rushed each other at
full speed. They collided, each with his hands clasped
tightly around the other's neck.

Juliette ripped her gaze off them to find Michael bat-
tling not one but two Adarians. His clothes were singed
in places, mementos from the lightning, but he'd obviously healed himself, and as he finished dealing with one
Adarian, knocking him to the ground with a blow or a
shove, another attacked, taking on his immense strength
and skill. Juliette was incredibly impressed with the former Warrior Archangel. He obviously still had most of
that warrior within him.

But the cold was getting to her now; the temperature
was continuing to drop. She was losing the feeling in her
fingers and toes. She looked away from Michael and his
opponents to find the dark-haired Adarian from Callanish standing twenty yards away, staring at her once again.
The expression on his face as he watched her was both
intense and unreadable. He looked troubled. His black
eyes sparkled like obsidian ice in this new field of hard
winter. He was the one controlling the temperature. He
was making it hard for her to think, to move, and probably making it difficult for the archangels to fight.

Lightning bolt him, she told herself. But even her mind
seemed to be stuttering now, slow and sluggish in the
freeze. She looked up at the pitch black above her and
tried to focus on the clouds she couldn't see. The ground
bucked beneath her, throwing her back into the car behind her. She hit hard, the wind knocked from her lungs,
and stars swam in her vision.

Why doesn't he just kill me? she wondered then, as she
slid against the car and curled her legs up to her chest.
The dark-haired Adarian was powerful enough to stop
her from fighting back. He controlled the air they

breathed and the ground they walked on. What was he waiting for?

She blinked away the pain from her impact and looked up at him again. Still, he watched her, his expression one of utter fascination. She felt like he was inside of her, listening to her thoughts and feeding her fear. She glared at him, hoping that for that brief, painful moment he actually *could* read her mind. *Bite me,* she thought at him.

"He will, little one, when it's his turn."

Juliette spun on the ground, her head snapping up to meet a pair of ice-blue eyes. A black-haired man hovered nearly upside down above her, unmoving in the freezing air. He was uncommonly handsome, reminding her instantly of one of the four favored. He smiled, flashing two elongated, wickedly sharp fangs.

Juliette screamed. A bloodcurdling howl of horror escaped her throat as she felt the earth drop down beneath her. Ten feet. Twenty. All at once, she was breaking through the bonds of gravity as the man with blue eyes and fangs ripped her away from the world and took her into the heavens.

CHAPTER THIRTY

"Juliette!" Gabriel saw Juliette being ripped from the ground and torn through the sky, but there was nothing he could do about it. His opponent took advantage of his brief lapse in concentration, taking him by the throat and tossing him to the ground so that the wind was knocked violently from his lungs. Gabriel rolled across the frost-covered ground, shoved himself back up, forced his lungs to expand, and called for his brother.

"*Uriel!*" he bellowed, but he needn't have bothered. Uriel had seen Abraxos take Juliette. His black and emerald wings exploded from his back, stretching to their full, impressive length in a heartbeat.

The former Angel of Vengeance leapt into the night sky, shooting across the darkness like a raven rocket. He didn't get far. As suddenly as he'd taken to the air, he was ripped from it, yanked to a halt by another insidious force field that wrapped around his airborne body and flung him to the ground like a rag doll. Uriel had enough foresight to brace for the impact and roll as he struck down, but the hardened air wrapped around him once more, picking him up and slamming him back down into the ground with vicious force.

Gabriel knew it was his own opponent responsible; he

could see the man's amber eyes glowing like double suns, burning with power as he flung the force field at Uriel. Gabriel shoved himself up from the ground, rushed the black man, and called his own power to the fore at the same time.

As they collided, the force field evaporated and Gabriel braced his hand against the Adarian's clothing, weaving gold into it with unearthly speed. The Adarian bellowed in agony as the gold began to sear his flesh.

Thirty yards away, Uriel once more pulled himself up off the ground and leapt into the sky. Gabriel watched him go with a mind-numbing sense of ambivalence. He wondered whether it was too late.

Azrael! As Gabriel wrestled with his smoking opponent, he once more called for his vampiric brother. Azrael hadn't come through the portal with Uriel and Michael, and neither had Max. They hadn't made it home yet; only Uriel and Michael had seen the wreckage of the mansion's main room and immediately put two and two together to come after Gabriel.

But Gabriel needed Az. If anyone could track down an Adarian turned vampire, it was an *archangel* turned vampire. Azrael was the very first vampire in existence; his powers measured greater than those of his brothers' combined, and he could perform scries at will. *Az! I need you!* Gabriel had no pride in that moment.

He picked his opponent up off the ground and flung him with all his archangel strength against a nearby boulder. The man went flying through the air, leaving a trail of smoke behind him like a failing jet engine. He struck the stone, cracking the rock beneath him with immense force.

Another Adarian was upon Gabriel in the blink of an eye. There were half a dozen of the powerful First Angels to contend with and Gabriel was already injured.

The wounds would heal at a faster rate than they would for a human, but not fast enough to give him back the strength he needed for this fight.

A shard blast went off, striking Gabriel in the back of the leg. He roared with rage—with more anger than pain at being wounded with the formidable, damnable weapons yet again. He spun, ready to face the man who had attacked him, but Michael was already on the guilty Adarian.

Gabriel's leg buckled, sending him to the ground in a spray of rimed mud and torn, crystallized turf. He gritted his teeth as his new opponent took advantage of his position and kicked him in the side, sending him skidding several feet across the ground.

Again, Gabriel rolled, coming to his hands and knees, but his right leg wouldn't cooperate; it was turning to stone from the knee to the hip.

"Gabriel!"

Gabriel blinked, recognizing the voice that barked his name. His head snapped up in time to find Max coming through a portal from the mansion and stepping away from the iced-over door of the car he'd just transported through. He was dressed in the same black fatigues he'd worn during the battle outside Dallas four months ago. Gone were the suit and glasses, and he carried a satchel over his left shoulder. Azrael was not with him. How had Max been able to find their location without Az?

And then Gabriel remembered Juliette mentioning Sam. *Lilith*, Gabriel thought. She must have told Max where they were.

Disappointment arced through Gabriel; Az was invaluable in a situation like this. But the disappointment was quickly overshadowed by a sense of relief nonetheless. Max had something black and silver in his hand. He threw it toward Gabriel, tossing it through the air with such superhuman speed that it blurred, forbidding anyone else from stopping it.

Gabriel reached out and caught it, ignoring the intense sting it brought to his hands as he did so. He recognized the weapon instantly. When the Adarian came at him once again, Gabriel spun and leveled the gun on the man. He pulled the trigger three times.

Three gold bullets embedded themselves in the chest of the Adarian, knocking him backward and bringing him to his knees. The man threw back his head in rage and pain, clutching at his chest with clawlike fingers. He bellowed his agony into the night as the gold bullet ate him up from the inside.

Gabriel leaned forward and tried to stand. Pain shot through his body from the shard-blast wound; his leg literally crackled when he put weight on it. He grimaced and shifted, placing his standing weight on one foot. There was a flash of light and he looked up to see the Adarian he'd been fighting disappear. The light swelled and then receded and with it went the injured man.

Gabriel's eyes widened. Another flash of light took one of Michael's opponents. Michael spun, ready to face the one behind him—but the Adarian stood back from Michael and allowed his hands to fall to his sides. He wore an enigmatic look on his handsome face, a knowing smile. His stark eyes flashed with secrets.

Another blinding flash and he disappeared as well.

"No," Gabriel muttered. *No, no, no.* They were leaving. They'd come for Juliette—and now they had her. Their task was done.

The Adarians were all stopping now, ending their struggles. The four remaining stepped away from the archangels and Gabriel's heart hammered painfully. He knew, in his heart, that as they dwindled in number on that rain-and ice-soaked field, so did his chances of finding Juliette again.

A fourth Adarian vanished in a flash of light. The temperature began to warm back up. Gabriel looked at Michael and their gazes met. As one, they ran toward the nearest Adarian, intent on trapping him there. However, the Adarian flashed out of existence before they'd made it halfway.

Gabriel had no idea how they were simply disappearing as they were. But he vaguely recalled them doing something similar after the battle in Texas. One by one, they had been recalled from the field—even the injured and unconscious. As they were doing now.

Desperation clawed at him. These vanishing men were his ticket to finding Juliette. And then a familiar sound had him whirling around to face the two cars that lay, almost forgotten, in the passing space beside the road. The door to the nearer car began to swirl, warping and vanishing behind an opening portal.

Gabriel froze, hope stubbornly burgeoning to life within him once more.

A black mass shot through the portal, creating a blast of wind that nearly knocked all three archangel brothers and Max to the ground. Gabriel could have shouted with joy as he straightened and tried to follow Azrael's streaking form. He would recognize the feeling of Az's power anywhere. It was like his signature—dark, potent, and fierce.

Az came to a sudden stop, hovering in the air before Gabriel.

"Abraxos took her," Gabriel told him without preamble. Azrael's golden eyes were glowing like fire, brutally stark in his perfect, angelic face. His long black trench coat hung around him like a holocaust cloak and blended with the pitch blue-black of his shoulder-length hair. He was a living shadow, punctuated by the intense, turbulent light of twin suns.

Gabriel looked him in those glowing golden orbs and whispered, "Please find them. Before it's too late."

Azrael did not waste time replying. He simply shot through the night with a second blast of wind so strong, it knocked Gabriel backward and temporarily blinded him. Gabriel lowered his arm and turned, looking in the direction that his brother had disappeared. There was no sign of him, of course.

He glanced around the road and its adjoining field. Michael, Max, and Uriel stared back at him. There was no sign of any of the Adarians either. The three archangels and their guardian were alone.

Their flying speed was dizzying—impossible. The wind was immense, buffeting her so hard she couldn't breathe unless she kept her head ducked and her face hidden in the curve of her captor's neck. He was holding her fast and firm against him, his right arm around her waist, his left hand behind her neck, bracing her almost gently. His thumb and fingers pressed threateningly to her pulse points.

This was Abraxos. She knew this now. It could be only he—the leader of the Adarians. But none of the archangel brothers had warned her that he'd become a vampire. And he was very much a vampire. She could feel the dark essence of his transformation like a label: "I am vampire." He wore it well. His tall, black-haired, blue-eyed badness was effortlessly scaring the shit out of her.

Juliette tried not to tremble. She tried not to break down and cry. But she didn't want to die. She had lived so many lives—and all of them had been wasted. Because not until now—not until *this* one—had she finally come to realize who and what she was. *Why* she was. Not until now had she found Gabriel.

And now she was ensnared in the arms of her killer.

Before her was the evil vampire. Behind her was a thousand-foot drop into the unknown. She was trapped.

Trapped.

. . . she willed her magic to remain within herself. She trapped it there, deep inside, forever denying the wizard her essence. . . .

Juliette frowned where she pressed her forehead to Abraxos's shoulder. Why was this line replaying in her head? Why now? Ever since Samael had leaned over to whisper in her ear, she'd been recalling the short paragraph she'd read in the history book Law had left in her cottage. What could it possibly mean?

Abraxos slowed, still clutching her tightly in his arms. Juliette chanced a look up, lifting her head. They were landing. The wind was changing. Juliette's hair whipped about her face for a moment as they descended and her stomach leapt up into her throat. She held her breath and hid her face again, unwilling to watch the ground come up to meet them.

In a few seconds, she felt the tips of her boots touching down and she braced herself. But Abraxos brought them in gently, setting her steadily on her feet before releasing his grip around her waist and neck.

"You can look now," he teased her softly. His voice was deep and pure and powerful and Juliette recognized that kind of resonance. The Masked One had it as well. Azrael. *It must come with vampirism,* she thought. Still, she'd heard Azrael say only a few words before he'd disappeared to "get dinner" after kidnapping her from the elevator in Sam's hotel, but from what she'd heard, Az was special even in this. The former Angel of Death's voice was literally mesmerizing.

Juliette took a shaky step back from Abraxos and glanced around. They were standing on a craggy, moss- and grass-covered cliff overlooking a turbulent North Sea. "Wh-where are we?" Her mouth wouldn't move quite right. She was either still very cold or terrified out of her mind. Probably both.

"We're on the cliffs just south of Stonehaven," he told her calmly. He gestured to the land behind him. "There's a golf course just over that rise."

She knew where that was. They were on the mainland now. Somehow, in the space of a few short minutes, Abraxos had crossed not only the water that separated the Hebrides from the rest of Scotland, but most of Scotland as well. They were now in the heart of eastern Scotland, a short drive from Aberdeen.

She felt her jaw drop open as she looked up at the Adarian vampire. Three hundred and fifty miles in five minutes. If he could do that—what else was Abraxos capable of? And how the hell was she still in one piece? Shouldn't the trip have ripped her hair out or frozen her solid or something?

Abraxos threw his head back and laughed, the sound deep and wonderful despite Juliette's fear and disbelief. "It is rather fascinating, isn't it, little one?"

Juliette blinked. "You're r-reading my mind."

"Of course," he admitted easily, shrugging his broad shoulders. He was dressed in a navy blue thermal shirt that set off the color of his eyes and black jeans with a black leather belt. To hear Eleanore speak of him, he'd always been the military type. But it would seem that turning into a vampire had brought out the *GQ* side of him.

Again, he chuckled, and the sound wrapped around Juliette like invisible velvet. "Are y-you gonna k-kill me or wh-what?" she stuttered, hating the way she couldn't stop trembling. She was about to die. It was a hard realization.

Abraxos watched her for a long, silent while, his sapphire eyes sparking with blue fire. "Why so eager, little one?"

"I don't l-like being tortured."

Abraxos raised his head in understanding, nodding to himself. "Something of which you would know much about."

So he knew about her past lives. She didn't know why, but for some reason that brought her some small sense of satisfaction. She wanted someone to know—to recognize all that she'd been through. Even if it was her killer who vindicated her.

"I am truly sorry for all that the Old Man and his four favored have put you through, little one. And I am sorry that it has to end this way in this life. You have something I very desperately need." He shook his head, shrugging as if helpless. "There is no other way."

"So do it, then," she hissed at him. She was growing tired of being told she was going to die. It would almost be better to just get it over with.

He smiled a small, strange smile that made him look poetically poignant. And then he sighed. "Very well. Wait here." With that, he shot into the sky, leaving a burst of tailwind so strong, it buffeted Juliette, causing her to stumble.

She caught her balance and blinked up at the place where he had disappeared. *What the fuck?* she thought. Where did he go? She couldn't even tell what direction he'd gone in.

"Wait here?" she screamed, calling into the night after him. "Like I can bloody well go anywhere!" She vaguely recognized that she'd picked up on Gabriel's mild-mannered swearing, but mostly, she was bewildered. Abraxos had left her on an outcropping of stone, a hundred feet above the water and rocks below. It was dark and there was nowhere for her to go. Even if she ran, she would probably fall off the cliff. It wouldn't be the first time.

And if she didn't fall—Abraxos would catch her. Of that, she had no doubts. She was trapped.

A cold breeze brushed by her, causing her to shiver violently. Juliette shoved her hands into her pockets to warm them. Once again, her fingers brushed against the smooth gold of the bracelet Gabriel had given her.

She frowned and pulled it out, looking down at its intricately carved surface as it shimmered vaguely in the moonlight.

Trapped. Trap . . .

". . . *Just put it in your pocket. It has the power to trap a person's supernatural abilities within their body. I want you to carry it with you. . . .*"

Juliette's eyes widened as a puzzle piece noisily slid into place inside her head. She glanced up at the empty night sky—and then looked back down at the bracelet once more. Gabriel had told her that the bracelet trapped a supernatural creature's powers within his or her body. Abraxos and his Adarians wanted to steal her power from her by draining and drinking her blood. But if she bound her power within her body . . . maybe it couldn't be drained along with her blood. Maybe it would stay put.

Maybe that was what the archess in the book Law had given her had done; she'd bound her abilities within herself, keeping them from the warlock in the process.

Juliette stared down at the gold wreath. She might die anyway, but if she did, she would at least deny the Adarians what they wanted and perhaps even spare the other archesses in the process.

Juliette turned the bracelet over, looking for some kind of catch or lever with which to open it. There was no way she could slide it over her hand. She was small, but the bracelet was perfectly round and smaller than the circumference of her hand. She'd never noticed before how small it was.

She held it up next to her wrist, squinting at the size. And then, as if to test it out, she bumped it against her arm. There was a quick blinding flash and Juliette jumped, squinting her eyes. When she opened them again, the bracelet was no longer in her hand. It was now on her wrist, and it seemed to wink at her beneath the moonlight.

CHAPTER THIRTY-ONE

K evin could feel that his men were returning to their temporary lair. It was a vibration in the air, a sense that they were no longer in danger. Long ago, Kevin had learned that he possessed the ability to recall his men to a certain location at a certain point in time.

The Adarians tried to stay out of human affairs; their wars and battles had nothing to do with the mortal world. Nevertheless ... once in a while, fighting was necessary, for Adarians were not the only supernatural creatures to inhabit the third planet from the sun.

Seldom, those fights went south. When this happened, Kevin's recall ability kicked in. Unfortunately, it was the only time he was able to use it. If he had possessed the power to call his men to him at any given moment, he would have had his hands on Xathaniel days ago.

The recall began when the Adarians were beaten—or when they had accomplished what they'd set out to do. In those instances, Kevin's men disappeared one by one and reappeared at a previously decided-upon location. In this case, the location was an underground compartment that could be reached through the very cliffs he had left Anderson standing on top of. These locations, or bunkers, were located all over the planet. They'd been created by the Adarians over the last several thousand years and reinforced over time.

Kevin made his way through the caverns' winding stone maze until he could hear his men conversing. At the entrance to the bunker, he shifted, allowing his body to turn to fine blue mist. The mist swirled, collected, and shot beneath the metal door they'd erected, into the cracks, and across to the other side. There, it collected once more, coming together in a sparkling blue dust cloud that quickly solidified to take on his familiar, tall shape.

"General," one of his men greeted him. But the man's voice was tight with pain and his teeth were gritted in stifled anger. Kevin let his eyes scan over the scene. Ely was there, bruised and bloodied, but standing tall and strong as ever. Mitchell was completely undamaged; he had that kind of luck in a battle. People tended to steer clear of him and his powers were immense. Luke was in the same shape as Ely—a bit worse for wear, but whole and healthy all in all.

However, all seven of the group of Adarians that had once numbered eleven were injured in some fashion or another. His vampiric hearing sensed their heartbeats. All were stable but one.

Kevin made his way to a brown-haired man who lay on a bloodied cot, his eyes closed, his handsome face pale. Kevin knew that behind the closed lids were a pair of blue green eyes so stark, they appeared to give off light even when they weren't glowing. His name was Puriel, but he'd gone by the name Paul for more than a thousand years. Paul possessed the power to control electrical fields, and much like an archess, he could even pull lightning from the skies to strike his opponents.

"Gold bullets, sir," another of his men informed him as he gazed down upon the fallen soldier. Kevin noted three entry wounds in Paul's chest. The archangels had learned to fight back, it would seem. *Almost too late,* he mused. As a newly formed vampire, Kevin found that gold had no caustic effect on him the way it had before. His Chosen would eventually possess the same immunity.

However, for the time being, his men were vulnerable to the metal, and one of them was dying due to it. But this was why he had come down here. This was why Kevin had left Juliette Anderson alone up top on the cliffs. He'd known there was a chance that someone in his party would need healing, and because he wasn't certain whether the healing-power transfer would work with an archess, he'd wanted to make sure his men were stable before he allowed Mitchell to have his way with the female archangel.

He'd left her up on top of the cliff because he hadn't wanted to subject his men to the danger of a terrified archess unless absolutely necessary. Archesses were far from helpless damsels in distress. If anything, they were more dangerous than their male counterparts.

Kevin turned and waved the locks off the metal door. It swung outward, opening up to the damp, salty air and the moonlit darkness of the night. There was no time to waste now. Paul's life force was fading.

Kevin shot through the exit and into the underground tunnels like a blue comet, and then burst through the opening beneath the cliff and up into the darkened sky. The blast of wind blew Juliette's hair into her eyes; he watched her where she sat against an outcropping of stone as he approached.

She'd curled in on herself, her knees to her chest, and now she slowly lowered her hands from her face as he touched down and strode toward her, his boots crunching on the rocks beneath him. She flinched when he lowered himself to one knee in front of her so that they would be eye to eye.

"Juliette, you are going to do something for me," he told her, allowing his vampire influence to pour over her.

She glared up at him, defiance oozing from her archess pores. He was impressed; any human on earth would have been coaxed into a state of mesmerism by his mere presence. But Juliette Anderson was an archess—and a pissed-off one, at that. She felt she had nothing to lose. There was no reason for her not to disobey.

But now was no time for her rebelliousness. "If you don't do this thing for me, I will go after your family," he told her calmly. She tried to look away from him, tried to break eye contact, but he grabbed her chin and turned her to face him once more. "And then I will go after your friends. And when I've finished with them, I will choose ten children and kill them off one by one in your name."

Kevin noted the fear sparking to life in her eyes. She felt good beneath his touch, reminding him of how perfect she was. She was an archess; no one had ever been created to more perfect specifications. Her skin was soft and warm and she trembled beautifully. Her straight white teeth were clenched in resentment and her hazel eyes flashed green with fury. He stared down into them and felt himself harden. He could hear her ragged little breaths and smell the adrenaline lacing her powerful blood. His teeth began to ache in his gums.

Somewhere close by, lightning crashed into the North Sea and thunder rolled closely after it. Kevin released her chin to let his hand slip to her throat, where he gripped her just tightly enough to drive his point home. "None of that, little one," he warned, knowing full well that the weather was responding to her anger. "If you so much as send a single spark into any one of my men, I swear, I will make those children suffer. Do you understand me?"

She nodded, her luminescent eyes wide, her pained expression exquisite to behold.

"Good." He nodded his approval, his gaze boring into hers. "Good girl." He stood, taking her with him, his hand still around her throat. She gasped and her hands came around his wrist instinctively. Kevin noticed something gold flash around her left wrist. He frowned, narrowing his gaze. He hadn't noticed it on her before. The surface of the gold wreath bore intricate engravings of wording that looked familiar to him. Ancient wording . . .

But there was no time.

Kevin pulled Juliette to him with his hand at her throat, and wrapped her tightly in his embrace. Once more, he took to the skies, diving over the cliff to the sound of her breath catching and her heart hammering wildly. He shot through the tunnels beneath the ground, one hand over her head to protect it from any near misses.

And then he was coming through the giant metal door and into the bunker. With a vaporous flourish, he landed at the center of the group of men and released Juliette, allowing her to stand on her own.

He steadied her with one hand on her shoulder as she pulled away from him enough to see that she was surrounded by Adarians. The five of his men who could stand slowly came to their feet, their stark eyes glued to the promising young woman who had been deposited into their ranks. Kevin recognized the emotions crossing their faces. They were angry, injured, in pain. They were hungry for revenge—and for other things.

Juliette spun a slow circle in their center, no doubt feeling she was surrounded by sharks. She was defenseless as long as she remembered his warnings. And his men all but knew it; the looks in their eyes were darkly promising. Juliette saw it, too; she did so unconsciously, he knew, but she backed up against him, her pulse so fast, he wondered if her little heart would simply give out.

He took advantage of the situation and bent over her

until his lips were next to her ear. "Heal him, little one." She stiffened in front of him as his words whispered across her skin, but he gestured over her to Paul's prone body and once more took her neck in his fast grip. "I will only tell you once," he added. And then he let her go.

Juliette took a slow, stumbling step forward, closing the distance between herself and the cot on which Paul lay. Kevin watched her carefully, ready to react should she try anything dangerous. The other men stepped back a bit, giving her room. But their eyes followed her like the eyes of wolves on little Red.

She knelt beside Paul's body and pressed her fingers to his throat.

"He lives, but barely," Kevin supplied, saving her the trouble.

She nodded her understanding and placed her hand palm down upon his chest. Several seconds passed and nothing happened. He could hear Juliette's pulse quicken once more. Kevin moved up behind her and knelt down. He placed his hand over hers and felt nothing. No heat. No warmth. No healing energy at all.

Wrath rushed through him, hot and red, and he stood once more, grabbing her with a fist in her hair and yanking her up with him. She gasped in pain but remained otherwise silent. He spun her around and brought his face to hers. His hand remained fisted at the back of her head, holding her immobile. "What have you done?" he demanded, hissing the words across her lips.

Juliette did not answer. Her eyes were fully green now, flaring with emerald fire as she glared up at him in utter defiance. Kevin grabbed her once more by the throat with his free hand and she again wrapped her fingers around his wrist.

He caught the glint of the gold band and paused. It seemed to shimmer more brightly than before.

He glanced up into her eyes and saw the answer there.

She couldn't hide it from him. He took the thoughts from the surface of her mind as if skimming a small pond for lily pads. He bared his teeth, flashing fangs, and then squeezed the hand around her neck. With his other, he released her hair and curled his fingers around the gold band, giving it a good yank. It was warm in his grip, but when it didn't burn, he could feel his men shift in stunned silence.

Still, the bracelet remained attached to her wrist, bruising her where he'd pulled against it. It wasn't going anywhere. He had to fight his own strength and his own anger now to keep from killing her outright. "Take it off," he commanded, growling the words through a clenched jaw.

"Bite me," she said, echoing the thought she'd hurled at Mitchell earlier that night.

"Fine," he replied, and without pause he fisted his hand in her hair once more in order to yank her head back, exposing her throat. He'd learned over the last few nights that there were two ways a vampire could bite an individual. He could just do it—and it would hurt, as if two fork prongs were being embedded into the side of the victim's neck. Or he could do it and flood his victim with an influence that took away the pain and substituted pleasure.

Kevin wasn't in a generous mood. And so as his fangs delved into the side of the archess's throat, he was struck with two things at once. One was her scream as the pain overtook her, buckling her knees beneath her. The other was the rush of pleasure he received at having her flesh between his teeth and her blood across his tongue. He swallowed, holding her limp body against him, and his pleasure spread, arcing through his entire body.

But by the time he'd swallowed his third or fourth mouthful, he was beginning to realize that there was something missing. It was blood and it was the sweetest blood he had ever tasted—but it was just blood. There was no magic in it.

He concentrated more deeply, willing her power to leave her body and enter his own. There was no change. Nothing happened and the archess was growing weak in his grasp. He felt her heart flutter and heard her moan in helpless pain, and he frowned against her neck. This wasn't right. *I'm killing her,* he thought. *And it's pointless.* The bracelet obviously kept her powers within her and prevented him from taking them through her blood.

With that bitter realization, he reined himself in and pulled his fangs from her throat. She was limp in his arms. He bent and lifted her, gazing down at the side of her neck where it was marred by two deep, angry red holes that dripped precious archess blood. "Take her," he told Mitchell, handing Juliette to the tall, dark-haired Adarian she'd been promised to.

Mitchell took her from Kevin's arms and Kevin turned and knelt beside Paul's prone form. His gut clenched; his heart ached. *Too many,* he thought. He'd lost too many lately. One of them by his own hand.

And the world was getting smaller.

But Paul's heartbeat was barely discernible now. He was nearly gone. It was do it this way—or lose all of him forever. Kevin bent over his fallen soldier and whispered into the man's ear, "Forgive me." With that, he turned Paul's head to the side and sank his fangs into the man's throat.

The Adarians around him were silent. It was as if they understood. Or maybe it was that they were too shocked—too afraid—to say anything at all. Whatever the reason, the room became a mortuary as Kevin drank Paul's blood and absorbed his power along with it. It was over in less than thirty seconds. Paul's heart stopped beating altogether and his life force slipped away.

Kevin extracted his fangs from his soldier's neck and

stood, wiping his mouth on the back of his hand. He could feel Paul's power there residing within him now—ready for the taking. He turned and looked at the archess in Mitchell's arms. Her eyes were open beneath half-closed lids; she was weak but conscious.

She watched him warily, hopelessly, and he approached like a wolf fresh from the kill. "How do I get the bracelet off?" he asked, allowing his power to pour over her. He didn't hold back. He bombarded her with its potency, wanting the truth and wanting it now.

She shuddered beneath the weight of his words and magic and groaned when it set off an aphrodisiac-like reaction within her body. Mitchell watched her knowingly and then glanced up at his general with dark, glittering eyes.

Kevin brushed the hair from her cheek and waited. Juliette's lips parted and she spoke, though the sound was a harsh, hoarse whisper, as her tender throat no doubt prevented anything else. "I . . . can . . . remove it."

"She speaks the truth," Mitchell said. He'd been in her head. But Kevin didn't need the affirmation; he'd been in there as well. The ability to read minds was a vampiric power, and his transformation into one of the supposed undead was complete.

Apparently only the individual who put the bracelet on could take it off again. She had already refused to do as much once. It had cost him the life of one of his men. And now if he didn't get it off her soon, it was going to cost Mitchell a healing power.

Kevin could feel Paul's stolen power add itself to the cocktail of the others he already had swirling inside. He felt volatile. Strong. "Take it off, Juliette," he commanded, using every ounce of his newly learned vampiric power to bend her will with his words.

Behind her, Mitchell shook his head as if to clear it and swayed on his feet. Kevin reached out to steady him with a strong hand. Juliette blinked once, and then shifted in Mitchell's arms. Kevin smiled as she began to reach for the bracelet with her other hand.

But the bunker was plunged into chaos before her fingers closed over the metal. The heavy bunker door came off its hinges and went flying into several Adarians against one wall. The ground, walls, and ceiling began to tremble, and the lights began to flicker menacingly. One of them sparked—and then they all went out.

CHAPTER THIRTY-TWO☉

There was a growling sound beside Juliette, then a
grunt of pain, and she was falling. But before she
could hit the ground, a second set of arms lifted her,
crushing her to another strong chest. She closed her eyes
and curled inward, feeling exhausted and dizzy and disoriented. Beyond the periphery of her senses were the
distant sounds of scrambling and scraping accompanied
by the shouts of the Adarians.

There was nothing she could do as her hair began to
whip about in a strong breeze as her captor began to
move through the darkness at roller-coaster speed.

"It's okay, Jules. It's me," came a deep voice at her ear.
She felt something incredibly soft brushing her cheeks
and caught the scent of spice or incense. She recognized
the voice, but it took her a minute of frantic mental fumbling for her to place it. It reminded her of the movie
Comeuppance. And then she remembered. Christopher
Daniels.

Uriel! Relief washed over her, though she knew she
wasn't out of the woods yet.

She turned slightly in his arms, enough to open her
eyes and look around just as he shot from the opening of
the underground caverns and into the moonlit night beyond. His massive black wings emerged above them,

stretching to their full length, and shimmered black and green, nearly iridescent. They beat the air with a hard and steady rhythm, taking them up to the top of the cliff.

There, he gently touched down, still holding her fast in his arms.

"She's injured," he said, gazing at someone over her head. She wanted to see who it was, but her neck hurt too much for her to turn her head.

"She's wearing the bracelet," Michael said as he stepped up to them. Juliette felt more reassurance wash over her at the appearance of the second brother.

"You did good, lass," Gabriel said. This time, Juliette did turn her head, despite the pain. The former Messenger Archangel was standing there beside her, his tall, broad form seeming to shield her from the world. His black hair billowed in the sea breeze, the five-o'clock shadow on his strong chin making him appear ever the rake. He was so gorgeous, her pain eased a little at the very sight of him. He looked down at her in Uriel's arms and his silver eyes claimed her as they always had. "That's my girl."

But then he somewhat reluctantly stepped back out of the way and Michael placed his hand to Juliette's chest. The familiar light and heat she'd felt when he'd healed her before returned once more and the pain in her neck gradually slipped away. But the weakness remained. She frowned, wondering what was different this time.

"I'm sorry, Jules," Michael said softly as he removed his hand. His stark blue eyes looked a tad bloodshot. "I can't replace the blood loss. It's not within my power."

Juliette could not feel disappointed. She was grateful that they were all there with her, to say nothing of the fact that the holes in her neck had been closed up.

"Thank you," she said softly, meaning it with all of her heart. "How are you here?" They were more than three hundred miles from the Hebrides. How had they all found her? How had they gotten there so quickly?

"Az found you," Uriel told her. "Then he contacted us and we used the mansion's portal to get here."

Speaking of the vampire archangel, where was Azrael? She glanced around and saw Max standing a few feet away. Only Az was missing.

Uriel's grip on her tightened suddenly as the ground beneath him began to buck. "Time's up," he muttered, beating his giant wings once to take them both into the air a safe few feet from the turbulent rock. Juliette looked down as the rock began to crack and separate, opening up like the gates to hell.

She squealed and ducked her face into Uriel's shoulder when the ground then exploded outward and dirt and stone went flying in a nasty, painful spray. Uriel curled his wings over her body and she could hear the stones buffet the thick, feathered appendages. Then he was spinning away from the new opening and depositing her on the ground a few yards away as two figures shot out from the depths of the crack—two blurs, one black and one blue.

Juliette found her footing and though she could still feel blood loss bending her knees, she retained enough strength in the heat of the moment to stand on her own. She had no choice. Because once the impressive struggling figures of Azrael and Abraxos had drilled their way to the surface, the other Adarians had followed. Now the six remaining soldiers engaged the four brothers and their guardian once more.

Juliette stumbled backward, trying to make heads or tails of the chaotic clash between Adarian and archangel. They were very nearly equally matched. However very nearly was not close enough. Not to ensure Juliette's safety—not this time.

"Take off the bracelet, Juliette," came a calm, cool voice from behind her.

Juliette whirled around to face the dark-haired man with piercing black eyes who read her mind and gazed at her as if she belonged to him. She was able to get a good look at him now that he wasn't freezing her with his power or knocking the ground out from under her.

As far as the tall, dark, and handsome thing went, he was a woman's wet dream. He was certainly tall, as all Adarians were. He was broad-shouldered and slim and wore dark jeans, boots, and a white button-down shirt beneath a black sport coat. His chin was stubbled slightly and his dark eyes sparked with specks of what she could now see were different colors embedded in the blackness. Like stars.

She wondered what his name was.

He smiled at her, shoving his hands into his jeans pockets. "Mitchell," he told her softly, taking a step toward her as he looked down at the ground. "Juliette, you seem to be a woman of integrity," he said then, his expression becoming contemplative. Behind her, lightning struck and thunder boomed, causing her to duck and cover her ears.

A few seconds later, she was straightening again and Mitchell was continuing as if nothing had interrupted him. "I've met a lot of women over the years," he told her, finally looking back up to meet her gaze again. He stepped forward. She stepped back. The sounds of struggle were all around her. "And I've been in their heads," he continued. "I've never been as impressed with any of them as I am with you. So, I'll make you a deal." He stopped and shrugged, his hands still in his pockets.

Juliette knew better than to say anything. Whatever he was up to, it wasn't worth letting her guard down. She watched him carefully as he finally took his hands out of his pockets so that he could pull a cigarette from the inside pocket of his sport coat, place it between his lips, and flick a lighter to life, shielding it from the ocean breeze. The end of the cigarette began to glow red and he extinguished the lighter and repocketed it. With utter calm and conviction, Mitchell took the cigarette out of his mouth and focused his dark, piercing gaze on her once more.

"If you grant me your word that you'll remain with me and give me your blood when I ask for it, I will let you live." He blew a small cloud of smoke, his eyes glinting as he watched her take in his words.

Juliette had no idea what to make of the offer. It was terrifying for her to think that her only two options in life now were to give herself over to an Adarian to be his eternal prisoner—or to die. The thought left her momentarily speechless. She stared up at the dark-haired man and opened her mouth to say something, but closed it again when she realized she had nothing to say.

What *could* she say? Even if she thought the offer sound and was crazy enough to accept it, how could he be sure that she wouldn't go back on her promise?

"As I said, Juliette," he told her, taking another drag of smoke and lowering the cigarette once more, "I know you're a woman of your word." He blew a small cloud. "Integrity, Juliette. It's what sets you apart from the others. If you make a promise, you keep it. Don't you?" His voice had dropped, becoming almost intimate. She was amazed that she could hear him even over the cacophony of battle going on around them. It was something about the voices of Adarians and archangels—they always managed to make themselves heard with perfect clarity.

"Abraxos would never let me live."

At this, Mitchell gave a small laugh. He shook his

head. "The General is in love with Granger. I don't have to be able to read his mind to know as much. He won't be able to kill her. He understands, perhaps better than anyone."

Juliette stared at him, shocked by the news. Abraxos was in love with Eleanore? Ellie had told Juliette about Abraxos—about how he'd appeared to her when she was a teenager. She'd had a crush on him. He'd been her first crush, in fact.

There was obviously more to it than that for Abraxos. And now everything Uriel and Ellie had told her about Kevin Trenton's drive to get his hands on Ellie made even more sense than it had before. Abraxos wasn't only bitter that he couldn't heal—he was bitter that Ellie wasn't meant to be his.

Despite the severely warped situation she was in, Juliette found herself reasoning. What Mitchell was asking her for made sense, in a way. If he really wanted her to live, then giving him nonstop access to her blood was as good as killing her. Once he used his dose of healing power, he could return to her for another. On and on. All he needed was her word that she wouldn't deny him.

She could even understand why integrity would be important to Mitchell. He could obviously read minds. She imagined that after centuries of reading duplicitous minds, he would long for the solid reliability of a mind that meant what it said. Nevertheless, Juliette was not going to let her empathy with the Adarian snap the trap shut. "What in the world would make you think I would ever make such a deal with you?" she asked him then, and though her own body was weak, she, too, managed to make herself heard.

Mitchell smiled and shrugged, dropping the cigarette to smash it under one boot. "I assumed you would rather not die."

"You assumed wrong," she told him. It was true. She had lived many lives—and died many times. And in all those existences, the most painfully grievous moments had been not when she was dead but when she'd been very much alive—and suffering. There were worse things than death.

Mitchell considered her answer for a moment, his gaze searching hers with uncomfortable intensity. "You are not afraid to die. I can understand this. After all, it's nothing new to you." He came toward her again and Juliette fought not to step back. She chanced a glance behind her and found that she had maybe three feet to go before she would be flush with the cliff's ledge.

"However, something in this life *is* new to you," he continued. "You've never truly loved before, have you, Juliette?"

Juliette's head whipped back around, her gaze cutting to his eyes. Trepidation unfurled within her gut. Dying was one thing . . . but this was skimming the edges of something more dangerous.

She said nothing. She didn't need to, though, and she knew it. She knew that the moment she thought of Gabriel and his silver eyes and his captivating brogue, he was reading those thoughts as well—stealing them from her in the most merciless and intrusive manner.

His smile was back. He cocked his head to one side, again shoving his hands into his pockets. "What would you do to save him, Juliette? Would you make a promise if his life depended on it instead of yours?"

Juliette froze. She thought of Gabriel and the life she had decided she wanted to have with him. Here. In Caledonia. She'd never experienced a sense of home before, not in all her many lifetimes. But Gabriel could give her that—Gabriel would give her that. She knew it in the very fiber of her being.

Unless he couldn't. Because he was dead.

She swallowed and nearly choked on the dry lump that had formed in her throat. Mitchell watched her for another moment more, and then he reached into the back waistband of his jeans and extracted a shard gun. He held it down at his side for a few short seconds—and then raised it, along with his gaze, until they were both directed at something above her head.

Juliette spun around to see Gabriel and another Adarian fighting several yards away. The Adarian had him around the neck in a fierce death grip. But the Adarian was also injured and bleeding from several wounds across his strong body. The fight seemed to be well matched.

Except that Gabriel's back was turned toward her. Juliette's heart flipped in her chest and her stomach turned. His broad back was the perfect target for Mitchell's shard gun.

"No," she whispered, having lost her voice.

"You have three seconds, Juliette. Take off the bracelet and I will consider it your vow to willingly join me. You will live—and so will your precious Messenger."

Juliette had no further time to think. Either she surrendered, or Gabriel would die. Fury boiled to life within her. She was so sick to death of people shooting Gabriel with those shard guns. How many times had Azrael said he'd been shot? And here was another Adarian again— threatening to do it some more.

With a bitter cry of frustration, Juliette curled her fingers around the bracelet and gave a quick yank, ripping the golden wreath from her wrist with a blinding flash. At once, she felt her powers swell, an influx of energy and ability that had been kept just out of reach while she'd worn the band.

Mitchell's dark eyes sparked and his cruel lips curled

up in a slow, satisfied smile. "That's better," he said, lowering the deadly weapon.

Juliette's heart was cracking open. Visions were flashing before her mind's eye. Gabriel at her doorway, the salt of the sea in his hair. Gabriel across from her at the breakfast table, laughing as he told her a story. Gabriel as he bent to claim her lips with his own while his body was buried so deeply within hers.

Gabriel, her archangel.

"Not anymore, little one," Mitchell said softly as he closed the distance between them so that he towered over her. He curled his finger beneath her chin and tilted her head so that she was looking into his eyes.

Her cheeks were wet.

"You've given me your word," he told her, his gaze intense. "And to make certain it can never be broken—" He released her chin, raised the gun, aimed it at Gabriel, and began to pull the trigger.

Juliette screamed, "Noooo!" She found herself rushing forward before she knew what she was doing. All she was consciously aware of was that she didn't want Gabriel to die. She couldn't stand the thought of him being shot again. Not even once more. Not when she could do something to stop it.

She ducked her head, using her shoulder like a football player. Using every ounce of her strength, she slammed into Mitchell's tall body, spinning as she did so. The unexpected impact gave her enough momentum to turn them both and keep going. One step, two ... The third crumbled beneath their booted feet as the cliff gave way underneath them.

Juliette closed her eyes when the sky opened up to embrace her. She'd been here before. She remembered the feeling. The air was open; there were no footholds or handholds in space. Time slowed. It very nearly stopped.

She sensed Mitchell pulling away from her, his own body falling as hers was. She let him go. It would be over soon.

There were precious seconds remaining. An eternity— and certainly long enough for her final, perfect sentiment.

I love you, Gabriel. Maybe they would meet again. She loved him, after all. *And I always will.*

CHAPTER THIRTY-THREE

What in the world could make Gabriel turn his back on a man like the Adarian he was fighting now? . . . It was a phantom of a thought, floating like a ghost in the back of his mind as he spun around, doing that very thing. But then he had his answer. It tumbled over the cliff in the form of a beautiful young woman, long hair flying, eyes closing, her body clutching to the enemy to take him down with her.

There was a sound, ripped from somewhere deep inside of him, but he didn't consciously make it. He only knew he was moving faster than he had ever moved before, following the image that took his heart with it.

He didn't reach her in time. Not to stop her. But his body, propelled by a love and loss too great to deny, left the safety of the ground along with her. He fell after her, clutching at empty air, his mind blacking out on all emotion save one.

That one emotion ripped him apart from the inside. It tore him open and left him gaping as he fell, exposed as he had never been exposed before.

A lifetime — several — passed before he'd made it far enough to touch her. Gabriel looked upon her lovely face, her closed lids, and her furrowed brow, and the world melted around them. His hand slipped around her wrist as the cliff face blurred beside them and the wind whipped through her hair. It was a final connection. If they were going to die this time, they would do so together.

Juliette opened her eyes. Gabriel's consciousness froze in confusion. Her eyes were glowing. Their hazel brilliance now burned like gemstones, luminous lamps of amber and emerald so lovely, he literally stopped breathing. It wouldn't matter in a moment; the world was about to end.

But Juliette blinked her glowing eyes and he felt her hand upon his cheek, warm and soft and pure. "I love you." She mouthed the words, but he couldn't hear them. The wind stole them from her.

They echoed in his mind.

"And I love you, lass," he whispered. They were words he had never strung together in that order before. Not until now.

Now, he thought. *Now we hit bottom—one hundred feet down. It's over.* He would not survive the fall. And if he did, he wouldn't want to—not without his archess. As his last act upon the earth, he used his grip on Juliette's wrist to pull her to him, hauling her into his arms to hold her tight.

He closed his eyes, his hand spanning the small of her back. And he waited.

And waited.

. . . and waited.

"Gabriel," came her soft voice, whispered across the curve of his neck.

Gabriel's hand moved up her back and stopped, sensing something different. It felt like a warp in the air, warm and nearly solid. Gabriel frowned, feeling strange. His body felt slightly numb. He no longer sensed the wind buffeting him. The sound of it was fading, being replaced by something oddly hollow. Like an echo.

He opened his eyes.

The cliff's blurring face was gone. The ocean's white-capped waves, frozen in waiting time, were gone. The night and its full moon were gone. The world had disappeared and all that remained were Gabriel and his archess standing together in a space of white fog and nothingness.

"Where are we?" Juliette asked. Her words bounced against the nothingness and were swallowed in its cotton.

"Nowhere," Gabriel replied. He knew what was happening. But the knowledge was like a slow drug, and its piggybacking epiphany of joy was gradual, as if affected to a sluggishness by the dense mist around them. "No' anymore," he whispered. "No' yet."

And then he looked down at the woman in his arms and gradually let her go. For the second time in the space of the last few eternal seconds, he could not believe his eyes. "Juliette . . . ," he gasped, utterly breathless at what he beheld. "My God . . ." His hand came up to cup her cheek. He could say nothing further.

There were no words.

Her archess eyes were glowing again, more stunning than anything he had ever seen. But even more bewildering were the massive brown and green wings solidifying at her back. The air warped around her, the shape of the wings shimmering and iridescent until, finally, they hardened into reality and Gabriel felt tears on his cheeks.

"My angel," he rasped, his breathing ragged with emotion.

"Gabriel," she whispered, and he watched as her own glowing eyes began to shimmer with unshed tears. "You . . . have wings."

It was hard, but Gabriel managed to pull his eyes off her form in order to glance over his shoulder. And she was right. Behind him in each direction stretched the magnificent plumage of two massive raven-black wings, run through with streaks of stark silver. "Wha' do you know?" he whispered, too struck with awe to say much else. Everything was happening so quickly.

He recognized it all now. Uriel and Eleanore had gone through the same thing. The two had shared the experience shortly afterward and the other three archangel brothers were treated to a preview of what they might expect once they found their own archesses. This was Gabriel's "choice." He was here with Juliette now to make a decision: stay on Earth or return to his realm with his archess. He couldn't believe it. It was truly coming to pass. It wasn't a joke, he wasn't being teased, and it wasn't a dream.

He looked back at Juliette. "You have them, too, luv."

She blinked, her pink lips parting with a catch in her breath.

"Go on, then," he said, tilting her head gently to the side with a curled finger beneath her chin. "See for yourself."

She turned and shrugged her shoulder. Her gasp indicated that she could see them. "Oh my God . . ." Her voice trailed off in wonder. "What— How—"

"You sacrificed yourself to save me," Gabriel said. He knew that now. It must have been why she had rushed the Adarian. He could feel it in his bones. "Didn't you, luv?" he asked softly.

Juliette turned back to look up at him with those incredible glowing eyes and he had to fight not to tremble. She was humbling him. He didn't deserve her.

She didn't answer. But when she blushed and ducked her head, he knew it was true. "And that's why we're here," he said, curling his finger beneath her chin once more. She turned her eyes to him again and he smiled. "Juliette, my sweet angel."

He had no more words and even if he'd had them, he

no longer wanted to speak. Right now, all he wanted to do was kiss her. Hold her. He wanted to know, for once and for all, that everything he was seeing was real.

So he bent over her and she closed her eyes. His lips brushed hers with a featherlight tenderness befitting angels. And then he pressed into her, claiming her mouth with his own, parting her lips and tasting her deeply. She was real.

She was very, very real. She was his archess and she would soon be his wife and he would make a home for them both. In Caledonia.

It never failed. Every time Gabriel kissed her, the rest of Juliette's world melted away. It didn't seem to matter what else might be happening. He simply subjugated her every sense, taking over without mercy. His kiss was a mandate, a cage, a lock and key—and as he tore down her defenses and ripped away her world, she could swear she heard the *click* as he bound her to him forever.

Her body heated up, her core melted, and she grew wet for him. A moan of longing and pleasure bubbled up from inside of her and he swallowed it, fisting his hands in her hair as if he couldn't get close enough.

Someone cleared his throat.

Juliette stilled, feeling strange suddenly. Their surroundings had changed. Sound was coming in at them once again: the wind, the waves. The air was colder. Gabriel was still kissing her, but the urgency of the kiss had lessened a little. He apparently sensed it, too.

Juliette opened her eyes as he slowly pulled away, lowering his hands.

"This is a familiar scene," said Michael from where he stood a few feet away, his arms crossed over his chest, his grin a mile wide. "Nice wings," he said, winking at Juliette.

She had no breath with which to speak at that moment; Gabriel had more or less taken it all. But she did manage to glance over her shoulder again. Vast brown and green wings unfurled from the center of her back. *Wings,* she thought. *I've really got wings.*

Tentatively, and not at all sure of the strangeness of the musculature, she tried to move them. They responded beautifully, curling forward and brushing their feathers along the ground — and then extending again until they were raised high on either side of her in exultation. She couldn't help but laugh then. The sensation was incredible.

"I have wings!" She giggled the words, turning once more to look up into Gabriel's glowing silver gaze. He was staring down at her with immense pride, his grin ear to ear. His own wings flicked behind his back and drew Juliette's wide-eyed gaze once more.

They were stunning, much more so than hers, in her opinion. Out here, in the black of night, they made him look like the tall, dark archangel he truly was. It was fitting. His colossal wingspan stretched more than ten feet in either direction. His feathers were a deep, dark pitch, shot through with marbles of silver that made them shimmer in the moonlight.

Juliette shook her head. This was all too much.

But then she frowned. Something niggled at her brain. It was quiet around them. Hadn't there been a battle going on only seconds ago?

Her eyes widened; she spun around, searching for Abraxos and his Adarians. But the cliff top was empty. A massive gash had been ripped into it from below and rocks and debris had been strewn all over it. However, the General and his men were missing.

She stepped around Gabriel and he let her go, turning with her. Max and Uriel stood to one side. Uriel's wings were gone. She wondered how he made them disappear. She supposed she would be learning very soon.

Both Uriel and Max watched her in silence. Max smiled a proud smile and Uriel nodded at Juliette's wings, chuckling softly.

"What happened?" she asked. "Where is everyone?"

"Once you fell off of the cliff, the Adarians began disappearing again," Uriel told her.

"And you've probably been gone a little longer than you think you have," Michael added. "It was the same way with Uriel and Ellie."

Juliette thought about that. The Adarians had disappeared? How did they manage that? She had a thousand questions, but they were stilled in her mind when she caught sight of the fourth archangel brother. He stood alone to one side, leaning against a tall boulder. His figure was partially hidden in shadow and his amber gold eyes reflected the moonlight with supernatural eeriness. Juliette could see that his black trench coat was stained wet in places. She swallowed hard.

He straightened and came away from the shadows then, a tall shadow of a man himself, utterly at one with the darkness. His boot stepped out into a shaft of moonlight, illuminating his impressive frame. Blood smeared his neck and part of his beautiful face.

Azrael had been fighting Abraxos. The two were probably the most powerful supernatural creatures on the planet other than Samael. They'd gone head-to-head, tooth and nail—and Azrael's still, calm facade could not hide the crimson evidence of the viciousness of that battle. Juliette wondered what had happened. Whose life liquid stained Azrael's clothing—the General's or Azrael's?

Az's golden gaze skirted to the wings at Juliette's back—and then to those that graced the back of his brother. A small smile curled his perfect lips, a smile that almost reached his eyes.

His gaze returned to Juliette and he nodded once,

slowly, as if in reverence. "Welcome," he said, his deep voice rumbling across the cliff's top with mesmerizing grace. *You are a very resourceful woman, Juliette,* his voice continued, but this time in her mind alone. *Intelligent, powerful, and kind. You are a true archess.*

Juliette wasn't sure what to say to that. But it turned out it didn't matter because Az cocked his head then and cut his gaze to Max, who had been watching him with an almost wary kind of care.

"I need blood," he said simply.

Juliette shivered.

Azrael's gold gaze sliced back to her. The gesture hadn't gone unnoticed.

"Of course," Max said softly. "We'll see you back at the mansion."

Az nodded once more and stepped back into the shadows. Juliette watched with wide eyes as his form seemed to melt into the darkness until she could no longer make it out. Within seconds, the unsettling reflection of his eyes was gone. And so was he.

"Wow," she whispered, shaking her head. "He sure has a lot of powers."

"Indeed," Max muttered, coming to stand before her. Gently, he grasped her by her upper arms and smiled down at her. "I never had any doubts that you had survived the fall, Juliette," he said softly. "I saw what you did. You sacrificed yourself for Gabriel—not once, but twice."

Juliette frowned up at him, not understanding.

But his smile never wavered and he went on. "You removed the bracelet," he said as his hands slid down her arms until he was taking her hands in his and turning her wrist over. The bracelet was gone.

Juliette shrugged. The tiny gesture was repeated with her shining, downlike wings, drawing a deep, wonderful chuckle from Gabriel. She glanced up at him and he gave her a knowing look.

"That, in and of itself, was enough for you to prove your love for Gabriel," Max said.

"Aye," Gabriel agreed, grinning widely. "Bu' she's a strong Scottish lass an' one manner of proof was no' enough for her, was it, luv?" He chuckled again, brushing the back of his forefinger down her cheek.

Juliette shivered again, but this time in pleasure.

"Okay, I think we've been on this windy precipice long enough," Uriel interrupted. They turned to watch as he strode across the hilltop in the direction of the golf course that Abraxos had said was over the rise.

Max, who Juliette noticed was no longer dressed in fatigues but was once more wearing a brown suit and glasses, shoved his hands into his trouser pockets. "Ah, Scotland," he said, as he looked around before following Uriel. The moon reflected off the lenses of his glasses. "I grew up here, you know," he said. "Jus' up the road in Aberdeen." He chuckled and Juliette stared at him as his accent changed from American to a Scottish brogue in a heartbeat.

"I can still remember feedin' the haggis to the family dog. Och, me mom did whip me fer tha' one." He shook his head as if lost in memory, and disappeared over the rise after Uriel.

Michael ran a hand through his blond hair and smiled to himself, following after.

Gabriel took Juliette's hand in his, weaving his fingers with her own. He bent over and whispered in her ear. "Never mind him," he told her. "That's jus' Max. It's somethin' he does."

Juliette nodded, not knowing what to think or say. It didn't matter to her, though. Not really. She felt light inside, free of worries and pain and longing. Gabriel gave her hand a knowing squeeze and led her after the others.

Juliette was surprised to see that less than a hundred yards inland was a small golf-caddie shack. Uriel raised his hand toward the door of the shack and it began to warp and waver. The portal swirled to life, and at its center crackled a lit fireplace and warm, comforting home.

The five of them made it through the portal in short order and Max waved it shut behind him.

Uriel looked up then as a figure emerged from one of the archways leading to another wing of the mansion. "Uriel," Eleanore breathed, her voice and expression oozing vast relief. She strode quickly toward him, looking as beautiful and slim and tall as ever. Juliette experienced the tiniest twinge of friendly envy over the girl's height, and then realized she was just glad to see the other woman. The other *archess*. It was almost like having a sister.

Uriel met her halfway and then embraced his wife tightly, tilting her head back to kiss her.

And Juliette remembered what Mitchell had said about Abraxos and his love for Eleanore. It was information that needed to be shared. All of it was: the fact that the Adarians planned to steal the archesses' powers by drinking their blood, the fact that the General was no longer affected by gold—all of it. She had much to tell them.

But she felt him then, his tall hard presence at her back like a sexual beacon. She closed her eyes as his arm snaked around her, his hand spanning across her abdomen to pull her up against his chest. With his other hand, he ran his fingers along the top ridge of her left wing. Juliette's head fell back upon his shoulder.

The sensation was indescribable. Gabriel's touch had always set her off—and now it set her off in an entirely new way. He bent to whisper in her ear. "I think I'm goin' to like these, lass," he teased her. "I canno' wait to see you in them and nothin' else."

CHAPTER THIRTY-FOUR

The next few days were somewhat of a blur for Juliette. Her parents had been brought back to the mansion. It was a feat worthy of angels—and only angels—as her parents seemed to be only slightly less stubborn than Eleanore's. It had taken all four of the archangels, Max, and both archesses to get the two couples safely sequestered in their own wings of the never-ending, space-defying mansion.

By the end of the following week, Eleanore was hounding Juliette about wedding preparations. Gabriel had proposed. He'd taken her to the Highlands, constructed a cottage for her as only an archangel could, and kept her in his bed until she'd agreed to become his wife. She'd played hard to get . . . until she was so sore from orgasming that she had no choice but to agree. And then Gabriel had kept her there anyway. For a few more days.

The stamina of an archangel was mind-blowing.

Now Juliette stood at the empty stone window frame of Slains Castle, looking out over the North Sea on a gorgeous early-April afternoon. The different colors around her were stark, and if painted, the viewer would have sworn they were imaginary. The water was turquoise, pure and perfect. The seagulls were a crisp, sharp white, the grass was beginning to green, and the moss on the cliff rocks was bright yellow. It was the rocks of the cliff that she gazed at now. Black. As black as her last name would soon be.

This was where Juliette wanted to get married. In this place, where she had lived, died, and found love. This place that had become more a part of her than any ground upon which she had stood.

These cliffs had seen her death. And now they would see her reborn—into a new life.

It hadn't been easy to secure the right to hold a wedding there. The owners of Slains were determined to turn the majestic, crumbling ruins into a string of summer homes. It would be yet another part of history—a part of her past—laid to rest and built over, all but forgotten.

Juliette smiled softly as the wind caressed her cheek, brushing her long hair around her face with the gentleness of a lover. She closed her eyes and breathed in. The air smelled like salt and wet grass and the dawn of a promise.

She opened her eyes when she heard the crunch of a boot behind her. She smiled, feeling his nearness like an approaching candle flame. Her green gaze skirted the blue horizon. "Have you ever seen anything so beautiful?" she asked.

There was a stretch of silence and then, in a soft voice filled with a depth of emotion Juliette had only recently begun to understand, Gabriel said, "No, lass. I haven't."

She turned to face him and was struck still and silent by the expression on his handsome face. His silver eyes pinned her to the spot, searing through to her soul, his brow furrowed with a near pain. The wind brushed his sable hair against his stubbled jaw, making him seem both vulnerable and strong. His tall frame was draped in the color of his name—the color of these cliffs. He seemed stricken as he stood there, taking her in. Juliette could barely breathe.

Gabriel allowed another eternal moment to pass and then strode toward her, slow and with purpose. She remained still, her head leaning back to take in his height. Her lips parted in awe as he came to tower over her and she drowned in the molten mercury in his gaze.

"No' in all my life," he said, not touching her—as if not daring, "have I ever seen anything like you."

Another beat of stillness passed between them, a silence so pregnant with need, it felt like the space between Adam's finger and God's on the Sistine Chapel. And then they were coming together, the both of them, of their own volition. Gabriel's arms wrapped around her, pulling her against him with indisputable possession. Juliette ran her fingers through his hair, fisting them in the softness of his wayward waves. They embraced in a passion unequaled, their lips connecting in an explosion of love and loss, memory and pain—and hope.

And after two thousand years of life and death and existence, Juliette at last felt that she'd come home.

"Good God, Jules, this is amazing." Sophie shook her head, her immense mane of golden hair shimmering down her back as she did so. "Where the hell did you find this man?"

"You mean this 'angel,'" Juliette corrected her best friend, shooting her a quick smile.

"Right. Angel." Sophie nodded. She hopped off the stone railing she'd been sitting on and brushed off her hands. "I'm not sure I'm ever going to get used to that." She sighed and turned to face Juliette, her golden eyes smiling. But it was clear to Juliette that there was still a bit of shock in those sunny depths.

It was understandable. Since the moment Sophie had arrived two nights ago, Juliette had made strides to explain the situation to her best friend—the *whole* situation. That meant coming clean about her ability to heal and how she'd had it for more than a year. And then enlightening her on the fact that Juliette was an archess— and her new fiancé was the archangel Gabriel.

To say that Sophie was surprised would be an understatement. But she was less surprised than Juliette's parents had been. Sophie had always had a very open mind. Juliette was fairly certain it was at least in part due to her upbringing. Or lack thereof.

Sophie was an orphan. She'd been orphaned as a child and handed over to the care of St. Augustine's orphanage in Pittsburgh, Pennsylvania. From there, she had been shuffled through three different foster homes. At the first, she had found herself despised by the woman who would have acted as her mother, because Sophie was growing into an incredibly beautiful and bright child. At the second, and at the age of twelve, she barely escaped the sexual advances of her would-be father. At the third, the threat of sexual abuse reached a new high. And in order to defend herself . . . Sophie had run away.

What she'd seen in the final years of her teenage life, she had yet to share in full even with Juliette. But Jules could just imagine. At twenty-seven years old, Sophie was now a uniquely gorgeous young woman. She was taller than most girls, standing at a lithe and willowy five feet and nine inches. She had a dancer's physique despite the fact that she actually hated ballet and thought it was the harbinger of anorexia. Ironically, Sophie herself didn't appear to have a single ounce of fat on her body.

Her skin was poreless, her lips were full, her breasts were pert, if a tad on the smaller side, and her amber gold eyes were unlike any Juliette had ever beheld . . . until she'd met Azrael, that was. The vampire archangel had eyes a little like Sophie's. Like candle flames—like fire.

It fit Sophie. A more fiery spirit Jules had never known. Her best friend was a spirit uncageable, unpredictable, and childlike. Sophie's lovely face lit up at the sight of everything from Strawberry Shortcake to Skela-nimals. She loved Saturday morning cartoons, insisted on eating her dessert before her main meal, and never failed to dress up in at least three different costumes on Halloween.

Halloween was Sophie's favorite day of the year, in fact. It was that part of her that made it easier for her to accept the supernatural nature of what Juliette had been forced to share with her over the last two days.

Sophie had no problem with things "not of this earth." She'd been subjected to the darker side of humanity and knew enough about its less redeeming qualities that it came natural to her to want to believe that there was something else—something more than what had been dished out to her so far.

Sophie hated the fact that she was too old to go trick-or-treating, so she always volunteered at Halloween parks and carnivals and she never failed to be invited by at least ten different guys to ten different Halloween parties. At these parties, she chose to forgo the expected slutty French-maid-type costumes in favor of those that more truthfully reflected her spirit.

She went as a ghost, as a fortune-teller, as a zombie pirate, and as a vampire. The vampire costume was her favorite, and when Juliette had once asked her why, she'd simply smiled, flashing her fake stick-on fangs. "Can you imagine me with a real set of these?" she'd replied. "No one would ever mess with me again."

That was understandable. A lot of men came on to Sophie. It was only natural that she would secretly yearn for some other means with which to defend herself. As far as Juliette knew, Soph had read every vampire book and seen every vampire movie in existence.

Juliette smiled at that thought now as she and Sophie descended the stone steps of Edinburgh Castle, weaving in and out of the throng of tourists also enjoying the site. Sophie had yet to meet the fourth archangel brother, Azrael. In fact . . . Juliette had yet to tell Soph that Azrael was a little more than just an archangel. Sophie had been overwhelmed enough to learn that one of the archangel brothers was Christopher Daniels, the star of *Comeuppance*. She'd almost asked Uriel for his autograph. It was even more surprising for Soph when she'd learned that another brother was the Masked One, lead singer of Valley of Shadow, an incredibly popular rock band that was now touring the US.

Jules wondered how Sophie would react when she learned that the Masked One was not only an archangel— but a real, live vampire.

Would she be elated? Or would she freak?

Time will tell, she thought as they passed through the Edinburgh Castle gates and moved out onto the cobble-stoned streets of Edinburgh beyond. Azrael was supposed to arrive that night, in fact, coming to Scotland just in time for Gabriel's bachelor party.

The wedding was in two days, Saturday night at Slains Castle—overlooking the North Sea. They were holding it at night so that Azrael could attend. Uriel had done the same thing. The four brothers were very, very close.

"Hey, did I tell you about the orphanage in Harris?" Jules asked, breaking the silence. She'd wanted to share this news with Sophie since she'd learned it. She figured that, as an orphan herself, Sophie would appreciate knowing.

"What orphanage?" Sophie asked.

"The one that burned down."

Sophie stopped and gave her a hard look. "Were the kids okay?"

"They're all fine. In fact, that's what I wanted to tell you. This adorable little brother and sister were recently adopted by a couple Gabriel and I know personally."

"That's wonderful!" Sophie exclaimed, her golden eyes lighting up with real joy. "Good parents?"

"Definitely. The new dad's a police officer—chief inspector, in fact. And the mom's a nurse at the hospital. It turns out they've been wanting to do this for a while, since the mom can't have kids of her own. Beth and Tristan took to them both right away."

"Kids know." Sophie nodded, still smiling brightly. "That's good news," she added. "Thanks for sharing." She turned the warmth of her smile onto Juliette, and Jules couldn't help but grin.

"You're welcome. I knew you'd appreciate hearing about it."

They lapsed into another silence for a few minutes. Sophie broke it this time. "I had no idea Scotland was so gorgeous," she said as they rounded the corner of a street that reminded Juliette of Diagon Alley from Harry Potter. "I mean, this looks like Diagon Alley," Soph continued, making Juliette grin widely. "I expect Hermione to come around the corner with a big orange cat any second now."

"You would love that, wouldn't you?" Juliette teased. Soph was a huge fan of Harry Potter. All that magic and the bad guys who weren't really bad guys. It was right up Sophie's alley.

"You know I would," Soph shot back, laughing as she said it.

"So tell me honestly," Jules teased her, "how long would it take for you to find your way to Snape's classroom and pretend you'd been a bad student who needed a spanking?"

Sophie's jaw dropped open. She gave Juliette a fake punch in the arm and then laughed. "Okay, okay, you foulmouthed little minx! Not long at all, actually."

Juliette giggled and the two moved on down the street. "Then I suppose it's a good thing wizards and witches don't exist, after all."

"Nonsense," Sophie replied. "If angels can exist, anything is possible."

"I guess you have me there," Juliette admitted. They moved in silence for a few moments, and Juliette didn't miss the plethora of bodyguards Max and the four archangels had hired to tail the girls. They kept a far enough distance behind her and Sophie to give the girls privacy, but close enough to frighten away the men who glanced their way.

Juliette looked over at her best friend. Sophie's smile was gone now and her attention seemed to be turned inward.

"You okay?" Juliette asked, wondering whether everything was finally getting to the girl.

Sophie looked up and smiled. "Oh, yeah. I'm fine."

"Wanna share?"

"I was just wondering whether witches and wizards are allowed to go back to Hogwarts even when they're adults, the way they can here in the Muggle world." She laughed softly, but there was a hint of something wistful to her laughter.

Sophie had never had a chance to attend a university or college. As a runaway, she'd gone straight into the work world, and though she would sometimes speak of attending classes in film or acting, she treated the notion as more of a pipe dream than anything else, no matter how much Juliette tried to encourage her otherwise. Juliette wondered now whether that was where this sudden wistfulness was coming from.

"You do know that Hogwarts is make-believe, right?" she joked, wanting to ease Sophie's pain if that was indeed the issue.

Sophie shot her a dirty look and *tsk*ed her with a shake of her head. "Shame on you, Juliette Anderson. And just when I was going to invite you to the Quidditch Cup next week."

The girls passed a candy shop and Sophie stopped, pulling Juliette to a halt beside her. "Wait. I gotta go in here."

Juliette rolled her eyes. It never failed with Sophie. She was all about immediate gratification.

The two entered the sweetshop and Sophie began filling a basket with treats. "So, what is this stag-party slash hen-party thing all about, then?" she asked as she picked out chocolates by the handful. "God, British chocolate is divine. I have to see if I can get some of this in my suitcase for the trip home."

"I don't know actually," Juliette replied, biting her lip to hide her smile. "I think I have to go and do some strange things like get a man's trunks and wear them and kiss ten guys or something."

Sophie's brows raised. She turned a doubtful expression on Juliette. "And Mr. Black is going to let that happen? The ten-kisses thing?"

Juliette blushed. Sophie had met Gabriel and was admittedly impressed with the archangel. She'd also made it very clear to Juliette that she was convinced no man had ever been more obsessed with a woman than Gabriel was with Juliette. So, she had a point there. Juliette would be shocked, too, if Gabriel actually allowed her to go and kiss ten guys. Then again—he was Scottish at heart. And this was tradition.

"Yeah, good luck with that, Jules." Sophie shook her head, rolling her eyes. "God, I can't believe the company you're keeping these days," she muttered, breathing out a sigh of utter fascination. She leaned in and whispered, "Archangels. And not just any archangels—but *the* archangels. And only Michael and Azrael have yet to find their archesses?"

Juliette glanced nervously up at the woman behind the counter several yards away, but the woman was wearing an iPod and was utterly oblivious to their conversation. The bodyguards were all outside on the street. She nodded at Sophie.

Sophie sighed heavily. "Too bad I can't be an archess with you. Damn, it would be so cool to be able to bonk some jerk-off on the head with telekinesis or set his shoes on fire like Drew Barrymore."

Juliette started to smile at that, but stopped. Sophie was right in a way. She was so beautiful and so special—and so *kind*, even after everything she'd been through. If anyone in the world deserved to be an archess, it was Sophie. The thought made Juliette feel inexplicably sad.

Sophie frowned as she watched Juliette's expression change. "Hey," she said, shaking her head. "I'm *kidding*. You can have the power, girlfriend. I'm not really into angels anyway." She smiled wickedly, flashing those perfect straight white teeth of hers. "I've always been more into the bad boys. You know that." She winked and Juliette felt instantly more relaxed.

"Fair enough," Juliette replied, picking out a package of Parma Violets for herself. "Only a bad boy could keep you in line."

"No one can keep me in line," Soph shot back, giving her a impious look over her shoulder as she took her basket to the front counter. "And I'm going to prove it tonight by making sure you kiss all ten men you're supposed to kiss, no matter what your betrothed has to say about it."

"Are you ready for this?" Michael asked softly as he adjusted Gabriel's collar. They were standing at the altar of a church in Cruden Bay, where they had gathered to get dressed for the wedding and sign marriage documents. Once they were finished, they would take a car just down the road to Slains Castle, where the ceremony would take place.

Juliette and her bridesmaids were there already, hidden from view inside an elaborate bride's tent that Michael and Max had built for them.

"I've been ready for two thousand bloody years," Gabriel replied, smiling as he said it. His body felt tingly; his chest felt light. He felt strange—in a very good way. "Is Az here yet?"

"I'm here," replied a deep, melodic voice. Gabriel turned as his incredibly tall, incredibly handsome vampire brother came through the front door of the church dressed in a black tuxedo that made him look like candy for a very wealthy, very beautiful sugar mama.

"You clean up nice," Michael teased the vampire.

Az shot him a fanged smile and then closed the distance between himself and Gabriel. "This is for you," he said as he dug into the inside pocket of his tux jacket and pulled out what looked like a parchment rolled up and wrapped with a ruby red satin ribbon.

He held it out toward Gabriel, and Gabriel looked at it warily. "Wha' is it?"

"Your wedding present," Azrael replied easily. "It's the reason I was late arriving at the scene during the battle with the Adarians the other night," he went on to explain. It had been a while since Gabriel had heard the former Angel of Death string together so many words at once. He wasn't a man who spoke without reason. Maybe he got out everything he wanted to say while onstage.

Gabriel raised a brow. "You got there in time," he said. He could tell Az felt bad about having shown up after Juliette had already been taken.

Azrael's smile turned warm. He obviously appreciated the sentiment, but again, it didn't require words to express as much.

Gabriel gently took the rolled parchment from his brother's tapered fingers and pulled the ribbon loose. It fluttered to the ground in a crimson flurry. Gabriel unrolled the tall piece of paper and began to read.

His eyes widened and his heart skipped a beat. He read it again.

And then he looked up at Azrael to find the vampire archangel watching him with twinkling golden eyes. "You're welcome," Az said softly. And then he turned and strode across the church toward the door once more. Michael followed him, a knowing smile on his face. Apparently, the Warrior Archangel had been in on the secret.

The two men were joined by Uriel, who appeared in the moonlit entrance, his green eyes taking in the scene. "You ready?" Uriel asked, his emerald gaze settling on Gabriel, who yet stood stock-still, frozen in shock at the front of the church.

Gabriel closed his mouth and swallowed hard. He glanced back down at the deed in his hands. He was now the proud owner of one Slains Castle on the coast of Cruden Bay, Scotland. That was, if his eyes weren't deceiving him and he wasn't dreaming. He exhaled a shaky breath and half smiled, half laughed.

He thought of the castle and he thought of his soon-to-be bride. And then he thought of how she would react when he told her the news.

"Yes," he said, nearly breathless with happiness. "Yes, I am."

EPILOGUE

The pipers played clear and true that night. The notes filled the sea air with a purity befitting the occasion. The crowd grew silent and stood as one as the first bridesmaid appeared at the end of the row and began to make her way down the aisle of crumbling castle walls and strewn rose petals.

Gabriel nodded at Eleanore, who smiled back warmly. She was stunning in the lavender bridesmaid gown they'd chosen, but Gabriel doubted the archess could look anything less than stunning, no matter what she wore.

She took her place on the left-hand side of the priest, across from Uriel, and turned to gaze down the aisle as the maid of honor came around the corner. Juliette's best friend, Sophie Bryce, was wrapped in pale lilac, the color of a Scottish thistle. Her fair golden skin and long golden hair were offset by the color to stunning effect. Gabriel had to admit that Juliette's friend was an incredible beauty.

She nodded at Gabriel, smiled warmly at Eleanore, and took her place in front of the other bridesmaid, across from Azrael, who acted as best man.

Gabriel nodded back at her, and some tiny part of him noticed that as she looked up and over his shoulder, something strange flashed in the depths of her sun-colored irises. But he could not concentrate on it; he was unable to. At the moment, his entire body was wound tight as a drum. His heart beat for only one woman that night, and if he had to wait much longer for her to walk down that aisle, he was going to break rank and leave the altar to find her himself.

At last, the pipers crescendoed and he felt his chest open up and his eyes nearly water with emotion as Juliette and her parents rounded the castle corner. "My God . . . ," he whispered, unable to help himself. He gazed at his chosen bride, his living, breathing angel—his archess—and felt his breath leave him. She smiled at him, her cheeks flushed, her hazel green eyes flashing with warmth and promise, and Gabriel Black knew then and there that he was forever ruined to find as much beauty in anything else in the world—ever again.

Azrael forced himself to remain where he was, standing there at the front of the wedding party behind his brother. He forced himself not to move. Not to speak. He was constrained to compel himself to do these things with every single inhuman fiber of his supernatural being, and it was one of the most difficult tasks he had ever undertaken. He had to rein himself in as he had never imagined he would have to. The vampire archangel called upon two thousand years of training on Earth and countless thousands of years of existence as the Angel of Death to find within himself the strength he needed to allow Gabriel to have the wedding he deserved.

Azrael marshaled himself to stillness.

But what he wanted to do was step around the groom, grab the golden-haired, golden-eyed maid of honor, and take to the skies with her.

Because she was the one. She was the woman he had been waiting for—looking for—night after night, for the last twenty centuries. Sophie Bryce was an archess.

And she was his.

Read on for a look at the new installment in
the sexy and enthralling Lost Angels series,

DEATH'S ANGEL

Available in January 2013
from Signet Eclipse

He's an archangel, Sophie told herself sternly as she tried with all her might not to fidget. She stared up the long aisle of decorated chairs to the altar before Slains Castle. Azrael stood there beside the groom, and to her, he was the epitome of everything desirable in a man. His incredibly tall, imposing form was draped in the color of night, and the suit was tailored to fit his extraordinary physique with absolute perfection. His sable hair fell in gentle waves to his shoulders and made Sophie's fingertips itch with the need to touch it. His skin was so fair, it was nearly translucent. He honestly looked like a vampire lord in that expensive tux, his gold eyes nearly glowing in their intensity, and it was making her a little nuts.

Juliette Anderson, Sophie's best friend, was getting married, and Sophie was the maid of honor. It was her job to stand there and be supportive, to take the bouquet and carry the train and all of that business. But as the vicar gave his Gaelic blessing to the gathered members of the wedding party and the pipers poured their bittersweet music across the castle grounds, Sophie could concentrate on nothing but Azrael.

Azrael the archangel.

Juliette had told Sophie all about him. He and his three brothers were the four favored, the Old Man's favorite archangels. Jules had hammered Soph with the news about them short hours after Sophie stepped off the plane in Edinburgh. Sophie had her own news that she'd been wanting to share with Juliette for the last three weeks, but when she'd seen the look on Juliette's face and caught the frantically anxious tone of her voice, Sophie's affairs had instantly taken a backseat to Juliette's and they'd remained there ever since.

Gabriel and his brothers were none other than the four most famous archangels in existence: Michael, the Warrior Angel; Uriel, the Angel of Vengeance; Gabriel, the Messenger Angel; and Azrael, the Angel of Death.

He looks the part, Sophie thought now as she again stole a surreptitious glance at the gorgeous man. He was too handsome. It was that kind of handsome that was difficult to look at.

According to Juliette, the four favored had come to Earth two thousand years ago in order to find something very precious to them: their mates. It sounded like something out of a werewolf romance, but there it was. Apparently the brother archangels had been given gifts by the Old Man in the form of four perfect *female* archangels, whom he called archesses. Before the archangels could claim them, however, the Old Man sent the archesses to Earth, and there they were scattered—lost to their mates for centuries. Until now.

For some reason the archesses seemed to be popping up all at once. *Well, maybe not all at once,* Sophie reasoned as she dutifully lifted the train of her best friend's gorgeous wedding gown and followed her down the aisle toward the altar. After all, Juliette was only the second archess to be found out of the four that had been created. Maybe it was only coincidence that she and the first archess had both made their appearances within months of each other. Still . . . two thousand years without anything, and then in the course of a few months, two archesses appear?

Sophie glanced furtively toward Uriel, the first arch-angel of the four brothers to have met his archess. He looked incredibly handsome in his fitted tux, with his piercing green eyes and wavy dark hair. Uriel had been surprising enough for Sophie to take in because he was also Christopher Daniels, the famous actor who played Jonathan Brakes, the "good" vampire in the hit movie *Comeuppance.*

Azrael was harder for Sophie to take in. Not only was he literally the most handsome man Sophie had ever laid eyes on, he was supposedly the lead singer for Valley of Shadow, which was at that moment the most popular rock band in the world.

Once she'd processed the information, she realized it made a lot of sense. *'Yea, though I walk through the valley of the shadow of death . . .' How fitting,* she thought.

As the enigmatic lead singer of Valley, Azrael always took to the stage wearing a black mask that hid half of his face from his fans. His voice crooned and hypnotized, pouring out over his audiences with immense influence.

Sophie had been a breathless, swooning fan of Valley of Shadow since its inception. She'd been as mesmerized by the Masked One's physique, charisma, presence, and ethereal voice as every other woman in the world. When she streamed his songs through her iPod, she was able to close her eyes and pretend that he was singing to her—and her alone. Hell, she even dreamed of him.

Oh jeez, she thought as that memory flushed her with both embarrassment and baffled anticipation. The bride took her place at the front of the altar, and Sophie held her bouquet as the ceremony began. Sophie couldn't be-lieve she was actually standing there, a few feet away from the Masked One. To say nothing of the fact that he was also an archangel. The Angel of Death, no less! Her mind spun with the implications.

He's looking at me. She could feel the archangel's

golden gaze searing into her from where he stood opposite her beside the altar. She forced herself not to meet his gaze. She couldn't do it again. Every time she glanced up at him, she felt that he was staring right through to her soul, reading her from the inside out, absorbing her very spirit with those piercing orbs of his. It was too much. And yet, even as she knew she shouldn't look at him again because of the way it made her feel—she wanted to.

She was a moth to the flame.

The vicar called for the rings, and Sophie actually felt Azrael's gaze lift. He gracefully pulled the set of heavy gold bands from the inside pocket of his black tux and handed them to the handsome groom. Gabriel took the rings with a very real smile and turned to face his bride.

Sophie found herself transfixed by the image of Gabriel sliding the band onto Juliette's slim finger. The knotted gold Celtic design winked in the moon- and candlelight, fitting Juliette's finger perfectly. It rested on her hand like a brand, final and complete, and Sophie imagined the tall and enigmatic Azrael sliding a ring on her own finger in the same fashion.

And then she blinked. Her heart thudded hard behind her rib cage. Where the hell had that image come from? It had appeared out of nowhere, clear as day, and now it was refusing to fade away. She could almost feel the physical weight of the metal on her finger—and the heat of Azrael's touch on her hand.

Sophie felt her face flush with embarrassment. If he only knew what she was fantasizing about in that moment!

With a small start, she realized that the ceremony was over. The pipers began to play "Amazing Grace," and Juliette and Gabriel kissed. The vicar said a few more words in Gaelic—which Juliette seemed to understand—and then she and Gabriel turned to head back down the makeshift aisle.

The moon was in its last night of being full above

them. Its blue-white light cast the decorated castle and its grounds into stark, beautiful contrast. Streamers and ribbons of lace and satin had been strung between stone columns and draped over the battlements of Slains Castle so high above them. The waves of the waning tide crashed against the rocks far below, and seagulls sang the last, piercing notes of their nightly lullabies.

Roses and lavender scented the air, which was unnaturally warm for this time of year. While the rest of the people who had gathered to see the wedding—namely, members of Gabriel's clan—were unaware of the reason behind the unseasonable pleasantness, Sophie knew that the warm weather was due to Eleanore Granger, the first archess to have been found by the four favored.

Eleanore was Uriel's archess. As an archess, she possessed powers much like Juliette's—a fact that Sophie was still trying to wrap her head around. Ellie and Jules could both control the weather to some extent, throw things around with telekinesis, and manipulate fire where it already existed, and most important, they could heal.

It was this power to heal wounds and sicknesses with no more than a touch that really set the archesses apart from every other supernatural creature in the world. And that was another thing Sophie had been forced to take in rather quickly. Apparently, archangels and archesses were not the only ones to inhabit the planet alongside unsuspecting humans. There were others out there—other beings with powers.

Still, none of the other paranormals possessed the ability to mend injuries and pain. This power belonged to the archesses and to Michael and seemed to be limited solely to them.

Juliette had sprung a lot on Sophie, to be sure. But luckily for Jules, Soph could handle it. She didn't have a lot of memories from her early childhood. But what she did have from those precious days, she held on to with an unequaled fierceness. She had had six precious years with her parents. They'd died in a car accident a week before her sixth birthday. Until that day, Sophie had been in paradise.

Her mother was an assistant curator at the American Museum of Natural History in New York. Her father had been a pilot. When he was out of town on a job, Sophie's mother would take her to the museum after hours and the two of them would explore ancient Egyptian tombs and tell ghost stories in what Sophie called the Whale Room.

Sophie's mom, Genevieve Bryce, had been a unique woman possessed of an open mind. Nothing was impossible to her. "'There are more things in heaven and earth, Horatio,'" she would quote to Sophie. It was one of the few things she could remember her mother saying. Such things as magic and miracles were not pipe dreams upon which to fantasize, but very real possibilities to Genevieve. This respect for a world greater than human knowledge was passed on to Sophie, even in the six short years she had been with her parents.

It was enough, luckily, because otherwise, what Jules had told her over the last few days would have sent Sophie to the loony bin. Or convinced her that *Jules* belonged in one, anyway. If Sophie hadn't been the person she was, Juliette would have had a much more difficult time bringing her best friend into the circle of archangel knowledge.

Now that she was here, witnessing the archangels' immense physical presence and stark gazes firsthand, she was definitely convinced that magic could exist. To say nothing of what Ellie was doing with her powers.

There was also the small fact that Juliette had actually shown Sophie her wings. Real honest-to-God wings. Apparently, Juliette could control when they appeared and when they didn't, which was fortunate, because the wings were massive and stretched to a good seven or eight feet on either side. Most impressive of all, perhaps, was the fact that the wings were actually *functional*.

That one hurt a little. Sophie was happy for Juliette and all that she'd found in the last few weeks. Jules deserved the best. She was a kind soul and always had been. She was empathic, understanding, and giving, and Sophie was lucky to have her as a best friend. That Juliette never judged Soph for her past or her lack of a family or "proper" education was like a gift from the Fates to Sophie. She didn't know what she would do without Jules.

And yet, when Juliette had spread those magnificent wings of hers and beat the air with them and risen from the cliffside where they'd been standing, Sophie had experienced a pang of something she'd never felt before toward Juliette. Jealousy. Envy.

It was a sour, bitter kind of feeling that left a bad taste on her tongue and coiled tightly in the pit of her stomach. She couldn't help it. She would give anything for the ability to leave the Earth's bonds and escape all that there was while she was trapped there on the ground. To rise above it all. She would give *anything*.

Gabriel and Juliette reached the end of the aisle and all of Gabriel's clansmen and clanswomen began tossing flower petals upon the couple. Hundreds of white rose petals cascaded down upon the bride and groom amid shouts of congratulations. It was a heartwarming scene, especially when combined with the gorgeous music pouring forth from the pipers, who stood like sentinels along the castle walls.

"My best friend's getting married," she whispered to herself, in awe of the event, the importance of which was finally hitting her as Juliette laughingly pulled rose petals out of her mass of beautiful hair. And then Sophie watched as Juliette's new husband leaned over and kissed her tenderly on the cheek. He closed his eyes, seemingly lost in the wonder that was his new bride.

And Sophie smiled. "Congrats, Jules. You deserve him."

Azrael stood still in the men's restroom of the portable guest- and bathhouse that had been erected outside of Slains Castle for his brother's wedding. He was alone, and the air was filled with the hollow sense of foreboding. There was a storm brewing. It was a hurricane, hot and windy and destructive, and it was ripping through Azrael's insides, begging to be released. He exhaled a shaky breath and pressed his forehead to the mirror in front of him, glancing up at his reflection as he did so.

Another human myth gone horribly awry. Vampires did indeed have reflections. It was the wraiths that didn't. Azrael bared his teeth and laughed a cold, hard laugh at the thought. The most asinine things were going through his head at that moment. The thoughts were like fireflies on a pitch-black night, chaotic and useless and utterly distracting.

Sophie's whispered thoughts echoed through his mind, taunting him: *I would do anything.* She'd been thinking about Juliette's wings and wishing she could fly. If she'd had any idea how dangerously tempting her thoughts were . . . to say nothing of her reaction to the image he had so carelessly planted in her mind of the wedding ring sliding onto her finger. He hadn't even meant to do it; he'd simply imagined it. However, he'd been in her head at the time, thoroughly rapt in all that she was, and she'd caught the impression clear as a bell.

Her heart had skipped, her cheeks had flushed, and her lips had actually grown fuller as blood rushed into them. Her eyes had become glassy and unfocused. Her breath had hitched. And Azrael lost a little of his sanity then and there at his brother's wedding.

He'd never felt like this before. Not in his two thousand years on Earth—nor in the thousands upon thousands of years before, in the realm of angels—had he lost focus in this manner. He felt like he had the flu. Vampires didn't get the flu. Archangels didn't get the flu. The Angel of Death most certainly did not get the flu.

Azrael swore under his breath—and the mirror in front of him cracked beneath his palm, slicing into the skin of his hand. He blinked and slowly pulled away, straightening as he turned his hand over and gazed down at the welling red line across his palm. Even as he watched, it began to heal.

Azrael looked back up at the mirror and glared at the evidence of his rage. Lightning had indeed carved itself across the glass, a reflection of the storm that raged within him and was now breaking free. *Get control,* he told himself sternly. He was the most powerful vampire on Earth. If he couldn't control his emotions, they would leak out in an incredibly destructive manner. Broken mirrors would be only the beginning.

He needed to think. He needed to plan. But Sophie Bryce was two hundred yards away, a walking, talking piece of the sun, and Azrael was losing it.

The lights in the men's restroom began to flicker and the shadows in the corners grew longer. The temperature in the room seemed to drop. Thunder rolled in the distance. Again Azrael swore. He was fighting a losing battle. The image in the broken mirror reflected a tall, broad-shouldered man draped in stygian black, his sable hair framing a strikingly handsome face that was entirely too pale. Eyes that were entirely too bright.

And fangs that were entirely too long.

With a great amount of effort, Azrael forced his fangs to recede. He couldn't get rid of them completely; his incisors would always be noticeably sharp and a touch longer than human canines. But with a good deal of concentration, he was able to make them look passable. This

...a learned vampire ability; new vampires had to practice and it could sometimes take years.

Azrael should know. When he had left his realm and traveled to Earth with his brothers two thousand years ago, something had happened to him. Michael's theory was that what Azrael had done up until then as the Angel of Death somehow negatively influenced Azrael's material form on Earth. Unlike his brothers, Az had been transformed into some kind of supernatural monster.

At the time, there was no name for what he was. The fangs, the nearly unquenchable hunger for blood, the new and horrid deadliness of the sun . . . these had never existed in a being until Azrael came along. He was the first vampire. He gave himself the name because it sounded right.

It took him months to learn to control the hunger. It had been a very painful period of time, and in the years since then, he had never forgotten the way it tore him up inside, shredding his soul like tissue paper. Now, every night as he awoke with the stars, he thanked fate that he no longer suffered. He still had to feed. It was necessary for the survival of a vampire to ingest human blood every night. But his need had become a simple understanding of his physiology—and an acceptance of the same. He considered himself immensely fortunate and never took for granted the fact that he no longer craved and hungered the way he had in those horrid moments of vampiric inception.

But tonight . . .

As Azrael stood in the men's restroom outside of the castle, he was gripped by acidic, mind-numbing fear. Because he felt it again. It was the same driving kind of need—one that shoved every other thought or desire or inclination ruthlessly out of the way and threatened absolute subjugation. Only this time, it was focused. Directed.

He hungered. He craved like a madman. But what he craved and hungered for was Sophie Bryce.

His archess.